CrossFire

Across the

Crossroads

Victor Bose

First published by Dog Ear Publishing
4010 W. 86th Street, Ste H
Indianapolis, IN 46268
www.dogearpublishing.net

ISBN: 978-159858-279-6

Printed in the United States of America

Part One

Present Day

1

Carol made herself a light tonic and settled down in front of the fireplace. She looked up over the mantle at the pictures that have adorned the room for as long as she had owned the place. Nathan and Carla McIntyre were on the right. They had given her a loving family to grow up into a noble citizen and a dedicated officer for the San Diego Police Department.

In the picture in the middle had Kyle and Bobby, her two sons in front with her husband Jack and herself behind them. Carol had devoted her life to give Kyle and Bobby the best she could afford. After Jack was killed by a gang member from one of her busts, Carol had been the dad and mom at the same time for the last twenty years. She had felt like giving up on life, but Kyle and Bobby had kept her going—their innocent faces, the silent hugs, had kept Carol from a total collapse. She had felt that life had been unfair—"Why me, God, why me?" she had asked the blue heavens. She never knew why.

Carol glanced over to the picture to the right and a flood of memories engulfed her mind. She had told Kyle and Bobby that the person in the picture was William McMillan and had avoided any further talk about him. Any attempt to discuss this man made Carol emotional and upset. Her sons learned over time that they should never mention William McMillan in their conversations. However, they knew that their mother had a profound reverence for that man, whoever he was.

"One day when you are all grown up, I'll tell you about him," Carol had said, "if I told you now, you may misunderstand this man, just like everyone did in his lifetime."

The shrill ring of the telephone jolted Carol out of her thoughts. It was Kyle calling in from the O'Hare airport, boarding a red-eye flight from Chicago. It was his graduation day at the Law School in the University of Chicago and Carol could not attend.

"It's ok Mom, I know you love me. I'll see you soon," Kyle had said, knowing what a stickler for duty his mother was. He understood her obligations very well.

"How was everything at the graduation, son?" Carol was genuinely interested.

"It was great Mom, I missed you. I am just boarding the plane and will see you tomorrow in San Diego at around seven in the morning, ok?" Kyle appeared to be in a hurry.

"Sure thing Kyle, I'll pick you up," Carol replied. "Kyle?"

"Yes Mom?" Kyle asked.

"My apologies again for not being around during your graduation, but you've made me very proud, my son," Carol was emotional.

"No worries Mom, I understand. Hey, I've got to go and I will see you tomorrow bright and early. I love you Mom," Kyle signed off.

Carol replaced the receiver in its cradle and looked up at the picture of William McMillan and murmured, "Kyle's grown up into a mature adult now, its time that he knows. He should know everything about what you and I had to go through twenty five years ago." But Carol could not figure out where to start.

She closed her eyes and let her thoughts wander a while before fatigue took over and put her to sleep in her couch.

2

Always an early riser, Carol was at the airport well before Kyle showed up dragging his luggage behind him. They shook hands and hugged, "Welcome home son and congratulations again on your graduation," Carol whispered.

"Good to be back, Mom. I've got to take care of my momma, you know," Kyle had a playful tone in his voice.

Carol slapped him lightly on his back and kissed his forehead.

"Your Dad's wishes have been fulfilled now, Kyle. You have graduated and have grown into a fine young man that I'm proud to call my son," Carol said as they rolled off the parking lot.

"Mom, can we visit Dad on the way home," Kyle asked.

"I was about to tell you the same, son, he'll love to have you with him today," Carol smiled.

They picked up a wreath of fresh flowers and headed off for the cemetery where Jack had been lying for the last twenty years.

"Our beloved Jack" the engraving read on the stone above the grave.

Carol and Kyle kneeled down where Jack lay. Carol tenderly brushed off the dry leaves on the grave and spoke softly, "Hello Jack, today I am missing you more than ever. You'll be very proud of your son, my dear, just like I am. Bless him that he may prosper in life".

Kyle lit a candle, placed the wreath on the grave, gingerly swept his hand over the grave, closed his eyes and prayed. They sat there in silence, mother and son in front of the grave of the person they both loved and cherished and who was so cruelly snatched away from them twenty years ago when Kyle was only a year old. The memories were still fresh in Carol's mind—his laughter, his love, his caring, they were so vivid in her mind—it was just only yesterday.

The distant clap of thunder cut into the silent conversation.

"We'll be back again, Dad. I love you," Kyle murmured.

As mother and son walked away, Carol asked, "Well son, what's next for you?"

Kyle smiled, "I want to join the SDPD, Mom. I've been thinking all about it for the past few months. You have discussed almost all different careers with me, but you never talked about yours. You've an illustrious career, Mom—everybody respects you, I am proud to be your son. I want to serve and to protect people just like you have, Mom. So I have decided to follow your footsteps and no, you are not talking me out of this," Kyle was rather emphatic.

Carol's jaw dropped. She could not believe what she had heard. She had left no stone unturned to steer Kyle away from a potential career with the police. She always ignored young Kyle's questions about her job. At the most she would make fleeting references to her work, but never encouraged Kyle for a career as a cop. She never had parties at home where her friends might praise her work and her heroics, lest Kyle heard those stories and grew an interest to follow her footsteps. She had even turned down three offers for promotion, to avoid the exposure that rank brought on a decorated police officer. She did not want Kyle to even consider joining the police. She feared what might happen if her son had to go through the ultimate test in life that she herself had to go through in the early years of her illustrious career. It was a scar that never healed. It was an agony that she still carried in her heart and would do so till the last breath of her life.

Carol was confused and they did not speak much all the way home. Kyle was talking, but all Carol answered were in monosyllables. Her mind was wandering far away to those days when she had to choose between her emotions and her sworn duty to serve and protect—she had chosen the latter. That never stopped to haunt her days and nights. Now Kyle wanted to become a cop and she did not know what to do. She felt alone and wished Jack was there with her.

"Are you ok Mom?" Kyle was shaking Carol by her shoulder, "you seem lost somewhere. I really want to follow your footsteps you know?"

Carol stared at her son for a while, nodded in apparent resignation, "I have never stopped you from doing what you wanted to do and I don't want to stop you now. The life of a dedicated police officer is not easy, my son, you might have to make some decisions that will haunt you all your life and will make you look back in utter helplessness".

"Kyle, the time has come, to share a secret of my life with you," Carol sighed. "I had kept this from you so long fearing that you may not fully understand it all. However, I feel that now you are matured enough and have the right to know. After you listen to what I have to tell you, if you still want to join the ranks of the men and women who have dedicated their lives to public service, I won't hold you back", Carol paused as if searching for words that failed to come.

She continued, "One question for you—have I been a good mother to you?"

Kyle was visibly surprised at this, he shrugged, "Of course Mom, you are the best God ever gave anyone for a mother, and I mean that in all seriousness. But if this is bothering you so much, I don't want to know."

As Carol pulled into her driveway, she said, "No, you need to know. Why don't you go freshen up first? I'll make us some lunch and then we can talk".

"Right Mom, I can't wait to take things off your chest. The car felt heavy there—you seem to be carrying a lot of weight on your shoulders," Kyle said jokingly and hauled his luggage away.

Lunch was a simple and silent matter and Carol was not in the mood to eat much anyway. After the dishes were done, Carol picked up a bottle of beer and said, "Let's go outside and sit in the porch son, it's warm in here," it was actually a perfect winter day in San Diego.

"Sure Mom", Kyle followed her out.

Once they had settled down on the porch, Kyle said, "Oh come on Mom, spill it now, you are killing me with this suspense."

Carol smiled and ruffled his hair fondly.

Part Two

About Sixty Years Ago

3

There was a light rain pouring down that day George was driving down in his pickup truck from Los Angeles. The roads weren't very slick yet, and there was this open stretch of road ahead of him after San Onofre. He decided to step on the gas and check out how well the truck performed on the road. Soon he was driving past the legal limit weaving in and out of traffic. Cars ahead of him saw a maniac who thought Interstate Five was some racetrack and moved over to the slower lanes to let him pass. George had felt a sense of power and thrill and stepped on the gas even further, "I'll slow down if I see any cops behind me," he thought.

He cranked up the radio and Elvis was bringing the house down— George was having fun. Ahead of him was a Ford sedan, but there was no sign that the car would move over to let him pass like all the other cars had done. He was almost tailgating that car, but still there was no sign of any intention that the driver would move over and allow George to zoom by.

"Move over, damn it, you are the slow one, so you move," George yelled out inside his truck. Still there was no sign that the driver ahead would oblige. The adjacent lane was empty and he could easily have passed the slower car, but George had no intention of yielding to a slower vehicle.

George flashed his headlights and was almost up to the rear bumper of the car ahead, but the driver ahead was apparently oblivious of him. "Ok, you son-of-a-bitch, you want to play rough, I'll play rough". George was out of his wits by that time.

He passed the car on the next lane, veered back into the fast lane ahead of the car, jammed his brakes hard and braced himself for the rear impact. Sure enough, the car behind rear-ended George and hit him harder than he expected it would. His head jack-knifed back hard and something like a hot bright whiplash shot through his head and almost knocked him unconscious.

George had only expected to scare the driver, but apparently he under-estimated the situation. He knew he was in big trouble—should he stop or should he run—he could not think straight. There weren't too many cars in the road, but drivers craned their necks to look. George decided to stop and talk his way out saying that he was rear ended. He pulled over about some fifty yards from the car behind and twisted around in his seat to look. The car behind was pretty much totaled in front and stopped broadside in the middle of the lane. George looked at his rearview mirror and cursed himself. He should have listened to the psychiatrist from the rehab center. She had cau-tioned him about his short-temper, but then it was too late now.

"Oh heck, that looks pretty bad! I just hope he is alive," he told himself.

He started to step out of the car, gingerly massaging his neck. He cursed himself again, "I'm supposed to be hit from the back and badly hurt. I better stay in the car till the cops arrive." He just sat there and rehearsed his story that he would tell, over and over in his mind.

The cops arrived and they arrived in force. The cruisers and a fire engine were already there and George could hear the wailing siren of the approaching paramedics. He wondered how the emergency crew always got to the scene so quickly, but collected himself to concentrate in the rehearsal of his story for the cops.

"Sir, are you hurt?" the officer came up to the driver's side and asked.

George grimaced as if in considerable pain. He clutched the rear of this neck, slowly turned towards the officer and silently nodded.

"All right, just don't move, Sir. I'll get help," the officer counseled and spoke on his radio, "We have an injury here, no fatalities, but rush in a medic."

George glanced at the rearview mirror to see that the paramedics were jumping out of their van and one of them was sprinting towards him.

George was helped out of his car and the medic got to work. No bruises, no broken bones, but George kept clutching the back of this neck and moaned in pain. The medic brought out a breathalyzer and tested George's breath.

"You are a very lucky man, Sir. Looks like you will be fine after a few days of rest," the medic was rather encouraging. "However, I am not so sure about the guy back there," the medic nodded towards the car behind, "he looked pretty bad back there at first glance."

George looked up to see the officer looking at him with a quizzical expression, hands on his hips. "Oh, I don't like that look," thought George.

"Officer Brady," the medic said, glancing at the name tag of the patrol officer, "This gentleman seems ok, but I would not recommend that he drives his car for a few days, so you might start making the arrangements. By the way, the BAC is normal."

Brady nodded.

The medic asked for George's license, completed his paperwork and handed the license to Officer Brady.

"Thanks Doc, we'll take it from here," Officer Brady shook hands with the medic who walked back to his van.

Traffic was literally crawling on the freeway with people slowing down to figure out what had happened.

"What can't you bastards mind your own bloody business and get moving," George spitefully shouted in his mind.

"Care to give me a statement of what happened out here Sir?" Officer Brady was kneeling beside George, "or if you wish, we can do this at the station."

George glanced over to the car behind him. It was totaled in the front and chances are that the driver was fatally injured, if not already dead. He wondered if he could gamble his way out. He concocted a story where he was apparently going at the limit and the driver behind was speeding like a maniac and rear-ended him before he could get out of the way.

"It could have been failed brakes or something. I just hope he wasn't drunk. Is he doing ok? Gosh, I can't believe this has really happened," George feigned genuine concern.

Officer Brady looked at him for a while, trying to look into George's eyes to catch some sign that could give him away. There were none. George seemed to speak the truth, but Officer Brady wasn't satisfied—it just did not sound convincing enough.

"I don't know yet, Sir, but I am going to find out. I'll have a deputy drive you home and have your truck towed to the police lot. We'll have to do some tests. Here's your license and the police report," Officer Brady handed George the paperwork. "Don't leave town without letting me know. My number is on the report as you can see. Now get back inside your truck and wait till a deputy arrives to drive you home." Officer Brady was courteous yet firm.

Another officer had approached them. He pulled Brady aside and started to talk in a hushed tones. George strained to hear the conversation, but nothing could be heard over the din of traffic, which was now moving a little quicker than before. The medics had placed the driver of the sedan on a stretcher and were loading him on the van—the ambulance had its lights flashing.

"Well Mr. Briggs," Officer Brady had walked up to George, "it looks real bad there. That guy is badly injured and has lost a lot of blood. Fractured skull, broken ribs, and wrist, probably a punctured lung, you name it. We'll drive you home and I want you to stay in town, till we complete our investigation. For your sake I hope your statement is exactly the way it happened, otherwise…" Officer Brady left the sentence hanging, tipped his hat and headed back toward his cruiser. The paramedics rushed off, lights flashing and sirens wailing.

George got back inside his truck. He closed his eyes and kicked himself for his foolishness. "I'm in big trouble. I just hope that guy doesn't make it— then at least I have a chance," he thought as the sirens faded away in the distance.

4

The courtroom was quite full for a case involving a traffic accident. Actually there were more law students than the general public present in the room. It was part of a program where the students are exposed to live proceedings in the courtroom to give them a flavor of how things get done in real life. The presiding judge had to first approve the presence of the students before they were allowed in.

Brant Sawyer was inevitably the brightest in the class and his teachers knew it. Brant was raised in an orphanage, but he appeared to have a spark in himself since his childhood that clearly showed through his calm and quiet self. He was brilliant in school, did not appear to have too many friends and kept to himself most of the time. The matron had endorsed that Brant be provided with the necessary scholarship at the UCSD to further his education. Brant was interviewed much to the satisfaction of the council at UCSD and he chose to take up law. He demonstrated his brilliance in the first three semesters and had made up his mind to specialize in criminal law. Brant had always preferred the last row in classes and that day was no different.

"I just like to observe everything and everyone. I can't do this if I am sitting upfront," Brant had told one of his instructors who had questioned his preference.

Judge Clark was presiding. George Briggs was being charged with reckless driving with the attempt to kill. He was also being charged with providing false information to a police officer, misleading and for obstruction of justice.

The Prosecutor motioned to a paraplegic seated in a wheelchair and gave a long account of how the defendant purposefully caused the accident on the freeway. The defendant even lied to the police officer and filed a false report on how the events had occurred. Her client had a perfectly normal life before the accident with a wife and two kids until George came along and took almost all of it away. Her client had been seriously injured and had become a paraplegic. He had lost his job and his family was in extreme distress.

"I'm toast," thought George, "why did he not just die?" He scowled.

The Prosecutor marched in three witnesses who gave sworn testimonies on how things had happened. All of them without exception described how George had been dangerously driving through traffic on that day and how they had wondered how far he would go before he was pulled over by a cop.

"Your witness," the Prosecutor had offered the defense lawyer to cross examine each witness.

After some customary probing questions, the defense lawyer had given up on each witness, there was no hole in their story, and everything led to the fact that George was indeed guilty. To top it all off the Prosecutor also presented some pictures of how the accident happened. Apparently one of the witnesses had kept clicking away. Her pictures showed clear evidence of how George had tailgated the victim, how he had overtaken the sedan and how the impact happened.

"Gosh, that son-of-a-bitch also lied to me even just before coming to court," the defense lawyer mused. "To hell with my so-called duties to my client, this guy deserves to be put away."

"I have no further questions, your Honor," the defense attorney said, much to George's surprise. He did not like his lawyer anyway.

"Driving is a privilege and not a right," Judge Clark said in his closing comments. "Such sheer lack of responsibility for fellow citizens, misdemeanor, obstruction of justice and lying to a police officer to top it off will not be tolerated in my court. Let my voice be heard beyond this courtroom that I won't be so lenient in the next case like this."

George was sentenced to 15 years in prison without the possibility for an early pardon. All his assets were to be seized, liquidated and the proceeds handed over to the victim. George's driving license was revoked and he could not ever get one anywhere in the United States.

George looked at the Judge with cold, furious eyes and glanced over this victim. He showed no emotion—probably his facial muscles were paralyzed as well, thought George.

He had inherited quite a fortune from his single aunt who had died a few years ago. George knew that all he had to do was to enjoy life—he did not have to work anymore with all the money that was passed onto him. All of that would be gone now.

George did not feel sorry for what he had done; he was going to pay dearly for it anyway, so he was square. "Gosh, 15 years is a long time. I'll be pushing forty by the time I get out," he pursed his lips, wondering how he was going to serve his time.

As George was taken away into custody, the courtroom started to clear. Brant however was engrossed in what he had just heard and played it on his mind over and over again.

"There's got to be a way the defendant could have been spared. I know there was a lot of evidence against him and he did look crooked, but there must have been something that the defense could have done. Maybe if they could…"

Brant's thoughts were interrupted as he felt one of his classmates shaking him by the shoulder.

"Are you in one of those spells again? It's over Brant, time to go," Mary was laughing.

"Yeah, I guess," Brant frowned, gathered his papers and followed Mary out.

5

"Patrol three two two, come in Patrol three two two", the radio crackled.

Bill picked up the handset, "Go ahead Control, this is Patrol three two two".

"We have received an emergency call from a crèche near to your current location. The caller has reported that two gunmen drove up in a black minivan and have rushed into the crèche. It should be full of little kids at this time of the day. It's called Baby Steps between Shelter and Main—address is one six three four Shelter Drive. Get there as soon as you can. I'm calling in other units to assist."

"Roger Control, we're on our way," Bill responded.

His partner John at the wheel of the police cruiser already had his lights and siren going and was screeching into Gibson Lane.

"Turn off your siren John and drop me off here," Bill called out.

"But Bill, we aren't there yet, it's still a block away," John was surprised.

"I know John, I don't want those guys to panic and do something foolish—we have kids in there. This is a one-way street, when the other units come in, pull them over here too and have them turn off their sirens as well. Then join me as soon as you can. I'm off," Bill was out of the car and sprinted away.

The cavalry was just arriving by the time Baby Steps came into view. Bill motioned the junior patrolmen to silence and called them over. "All right guys, we need to circle the building. Take cover of the bushes around and crawl into position. I don't want you to be seen. I'm the only one dressed in civilian clothes, so I am going in. Don't move till I tell you to. On my word come in, and for God's sake, remember there are kids inside."

Bill walked up to the glass doors of the crèche, the curtains were drawn. He gently nudged it, trying to push it open—it was locked as he expected. He looked around and there was that black minivan parked across the street. He knocked on the door and stepped back two paces, with his hands clasped in front of him.

Inside the two gunmen were startled at the knock. "What do we do, Marty?" Budge asked nervously.

"Oh darn it, who the hell is that? Let me think," Marty said. He glanced around the room full of frightened children and then saw Joan and Mrs. Burns trying to hug as many children as possible, trying to shield them from the view of the two hoodlums. He beckoned to the fifty five year old owner, Mrs. Burns to take all the kids into the adjoining playroom and motioned Budge to lock the room. "Leave that girl in the pink and white skirt behind," he ordered.

"You stay right here, miss," Marty ordered Joan, "with that girl. I'll need you both." He motioned Joan to the window and said softly, "Look through that window and tell me who it is. No wise or funny stunts miss, or this sweet girl won't remain pretty any longer."

Joan peered out and saw a stranger in civilian clothes—she was crestfallen. She hoped it was a police officer. The man looked well built, strong—she had never seen her before. Joan mused, "Maybe someone who wants to visit our facilities. Well he picked a wonderful day to visit," she thought.

She came away from the window and played the biggest gamble of her life. "He is the father of one of the kids here, probably wants to pick up his daughter," she turned to Marty. "It is not usual to have our doors locked at this time of the day, you know?" and left that phrase hanging.

Realization dawned on Budge. "What do we do Marty? Should I bust him? I can you know," Budge asked nervously.

"Shut up you bloody idiot, I told you not to use my name," Marty was furious. He continued, "You do that and this place will be swarming with cops in no time. If we don't let him in, he will get suspicious and probably call the cops anyway. You heard what she said—it is unusual to find the doors locked from inside at this time of the day. Darn it, we'll have to bring him in. You cover the girl."

"You listen to me very carefully miss", Marty said turning towards a flustered Joan. "Go and open that door very slowly, one wrong move and both you and the sweet doll there are dead. Do you hear me? Get that guy in and shut that door again as soon as he gets in. No tricks babe, I am going to be your shadow. Wait till he knocks again."

Bill motioned to his men waiting in the shrubs, indicating that they should move in closer, but remain out of sight. He stepped up and knocked again, this time a little longer than the first time, "Hello, is there anybody in there?" he shouted and stepped back a couple of steps again.

"Ok miss," Marty whispered. "Open that door and let him in, and I don't want to remind you to be very careful".

Joan prayed, "Oh God, I hope this will pass soon" and opened the door. "Oh Mr. Stockton, how are you?" she said and opened her eyes wider than usual.

"She's smart," Bill thought and said aloud. "Hi there, is everything ok? I got off early from work and wondered if I could pick up my child on the way home."

"Sure Sir, please come in", Joan said in a nervous voice. "Where have I seen this man before?" she thought, but could not remember.

Bill made his final signal for his men with his hands behind his back, motioning them to take positions near the door, but remain in the cover of the walls. He stepped in.

He was actually yanked in by someone and thrown to the floor on his face. He turned over on his back, palms out with his hands in full view. "Shut that door miss," Marty barked and Joan quickly complied.

Bill quickly surveyed the room. One guy was to his right, had a revolver in his hands and was holding on to a little girl. She looked visibly scared. The other guy had a Magnum in his hand, safety catch off and was pointed down towards him. "That's a big gun for a guy his size," Bill thought, "I wonder if he can use it right."

The girl who let him in was standing in a corner to his left looking at him with an apologetic expression in her face. Further left was a door to a room that was locked. "That's probably where the other kids are", Bill reasoned.

Marty was talking to him, "On your knees mister, hands behind your head, very slowly now".

"Let me waste him Marty", Budge said nervously, "I don't like it. He looks like a bloody cop."

"Will you shut up? For crying out loud, I told you not to use names, you idiot" Marty shouted, without taking his eyes of Bill.

"Ok, so we have Chief Marty and Mr. Loudmouth" Bill mused. He looked at Budge and looked at those nervous and wicked eyes, "The jittery type", he thought.

Bill looked at Marty and appeared scared. He started talking in very hysterical tones to Marty as he pulled himself up to his knees.

"What's going on? Who are you guys? What have I done? What do you want? What have you done to my child?" Through the corner of his eye, Bill saw Budge release the little girl who ran over to Joan standing in the corner and tried to hide herself in Joan's dress and shut the world out of her view.

Budge hurried over to Bill shouting, "Shut up, shut up, you're a copper, aren't you? You can't fool me. Let me do him in Marty," Budge pushed Bill down on his knees as Marty in a reflex action lined up his Magnum towards Bill. Marty was visibly irritated at the repeated use of his name and looked up to speak to Budge.

Bill was on his knees now, Marty's gun almost touching his forehead. He glanced up and saw Marty's attention turned towards Budge who was standing a few paces away to the right.

Bill used his left hand to grab Marty's hand that held the gun and slid his finger in the trigger. In the same smooth action, his right hand grabbed Marty's elbow, folded the arm till the gun was pointing towards Budge. Then he pulled the trigger. All of this happened in almost one motion so suddenly, the heavy recoil from the Magnum almost broke Marty's wrist, the bullet hit Budge on his right shoulder, throwing the revolver flying from his hands and Budge shrieked out in pain. Bill punched out hard on Marty's jaw as he stood up on his feet.

The quickness of the events stunned Marty as the policemen waiting outside crashed in through the door. Soon they had Budge in handcuffs—he was screaming and crying in pain, blood was pouring from his right shoulder. Marty was still stunned as he got pinned down on his stomach and was promptly cuffed by an officer.

"Are you all right, Sir?" an officer asked Bill.

"Yes Bobby, I am, thanks. Please have this area cleared as soon as you can—there are kids in here", Bill replied adjusting his jacket in place.

He turned towards Joan who stood wide-eyed as she held the little girl. She peered at Bill with those small blue eyes and wept softly.

Bill walked over to Joan and nodded, "You're ok, ma'am?"

"Y-Yes, thanks," Joan stammered. "She's a little upset though", Joan said looking down on the little figure clutching at her dress.

Bill sank to his knees and ruffled the child's hair, "It's all over now, sweetheart, it's just a bad dream", Bill whispered in the little girl's ear and held her hand. "You were very brave, please don't cry my dear".

Something in Bill voice was so father-like and reassuring; the little girl slowly turned towards Bill and wiped her tears away.

"There you go, girl. What's your name?" Bill asked softly.

"Julie", she replied.

"What a sweet name! Do you want to go and meet your friends?" Bill asked. The girl nodded.

Bill beckoned to Joan to open the door to the second room. There were about twenty kids huddled around Mrs. Burns, all looking towards them with confused anxiety in their eyes.

"Hello ma'am. I'm Detective William McMillan, SDPD. You are all safe now, it's over," Bill spoke in a comforting voice. "We will clear things up very quickly and leave you alone. Can you please call all the parents and request them to come by to pick up their kids as soon as possible? I'm afraid this is a crime scene, so we will have to ask you leave a spare key with us, for further investigation in this matter. You can be back to this place within the next forty eight hours, you have my word. I'll have two officers posted outside. If the two of you need escorts to go home, just let them know and they will arrange everything."

With that Bill stepped out and directed an officer accordingly.

He was about to leave, when he heard Joan calling him, "Detective McMillan?"

Bill turned and approached Joan. Mrs. Burns was at her side.

"Yes ma'am?" Bill asked.

"I wanted to thank you for what you did. Thank you very much for saving our lives and the kids. We are in your debt", Joan said with a sparkle in her eyes.

Bill looked at her and waved his hand dismissively, "You did something very brave today. A lesser woman would probably have reacted otherwise, Miss."

"Joan, Joan Higgins," Joan volunteered.

"Yes, Ms. Higgins, you were very brave today. That was very sharp thinking on your part. Thank you for warning me with those wide-open eyes. By the way, just to set the record straight, who is this Stockton guy?" Bill asked jokingly.

Joan blushed, "It was instinctive, I pulled the name out of the air—but you did all the hard work".

Bill laughed and nodded in understanding. He felt like spending a little more time with Joan—he felt strangely drawn. But he had to wrap this ordeal up first. "I'll come by later to check things out. Till then take care", Bill replied. He nodded to Mrs. Burns and to Joan and walked away.

Mrs. Burns glanced towards a beaming Joan as Bill walked away. She nudged Joan, "He's handsome and pretty smart, huh? I'd go after him if I was your age, but you know what, I think I'll just step aside for you," she teased.

Joan blushed, "Mrs. Burns! I now remember where I saw him. He was in the newspapers last April on that Vista homicide case. He busted a gang in Vista with the help of only four police officers. He was honored by the Mayor for that effort".

Mrs. Burns laughed, "Well, you had a first hand experience of his work and I think I'll be correct to say that a little fondness may be in the air. By the way, I noticed his ring finger was empty, so get on with it girl!"

Joan laughed her short laugh and shook her head and walked inside.

6

Bill was in the newspapers again the next morning. Chief of Police McArthur was all praise for the most efficient asset in his force. He lauded Bill for his bravery and speedy resolution of the most delicate situation. Bill's statement about Joan's contribution on the rescue operation had found coverage in the press as well.

Joan called Bill that evening after work. "Detective McMillan, this is Joan Higgins," Joan said expectantly.

"Hello Ms. Higgins, I guess you are famous now," Bill sounded friendly.

"Joan will suit me fine," Joan paused and continued, "Well, you see, I am a little embarrassed at all this press. I just did what my instincts told me to do," Joan's the shy type, Bill reckoned.

"Well, your instincts do you credit, miss. We are always looking for resourceful young people like you in the force, you know," Bill was probing.

"Oh Detective McMillan, you are stretching this too far," that shyness showed again in Joan's voice.

"If you don't mind, um…," Bill paused, "Joan," he paused again, "can I ask you a question?"

"Sure Detective," Joan was inquisitive.

"Well, you see, I was going to take the weekend off and head towards Santa Barbara for a day trip. I was wondering if you are free this weekend, you might want to give me company," Bill crossed his fingers hoping Joan would agree.

"Sounds like fun, Detective. Are you sure that you want my company? I am not the talkative type, you know," Joan tried to not sound overly enthusiastic.

"Thank goodness for that. In my business, I have been known to make people talk," Bill laughed. "I will pick you up at your house this Saturday at around seven in the morning. I hope it is not too early for you," Bill offered.

"I'm an early riser, so seven o'clock will be fine. I will see you then," Joan sounded happy.

"Good, till later then. By the way, my friends find it easier to call me Bill."

They laughed and hung up.

Bill picked Joan up in the morning and they drove off towards Santa Barbara. It was going to be one of those gorgeous Southern California spring days with clear skies, comfortably warm with a light breeze blowing in from the ocean. Traffic was pretty light on that Saturday morning and they talked like long lost friends.

Joan was the only child of the Higgins family. She was fun loving, gregarious and loved children. The trait that stood out was her sense of independence, strength of character and of course her short laugh that lightened up her eyes and genuine happiness radiated on her face.

The miles seemed to melt away as they exchanged stories about their lives. They reached Santa Barbara well in time to catch a scrumptious lunch and headed for the beach. They walked bare feet on the soft sand, and talked like long lost friends. At times they would sit and watch the kids play and laugh at their antics.

Bill and Joan shared their lives with each other and seemed to be in a hurry to open their hearts and talk about their joys and sorrows. They seemed to find trust and comfort in each other. They would laugh and rejoice the good times and comforted each other when the chips were down. By the time the sun dipped below the orange ocean they had developed a sense of bonding like only two very close friends can have and neither could figure out how things happened so quickly and smoothly the way it did.

The gulls were returning to their nests and Bill said, "Well Joan, looks like we've got to get going now, we have quite a drive ahead."

Joan nodded and sighed, "I guess you're right. Can I ask you a personal question?"

Bill laughed, "You mean something more personal than we have already spilled our hearts out on? Sure, bring it on."

Joan smiled, "Do you really enjoy your job? I mean it's so dangerous, living your life on the edge all the time."

Bill laughed, "Boy that's a loaded question!" He paused as if collecting his thoughts. "I would not do anything else, really. I chose this career because I wanted to serve and protect the community I live in. It's not always that I get to pull off those stunts like I had to at the crèche, but such situations do arise and I feel a sense of pride to wear my badge and protect innocent lives from danger. Quite honestly, there is too much of filth in our society. I cannot discuss all my cases with you, but some of them just fill you with disgust. There is danger involved—no question about that and I do get to live on the edge from time to time, as you say. But then, when I see the frightened face of a little girl or the corpse of an innocent man who has been brutally put to death or when I see a dealer pushing those drugs to youngsters it just makes my blood boil. Commitment to serve and protect is an overpowering emotion, Joan, you have to experience it to know it. I guess when one is committed to public service, danger comes in at a distant second," Bill paused. "Yes, I do love my job; it makes me feel that I am giving something back to the community that has given me so much."

He paused again and looked at Joan with mischievous eyes, "My job has perks too. I get to meet some of the most charming people there is around," he smiled and continued in a more serious voice, "but I'd say you are special. I can't say I've met anyone like you Joan, and no, I have not said that to any other woman until now."

Joan laughed, "That's not a bad pickup line, you know."

Bill grinned, "Well, I'm trying you know, I am not the expert at this."

Joan laughed her short laugh again.

They sat in silence for a while then Bill said, "I hate to do this, but like all things I guess this day comes to an end too. We've got to go, if that is ok with you."

"Yep, let's hit the road. I'm buying dinner on the way and you don't have to be chivalrous," Joan offered.

Bill shrugged, stood up and held out his hand. Joan grabbed it and pulled herself up.

Dinner was a full five course meal at the restaurant in Malibu and Joan was a gracious host. Bill offered to split the charge, but Joan dismissed it saying, "Well I like to give back too, in my special way," she grinned. "But I don't want to insult you. I just want to do this, please."

Bill gave up, "You sound like a woman who doesn't take no for an answer!"

Joan chuckled, "Depends on what the question is, Bill. But you do seem to be a rather intelligent man."

"The day was too short, I think," Bill said as they pulled up on the curbside in front of Joan's apartment building.

Joan nodded thoughtfully, "Agreed. Maybe we should do this again sometime."

Bill parked, came by the passenger's side, and pulled it open for Joan to step out. "Absolutely, I'd like to see you again."

Joan opened the entry door to her house and offered, "Would you like to come up for some coffee or a drink?"

Bill hesitated, "I'd love to Joan, but can I take a rain check on that?"

Joan grinned and nodded, "No problem Bill, I did keep you long today."

Bill shook his head dismissively, "No you did not—it really was one of the better days of my life." With that he reached out, kissed Joan lightly on her cheek, patted her forearm and wished her goodnight.

7

"It's so completely frustrating, Josh," Dave Reynolds was clearly not happy that day. "At this rate I will soon need a psychiatrist. I don't think that son-of-a-bitch manager will give me any slack. Underpaid and overworked, that's what I am, man. Life just sucks, playing dog to the stinking rich. I wish I had a million bucks. I'd buy out this company and kick that bastard's sorry ass out."

Dave had a wild childhood. His birth mother passed away when he was just a year old and his father remarried. His step mother cared for him, but that was more out of moral duty than anything else. His father worked as a janitor in Los Angeles airport and was an incorrigible alcoholic. His parents seemed to find their recreation in fights and arguments, which were pretty much a routine occurrence. It was difficult to say who had the last say, but then with Dad passed out under the effects of cheap vodka, his mother's curses resonated through the silence.

Dave lost his father by the time he completed his fourth birthday—cirrhosis of the liver was what the doctor diagnosed. His mother moved to San Diego where she had family. She managed to get a job as a waitress in an ethnic restaurant and enrolled Dave in a public school. She never remarried and spent the rest of her life providing for Dave before she was killed in a road accident. Dave graduated from school and used his modest inheritance to complete training as a private security guard.

The job placement office at the school fixed him up with a private security company. He was placed on probation for a year. The pay was just barely enough to pay the rent and cover a few simple meals a day. The time in probation was very difficult for Dave. The company often exploited Dave with longer work hours, minimum pay and even delayed his confirmation as a permanent employee.

His company was contracted by an old woman who had inherited her husband's sprawling estate in Del Mar and Dave was given his first assignment as an in-house security guard. That was when he met Josh Timmons. Dave had the morning shift and Josh relieved him at six in the evening.

At first it was a short change of guard between Dave and Josh, a cursory handshake and goodbye. After a while Josh started to report for duty fifteen minutes early and spend some time catching up with Dave. The fifteen minutes increased to half an hour and went up to an hour before Dave started to reciprocate with the same favors every morning.

Josh was quite a different character. He was a private security guard like Dave was and of the same age. However that was where the similarity ended.

He seemed to have a spark in his life that Dave could not comprehend. Josh appeared to be too smart to be a security guard, which often baffled Dave.

Josh was the ambitious type and had discussed with Dave that the job of a security guard was simply a stepping stone for him. He had big plans for the future and the job was the first step in the right direction. However, he never discussed what his plans were which aroused Dave's curiosity all the more. "All in good time brother, when there is a good time," Josh always side-stepped Dave's questions.

They became good friends and saw each other and confided in each other more than ever before—at least that was what Dave understood. Josh still held matters close to his chest, but with every passing day he felt increasingly confident that Dave would be the right person to have as his sidekick. Dave was still rough around the edges but Josh thought he could mould him into shape.

Dave hated his job and Josh was well aware of it. But hatred needed to transition into frustration before Dave could be of any use to Josh. He knew he had gained Dave's confidence but he just waited for the appropriate time to approach Dave with his plans. "Why don't you try something else for a living Dave? This job seems to take a lot out of you," Josh had counseled.

"I don't have the skills to do anything else, man. You're right, this job is draining the life out of me, but at least it pays the bills," Dave sounded like a cornered animal that had no escape.

Josh only shrugged.

"You are the guy with the bright ideas Josh. Got any for me?" Dave asked quizzically.

Josh smiled and said, "I'll work on it. At times when rules work against you, bending them a bit can work to your advantage. Why don't you ask for a raise?"

Dave was surprised, "You're telling me that asking for a raise is the brightest idea you have for me?"

Josh mused, "A little more over the edge, my friend." He patted Dave on the back and said, "Hang in there buddy. I was talking short term."

Dave went straight to see his manager that evening and demanded a raise. The manager laughed at him, "What do you think you have done so special that I should even consider a raise?"

Dave was adamant, "These are long, boring twelve hours every day we are talking about, Mr. Platt. I read the newspaper fifteen times over by the end of the day. The old lady seldom comes and goes and nobody visits her. What security is she worried about anyway? Have you any idea how boring it is to stare at a bunch of television monitors every day? The images never ever change during the day. So I am requesting a transfer to another client or a raise. I need some motivation, you see?"

The manager leaned back in his chair hands clasped behind his head and listened to Dave complaining. "Are you finished?" he asked.

"Yes Mr. Platt, you've…" Dave did not get to finish his words.

The manager continued, "Well Dave, the requirements of the job were made clear to you before we accepted your employment application. You agreed to those requirements. So I cannot quite understand the reason for your complaint. Nobody said this was going to be easy, which is why everybody is not lining up on my door asking for a job, thank God."

The manager paused for effect and continued, "I have three options for you Dave. The first, be happy with what you have. The second consider swapping shifts with Josh every other week—one week you take the night shift and the next week, work on the day shift. If none of these options look good for you, it brings us to the third option—quit the job. A raise is out of the question at this time. The client is not going to pay us any extra, so I cannot pay you any extra either. Why don't you go home take a warm shower, think about these options and let me know what you decide? Does that sound reasonable to you?" Dave stared at him for a while, slowly nodded and left the office.

Dave drove directly back to work much to Josh's surprise. "Boy, you're too early for your shift, you know?" Josh said jokingly.

Dave collapsed in a chair, held his head in his hands and ran his fingers slowly through his hair. He looked up and said, "I went to see the manager after I left and had a chat with him about the raise."

Josh handed Dave a beverage can and asked nonchalantly, "You don't waste too much time, do you? How'd it go?" he asked a rhetorical question.

Dave gave a complete account of what happened as Josh listened intently. "Well, the man has a point, if you really think about it. If you want to swap shifts with me, I'm ok with that, no big deal there," Josh volunteered.

"It's so completely frustrating. Swapping shifts is not going to bring me any extra money," Dave was almost shouting. "At this rate I will burn out right before your eyes. Gosh I need a shrink!"

"It's time my friend, you are ready," Josh mused. He paced the room and could feel Dave's eyes following him. "Hmmm…I see we have a problem here then," Josh said in a barely audible tone.

He paced a little more as if deep in thought. Then he stopped and grinned, "I think I have the perfect thing for you. This will change your life forever. If money is what's bugging you; then I have a solution for you my friend, you will be rolling if not swimming in cash. But it is going to take some effort on your part and will require a fair amount of patience and perseverance. I've known you for a while, so I know you can do it. However, you will have to trust me and do exactly as I say. The smallest oversight or the simplest mistake can bring you down faster than you can bat an eyelid. So the risks are high, but the rewards far outweigh them. Interested?" Josh asked an attentive Dave.

He already knew the answer—Dave would try anything different at the moment.

"I'm yours, buddy. I'll do anything to get out of this cage Josh," Dave sounded beaten.

Josh walked up to him, slapped his left arm and smiled, "No worries, that's what friends are for. I've brought in my dinner. Why don't you go grab something and come back? We can talk afterwards?"

Dave jumped on his feet, "You won't even notice I'm gone."

He was true to his word. He even brought along a six pack and offered Josh to help himself.

Josh grinned, "I'm still on duty, so I won't drink. The most important essence of what I am going to tell you is patience and discipline—it's got to start now. You just can't afford to compromise on discipline."

He paused as a familiar car showed up in the driveway. "Is that you Mrs. Scott," Josh spoke to the microphone.

"Yes Josh, open the gate please," the woman's raspy voice sounded through the speaker.

"Right away, ma'am. Good night," Josh punched a button and watched the television monitor as the gate opened and the car came through.

"That was all the excitement for the night, I guess," Josh watched the gate close shut and turned to an expectant Dave. "Are you ready?" Josh asked.

"Get on with it," Dave urged him, "this suspense is killing me."

Josh grinned, pulled his chair close to Dave and laid out his plan. For the greater part of the next hour, Josh spoke and Dave listened intently. "So that is the plan, my friend. I have thought this through every possible angle that I could think of and have tied up all the loose ends. We will need to modify this as we go along, but that is the basic structure of what we have ahead of us," Josh paused, unscrewed the cap of the bottle and gulped down a generous swig of water.

He looked hard at Dave and continued, "So what do you think? Are you willing to work with me on this?" Josh hoped for Dave's sake that he would agree. Otherwise Josh would have to kill him—Dave just knew too much.

Dave was bewildered and unconsciously his jaw had dropped at what he heard. He stood up, hands in his pocket and started pacing the room deep in thought.

Josh watched him in silence and didn't feel so sure about Dave anymore. He wondered how he was going to kill Dave. He cursed himself, "I should have studied Dave more closely before I spilled my heart out. Bloody hell, it's too late now," Josh thought. Dave knew it all and with every passing moment Josh felt increasingly certain that Dave would decline his offer and he would have to start all over again to search for another partner and re-start the grooming process. But for the moment, he needed to figure out a way to kill

Dave and within the next few hours—Josh just could not afford to let Dave out of his sight alive—he knew too much.

Josh looked outside the window. The estate was on a cliff and the road behind the gate to the estate was a steep downhill that hugged a rather deep canyon. So if he could snap the brakes on Dave's car and cut open the fuel lines on the undercarriage that might just do the trick. All he had to do was to divert Dave's attention for a while, get him out of sight and…

"Brilliant," Dave almost shouted out, breaking Josh's train of thoughts. "Simply brilliant, Josh. Man, I've got to hand it to you. You are a genius, I always knew that." Dave was beaming and vigorously shaking Josh's hand in excitement. "You little devil, so this was what you had in mind all this time? Why did you not tell me before?" Dave's questions were like rapid fire—he didn't seem to care about pausing for answers.

Josh was laughing, more out of relief than anything else. "Hey, I need my arm, let go now." Dave released his grip on Josh's hand and apologized.

"So are we on, right?" Josh asked.

"Are you kidding me? Of course we are on. What the heck are we waiting for? Let's get started, man," Dave was ecstatic.

"Very well then," Josh said calmly. "From this day, we are partners, each of us have some groundwork to do as you know now. Secrecy and discipline will be the key to our success," he ended.

"Right on, Josh," Dave still could not control the excitement in his voice. It was an adventure he was about to embark on and made no attempt to hide his feelings. He gave Josh a friendly hug, clapped him on his arm and said, "Josh, you're all right you know? Thanks so much for letting me in."

Josh grinned, "Go get some sleep now; you have the morning shift remember?"

Dave nodded and drove off.

Josh splashed some water on his face, looked at himself in the mirror and murmured, "Here goes the neighborhood."

Two weeks later both Josh and Dave handed in their resignations. Josh started his training at the Police Academy while Dave signed up at the Fire Academy.

8

Bill proposed marriage to Joan on her twenty-fifth birthday. Joan had almost finished her glass of red wine in the restaurant when something solid appeared to move and a subdued tinkling noise came from inside her glass. A startled Joan looked closely and fished out the sparkling diamond and blood red ruby ring. She looked up to find Bill already kneeling beside her with a mischievous smile in his face.

He held her hand and said, "Will you marry me, Joan?" Bill sounded like a schoolboy on his first date, nervous and anxious.

Joan blushed, still recovering from the pleasant surprise, "Yes, yes, yes," she hurried. Bill hugged her and they kissed as the other guests turned around in their seats and started to applaud. "Congratulations and good luck," they yelled.

It was the culmination of three years of courtship as Bill and Joan grew closer to each other. She was apprehensive of Bill's job in the beginning, but over time she got used to it. Bill was highly regarded in the community and among his colleagues and was often quoted as a model citizen and public servant. He loved what he did and he loved Joan dearly. He could not have hoped for a better woman to come into his life and he made no secret of it.

One of his favorite lines to Joan was, "Hey I found you in the line of duty. Who says police work is dangerous business, unless of course you are indeed more dangerous than you look!"

Joan laughed, "I just can't win against you, can I?"

They found a nice little three-bedroom house in Carlsbad with an unobstructed view of the Pacific and immediately fell in love with it.

"This is where I'd like to stay and raise our family Bill, but can we afford this?" Joan whispered softly to Bill, clinging on to him. The realtor purposefully stayed away to allow some privacy.

"I think we can manage, sweetheart. It will be a little tough, but we'll get used to it after a while, I guess," Bill replied. "It is so peaceful and beautiful out here," he murmured to Joan as they looked over the edge of the ground dropping to the lush green canyon below.

"The canyon, the ocean in the distance, the blue skies, this little garden and we're perched right on top of it. Yes, this is where I would like to live and grow old with you my love," Bill said lovingly.

Joan snuggled close to him and peered up at him. Bill looked down on those gorgeous blue eyes and hugged her tight.

They placed an offer below the asking price and to their surprise it was accepted right away. The owner had relocated and needed to sell his property quickly.

Bill and Joan spent the next three months decorating their new house, but decided to start living in it only after they got married. Joan had more spare time than Bill and she made the most of it. She had a keen eye for detail. The home that she and Bill wanted was finally theirs and she was going to pour her heart out and deck it up exactly the way they both wanted.

Their eyes were glued into each other as they exchanged vows. It was unrehearsed for both of them but words came to them naturally. They were oblivious of the other people at the wedding—nothing else in the world mattered now that they were bonded in matrimony. They exchanged rings as if in a trance.

"You may now kiss the bride," the priest motioned to Bill. It was a hushed silence as Bill and Joan held each other with sheer admiration, their eyes were talking without words being spoken. Bill held Joan in a fond embrace and they kissed passionately. The wedding party stood up and burst into a loud applause.

Captain Becker from the precinct was in full uniform. He walked up to Bill and Joan and personally congratulated the couple. He looked at Joan and said, "I am very happy for you Mrs. McMillan. At the risk of stating the obvious, Bill is not only a very accomplished officer but a very kind, honest and passionate human being. The Department is proud to have him in the service. I wish you the very best in your married life. You both look wonderful today."

He turned to Bill and said, "I thought about telling you this when you rejoined duty the week after, Bill, but no other time is better than now."

He stepped back, stood in attention and called out loudly, "Detective McMillan, the Department requests you to turn in your badge as soon as possible," he paused as Bill's contented expression changed into confusion and a sudden silence fell among the guests.

Captain Becker sounded serious and hurried on, "is that clearly understood Lieutenant," he stressed on the rank and paused for effect, "McMillan?" He laughed as he saw Bill's face brighten up and break into a wide grin and the guests roared in cheer.

Bill was incredulous and instinctively snapped into attention, "Lieutenant? You are not joking are you Captain?"

Captain Becker laughed loudly, patted Bill in the back and said, "No I am serious about this. I received the paperwork yesterday, so I thought today will be a good day to tell you about it. Well deserved, my boy, you are an asset to the city and to the SDPD. Take some time off and enjoy the company of your lovely wife and we will see you when we see you, Lieutenant."

"I'm speechless Captain Becker. Thank you so very much. I am blessed," Bill said as he shook hands with Captain Becker.

He squeezed Joan's shoulder and whispered, "There is indeed a God, but you are my lucky star, Joan. With you by my side, everything is possible. I will always love and protect you, my angel."

Joan whispered back, "I am proud of you darling, my life is complete with you as my husband. There's nothing more I want from life." She smiled, nodded at the guests and said, "I guess we better take care of them now. You don't want to be an impolite host, do you?"

9

Josh graduated from the Police Academy and joined the SDPD as a Junior Police officer. He was a sharp cadet and excelled during his training. The chief had only positive comments to make about Josh to the Captain of the Central Division, where Josh was to start his career in law enforcement. "The kid holds a lot of promise. Hold on to him and he will make you proud," the chief had said about Josh.

Josh rode along on patrols as an observer for a few months. A first hand experience on how the pros handled incidents was exciting for him—he was learning all the time. He was liked by everyone he worked with and he quickly made friends with fellow officers. He needed to work only four days a week, but voluntarily worked weekends—Josh was a voracious learner.

Soon he was into active law enforcement, reading rights to people, for the first time in his life he used his handcuffs to arrest a man who had broken into a drunken frenzy at home and had critically wounded his ten year old son. It felt good to enforce the law, it made him feel powerful.

"How'd you feel?" the Detective had asked as they drove down to the station afterwards, "That was your first arrest".

"There's a lot of room for improvement, Detective," Josh waved his hand in dismissal. He clearly wanted to set the bar higher for himself.

Josh was closely supervised—not that he needed much supervision. Josh was also willing to take up mundane duties—he spent the whole day observing people during some convention in the city. His colleagues were complaining by lunchtime, but Josh seemed to find his own amusement. "Somebody's got to do it," he said to the other officers on duty, "nothing wrong if that somebody is me."

While Josh established himself as a promising young police officer, Dave was shaping his career in the Fire Department.

The Fire Chief spoke to the group of newly promoted Fire Lieutenants, "You have joined the elite group of people who have sworn to serve the people of San Diego with care and compassion. You have sworn to protect lives, property and the environment of our fine city through fire suppression, rescue, disaster preparedness and fire prevention. You have demonstrated that you have the ability and the leadership qualities that are required to serve the community and lead the brave men and women who serve under you. This department has a long legacy of honesty, courage, efficiency, dedication and selflessness in order to protect the community we serve. You will be expected to live up to that legacy and carry it beyond. You will become the role models of those that follow you and be the pride of those that you report to. My personal best wishes to you and congratulations on your promotion to Fire Lieutenant. God Bless you all!"

As Dave walked away from the group, he felt a sense of pride at what he had achieved in such a short time. It was not an easy ride. It was just a little over a year ago that he had joined the Fire Department as a Firefighter after completing the Fire Academy with high honors. Josh had advised that he had to work real hard and prove his worth in pretty short order. He had to win over the confidence of his Fire Captain as soon as he could so that he could rise through the ranks quickly. It was very critical that both he and Dave got off to a huge start in their careers, it was critical to the plan.

"Life is better than before, but the best was yet to come," Dave thought.

So Dave dedicated himself to his job. At times he would work two shifts, and volunteered his time for his colleagues who wanted to take some time off. He pitched in for them and seemed always available to help. His supervising Lieutenant had cautioned him that overworking would burn him out, that it would tire him out making it difficult to perform his duties. But Dave went on and on, he was what they called 'Mr. Dependable'.

He was an avid learner just like Josh. For the first three months as he went out on calls in the fire truck as an observer. He watched intently what everyone did to bring fires under control.

From the third month onwards, he was allowed to actually participate in fire fighting calls. At first, he was only allowed to operate the water valves on the truck while the more experienced men fought the fire. "You did well there kiddo," the veteran firefighters used to tell him after they returned signed and exhausted from another battle with fire.

Six months later, his Lieutenant started him off with small fire containment jobs and Dave performed the call of duty in copybook style. He considered fires to have life. "Think of it", he told his Lieutenant one day, "the fire is born just like a life would be, the fire has motion just like a life would have, the fire has a core from where it starts just like life does, the fire would spread its reach if not controlled just like life would, one fire could start other fires just like life could reproduce itself, fire would give you life just like life could, fire would kill just like life could and," he paused, "the fire would also die just like life could. So a fire has life in my opinion."

His Lieutenant looked at Dave with surprise. It wasn't every day that a philosopher came to work for him. "You should have been a philosopher or a writer, Dave. That is the weirdest comparison I've heard," his Lieutenant had said with a wide grin, "But tell you what, you do have a point."

Dave almost had a respect for fire—he could anticipate how a fire would react as he fought to control the damage. Dave learned to assess the damage long before the fire could be contained. He sought out and contained the source of fire first. It did not take a long time before his Lieutenant was asking him for suggestions to control incidents more efficiently. Dave was intense and passionate about his work and it was as if he and the fire became one when he arrived on the scene.

10

Judge Baker held the court in the trial of Ray Ortega against the City of San Diego. Ray was charged with illegal possession and trafficking of prohibited drugs. For the last three weeks, Jamie Dawson, the District Attorney battled with Brant Sawyer who was representing Ray. It appeared that Brant had a counter-argument for every argument. Jamie had brought in several witnesses, who started with very convincing statements, but all collapsed in the wave of Brant's cross examinations.

There was a hung jury last evening—the twelve jurors knew in their hearts that Ray was guilty. His cold and emotionless eyes told them nothing, but somehow they knew Ray was guilty. They were inclined to vote against Ray, but Brant's counter arguments were so convincing, none of them could be sure. "You are to express your unbiased opinion based on the facts presented in the courtroom, not by any personal prejudice," they were told during the jury briefing. They all had a personal opinion, but the facts were really not convincing enough to indict Ray.

With twenty years in the courtroom, Judge Baker could also tell the defendant was guilty as charged and God only knew on how many more counts of unlawful acts. But there just wasn't any conclusive evidence from the proceedings of the last three weeks. "This young lawyer has a unique style of cross-examination—very convincing. I'll have to watch him a little closely," he mused.

"Have the jury reached a verdict?" Judge Baker called out.

"Yes your Honor, we have," the juror nearest to the Judge replied.

Ray nervously glanced at Brant and Brant winked back at him. "Take it easy, you're out in five minutes", counseled an emotionless confident Brant in a low murmur.

"Very well then", the judge was speaking, "what say you?"

Ray looked up at the juror who held a piece of paper in his hands and briefly closed his eyes in anticipation of a ruling against him. The juror hesitated a little, glanced at Ray who was looking at him with the same cold and emotionless eyes, turned his attention to the paper in his hand and read out loud. "On the charge of illegal possession of prohibited drugs, the jury finds the defendant," he paused, looked at Ray briefly almost not believing what he was reading and declared, "not guilty". A loud murmur spread across the room of people starting to talk to the next person with utter disbelief.

Judge Baker beat his gavel for silence and motioned to the juror to continue, who paused and looked at Ray again and was surprised to see the pursed lips and almost the beginning of a smile, for the first time since the trial started.

He turned back the paper in his hands and read out loud, "On the charge of illegal trafficking of prohibited drugs, the jury finds the defendant not guilty." There was that proverbial pin-drop silence in the courtroom, all shocked with sheer incredulity.

Ray was now grinning broadly and Brant had a controlled happy expression in his face, another mission accomplished.

The DA looked at the judge drained of all emotion; she had sensed this was coming. Judge Baker was speaking again, "Thank you. Please be seated. Our founding fathers have given us the counsel to hold nobody in this country guilty unless proven to be so through conclusive evidence. This court has been unable to provide suitable evidence that might prove that the charges against the defendant were valid. Mr. Ray Ortega, you are acquitted without charge, you are free to go. However, this court reminds you that when there is smoke there is fire. Please ensure that you stay clear from trouble in the future, so that we don't ever have to meet again in this courtroom. This case is hereby closed". He punched the gavel and the court burst out into pandemonium.

Ray was beaming and shaking Brant's hand profusely. "This is unbelievable, you are better than the boss said, amigo," Ray said in almost a whisper, "You did great".

Brant was not amused. He had learnt to keep his distance from his clients. He never expressed any emotion and always remained calm and composed. That was exactly the reason why he was revered by his clientele—a very special one at that. "Just remind your boss that he's got a payment to make," Brant murmured to Ray. "See you around", he gathered up the papers in his briefcase and prepared to leave.

Josh Timmons was seated four rows behind the defendant's bench. He had been following Brant for the past six months. He thoroughly enjoyed the manner in which Brant argued for his clients. Josh had not missed even one trial where Brant was defending the accused. Brant always seemed to represent the dregs of the society, he obviously enjoyed challenges. So far there was not a single case that Brant had conceded to the DA or to anyone. Narcotics, homicide, robbery, Brant was adept at all of them. He could almost foresee what was coming and always seemed prepared with a counter argument. The manner in which he cross-examined witnesses was a treat to watch. Brant was good, very good; he definitely seemed to have gained the confidence of the not-so-perfect citizens over the past six months—he had an unblemished record.

Josh had followed Brant even outside the courtroom. He never met a client outside his office. He lived in an oceanfront home in La Jolla. Brant was not married but saw several women—nothing steady or regular. Brant drove a Rolls Royce to court and a Bentley convertible at other times. Brant always patronized designer labels for his clothing. So with that flashy lifestyle, truly

Brant was earning and earning good. Brant knew what he was doing and was doing it very well.

Josh was interested—very interested in Brant. "A lawyer like Brant can be the next critical partner to help me fulfill my dreams," Josh thought. But he had to be careful. He had graduated from the Academy and had been a cop for over a year now. Josh never wore uniform to court. His badge however enabled him to gain entrance into the courtroom anytime he pleased. He had witnessed several trials and studied the defense lawyers intently. Nobody came close to Brant—his style was something so vibrant and so effective.

While Brant walked out of the courtroom, his eyes caught Josh looking at him with a thoughtful expression. "I've noticed this guy in all my trials for the last six months. He has never tried to speak or react in court, just seems to be watching the trials. Weird, maybe just a coincidence, or maybe he is just a fan", Brant thought and smiled to himself.

The DA rushed up to catch up with him. "That was very good Mr. Sawyer. Your client is as guilty as they can be; everybody knows that, you know that. Be careful of the company you are keeping these days, Mr. Sawyer. See that you lock your doors when you sleep at night", she counseled—obviously in sheer frustration.

"Madam District Attorney, you could not prove him guilty, could you? I would also hazard a guess that you have also heard what Judge Baker just said in plain English a few minutes ago. So my client is a free man. Which part of all this can a decorated woman in your position not understand or accept?" Brant paused. "I'd say you get over it ma'am. Your concern for my continued good health fills me with the utmost sense of gratitude," he continued sarcastically, "you take care of yourself now." Brant tipped his hat and walked away.

District Attorney Jamie Dawson stood there, shaking her head. "One day Brant, one day I'll pull that veil from your face and have my last laugh," she murmured as she watched Brant get into his gleaming Rolls and screeched away. Jamie looked at her watch and grimaced as the pangs of hunger gripped her.

Josh heard the conversation and smiled to himself. His mind was overflowing with thoughts and ideas of his grand plans for the future—he could almost reach out and touch it. A Malibu mansion with a private beach, a private yacht that could take him to the Caribbean whenever he wished, a fleet of expensive cars…

The driver honked and yelled profanities to wake Josh out of his daydream. He realized he was in plain clothes and off duty, and he was walking straight in the middle of traffic. He waved apologetically and crossed over to the other side of the street. He could have taken his car, but hopped on a bus to National City. "I've got to tell this to Dave," he thought.

He met Dave at the bar off Main Street. Dave was already into his second beer when Josh arrived. The bar was pretty empty, but then on a Wednesday afternoon, there was never a big crowd.

"I have been waiting for you. So, another victory for Brant, I guess?" Dave asked—he already knew the answer.

"No credits for guessing the obvious, Dave. I tell you, this guy is bloody good. Just the usual for me, George", Josh nodded to George, the bartender across the counter.

George filled up an oversized glass and pushed it over to Josh.

Josh gave a detailed account of the proceedings in the courtroom as Dave listened intently. "We have been following his trials, for six months now Josh and though the results are always obvious it is intriguing to hear the details of every trial," Dave said. "It looks like we have found the missing link in our plans. Now we have to approach him and see what he can do for us".

Josh nodded, "Yes, but like you and I, Brant is still at the beginning of his career. There is a time and place for everything and now is not that time." Josh paused as if in deep thought and murmured, "You're right, Brant is the missing link. But there is another one we need."

Josh looked up and noticed the big bulk of George appear behind Dave. He had his jacket on and George had a friendly smile on his face. "Gentlemen, I am leaving a little early today—the boys are having a bachelor party for a friend." He turned around and nodded towards the bar, "My manager, Kurt will take care of you if you need anything else—just holler and he'll be around. So if you'll excuse me, I'll take your leave today."

Josh nodded and said, "Sure thing George, go have fun and we'll see you later." Josh looked pensively as George walked away—for a man his size, he moved rather smoothly, almost cat-like in his gait.

Dave caught his look, glanced around to see George leave the bar and just stared there for a while. He held his gaze and said softly, "Can George be the one we are looking for?"

"What, so now you've started to read my mind too?" Josh was amused—he had picked Dave well, he thought.

"I've been around you for a while, you know. One gets to know such things. Jeez, if we were otherwise inclined, we could have been married," Dave joked.

Josh grinned and said, "Someone like George could turn out to be very useful, but I need to dig into his background."

Dave frowned, "Shouldn't be too tough to get some information on someone like George. I wish we knew his last name, you could have done some research on him."

Josh looked at Dave with unseeing eyes—his mind was churning. "We can fix that," he told Dave. He raised his hand to catch the attention of the manager behind the bar, who nodded and walked over.

When he approached, Josh smiled and said, "Hi there, your man Hurley said that you'll take care of us, since he had to leave early."

The manager looked puzzled and narrowed his eyes, "I'll definitely take care of you gentlemen, but," he paused as if uncertain and continued, "who's Hurley?"

Josh had a surprised expression in his face, "Your bartender, isn't he George Hurley?"

The manager let out a short laugh and said, "Oh no, his last name is Briggs."

Josh looked at a surprised Dave, laughed and said, "I can't believe it. We're coming here for over a year now and we always thought George's last name was Hurley."

Josh shook his head from side to side, looked up at the manager and said, "I apologize. George is a good man. How long has he been working for you?"

"Oh just over two years now," the manager said.

"Good to have a man like him around. I was wondering if you could bring us two Heinekens, please," Josh asked.

The manager bowed and said, "Coming right up gentlemen." He left.

Dave was smiling when Josh looked at him and said softly "You wily fox, that was very clever."

Josh grinned, "As Sherlock Holmes would say—Elementary my friend, elementary."

11

They found fingerprints on the gun that was allegedly used in the crime and ballistics confirmed the bullet to match the bullets from the gun. The case was easy and there was no doubt on how the ruling would go. On the day of the trial, Josh was supposed to accompany Detective Glover to Court and observe the proceedings. Detective Glover was to testify in Court since he was the senior officer who had arrested the suspect.

However Mrs. Glover went into labor which kept Detective Glover out of court. The judge had consulted the two opposing attorneys and summoned Josh to substitute for Detective Glover. Josh was excited—this was new to him. Josh walked into the courtroom on time and looked around the familiar surroundings, a room that he had frequented so much in the past. He looked over to the defendant's bench and saw what he had least expected.

Brant Sawyer was defending the man Josh had arrested. "You must be kidding me", he murmured to himself. He blinked and looked again—Brant Sawyer was still there in the flesh, calm, composed, expressionless and radiating confidence around himself. "This is going to be a very interesting experience", Josh thought.

Soon the Judge announced that Josh was substituting for the Detective and was also involved in the arrest. Brant appeared to review some notes intently. Josh took up the witness stand. After the regular oaths were taken, the Judge called the DA to question Josh.

Josh glanced over at Brant and thought that he had caught a surprised look on Brant's face as Brant saw Josh in the witness box. "I think he recognizes me. This is a nice way to get introduced", Josh told himself.

Brant did indeed recognize the man who had been consistently appeared in his trials for almost a year now. "So you're a police officer, huh?" Brant mused.

At the District Attorney's request, Josh described the crime scene as vividly as if it were happening right in court. He and Detective Glover had apprehended the defendant at the home of his deceased partner with a gun in his hand. They had found the victim, a Mark Sommers, lying in a pool of blood pouring out of his forehead and chest. He had been brutally shot three times—twice on the chest right through his heart.

The DA produced reports of fingerprint matching and ballistics that verified that the bullets found in the victim's body were indeed from the gun taken from the defendant's hand at the time of arrest. The court clerk was typing away furiously as the DA and Josh went through the routine events that followed.

"No further questions, Your Honor", the DA declared, "your witness," she offered, looking at Brant. Brant just sat there looking at Josh for a while. He had a deadpan expression in his face. Actually Brant was assessing the situation and lining up questions in his mind.

"Thank you for that account, Officer. How long have you been serving the SDPD?" Brant asked.

"Objection, Your Honor", the DA interjected, "Officer Timmons is a sworn officer and his length of service has no relevance to the case".

The Judge nodded, "Sustained, please keep your interrogations focused on the case Mr. Sawyer".

Brant nodded in acceptance—his question really was out of personal curiosity than anything else. He turned to Josh and asked, "Can you describe to the court how you got to the crime scene?"

"I was on patrol with Detective Glover, when we were directed to go to the crime scene. Apparently someone had called Emergency and reported seeing a person enter the house of the deceased, carrying a gun in his hand. We had rushed to respond. It took us about four minutes to get there. We knocked on the door and nobody responded, so we had to shoot the lock and enter the house," Josh responded.

"And what time was it when you received the message from the control station?" Brant asked.

"It was five to nine, late in the evening, I had glanced at the clock in the police car when the message came in," Josh replied.

"I see. What happened when you entered the crime scene?" Brant asked.

"We found the defendant standing over the body of the deceased with the gun in his hand. The defendant had a dark patch on his left jaw as if someone had hit him. He was bleeding from his nose and had a lump on his head," Josh replied.

"So you assumed that the defendant had shot the victim and hence arrested him, is that correct, Officer Timmons?" Brant asked.

"Well, clearly there was fight and there was nobody…" Josh had started to speak.

Brant interjected, "A Yes or and No is all I need to know Officer".

Josh was well aware of Brant's aggressive nature when he cross-examined witnesses and replied, "Yes".

"So you assumed the defendant as guilty and arrested him. Did you check to see if anyone else was in the house?" Brant asked.

"Yes that's routine. As Detective Glover disarmed the defendant and cuffed him, I checked the house and found no one," Josh responded.

"Did the defendant attempt to resist arrest?" Brant asked.

"No, I guess he panicked and…," Josh started to say and mentally kicked himself for volunteering additional information.

As expected, Brant interjected, "The court will record 'No' as your answer. The Court is not interested to know what you guessed or you assumed, Officer, since those are not considered substantial evidence," he paused, "I'm sure you are aware of that."

Brant walked over to his desk, picked up some papers scanned it quickly and read, "The police report here states that there was a broken kitchen window in the house of the deceased." He turned to Josh and asked "Did you see that broken window, Officer?"

"Yes, I did," replied Josh, careful to say exactly what he was being asked.

"Good. Did you see broken glass on the floor, Officer?" Brant asked almost instantaneously.

Josh thought a while, trying to remember the scene and replied, "No, I can't remember seeing any broken glass on the floor."

Brant nodded, Josh thought he caught a faint smile fleeting through Brant's lips, but it might have been his imagination. Brant referred to his papers again and said, "The police record here also says that two wine glasses were found, both almost half full on the kitchen table. Is that correct Officer?" Brant asked.

"Yes, we did find two wine glasses as you mention. The two men had started out on a drink, as was confirmed by our forensics expert—they found lip impressions on the rim of the glass," Josh replied.

"Thank you Officer, your testimony has been very valuable to this court," Brant turned to the Judge and declared, "No further questions at this moment your Honor, but I would request your permission to have Officer Timmons remain in court a little longer, should the need arise for some additional questions."

The Judge nodded in approval as Josh stepped down, pondering what Brant was up to. He had witnessed Brant's style for almost a year now and could almost predict his next move. But this time Brant did not seem to give anything away. "What are you up to Sawyer?" Josh thought.

Brant turned to the Judge and announced, "Your Honor, I had requested the presence of the emergency line operator who answered the telephone call for help on the day of the murder. Is she present in the courtroom today?"

The Judge called out, "I'm told she is. Would Ms. Benson please rise?" Brant joined everybody else in the courtroom to turn and see a woman in her mid to late twenties stand up.

"Thank you, your Honor. You may please be seated, Ms. Benson. I'll have questions for you later," Brant motioned to the woman.

"I would now like to ask the defendant to take the stand, Your Honor," Brant requested.

The Judge called the defendant to the stand.

"For the record, Sir, please tell us your name and your occupation," Brant asked the defendant.

"My name is John Carter and I own a restaurant," he paused and then continued, "used to co-own the restaurant with Mark," he paused again, "Mark Sommers, the victim."

"You have been charged with murdering your partner, Mr. Carter. Did you kill Mr. Sommers?" Brant asked.

"No I did not", the defendant replied with all the conviction that he could summon in his voice.

Brant let out a short laugh and said, "Mr. Carter, Officer Timmons here just testified under oath that he found the gun in your hand when he entered the scene of the crime—the same gun that was fired to kill the victim. You were also bleeding and apparently someone punched your left jaw. Still you expect us to believe you did not kill your partner?"

"Yes, I did not kill Mark, it was a guy wearing a ski mask who killed him," the defendant declared nervously.

"Oh, so there was another person. Do you know who it was Mr. Carter?" Brant asked.

"No, I don't. I could only see his eyes and he did not speak a word," the defendant stated.

Brant acted as if he was confused and said, "I am confused Sir. You are saying there was another person who shot your partner, but this police report does not mention anything about such a person being present. Please tell us what happened that night."

"I had gone to Mark's house that evening to discuss some business matters. About a quarter before nine there was a knock at the door. Mark was preparing a drink and asked me to answer the door. I released the deadbolt and just started to open the door when I felt the door being kicked in. I was thrown to the floor and this heavily built masked man entered the house and locked the door behind him. He motioned me to keep quiet and gestured me to stand up. When I stood up, he started punching out at me. His first punch hit my nose and dazed me. I tried to duck his next one, which struck my neck on my left and knocked me off my feet. Mark had heard the sound of the door being kicked in and the thud of my fall, and wheeled his chair to the front door. He," the defendant was interrupted.

Brant was warming up, "Wait a minute you said your partner wheeled in his chair. What does that mean?"

"Yes, Mark was a paraplegic and always moved around in his wheelchair," the defendant answered.

"I see, how interesting. You mean the victim could not walk?" Josh asked.

"No, Mark became a paraplegic from the hip down after an accident many years ago, though his hands functioned just fine," the defendant replied.

Brant looked at him thoughtfully, stole a quick glance at the Judge and without a change in expression said, "Please continue. What happened after that?"

"Mark was surprised just as I had been when he saw the masked figure in his house. He had started to ask a question, but before he could speak, the man shot him in his forehead. I tried to pick myself up, but the man shot Mark twice on his chest. Then the man rushed over to me and struck my head hard with his gun and I fell unconscious," the defendant paused. "The next thing I remember was the sharp crack of another gunshot, sound of breaking glass from somewhere at the back of the house and two Police Officers barging in through the door. I tried to sit up still concussed and confused and noticed that I was holding a gun in my hand. Mark was lying in a pool of blood. The Officers pinned me down, kicked the gun away from my hands and handcuffed me," the defendant concluded.

"Can you describe the killer?" Brant asked.

"He had a ski mask, so I could not see his features, but he had blue eyes. He was heavily built, had a light limp on his left leg. He was wearing black leather gloves, short sleeved shirt, jeans and tennis shoes. I am pretty sure I saw a scar on the outside of his right arm just below the elbow, a scar that comes from a stab wound. But things happened so fast and so suddenly I cannot remember any other detail," the defendant sounded tired.

"Thank you," Brant said, turned and nodded to the DA suggesting that she could ask her questions.

"Mr. Carter, I am looking at these bank records of your restaurant," District Attorney Jamie Dawson began. She walked over to the courtroom clerk and handed a copy for the Judge, "business has not been good for a while, am I right?"

The defendant replied hesitantly, "Yes, we have been having problems for the past year. For some reason, we have not had the steady flow of customers as we had before."

"And what may be the reason for that Mr. Carter," Jamie asked.

"Our cook decided to quit one day and we brought in a new cook. Business has never been the same again," the defendant said softly.

"How was your relationship with your partner?" the DA asked.

The defendant hesitated and said "We were very good friends and like all good friends, we agreed on matters and disagreed on others. It was good partnership."

Jamie snorted, turned to the Judge and said, "Please let this be on record, Your Honor, the defendant had disagreements with his partner. Here is a written statement from Jimmy Garcia, the ex-cook at the defendant's restaurant and he will be happy to testify in Court if needed. The statement clearly states that the victim had started to embezzle funds from the restaurant and had started to make false accounting entries in the books. He even asked Mr. Garcia to use stale meat and vegetables to save on expenses. He had also threatened to fire Mr. Garcia, if he told anyone about it. Mr. Garcia summoned enough courage and complained to the defendant," the DA stopped reading, looked at the defendant and asked, "How am I doing so far, Mr. Carter?"

She looked away from the defendant—apparently not interested in his answer and continued, "Mr. Garcia's statements mention several occasions when the defendant and the victim had heated arguments and the defendant repeatedly telling the victim, and I quote here, 'The restaurant is my childhood dream. I have spent every cent that I have to make the restaurant as popular as it is today. If you continue to do what you have been doing, we will have to go our separate ways,' unquote. The victim even fired Mr. Garcia for complaining to the defendant," Jamie put her papers away.

She turned to the judge and said, "So Your Honor, the defendant's motive to commit the murder is clear. The victim was trying to destroy the defendant's childhood dream. He could not tolerate the misgivings of the deceased and decided to kill him," the DA had walked over to the defendant's stand, turned to look squarely at this eyes and almost shouted, "Is that not true, Mr. Carter?"

The defendant was shaking his head in denial when Brant stood up and calmly said, "It's a statement from someone who has not been sworn in court, Your Honor. This is inadmissible evidence."

The Judge nodded and called, "Sustained. Please present the facts Madam District Attorney and be careful with your questions."

"Yes, Your Honor", the DA collected herself and said in a subdued voice. She approached the box, "Mr. Carter, my reports here say that you took some acting lessons a few years back. Did you plan to become an actor?"

The defendant looked at her and said, "Yes, I wanted be an actor and had taken some lessons in acting. Actually, I even thought of professional acting as a career before I realized that was not something I wanted to do," the defendant replied.

The DA laughed and said sarcastically, "Your lessons came in real handy, did they not Mr. Carter?" the DA asked. She turned to the Judge and said in a confident voice, "There was no heavily built man in the scene of the crime, Your Honor. It was the defendant himself who called Emergency after he had committed the murder, so that we overlook him as being the suspect. He then punched himself in a few places and knocked himself out with his own gun, just to prove to the authorities that he was attacked as well. As Officer Timmons said, it took them four minutes to reach the scene of the crime after they were alerted by the police operator. The defendant had the time to return back after calling the police. Then he knocked himself out but was too late to toss the gun away before the Police went in," the DA turned to the defendant—she was on a roll, "You are not a professional actor nor a professional killer, so you fell short, Mr. Carter. This man is guilty, Your Honor—it is as clear as daylight," Jamie concluded.

The Judge made some notes and asked Brant, "Do you wish to cross examine the defendant Mr. Sawyer?"

"Yes Your Honor, thank you," Brant said. He looked at Jamie and stared at her for a while and said, "That was a great piece of imaginative deduction Ma'am District Attorney; you do have a fertile mind." A low murmur spread across the courtroom and the Judge beat his gavel to bring silence.

The DA scowled.

He turned to the defendant and asked, "On which part of your body did you get injured on the night of the crime?"

"He punched me on my nose first, then he hit me right here," the defendant touched the left of his neck.

Brant consulted his notes and said, "Yes, the medical report from the paramedic who examined you indicates that you were pretty badly bruised on the left of your neck. The report further says that you had a bruise on the upper left side of your head." The defendant nodded in approval.

Brant reached inside his lapel pulled out a pen and suddenly threw it at the defendant yelling, "Catch it." The defendant was visibly startled and instinctively stuck out his right hand to pluck the flying object out of the air. "Good catch, Mr. Carter. You just proved that you are right handed," Brant smiled briefly.

"Phew, you could have just asked me," the defendant said returning the pen back.

"Sure, but the court needed to know for sure that you indeed are right handed," Brant declared. "I can understand a right handed person punching his own nose hard enough to make it bleed. However it is difficult to believe how a right-handed person can hit himself so hard and so effectively on the left of his neck and the upper left side of his head to cause such injuries as Mr. Carter has suffered," Brant paused as if in thought and said, "Actually I believe it is impossible, would you not agree Ma'am District Attorney?" Brant casually looked at the DA, who scowled and tried not to look at Brant.

A light murmur broke out in the courtroom and Judge beat his gavel to silence the audience.

"Very good Brant, very good," Josh mused.

"Your Honor", Brant was saying as the pandemonium stopped, "I would now like to call Ms. Benson to the witness stand, please."

A woman in her late twenties took the stand.

Brant approached her, "Ms. Benson, how long have you been working as an Emergency line operator?"

"That will be five years next month, Sir," she replied.

"Do you remember the exact time when you received the distress call?"

"Yes Sir. It was six before nine as I have logged in the call register," she said emphatically.

"Ms. Benson, please be very careful when you answer this question," Brant was building another crescendo. "You have heard the defendant speak in Court today. Do you think defendant could have been the caller?" Brant asked.

The witness thought for a while, looked at the defendant and said, "We get so many distress calls throughout the day, it is very difficult for me to remember any particular voice. However, I do recall that the caller had a rather deep voice and an exceptionally strong emphasis on the letter 's' when he spoke—it sounded more like 'sh'. I did not catch that emphasis when the defendant was speaking today."

"Did the caller leave a name and contact information?" Brant asked.

"No Sir. The caller would not give his name or contact information. He just said that he had seen a person entering the house of the deceased with a gun in his hand. When I asked his name, he would not say. All he said was that he did his duty as a citizen to report the incident and would not take any other responsibility or obligation and that it was up to me to send in help or to ignore the phone-call. Standard operating guidelines require us to send in help whenever we receive such distress calls and I promptly called the police."

"Thank you Ms. Benson, you did the right thing. No further questions. Your witness," Brant offered to the DA.

"No questions," the DA looked already defeated.

In the summary speech, the DA continued to maintain that it was the defendant who was indeed guilty and had planned out the murder meticulously and had carried out according to plan. The DA even suggested that a fight had broken out and that the deceased had knocked out the defendant after he had been fatally shot. The jury listened intently.

Brant started his concluding statement, "First of all it is clear that the defendant was not the person who had called the police control room to report the murder. Ms. Benson's testimony proves that beyond a doubt. It is impossible for a right-handed person to self-inflict such heavy injuries on the left of one's neck and head as my client had suffered. There is no circumstantial evidence against my client, the gun was planted in his hand by a third person, who we believe was heavily built, wore a ski mask and was ruthless enough to kill a paraplegic in cold blood. My client is not guilty," Brant concluded and took his seat.

"Has the jury reached a verdict," the Judge said looking up from his papers as he finished writing his notes.

"Yes we have your Honor."

The judge read the verdict, "This court finds the defendant not guilty of murder. As Mr. Sawyer mentioned there is no circumstantial evidence to implicate the defendant. The defendant is to be set free, however the court directs him to stay within city limits until such time that the actual killer is apprehended. The court also orders the police department to keep this case open and resume investigations to bring in the criminal to justice. Court is dismissed," the Judge beat his gavel again and stood up.

Josh turned to see the familiar scene of people profusely congratulating Brant who silently nodded in proud acknowledgement. He slightly bowed to the ladies and nodded to the men, shook hands with the defendant, gathered his papers and started to leave.

As he passed Josh, Brant glanced at him and softly murmured, "Case is over Officer Timmons, just like the ones before. Good day to you", and walked away without breaking step.

Josh caught up with Brant and said, "Congratulations Mr. Sawyer. Maybe we can get together sometime for a drink or something, nothing professional, I promise."

Brant was not surprised at the invitation. "I'll take you up on that. Let me know when you have time and we can get together. Here's my contact number," Brant replied as he handed over a business card to Brant.

Josh watched as Brant drove away in his Rolls and mused, "Are you just being friendly or do you have something in your mind? But you know, Brant, you are bloody good at what you do". He sighed as he remembered the Judge's orders to find the real killer, "Where on earth do I find the real killer now. I don't even know where to start."

12

Josh logged into the criminal database and searched for 'George Briggs'. He had promised Dave to run some checks on the bartender. George appeared like someone who might have a criminal record. The computer displayed three matches. Josh jotted down the carousel and docket numbers for the three matches and placed a call to Records Management.

"Smithy, this is Officer Timmons. I need a favor from you. I am looking for some information from our records. I'd like to come by around six this evening and do some digging. Are you planning to be there?" Josh asked.

"I'll be leaving at six tonight Officer, the missus has a party planned. You know how it is," the clerk said.

"Sure, I understand Smithy," Josh honestly had no clue how it would be if some wife had a party planned and the husband did not show up on time.

"But, Fred, the new hire will be here for the night shift and he can help you. However, if you have a carousel and docket number, I can look them up and keep them ready for you to pick up," the clerk said.

"Actually you know I don't have those numbers yet," Josh did not want to go on record anywhere. "But I will try to get them before I get there. Thank you as always."

Josh purposely showed up at the Records counter at seven—Smithy would definitely be gone by then. He was right. A young man was behind the counter preparing some dockets. Josh walked up to the counter and introduced himself. The clerk nodded, "Yes, Officer Timmons. My supervisor told me to expect you at around six."

"I know, something came up and I could not make it. I need to look at some files," Josh had a serious tone in his voice.

"Sure Sir, do you have the carousel and docket numbers to those files? I can get them for you," the clerk offered.

Josh nodded at the desk behind the clerk and said, "Seems like you have quite a workload there. Why don't you work on them while I look for those files myself? I have the numbers with me, so I'll help myself."

The young clerk hesitated and pushed a button to open a door beside his counter. "Thanks Officer Timmons, yeah I have quite a few records to pull. Are you sure you can locate those records?"

"Don't worry. I've been here before with your boss. I think I can find my way," Josh replied as he passed through the door and shut it behind him.

"Ok then. Just yell if you need help," the clerk turned back to his desk.

"Will do, thanks," Josh replied.

Josh located the first 'George Briggs' and frowned, it wasn't who he was looking for. The second file had 'Deceased' marked in big red letters on the front page inside the file. Josh put the file back into the cabinet and referred his note for the carousel and docket number of the last 'George Briggs'.

Josh pulled out the folder for the last 'George Briggs'; flipped the cover and picked up the picture—it was dated almost seventeen years ago. Josh frowned and picked up another picture that was dated more recently. The frown turned into a smile as Josh murmured, "Gotcha, my friend." The profile page had a 'Released' mark in bold red letters and dated couple of years ago— the same date as in the more recent picture. The man in the picture was indeed George Briggs, the bartender the Josh was looking for. He put the picture back, picked up a few more files from the cabinet in random and settled himself into a chair to read George's file.

Josh intently read the transcript of the court proceedings that took place almost seventeen years ago that had placed George behind bars on the charges of dangerous driving, obstruction of justice and something about providing false information to a police officer. Josh flipped over to the page where the sentence was recorded—fifteen years in prison with all assets being liquidated and transferred to the victim. "A pretty stiff sentence, I guess," Josh mused.

"Did you find what you were looking for Officer Timmons?" the voice of the records clerk broke through Josh's concentration.

"I don't think so, I was looking for some profiles and," Josh nodded at the files in front of him, "looks like there is no record here."

"Not a very fruitful search, huh? I'm sorry to hear that, sir, especially after over three hours that you have been here," the clerk was genuinely sympathetic.

Josh glanced at his watch and was surprised. It was indeed past three hours since he had got in. "Well, that's how it is, Fred. You win some and you lose some," Josh said in a tired monotone. "I'll return these back to where they came from and get out of your hair."

"Take your time, sir. As always, I am here to help if you need me," the clerk offered.

"I will, thanks," Josh replied.

He watched the clerk leave and picked up the most recent picture of George. "So that's your story? I wonder if you still have any juice left in you after seventeen years." Josh murmured.

Josh got up and replaced the files in their appropriate cabinets and started to leave, his mind deep in thought. He was about to step into the front office when realization hit him like a sledgehammer between his eyes. Josh stopped, whirled around and almost ran back to the filing cabinet. He almost yanked the handle of the cabinet and pulled out George's file once again.

He flipped over to the page where the sentence was recorded and read it again. It said, 'The court further orders that all assets of defendant be liquidated and handed over to the plaintiff who has been wrongfully disabled for life as a result of the defendant's irresponsible and reckless action'.

Josh stopped reading and closed his eyes. "Could there be a connection here?" Josh wondered. He turned his attention back to the file and turned to the first page of the transcript. Beside 'Defendant' it read, 'George Briggs'. The line below read 'Plaintiff', followed by 'Mark Sommers'.

"You bloody son-of-a-bitch," Josh murmured and shook his head incredulously as the realization sunk in and everything fell into place. Josh replaced the file, thanked the clerk in the front office and left. "I just killed two birds with one stone. This is my lucky day today," Josh grinned as he looked up at the clear night sky.

He approached the house where Dave lived and saw his car parked on the curb. Josh impatiently knocked on the door. After the fourth knock, Dave opened the door—he had a bathrobe on.

He looked irritated, "What the hell do you…" Dave stopped as Josh almost brushed past him into the house and sat down on the couch.

"Sorry Josh, I didn't know it was you," Dave was apologetic. "What's up buddy, you look excited."

"You bet I am," Josh sounded happy. He glanced over to the adjoining bedroom, nodded in that direction and asked, "You've got company in there?" He knew Dave dated women.

Dave hesitated and sounded embarrassed, "Well, yes, you caught us at a bad time. But I can ask her to leave if you've got something important to discuss."

Josh stood up, slapped Dave lightly on his shoulder and said, "I'm sorry, I should have called first. I'll see you outside in my car in ten minutes. It's about George," he said and pulled the entry door shut after him.

Dave looked at the closed door in wonder. He pulled on his pajamas and walked out to the street.

"Our friend George has an illustrious record as I just found out and believe it or not I have pretty substantial proof that he still has it in him to be useful to us," Josh said calmly as Dave seated himself in the car.

"No kidding! Are you going to tell me about it or not?" Dave was excited—knowing Josh for all these years, Josh never indulged in small talk.

Josh laughed and explained what he had discovered on George's profile. He paused and glanced sideways at Dave, who was grinning broadly. "Impressed already my friend?" Josh asked.

"You bet! But how do we know for sure he will work for us?" Dave was impatient.

"Hold you horses, buddy," Josh laughed, "you are an easy man to please. I have only completed half of the story. What I am about to tell you will blow you away," he paused again. "I am sure you have read about the Sommers murder case where the jury released the suspect and ordered the police department to find the real killer. Does that ring a bell?" Josh asked.

Dave pondered about it and said, "Yes that was about a few weeks back."

"Exactly. As a matter of fact I was the officer who had been in the scene of the crime and had to testify in court. The department has put me in charge of this investigation," Josh grinned at Dave's quizzical expression.

"Go on, I am not sure I understand the connection here," Dave seemed puzzled.

"Well, Mark Sommers the victim became a paraplegic seventeen years ago in a road accident. Our friend George was in road accident too seventeen years ago and it was a Mark Sommers who pressed charges against him. The judge had thrown George behind bars and had ordered all his assets be liquidated and transferred over to Mark Sommers. Are you still with me?" Josh paused.

Dave leaned back on his seat and shook his head. "So you think George finished his jail time, researched Sommers, waited a while and then had his revenge?" Dave said as he connected the dots in his mind.

"Can there really be any other explanation?" Josh stared at the road ahead and murmured softly. "I'll just have to prove this for certain."

"Well, are you going to put him away again?" Dave sounded doubtful.

Josh laughed out and said, "What good does that do to us to put away such a resource when we can use him to our advantage. The fact that we know his dark little secret gives us the required edge. Fear is a key motivator my friend. I think we'll give him a chance at life as long as he agrees to dance to our tunes."

"What are we going to do now?" Dave asked.

"We need to keep tabs on George. He does not know what we do for a living and I intend to keep it that way for a while. Let's get a little friendly with him. The time is not right to approach George just yet, but he'll soon have no option but to follow our lead. I have to demonstrate to the court that I am still investigating the Mark Sommers case, I'll fix that. If George decides to play with us, and I am sure he will, the case will stay open for a while. It will eventually be closed as unresolved," Josh replied calmly staring at the road ahead as if he could predict the future.

"I've signed up for narcotics training, starting next month, Dave. We have to get aligned with Brant and get George to work for us, and then we're all set for some real work," Josh continued.

"Everything is going per plan," Dave murmured. Josh nodded in approval.

13

"Lieutenant Bill McMillan reporting Sir," Bill called out as he saluted the instructor. He was one of the ten officers who were hand-selected to participate in the 'Supercops' program.

Over the years Bill had earned the respect and confidence of his fellow officers and Chief Miller had his eye on him as his potential successor as Chief of Police. So when the Governor disclosed his plans for the 'Supercops' program to the Chiefs of Police, it did not take long for Chief Miller to offer up his prodigy, Lieutenant McMillan for training.

"Welcome back Lieutenant, please take up your position," he instructed to the group lined up in the firing range. "Fire at will gentlemen, the top three Officers get to advance to the next level of training. Take your time."

The deafening sound of gunfire subsided but one gun continued firing in slow regular intervals. Bill seemed to be in no hurry to empty his gun as the others waited and watched in awe as his bulls-eye already had its center pierced and had a small neat circle punched with bullet holes all around it. The last bullet went through the bulls-eye a little to the top left of the circle that Bill had punched out. It almost appeared that Bill had placed a checkmark in the circle that he shot out in the target board.

He placed his weapon down and removed his head gear to be greeted with applause, the instructor was smiling broadly, visibly proud of his most able student. "You're such a show off," one of the Officers commented playfully. Bill grinned and waved his hand in modest dismissal.

The instructions were clear, first of all, one had to fire at will, in other words, one had the luxury to take his time to aim and shoot. Secondly, only the top three would be allowed to proceed to the next level, in other words, one had to be extra watchful —no rush, no macho shooting, everyone had to pace themselves to qualify for the remainder of the program. The group was dismissed after being told that the training was complete and that they are to await orders for assignments.

"That was some neat piece of shooting Lieutenant. Where did you learn to shoot like that?" the instructor asked as he shook hands with Bill.

"I learned from the best, Sir—'guess I just got a little lucky there," Bill said humbly.

"Lucky my left foot, Lieutenant—I know that grouping was well intended," the instructor nodded at the target board. "I'm glad you're here, Lieutenant, we have some hope yet I guess," he finished.

That afternoon, Bill and the other two officers were directed to report back to the training facility the next morning. The three men had re-grouped in the designated room and were busy in animated conversation, when the instructor walked in with the Chief of Police. The group fell silent, stood up and held their hands in salute, a little surprised at the Chief's presence. The Chief and the instructor saluted back.

The instructor took up his stand in the lectern and said, "You had been told that your training was over and that you are being trained for a special program but that was all that you knew. Well, that was the story for the rest of the group. The three of you have excelled in your training and you are the chosen group who will know what this is all about. For you the training is not over, it was just the beginning. We did not reveal all the details to the larger group on purpose. You will be sworn into complete secrecy—your lives could possibly depend on it. Please rise now to take your oath from the Chief."

The Chief of Police took the lectern and swore in the three Officers and then motioned them to take their seats. "Now that you are sworn in, this is as good as it gets. The Governor had announced a program to deal with corruption among police officers to investigate the growing number of cases in record that make us believe that some of our very own have started to abuse the power of the law vested upon them. They have also been suspected to support criminal activity for handsome kickbacks. However, we don't know who they are and how they operate," the Chief paused for effect and scanned the faces of the men.

"To this effect," the Chief continued, "the Governor has obtained the support of Senator Jones who in turn has helped us secure the services of the FBI. Your instructor here is not who you have been told so far. This is Agent Brendan Miller, who specializes in anti-corruption, espionage, narcotics, homicide and undercover operations. We have named this as the 'Supercops' program, because once you are through the grueling five weeks, that is really what you will become—Supercops. Each one of you have demonstrated in your career to be upright, competent and dedicated men, who are willing to take the necessary risks to make our cities better places to live in. Any questions so far?"

"No Sir, this is intriguing, please continue," Sergeant Carvey glanced at the other two officers and said on behalf of the group.

"Very well," the Chief resumed, "Agent Miller will explain during the course of the training program how you are required to maintain the dual identity without raising suspicion about your primary focus in your jobs. Remember that secrecy is the key to the success of the program and is critical for the safety and well being of yourselves and possibly your families. We recommend that you also do not discuss any activity about the program with anyone—family included—this is for your added protection. So far you have undergone physical and weapons and unarmed combat training. Next two weeks will teach you special surveillance techniques, use of special equipment to assist you in surveillance and of course working under cover without giving your position away. You will learn self-preservation procedures in emergencies, incident logging and reporting procedures and techniques on how to handle suspicious activity. Your suspects may as well be colleagues from your own precinct, so you will have to be all the more careful," the Chief paused to wet his throat.

"Without mincing any words, let me tell you that this is serious business, you will be at risk all the time, but the service that you will provide will make our workplace and our jurisdictions better places to live in. Each one of you will be assigned a special code which is what you will need to use whenever you communicate with each other or file reports to me and me only. Nobody apart from the Governor, Senator Jones and the five of us in this room is aware of this program—I'm sure that you understand the need for secrecy. With that, I will be happy to answer any questions that you may have," the Chief paused and emptied a glass of water.

There was a long silence as the three officers exchanged glances and assessed what they had just heard with mixed feelings of pride and apprehension. "Permission to speak freely, Sir," Bill spoke softly.

"Absolutely Lieutenant, no reason to hide anything between ourselves from now on," the Chief replied in an encouraging voice.

"The three of us have families to support. Lieutenant Pace and his wife just had a lovely daughter born to them. I know that secrecy is the key and we will all abide by your instructions. However just like anything else, there is always that chance that our cover gets blown, which could put our families at risk. Can you help us protect our families should anything go wrong?" Bill asked with genuine concern showing in his voice.

The Chief smiled and said, "I did not talk about the compensation part of it yet. The Governor has authorized two million dollars of life insurance policy for each one of you, where the State picks up all premium payments on your behalf. We cannot increase your salaries for the added risk to your lives because that would raise some eyebrows. So the State will pick up your mortgage payments and make payments on your behalf. These two instruments by themselves ensure that your families are financially protected. We will install a security system in your home and in your car. This will be continuously monitored. When activated, help will be on its way immediately and I will be notified as well. Each one of you and your spouse will be made aware of the security system activation procedure. If you realize at any time that you or your families are at risk, I can authorize around the clock protection for your families. I have complete faith in your own judgment and discretion. So I know you won't cry wolf unnecessarily while making that request for protection. We may have to pull you off the program if you feel that your cover is blown—this is for your own protection and possibly that of your family. Are there any other questions gentlemen?"

The three officers were breathing more easily now—the concerns had made way for excitement and eagerness—they were ready for action.

"Well then, good luck and God bless. I am proud to have the three of you in my command; I mean that in all seriousness. With your help, we will clean up our institution and soon this program will spread to the other counties and cities of California. I will hand it over to Agent Miller now and take your leave," the Chief concluded. He came by and shook hands with each one of the Officers and excused himself from the room.

The next two weeks turned out to be very intense, the three Supercops were intrigued with the level of detail that was covered in training—the art of blending with the crowd, surveillance techniques under cover, emergency self preservation procedures, the art of following without being followed, evidence documentation and filing procedures were some skills that were explained almost every day.

The sessions on narcotics were a revelation in itself for the three Supercops. They were instructed on essential drug detection and identification procedures and were offered case studies on drug related incidents, including the techniques on how to monitor activities of narcotics agents who may be working under cover.

"Remember that the person you are following is a cop and is a trained professional as well, who has been groomed on some of the skills that you are being exposed to now," Agent Miller had cautioned.

"That person obviously should not know that they are being tailed and in your best interests you would want to continue to keep things that way. In case studies we have always seen that corrupt cops never work alone—there is always a group of at least two or three cohorts involved. Such cops could make unconstitutional searches and seizures, or even put away a portion of the money they might have seized from buy-and-bust operations. Some of them have been known to even put away portions of seized drugs, for their own use or for resale to other drug dealers for large amounts of cash. We have had cases where we have found narcotics agents giving false testimony in court and get paid for that by the drug mafia. These are the cops you would need to watch out for. They would be ruthless people and would not hesitate to bring you into harms' way if they figure out that they are being tailed," Agent Miller instructed.

"We have information that there is a rather organized chain operating between San Diego and Los Angeles, but so far we have not been able to figure out how the stuff gets moved around. The narcotics guys of all the three counties have been super busy these days. Several arrests have been made that should have stemmed the flow of drugs from across the border, but they still keep moving around in this area," Agent Miller paused for a while for a quick gulp of water.

"You are not expected to investigate or arrest any drug dealers—that is the job of the narcotics guys. Your job is to monitor the activities of these narcotics operatives in the field, without making your presence known to them. No training can teach you everything, our training is based on what we know. What you experience in the field might be totally different. Use the knowledge that you are getting now and use your own discretion to act appropriately in the field," Agent Miller was wrapping up for the day.

"For the remainder of this week we will discuss embezzlement of public funds, where cops are suspected to be involved and how you would investigate on their activities. Next week we will look at some actual case studies that will require you to apply the skills that you have learned. Enjoy your evening gentlemen."

The next two weeks were fast paced and intense and exciting. The three Supercops-to-be were intrigued by the training and the steps that they would have to take in order to maintain the secrecy of their mission.

The Chief of Police was back on the last afternoon. "Agent Miller here tells me that the three of you have been rightly chosen for the job. I offer my personal congratulations on the successful completion of the training program to the three of our first Supercops. Each one of you will work independently of each other in three different areas."

"Lieutenant Walker, you are being placed in charge of investigation on several complaints of police brutality and cover-up efforts made by fellow police officers to protect their partners. We have reason to believe that our officers have acted in a manner that is not befitting the SDPD, but we have been unable to prove any charges against them," the Chief said.

"Sergeant Carvey, you will be in charge of investigating how we are losing track of public money—we suspect that police officers are actually involved in embezzlement of funds and grants that are released by the State and the City government," the Chief explained.

"Lieutenant McMillan," the Chief paused as Bill stood up, "You are being placed to investigate the activities of our narcotics officers. In spite of several arrests and convictions of people involved in cross-border drug trafficking, our schools and parks are not safe from these drug peddlers. Police departments from our Northern and Eastern precincts have complained that our borders are too relaxed to control the entry of controlled substances in the country across international borders. I have been taking a lot of heat about this and I have not ruled out the possibility of our own officers being involved in some manner," the Chief paused, as if to think.

"I sincerely hope that none of our officers are involved in any unlawful or any clandestine activities that would tarnish the name of San Diego's finest and I am turning to the three of you to help me prove that not only to myself, but to Governor's office as well. I have always believed that I lead an honest operation out here, but I guess reality is probably telling a different story. I trust that with your training, your inherent sense of dedication and commitment to serve, we shall be able to clean things up in short order. You know the drill for any and all communication between yourselves and with me. You will work independently of each other but have none other than each other to support if needed. So work as a team where each one has a critical role to play. Good luck and God bless," the Chief saluted as the three Supercops returned the gesture.

14

"You will have to act like them, talk like them and gel into their lives in order to work undercover. This is serious business and can cost you your life if you raise even the slightest suspicion. Under no circumstances can you carry anything identifiable in your person, or be seen with a police officer. You will be watched at every step of the way, especially when you start infiltrating the ranks. We will set you up, but after that you are on your own. You will not contact any of the listed phone numbers. Whenever you have something to report back you will call a special number that you need to memorize. When you call, use a public phone; don't use the same phone twice within the same month. We will act accordingly based on the information that you provide. Again, you have chosen one of the more dangerous jobs that a police officer can do. Make no mistake, I am," the instructor stressed, "trying to scare you. Stay scared and stay alive. If there is anyone in this room who would want to opt out, now is the time", the Instructor paused and looked over the room of wannabe narcotics officers.

"Sir, I have a graduate degree in Chemistry from UCLA, I wanted to work in the labs that analyze and research on narcotic substances," one of the officers said as he stood up. "Moreover," he paused and looked down at the floor, "I have a wife and a newly born son to protect. I am not sure I will be successful as an undercover agent."

"That is just fine, Officer. The Department needs chemical analysts like you as well. We cannot have everyone running around as undercover cops. I'm sure you have made the right decision to opt out. I shall make a note of your preference and speak to the Captain about it. The next proceedings of this class will not interest you, so you are excused. Good luck to you, Officer," the instructor concluded as the officer excused himself from the room.

"That was a very candid and honest decision and I applaud the officer for that. We are not looking for people who would jeopardize themselves and the Department with macho heroics, but people who are willing and passionately wish to assume risks involved in the life of an undercover cop. Anyone else who wants to opt out? I don't need reasons, just your decision to continue with the program or to move on," the instructor surveyed the room once again as three other officers rose, thanked the instructor and excused themselves from the company.

"Well then, now that we have taken care of the basics, lets get on with the rest of this course," the instructor said. Josh turned around to survey the group—only four officers remained, including him.

"Well, at least I know who are in the same class," Josh mused.

The three days turned out to be very interesting for Josh. He learnt about money flashes, buy and bust operations, drug identification, clandestine lab operations, undercover officer safety—Josh was intrigued.

He spoke Spanish fluently, which was one of the preferred qualifications an undercover cop needed to have to operate in the San Diego area. Appearance and behavior was important for an undercover cop, the cop needed to walk the walk and talk the talk.

"You must never let your guard down; even when you think you are safe and carry your loaded weapon all the time. We will issue a special weapon to you; it is not a standard police issue, but a weapon all the same. If you have to reveal your weapon they won't know it is a police registered weapon. Let them know that you are carrying, only if you have to reveal—they know you are, because they all do. Try not to get into an argument or do anything that would compromise your position. We shall study some real life accounts of undercover operations that this department has undertaken and discuss lessons learned. We learn new things after every operation and that makes us safer each day. Having said that I would not belittle my statement earlier that this is risky business and you can never relax," the instructor concluded for the day.

Josh drove off home after class and pondered over things that have happened in the past few years and concluded that everything in his plan was still on schedule. "So that's how you work as an undercover narcotics cop, eh? I have the end in my sights now," he thought, "soon I will be operating undercover, undercover," he laughed aloud.

It was not too long before Josh completed his training was ready for active duty. Lieutenant Prescott took Josh under his wing and assigned Josh to perform surveillance runs for a while.

"This is a hot potato these days, Josh," Lieutenant Prescott said in his briefing. "We have a drug ring operating in Southern California. Incidents have occurred in Los Angeles, Irvine and San Diego that appear to be related. We don't have proof to ascertain that they are related, but they could be— these guys have a brotherhood of sorts".

He picked up a file from his desk and said, "Here's a file for you to study and figure out your approach. You obviously do not have jurisdiction in Los Angeles and Orange County, but I need you to work on our end of the shop. We have reason to believe that the drugs are entering the country from south of the border. The border patrol has not apprehended anyone in possession of large quantities of prohibited substances, so we cannot be sure. You may contact the boys working in LA and Irvine if you need to. I have already informed Detective Brady in Irvine and Detective Connor in Los Angeles about you," Lieutenant Prescott finished.

"Thank you Sir. I'll do my best", replied Josh as he picked up the file and sat down at his desk to study the contents. The section on Los Angeles was confusing at best, not for the contents, but for the lack of pattern among the different cases and gangs on record. It was difficult to believe that they were all related, but it could be that these are different gangs working in collusion with each other—it's the brotherhood, Josh reckoned.

The section on Orange County was not as detailed, drugs were showing up in schools, nobody knew from where they came from. Interviews with students who were apprehended for drug abuse turned up nothing substantial. It was not the same person, or the same spot where they could buy drugs. News would somehow spread on where drugs would be available—sometimes as far north as Burbank or as far south as San Ysidro near the border with Mexico.

The section in San Diego was more interesting. There were records of some drug related arrests, court cases and trials. Josh was almost expecting this and sure enough there it was. Twenty four cases were documented that resulted in only six guilty verdicts. For the rest of the cases, the defendant was either released on bail or ruled not guilty. On the first twelve of the acquittals Brant Sawyer was listed as the defendant's lawyer. Surprisingly, for the last two years, there were none listed under Brant. For the last two years the cases had other lawyers listed. It was mixed bag between not guilty and released on bail verdicts among the three of them.

"Whatever happened to you Brant, suddenly lost interest in narcotics in spite of twelve successful trials?" Josh pondered and pursed his lips. He decided it was time to meet Brant. He dialed Brant's number.

15

Brant picked up after the fourth ring and immediately recognized Josh. "I have a client appointment on Saturday and Sunday this week and will not be able to make time to meet you. However, I can meet you next Saturday evening if you have the time," Brant offered.

"That will be fine," Josh replied. "Working very hard, Mr. Sawyer—weekends too?" he asked.

Brant laughed a short laugh and said "Well, Officer a man has to earn his daily bread, you know?"

"I know exactly what you mean," Josh countered and hung up.

Josh stationed himself a few houses from Brant's residence in La Jolla early that Saturday. Brant had said he would be busy and Josh wanted to check him out. He was in an unmarked police car, dressed in casual clothes, sunglasses and a baseball cap—there were no telltale signs that he was a cop. To a passerby, he was just a tourist taking in the magnificent views of the ocean in a clear weekend morning.

It was almost ten o'clock in the morning when a metallic green sedan drove up to Brant's residence. A middle aged man wearing an expensive looking suit exited the car, quickly glanced up and down the street, went up to the front door and knocked. He was carrying a small briefcase. The door opened and the man walked inside as Josh peered through his binoculars. He noted the plates of the sedan in his notepad and thought, "Nothing unusual there, just another moneybag of a client, I guess."

Josh surveyed Brant's home from his car. "That house could not have been cheap to buy. Brant's making more than a decent living. Rich clients and a streak of favorable verdicts in the courtroom…" Josh picked up his binoculars again as he saw the man come out of Brant's house, and walk up to his car, opened the rear passenger door and tossed his briefcase on the seat. He quickly glanced up and down the street, got behind the wheel and drove off.

Josh pursed his lips, thoughtful, as the sedan passed him on the other side of the street. Five minutes had passed when the garage doors to Brant's house opened and Brant drove out in a sedan that was also metallic green. Curiously it appeared to be of the same make as the car his client used. If the plates weren't different, one would easily have confused one car for the other. Josh ducked down as if to pick something up from the floor as Brant glanced to his left to check oncoming traffic and took a right turn. Josh allowed Brant to head out about a hundred yards before he started his car and followed.

Traffic was pretty thin on the Saturday morning, so it was not too difficult to keep up with Brant. Brant moved into Interstate Five and headed north towards Los Angeles. "Just an ordinary client call, I guess, though that car seems a little too run down for someone who owns a Rolls and a Bentley," Josh pondered as he noted the plates of Brant's car and followed at an innocuous distance. He kept changing lanes from time to time, so as not to arouse Brant's suspicions in any manner.

Brant moved into the exit ramp in Del Mar. Josh allowed two cars to get ahead behind Brant. Brant turned right at the intersection and Josh followed. Soon Brant turned into the parking lot of a grocery store. Josh drove straight ahead, turned the corner and turned right again into the parking lot. Brant was still in the car. Josh parked a few parking lanes away with his back towards Brant, shut his engine off and looked up at the rearview mirror.

Brant got out of the car, quickly looked around so see if anyone had any particular interest in him. He turned, apparently satisfied and entered the grocery store. Josh thought of calling his surveillance off, "the man's doing some grocery shopping for goodness sake, how suspicious can that be?" Josh reasoned with himself. On second thoughts he decided to stay put and just follow Brant around for the day.

Josh picked up his water bottle, twisted the cap open and looked back at the rearview mirror. His eyes widened as to his complete surprise, the man he had seen that morning at Brant's house, came out of the grocery store, unhesitatingly walked straight up to Brant's car, got into the driver's seat and drove away.

"Boy, am I imagining things here?" thought Josh, visibly confused. "Why did that guy take Brant's car? Whose car was Brant driving?" Josh wondered.

"Come in Control, over" Brant activated his police radio and spoke to the microphone, careful not to take his eyes off the rearview mirror.

"Go ahead Detective Timmons, over," radio crackled. "Cathy, can you please run a plate for me as quick as you can? It is Alpha Bravo Two Nine Yellow Six Zebra, over."

"Sure thing, please hold on for a moment, over," the operator replied.

Josh's mind was racing, he was thinking about too many possibilities based on the events that had transpired in the past couple of hours and none of them seemed to make any sense.

The voice on the radio crackled, "It is registered to a Brant Sawyer at Two Four Three Five, La Jolla Village Drive in La Jolla. Is he not that famous lawyer we read about from time to time? Any trouble Detective, over?"

"No, just checking. Thanks for that info, as always you've been a great help. Till later, over and out," responded Josh, his unblinking eyes glued to the rearview mirror.

"What are you up to Brant? I do not like this. Actually on second thoughts, maybe I do," Josh thought as he turned around to quickly scan the other cars that were parked in the lot. Just as he had expected, the other sedan was parked in the parking lot, not too far away from where Brant's car was parked.

Exactly as Josh could predict, Brant came out of the store shortly, with a grocery bag in his hand, walked unhesitatingly over to the other sedan, again quickly surveyed the parking lot, got behind the wheel and drove off.

Josh sat up, let Brant leave the lot and then followed him. Brant headed back to Interstate Five and headed north again towards Los Angeles. Josh called the Control Room again as he kept up with Brant at an innocuous following distance.

"Cathy, I need you to run another plate for me. Charlie Delta Five Alpha Eight Two Roger, over," Josh was in touch with the Control Room operator again.

After a while her voice crackled on the radio, "This plate is registered to Alejandro Garcia of One Six Nine National City Blvd, National City, over."

"Thank you Cathy, over and out," Josh responded.

The operator acknowledged as Josh closed the call and kept up the pursuit. "If he goes any further, he will be out of my jurisdiction. I cannot follow him beyond the San Diego county line, so if he is going further north, I will have to give up the pursuit real soon," Josh thought.

Brant kept on driving north towards Los Angeles past the last exit in Oceanside. Josh had to exit the freeway, turn around and head back southbound to San Diego. "You are up to something, my friend, looks rather fishy and very well planned. I wonder what," Josh murmured to himself.

Josh rushed back to the station and searched the computer for a record on Alejandro Garcia at the National City address. He was not surprised when the computer returned a positive match and provided the carousel and docket number information for the record. Josh called the Records Department, "Smithy, can you please pull a file for me?" and read out the details. "I'll come by in about an hour to pick it up". He listened said his thanks and hung up.

As promised, Alejandro's record was waiting for Josh when he arrived. "Here you go Officer Timmons," the clerk pushed a manila folder towards Josh.

Josh thanked the clerk, found an empty desk and examined the contents. Apparently, Alejandro Garcia was once apprehended for illegal possession and distribution of prohibited substances, but was released as a free man when no conclusive proof could be presented that could result in a guilty verdict. The lawyer who tried the case was Brant Sawyer. Josh raised his eyebrows more as a validation of his subconscious suspicions, than as a surprise. Josh finished reading the transcript of the case and smiled—it was the typical Brant style of arguments and counter-arguments that led to the acquittal.

He returned the file and went on to see Lt. Prescott. "Lieutenant, I need a tap on a suspect's telephone. What do I need to do to get that organized?" Josh asked.

"Seems like you have been busy, what's going on?" Lt. Prescott asked.

Josh had anticipated the question and had already cooked up his story. He pulled out a chair as if to think before answering, sank down into the cushion and said, "I was investigating the list of narcotics related cases in the San Diego area and have made a list of those who have not been convicted. This person is at the top of the list. I want to make sure that he is really living an honest life and is not up to something, so that we can get a warrant out for a search of his residence or maybe a potential arrest. This is why I need to monitor the phone calls made to and from his house, just in case my hunch turns out correct. If you could please sanction a day or two of phone tapping, that would be great and I will take it from there," Josh concluded in a very earnest voice.

Lt. Prescott had the reputation of allowing some free rein to his subordinates to take responsibility for their actions and accelerate the process of becoming more independent, especially for those who would become undercover narcotics cops. He listened and agreed to authorize a warrant for the phone tap. "Just be careful that this does not backfire on you or us. The quicker you can close the tap the better it is. Folks are getting very jittery these days if they find that their phones have been tapped," Lt. Prescott counseled.

"Thank you Sir. This will only take a few days hopefully. I would probably move on to the next one in the list if I don't find anything out of line with this guy," Josh replied.

The tap was placed and Josh put two groups of two cadets to monitor Alejandro's phone. "I want transcripts of each and every word of each and every phone call that goes in or out of the suspect's house and I want you to take close pictures of each and every person that goes into or out of that house. Eight hours every day for each of you on this. I will take the night shift and come to relieve you. Keep me posted on anything that you find unusual," Josh briefed the four officers in the police van. The van had the appearance of an electric power company repair vehicle parked on a side street with a clear view of Alejandro's front porch.

There were two cadets dressed as mechanics outside the van trying to work on some power cables as if they were preparing for a repair job. To a passerby, it was a routine electrical maintenance crew on duty. "All right, let's proceed with the test," said Josh as he hopped out of the van, walked over to the public phone across the street and dialed Alejandro's number.

A man answered the phone as Josh spoke, "Good afternoon Sir, may I speak with Mr. Alejandro Garcia?"

"This is he and you are?" Alejandro replied.

"Sir, this is Tim Bates and I am calling from Coastal Vacations to congratulate you on being selected in our random drawing for a free three night's vacation at our beach resort in Puerto Vallarta, Mexico. All I need from you is your approval to send you the certificates for you and a companion. You will need to pay only $10 for document processing and mailing fees after you receive the vacation certificates. We will confirm your reservations once we receive your $10 payment. May I…" Josh started to ask.

Alejandro interjected, "How long would the certificates be valid?"

"They are valid for a full one year Sir," Josh replied.

"Hmmm…So $10 will get me those 3 nights in Puerto Vallarta? This isn't some cheap joint out there, right?" Alejandro asked, clearly interested.

"Oh no, Sir, this is a five star resort on the beach," Josh replied.

"Ok, why don't you send me the certificates and let me look them over? I'll decide after that," Alejandro said.

"Sure Sir, I will put them in the mail today itself. You will have to call us at the number on the certificate to have them validated. Thank you Sir and have a great day," Josh replied and signed off.

"What a sucker," Josh said to himself and walked back to the van. "Did you get all that?" Josh asked the officers, who were laughing among themselves.

"Sure we got all of that. Jeez Sir, you have a career as a telemarketer there. He fell for that gag hook, line and sinker," one of the cadets said.

Josh smiled and waved his hand in dismissal as he listened to the tape being played back with the entire conversation that he just had with Alejandro. At the end, he was laughing too.

"All right, you guys are all set. Keep me posted", Josh said as he got out of the van and walked away past the block to his car parked on a side street. "I better go home and catch some sleep. Looks like a long night ahead," thought Josh as he headed home.

The alarm clock woke Josh up at eight o'clock. He freshened himself, dressed and went out. He parked the unmarked police car a block away from the place where the van was parked, and walked the way over to the van. He scanned the street up and down to make sure the no one was watching, before knocking on the door. The two junior officers greeted him as he entered the van and shut the door.

"Any traffic yet?" asked Josh.

"No Sir, nobody came out and none went in—no calls yet. As you can see, the lights are still on inside the house," the officer reported.

"Hmm..," pondered Josh. "Well, you guys are off for the night. I will take over from here. Do me one favor before you leave. Joe, I need you to walk up to the house, knock on the door and see if anyone is really in. Make an excuse that you have the wrong address, apologize and leave. The police car is parked a block away to the right. Put your hands in your pockets as you pass this van to signal to me that there is someone in the house. You guys can then leave for the night. Thanks for the help, gentlemen".

The two cadets nodded, exited the van and both walked away from the van towards the car parked away from the house and the van. As Josh peered through the windscreen after five minutes, one of the cadets appeared again on the other side of the street, walked past the van, went up the porch of Alejandro's house and knocked.

Shortly afterwards, the door opened and a man came out. Josh peered through his binoculars as he saw Joe having a short conversation with the man, who appeared to be built like Alejandro, but he could not be sure—it was a little too dark to be certain. He saw the cadet apologize and come away as the door closed shut. The cadet walked past the van with his hands in his pockets. "Well, I know there is someone in the house, but you did well," Josh murmured to himself, "I need to know who that man is."

Josh activated the radio and hailed the cadet who should already have reached the police car by now. "Joe, that was very good work. Can you open the glove compartment and pull out the yellow cover from there," Josh paused to allow the cadet some time.

"Got it, Sir," the cadet reported back.

"Good, does that photograph match with the guy who opened the door for you?" Josh asked.

"You bet. He appeared to have been on the bottle for a while", the cadet replied.

"No offense for drinking at home, Joe. But thanks again. You guys take off now and I'll see you tomorrow again," said Josh as he shut the radio off.

He poured some hot coffee from his flask and continued his vigilance. It was a quarter past the eleventh hour at night, when the telephone beeped. Josh snapped up the headphones to listen.

The caller was saying, "Rough day today. Nightingale will rendezvous at around exactly sixteen hundred hours tomorrow."

"Confirming rendezvous," Alejandro replied and the line went dead.

Josh removed his headphones as he saw the lights go out in the house. Evidently Alejandro was waiting for the phone call.

"Who the heck is Nightingale? It could not be someone's real name— probably a code name of sorts. Where is that rendezvous with Nightingale? Must be a pre-arranged location," Josh reasoned to himself.

The night passed without further incident, the bogus work crew and the two junior cadets reported back to the van at the crack of dawn. Josh went back to the station for some administrative work and then headed home for a short nap.

On a hunch, he dialed the Brant's home number. Nobody answered the phone as Josh had expected. He was getting ready to get back to the stakeout van with the intent of following Alejandro for this four o'clock appointment, when the phone rang and one of the cadets on duty called, "We have movement here Sir. It appears that our friend is planning to leave. His garage doors just opened, so we are expecting him to drive out any moment now."

"Ok, you need to stall him. It will take me about fifteen minutes from now to get there. Drive the van up to his house and block his driveway. See if you can delay him a little. Tell him you have a breakdown or something. Go now. Keep this line open." Josh directed and rushed out to his car.

He heard the van starting up and then stop shortly afterwards. The door opened and was banged shut as the cadet in the van said, "We are parked across his driveway Sir. He was just starting to back out from the garage. Carey is already talking to him."

"Good, I am not too far away, should be there in about another six or seven minutes. But whatever you do, don't let him drive away before I arrive," Josh counseled.

"Roger Sir," the radio fell silent.

It was after about four minutes that Josh heard the officer try to start the van, but the engine choked and spluttered, but did not start. "What's up partner?" Josh heard Carey's voice.

"The stupid van won't start—told you this one's nothing but trouble," Josh heard the other cadet shout.

Carey was shouting, apparently to Alejandro, "Sorry Sir, our van is not starting up, would you mind giving us a hand to move it away from your driveway? We are extremely sorry for the inconvenience."

"Good man, Carey, smart thinking," Josh said softly. He heard Alejandro getting out of his car and literally slam the door shut, frustrated. He was swearing profusely as he reluctantly went to the back of the van and helped push the van away from his driveway. Carey was at the controls inside and pushed the brakes on just a little so that it took some extra effort to push the van and hence buy time for Josh to arrive.

Josh drove into the street and said in a low voice, "All right Carey, I can see you guys, you can call off the act now. I've got it covered now. That was great work—both of you."

"Thank you Sir and good luck," Carey replied as he released the brakes and started the engine.

"Phew, thanks a lot Sir, we would have been stranded without your help. Please accept our sincere apologies for the trouble, Sir. You have a great day now," Carey told Alejandro.

Alejandro grumbled, visibly frustrated and walked back to his car. The van was already pulling away as Carey's voice came on the radio, "All yours Sergeant Timmons."

"Thanks Carey, you did great. You have a promising career ahead of you," replied Josh.

"Thank you for the opportunity Sir, that's why I work with San Diego's finest. Over and out," Carey laughed and signed off.

Josh watched from a distance as Alejandro backed out of the driveway in Brant's sedan and drove off towards the freeway. Josh followed as he checked his watch—it was five minutes to four, and Alejandro was late for his rendezvous.

Alejandro was speeding. Josh checked his speedometer—he was doing eighty five already to keep up with the car ahead. As usual, he was weaving through traffic, changing lanes from time to time. Alejandro turned on his signals to take the La Jolla Village Drive exit from the freeway. Josh followed at an unobtrusive distance behind. Alejandro drove into the parking lot of the shopping mall, parked the car away from the shops and department stores. There weren't too many cars parked in the vicinity. He exited and walked towards the shops.

Josh parked his car at a spot here he could see the entire parking lot. He quickly scanned the lot to see if he could spot anything unusual, but it was just the regular sight of shoppers going about their business.

Josh looked at his watch—it was quarter past four. He looked up just in time to see the sedan that Alejandro was driving the day before, appear on the ramp. The driver drove right inside the covered area and settled down on a parking spot. Josh peered through his binoculars as Brant came out professionally dressed as ever. He quickly glanced around to see if anyone was unusually over-interested in him, locked the car and also entered the shopping area.

Josh pondered, "Hello Nightingale! Who are you helping my friend?" Josh tried to make some reason out of all the events in the past two days and none of them seemed to tie together. He thought about following Brant to the shopping mall and was almost about to exit his car when he saw Brant reappear and this time walk directly over to his own car. After a quick and seemingly casual glance all around, Brant entered his car and drove off.

"Here we go again," thought Josh as he followed at a reasonable distance. The rest of the drive was uneventful as Josh watched Brant drive into the garage in his house.

Josh dropped off the unmarked police car at the lot, picked up his own car and drove home. He entered his apartment to see the lights flashing in his answering machine. He hit the play message switch and was headed to the refrigerator for a beer as Brant's voice came on.

"Hello this is Brant Sawyer. I sincerely apologize for this, but I'm afraid, we will have to postpone our meeting on Saturday as I had promised earlier. Something very important has come up and I will have to work on a case urgently—I'm sure you will understand. Please call me so that we can reschedule our appointment, if you are still interested. So long Officer," the message ended as the machine announced that the message was left at ten minutes after five.

The next morning Josh called Brant, "Mr. Sawyer, and thank you for your voicemail last evening. Sorry, I came home late yesterday, so I did not want to disturb you at that hour. Very busy these days, huh?" Josh asked.

"Oh, yes, I had a very busy weekend. I had to meet this client this weekend as well. Sorry, I cannot discuss any further details about it—the client-lawyer relationship, you know?" Brant replied.

"Sure thing, I understand," said Josh, "So I guess you will be busy this Saturday, is that right?"

"Yes, I'm afraid, we'll have to cancel our appointment," Brant said.

"No problem, nothing's more important than the call of duty. I'll check back with you in a couple of weeks and see if you have some time to catch up socially," Josh said.

"That will be perfect. Till later then," Brant hung up.

16

Josh was going to follow Brant wherever he went on Saturday. The past events seemed very odd and his curiosity was piqued. He packed a set of overnight clothes, picked up his camera along with a powerful telephoto lens. He was going to use his personal car—it would help maintain a low profile while he followed Brant.

Josh was parked down the street with a clear view of Brant's house early on Saturday morning. The sun had peeked above the hills and the morning joggers were taking in the clean fresh morning breeze from the ocean. Josh sipped his coffee and watched Brant's driveway.

Shortly after eight o'clock, Brant's garage door opened and he backed out of his driveway in his nondescript green sedan. He turned around and headed off towards Interstate Five. "Another trip towards LA, huh Brant?" murmured Josh.

He followed Brant along the freeway as he drove past Del Mar and picked up the Encinitas Boulevard exit this time. Soon afterwards, Brant drove into the parking lot of a grocery store. As Josh had guessed, Brant and Alejandro swapped cars exactly in the same manner as the last week and Josh snapped them up in his camera. "No points for guessing this one," Josh murmured, "Clever, very clever indeed. You guys don't use the same location a second time for your car swaps. This time, I am right behind you pal. I need to know what you are up to—from the looks of it, something just does not look right."

Brant continued north on the Interstate past the San Diego County line with Josh following at an inconspicuous distance. Since Josh was using his own car, his movements could not be tracked by the station. It was also officially his day off, so he could follow Brant as far as he would go. Brant appeared to be a very cautious driver—a little too cautious, Josh thought. But then Brant had to be careful, since he was not driving his own car and would want to avoid any situation that would raise unnecessary questions.

"Very smart thinking, Brant, you seem to be smart even out of court" Josh pondered. Brant drove past the Orange County line and into Los Angeles County. He picked up the first exit in Commerce and drove into the covered parking lot of a hotel. He tossed the car keys to the valet and walked into the lobby of the hotel carrying an inexpensive leather briefcase in his hand.

Josh watched an incredulous smile light up the valet's face as he looked at the one hundred dollar bill in his hand as a tip. He parked the car and was walking back towards the hotel entrance, the ear to ear grin still visible. Josh pulled up right in front of him and stopped him in his tracks.

The grin disappeared and the valet was about to speak when Josh got out of the car and flashed his SDPD badge. The surprise gave way to fear and nervousness as Josh beckoned him to get in his car and the young valet meekly obliged.

"What's your name kid?" Josh asked in an officious tone.

"Lance, Sir, Lance Barnaby," the valet said nervously.

"Lance, how long have you been working for the hotel?" Josh asked.

"Almost three years now Sir," the valet replied.

"Do you know the man whose car you just parked?"

"No Sir, I am here everyday but have never seen him before," Lance said with a definite conviction in his voice.

"What was that smile all about then?" Josh had seen the hundred dollar bill tip, but asked just the same.

"Well Sir, it is not always that a guest gives you a hundred dollar tip for parking the car," Lance said nervously.

"No kidding! A hundred dollars tip, huh? Good for you. That guy is a felon and I can throw you in for collaborating with him," Josh said quickly saw the fear in the valet's eyes and he hurried on, "But I will let you go, if you do a small job for me. But first, you better give that hundred dollar bill back to me—you would not want to take stolen money, would you?"

"Yes, Sir, No Sir," the valet was visibly nervous and he handed the bill over the Josh who made a show to examine if the bill was counterfeit money. "Thanks for the evidence, kid, this is counterfeit money. You don't want to be caught peddling this stuff," Josh said—there was nothing wrong with the bill.

"Sir, I will do anything for you, I have never seen that man. I need the extra money from tips for my studies and I will be thrown out of the job if the manager comes to know that I got into trouble. But of course I don't want any counterfeit money. Please Sir, I have done nothing wrong," the valet pleaded.

Josh looked at him and let a few moments pass in silence. Then he said, "What kind of identification are you carrying?"

Lance hurried to dig out his driver's license from his wallet and handed it over to Josh. Josh confirmed with Lance that the address was current and copied the information in his pad. The address was an apartment building a block away from the hotel.

"What's your telephone number at home?" Josh asked and noted the number as the valet hurriedly rattled off the digits.

"Ok Lance, I believe you," Josh said as he handed the license over to the valet, "Here's what I want you to do. I want you to take that car and drive it home. Park it there out of sight from the road and run back here. Is that understood?"

Lance nodded and started, "But the manager will…"

"Don't worry about that. I will talk to him right away and tell him that I have temporarily enlisted you. Now go and rush back, report back here—you have seven minutes and the clock starts now." Josh smiled as the valet almost ejected from the passenger's seat, got into Brant's car and drove off, tires screeching.

Josh parked, got out, opened his trunk, picked out two license plates, switched the front and rear plates of his car and waited in the deserted parking lot. He picked up a small gadget from a gym bag and put it in his jacket. He looked at his watch, five minutes gone and Josh was getting impatient. Seven minutes were almost up when Lance sprinted back, gasping for breath.

"Very good Lance, you did well. You should try for the Olympics, seriously," Josh said earnestly. "When do you get off?"

"My hours are till two in the afternoon Sir," Lance replied.

Josh glanced at his watch—it was a little past eleven. "Ok, go to the manager and tell him that you are not feeling well and need to leave early. Go home and await my instructions on what to do next. I will call you. Thank you for your help."

"Yes Sir, thank you Sir," Lance said as he rushed back inside the hotel.

Josh walked up to the registration desk in the lobby and smiled at the girl behind the front desk. He saw a waiter pushing a cart, obviously carrying lunch for somebody.

"Good morning ma'am. I was supposed to meet someone here in the lobby about half an hour ago. His name is David Seaborne," Josh described Brant, "he is always very well dressed, has blonde hair, about six feet four inches tall and would weigh about two hundred pounds. You could not have missed him if he came in and passed your desk. I have not heard of any woman who has given up the opportunity to give him a second look—heck even my wife checks him out when he is around," Josh laughed.

The girl thought momentarily and broke into a knowing smile. "I don't know him by his name Sir, but I think I know who you are talking about. Yes someone like that came in about ten minutes ago," she grinned, "you are right about that second look, thing. He is rather attractive, I'd say. He was going to meet one of our guests," She punched a few keys in the computer and reached for the phone and said, "I can call up Mr. Myers in room one fifty five and tell him that you are here. Your name is…"

"Buz Clark, but you wouldn't want to do that, miss. You see, I was his best friend from college and meeting him after five years. I called his office and they said that he would be here. I want to go up to and spring in the surprise. Incidentally Myers is a colleague of mine as well—he works for me," Josh smiled.

The girl was obviously bored that morning with not too many guests needing service and welcomed the opportunity for some light conversation. "All right Sir, the room is on the lobby to your left, behind the elevators. Have fun," she said.

Josh smiled and looked at the badge that the girl was wearing. "Thank you Martha, you have been very friendly and helpful."

Josh started to walk away then quickly returned to the front desk. "Actually Martha, I would request a special favor from you. Just to add to the surprise, it would be great if I could get a bottle of your best champagne and some *hors d'oeuvres* delivered to the room before I pop in," Josh said in a playful tone.

More fun—the agent was excited at the prospect. "Sure Sir, we can get that taken care of," she said.

"Great, and one more thing, just have the waiter say that the champagne is a courtesy gift from the manager. Can you please take care of that?" Josh asked.

The agent laughed, "Boy, you gents will get a kick out of this; I can almost imagine the surprise in their faces."

Josh looked at her for a while as she finished laughing. "You look very pretty when you laugh that way, Martha," Josh paused a while to see Martha blush and continued, "I was just complimenting you. Hey, I am happily married man, just so that we are clear I am not flirting with you," Josh laughed.

Clearly there was a rapport established with Martha. "That would be a ninety dollars even Sir," she said as Josh pulled out his wallet and took out the hundred dollar bill that he had taken from the valet. The agent told him that her shift changed at two o'clock, when her replacement arrives.

Josh asked, "Do you mind if I talk to the room service guy and give him instructions on what to say when he delivers the champagne?"

"Oh no, not at all Sir, it's best that you tell him directly. One moment please," she dialed the restaurant and requested that the room service waiter speak to Josh for instructions. Josh thanked Martha as a guest approached the front desk.

Martha got busy as Josh excused himself and waited. Shortly he saw the room service waiter push a cart into the lobby as Josh walked up to him. "Hi, is this for room one five five?" Josh asked. "I am the guy the front desk lady mentioned, to give you instructions, Bob," Josh said reading the waiter's name tag.

"Yes, Sir, what can I do for you?" the waiter was friendly.

"Well Bob, this is going to be a surprise for my friends that I am meeting after five long years. They don't know I am here, so you need to tell them that the champagne is a courtesy of the hotel manager. I will come in a little later to surprise them. Is that ok?" Josh asked.

The waiter nodded and continued on towards the room as Josh stopped him. "Oh, I forgot to ask Martha in the front desk to be there for another ten minutes in case my friends call the front desk to check. Would you mind going and let her know that? My name is Buz, tell her that and she will understand. I'll wait for you here."

The waiter left the cart with Josh and went around the corner to convey the message to Martha. As soon as he had turned the corner, Josh reached into his jacket pocket and removed the device that he had brought along and attached it to the underside of the cart beneath the sheet of white cloth. Josh had hoped that the magnetic base on the wireless microphone would lock on the underside of the cart and it did instantly. Josh smoothened out the wrinkles in the cloth as Bob reappeared in the corridor.

"Done Sir, it appears that she was going to stay at the desk for a while anyway," Bob said with a courteous smile.

"Thank you Bob, I truly appreciate the help. Would it be possible for you to leave the cart inside the room? I have to get some gifts from my car, so I will need a place to keep them and the cart would be perfect for that purpose."

"Yes, that will be fine Sir, we have a few more where they came from," the waiter said.

"Thank you very much again Bob," said Josh as he took out a twenty dollar bill and handed it over to the waiter as a tip. The waiter was visibly pleased, nodded and headed off. It was the first floor and incidentally adjacent to the hotel's garage.

Josh rushed out of the building through the back door, back into his car, put on his headphones and activated the recorder.

He heard the knock on a door, "Room Service with special compliments of the manager," Bob declared.

The door opened, "We didn't order anything," a voice said.

"No Sir," Bob said hurriedly, "this is complimentary from our manager in appreciation for your stay with us."

"I see," the voice said, "I can't say no to such graciousness. Come on in."

"Thank you Sir." Some silence, followed by the shutting of the door and Bob was out.

"This is real fine champagne," the voice said, "I guess we got lucky with some promotion," some laughter followed.

Brant apparently was a consultant lawyer for a person who was under trial for some drug related charge, in addition to carrying an unlicensed firearm in person. There was another lawyer in the room who Brant kept referring to as Dillard and another man by the name of Rusty Jones who seemed to be calling the shots. It appeared that the defendant was indeed guilty, but it was Brant's job to help Dillard prove things otherwise.

Josh heard Brant explaining, "I don't care if you think or even know that your client is guilty. I don't need to tell you that the law states that nobody is guilty till proven guilty in court. So you need to think and convince yourself that your client is not guilty and fight for him."

Brant went on to explain how Dillard needed to argue the case, what kind of counter questioning and argument could come from the public prosecutor and how he needed to present his argument to cause a mistrial.

Rusty was quite aggressive and threatening at times to Dillard. He stressed that the defendant had to be acquitted at any cost; otherwise Dillard would face dire consequences. Brant had to calm Rusty down several times so that he could continue his coaching.

Josh sat there listening to Brant as he dissected the facts of the case into the essential elements, analyzed each one of them, developed arguments around them and ultimately came up with a plan of action that would be sufficient to prove that the defendant was not guilty.

Josh looked at his watch—it was close to three hours when Dillard left the room to prepare for the trial.

Rusty said, "Brant, my friend, I wish you could work in my neck of the woods as well, but I understand your reasons. It is a good cover for our operations."

Josh could hear the sound of a briefcase latch clicking open and heard Rusty say, "Good, very good Brant, fresh meat from the South. This is worth over two million greenbacks from those junkies."

The sound of the briefcase shutting was followed by the sound of another briefcase opening and Rusty was speaking again, "Here you go my friend. That's half a million in cash for your courier services and expert advice for the last month—with your advice we were able to get two of my boys released on mistrials. They are following your advice to stay low for a while. You are a big part of my operation Brant, only if these stupid lawyers out here could be at least a little smart like you."

Brant was saying, "I should thank you, Rusty for engaging my services. The courier part of it is no big deal. Alejandro does a good job of making things look very innocuous. I like the green and you have been a good paymaster. It is always a pleasure to do business with you, my friend. I better head out now and see if I can catch some of my weekend."

"Yeah, I am checking out too. You take the champagne Brant, you earned it. I'll thank the girl in the front desk on my way out. Quite a hotel I must say, serving expensive champagne for just checking in for the night. By the way, this thing with Alejandro—working out well for you, I guess?" Rusty asked.

"Yes, of course, it is very convenient and my movements cannot be traced," Brant replied. Josh heard the door open and close.

"So Brant is ferrying over drugs for Rusty from Alejandro," Josh murmured to himself. "Lance should have already gone home," Josh glanced at his watch—it was past three in the afternoon. He turned off the tape recorder—the entire conversation was recorded.

Josh waited in his car, camera ready in his hands to see Brant come out of the hotel carrying the champagne and a briefcase. He was accompanied by a man who appeared to be slightly overweight, sporting a ponytail and a goatee beard. Josh clicked away several close shots both individually and showing both men shaking hands with each other.

Rusty walked over to a Cadillac and drove away as Brant turned around trying to find the valet. He did not find Lance anywhere around and headed back inside the hotel. Josh started his car and parked near to the lobby entrance and hurried into the hotel lobby, hoping that Martha in the front desk would really have left for the day. He did not want to be recognized when he met up with Brant.

Josh entered the lobby and to his relief, there was another girl in the front desk and she was talking to Brant, who obviously was asking for the valet whom he had given his car keys.

The girl had an I-don't-know look in her face—Brant appeared frustrated. Josh walked up to the front desk, making a show as if he was trying to pull his wallet out of his pocket, as if he was completely oblivious that Brant was standing a few feet away from him.

Brant's mouth fell open, as if he had seen a ghost when he saw Josh standing a few feet away from him at the counter. Josh saw from the corner of his eye that Brant quickly moved away from the front desk, almost in reflex action, exactly as Josh had anticipated.

Brant could not afford to reveal the fact that he was in that hotel, when he had told Josh earlier that he would be busy with a client in San Diego that Saturday. Furthermore, he could not say that his car was stolen. If he did, Josh would offer to help without a doubt. Brant would have to reveal the license plates or registration papers of his car, which did not belong to him in the first place. Brant would not want any attention drawn towards him. Moreover, he was carrying a briefcase with half a million dollars in it in cold hard cash—that would be real hard to explain to a cop.

Josh picked out a paper from his wallet, referred to it and spoke to the girl at the front desk, "Good afternoon ma'am. I would like to talk to one of your restaurant staff, his name is Bob."

The girl had a startled expression on her face at Brant's abrupt change of behavior, but she looked away from him and turned her attention to Josh. "Sure Sir, one moment please," she said as she dialed a number for Bob. She listened for a while and replaced the receiver and said, "Sir, Bob is on a room service call and will return shortly, if you could please wait here, he will come by soon."

"Thank you ma'am, I'll wait for him here in the lobby," Josh said as he turned around to see Brant seated in a sofa in the lobby with a newspaper opened fully to cover his face, the briefcase was on the floor next to him—completely hidden by the newspaper. A large group of people approached the front desk trying to check-in and the front desk got busy.

Brant was clearly trying to hide—he was in obvious dilemma and nervous and was not thinking straight. For the first time in his life, he felt a sense of fear, a sense of anxiety that confused his thoughts even more. He could not stay longer because Josh would definitely recognize him if he saw him. On the other hand he could not leave because he could not find his car or the valet.

His worst fears came true as Josh walked straight up to him and asked, "Excuse me, Sir. May I borrow the Sports page if you are not reading it? I've got to kill a few minutes here."

Brant was caught and he knew it, there would be no way out of this, he thought. His mind was racing, trying to cook up a story for Josh. He was about to lower the newspaper to respond to Josh's request when Bob, the waiter at the restaurant came up to Josh and asked, "You were looking for me Sir?"

"Oh, yes, Bob, I did not expect you to come so soon, but thanks for coming anyway," Josh said. Bob had turned around by that time and the front desk was busy checking in the large group of guests, so nobody noticed Josh pick up Brant's briefcase. Brant heaved a sigh of relief as he heard the sound of receding footsteps on the hardwood floor—he kept the newspaper up a little longer oblivious that his special prize had been hauled away. Josh and Bob were already out of hearing distance.

"Remember me, Bob? I'm the guy with that bottle of champagne delivery for room one five five…" Josh started.

The waiter broke into a smile, "Oh, yes, of course I remember you Sir, and what can I do for you now?"

Josh appeared to be embarrassed, "Did you remove the food cart from the room?"

"No Sir, I was going to get there after I met you, the front desk called to say that the guest had checked out. Why do you ask Sir?" Bob asked.

"Well, Bob, you see, I had taken my pen out to write my contact information for my friends and left it on the cart. I had forgotten all about it when I realized that the pen was not with me. It is a very favorite pen, it was a gift from the missus on our first anniversary and I have not parted with it for the last five years. I've got to get that pen back, you know."

"Yes, of course Sir, if you will please come with me, I will open the door for you and you can get your stuff," Bob sounded helpful.

Josh followed Bob into the room. The cart was there, but there was no pen on it. "Well Sir, it is not on the cart, are you sure that you did not pick it up? Maybe you can check your pockets one more time—it happens to me too at times," Bob grinned.

Josh made a show as if he was searching his pockets for a pen that never was there and said, "No, I don't have it. Can you please check the bathroom for me? I might have left it there when I used it. I will check the room, if it has dropped on the floor."

Bob went off to check the bathroom. Josh reached beneath the cart, removed the microphone, he had placed there early that morning, placed it in his pockets and continued with his futile search for his hypothetical favorite pen that his hypothetical wife had given him in their hypothetical first anniversary.

Bob soon came out announcing that he had no luck in the bathroom either. Josh responded likewise and appeared visibly disappointed. He thanked Bob for letting him in the room and walked out.

He quickly looked up and down the lobby, saw nobody and walked towards the back entrance of the hotel into the parking lot. The briefcase was solid evidence against Brant and Josh was not going to let that opportunity pass. Josh put the briefcase in the trunk of his car and walked back into the lobby—it was time to confront Brant.

17

Brant had heard Josh and a guy who he addressed as 'Bob' walk away. His mind was still racing. He had to get his car and get out as soon as he could, but apparently the valet he had given the car keys in the morning had left early and the new valet on duty was not able to locate the keys. His car could have been stolen, but there was nothing Brant could do to report that—it was not his car, a fact that cops could find out real soon. There would be some very uncomfortable questions to answer if the apparent theft of the car became known.

Brant had heard the large group of people trying to check in and some of them even had approached the seating area and had started chatting. He could not see the group through the newspaper, but that did not matter—he needed a way out and fast. "Maybe the car is in the parking lot," he thought desperately, "I'd rather go and check. Alejandro might have a spare key in his glove compartment. I could try to open the lock, get in and drive away."

Brant slowly lowered the newspaper and peered around. There was no one paying attention to him, Josh was nowhere in sight, there were a bunch of college students seated on the sofas in the seating area of the lobby and they were engrossed in juvenile chatter. Brant put the newspaper aside and got up, reaching for the briefcase that he had left on the floor beside him.

To his utter shock, the briefcase was gone. Brant frantically looked around, under his sofa and all over the lobby, but the briefcase was nowhere to be seen. "Oh my dear God!" he thought, "Half a million dollars and all my confidential documents are in that briefcase."

He looked suspiciously at the group of college students, who were still engrossed in their own conversations, rather oblivious of Brant's presence. None of them appeared to know anything about it, but he interrupted their conversation anyway and asked about his briefcase. All he got was blank stares and head shakes in the negative.

For the first time in a long while, Brant was in sheer panic. He told himself that he needed to clam down and think, but the circumstances were too overwhelming. The mounting stress totally drained him. There was his missing car that nobody in the hotel seemed to know about, there was Josh in the premises who could emerge and recognize him any moment, and now there was this missing briefcase with all his confidential documents and the money in it.

He ran his fingers through his hair, collapsed into a sofa with utter desperation and held his head in his hands, trying to focus on his options. There were several that floated across his mind, none of which made sense and each of them wilder than the previous one. Brant was in hot water and he knew it. He leaned back on the sofa to see Josh standing a few feet away from him.

"Is that really you, Mr. Sawyer? Oh dear, is everything ok? You're pale—you look like you've seen a ghost or something. Hang in there, let me get you some water to drink," Josh said as he purposefully hurried into the restaurant.

Brant was sweating, his face had turned pale as if he was going to have a seizure. The Brant Sawyer brand of sophistication and swagger had gone and had given way to a beaten and cornered individual—it is only going to go downhill from now on. Josh had seen him, that too in such a distressed state, so obviously the usual questions would follow. Brant stopped thinking, resigned to what had to happen and closed his eyes.

Josh was back with a glass of cold water on one hand and a wet towel in another. Brant sat up as Josh shook him on the shoulder. He emptied the glass—he needed that desperately, hoping it will help clam him down. He took the towel from Josh's hand and wiped his face and neck with it, then buried his face in the towel and sat there in silence for a while.

Josh smiled to himself, let a few moments pass and said with concern in his voice, "Mr. Sawyer, I think we should call a doctor, you don't look too well."

Brant looked up and waved a hand in dismissal at Josh, "No, that would not be necessary Officer Timmons, I am feeling better now. Thanks for the help. I wasn't feeling well a little while ago, could be my blood pressure acting up again."

"Well, why don't you rest a while before you leave? Are you staying here?" Josh asked. He was thoroughly loving every moment of this cat and mouse game—he was the cat and the mouse was trying real hard to hide from him.

"No, I am not. I was here to meet a friend after my client in San Diego cancelled his appointment," Brant murmured the answer.

"I see, well, rest a while. I don't think you should drive in this condition," Josh said in a comforting voice. He continued with candor in his voice, "What is it this time—the Bentley or the Rolls?"

Brant hesitated a while, looked away from Josh, so as not to make eye contact, then said, "Actually I had car trouble in the morning, so I took the train this morning from San Diego to Union Station. I took a cab from the station to this hotel."

Josh smiled and thought to himself, "Lying in your teeth, huh, Brant? Let's see how far you want to go."

Aloud, Josh said, "Oh I see, these stupid machines, you don't know when they act up. Well, Mr. Sawyer, why don't you stay right where you are for a while? I have some work to do—won't take me more than half an hour to finish. I will be driving back to San Diego so I can drop you off at home."

Brant started to object, while Josh said dismissively, "No, I don't want to hear it. San Diego cannot afford to lose a lawyer such as you, Mr. Sawyer. I'm sure you would have done the same for me if I was in your place. Besides, leaving San Diego's top lawyer high and dry on the road, would simply call for bad press," Josh added jokingly. "You just stay put here and I'll be back within half an hour and we can drive home, ok?"

Brant nodded in resigned acceptance.

"Traveling ultra light, Mr. Sawyer? You are not carrying your famous briefcase I see. This must be a social visit, eh?" Josh tried to sound friendly.

Brant opened his eyes just a little, his face ashen and said, "I lost it, must have been stolen in the train this morning."

"Oh you poor liar," Josh thought.

Aloud he said, "Really, I'm sorry to hear that. No wonder you look so beaten down. I could put a trace on it, but it could be like searching for a needle in a haystack. Moreover, the guy who stole it must have already removed the contents and thrown the briefcase away. You did not have any money in it, I hope?"

"No money in there, but I had important papers in there, my wallet is still in my possession," Brant still looked pale—another lie.

"Ok, good. Well, just hang in there a little longer, I'll be back soon and we can head back home," Josh said in a sympathetic voice and left.

It was thirty minutes past four in the afternoon and Josh went directly into the pharmacy down the street that had one-hour photo service. Josh pulled out his badge and requested the attendant to develop the pictures as soon as possible, indicating that he urgently needed the roll to be developed. The attendant promised to have his photographs ready in thirty minutes.

Josh called Lance and asked him to drive the car back to the parking lot in the hotel at fifteen minutes past five pm, "Don't be late, Lance," Josh said in a commanding tone, "lives depend on this," he ended dramatically.

"Yes Sir, I will be there," Lance promised.

Josh looked at his watch—there were still about fifteen more minutes left before the prints would be ready. He was starving. He stepped out of the pharmacy and into the restaurant down the street for a sandwich. Surprisingly, he saw Rusty behind the counter. Josh walked up closer towards Rusty, who was serving another customer ahead of him.

"Hey Matt, how are things, bro?" Rusty asked. There could have been no mistake that it was Rusty indeed. Josh immediately recognized the goatee that Rusty had and the voice was further confirmation that the individual was the same person Brant was with earlier in the day.

While Josh waited his turn, the customer by the name Matt ignored the question and said, "Give me the usual and here's the jacket that you had ordered." Josh saw Matt hand over a large packet over to Rusty. "I'll eat while you try it out," Matt said.

Rusty nodded, handed over an order of chicken fingers and coffee to

Matt and called in another person from the kitchen to operate the counter. He looked up at Josh and said, "He will help you Sir."

Josh nodded.

Rusty picked up the packet that Matt had given him, and disappeared into the kitchen. Josh ordered an order of chicken fingers as well and looked at his watch, still another ten minutes to go for the photographs to be ready. Josh settled down with his food on a table just next to where Matt was seated.

"I wonder where that gash on your left check came from," mused Josh when he picked up the two inch deep gash on Matt's left cheek. The scar showed prominently on the dark skin. Rusty came back shortly just as Josh was about to get up and leave.

He was carrying two regular sized carry-out boxes and came up to Matt, "The jacket fits me just perfectly, here's the payment and some more for the missus and kids. Don't worry, compliments of the house," he said as he placed a hundred dollar bill beside Matt. "It's good doing business with you, bro" and he walked off to resume position behind the counter.

Matt wiped his hands off in the napkin, left his unfinished food, picked up the bill and the carry-out boxes and left the restaurant. Josh allowed about fifteen seconds to pass before he too, dumped his unfinished food in the trashcan and left the restaurant. It was not too difficult to spot Matt, who was inside his car and closely examining the contents of the carry-out boxes.

"That's odd," thought Josh, "why would he leave almost half of the food behind and then be so very interested in the contents of the box that apparently also contained the same stuff?"

Josh casually walked past Matt's car and was able to catch a quick glimpse of the contents of one of the boxes that Matt was examining so closely. No chicken fingers there—the box was almost stacked with plastic packets of what appeared to be a powdery substance.

Matt sensed someone approaching his car and quickly shut the lid of the box he had opened. Josh walked by and entered the pharmacy, feigning ignorance of what he had just seen. "I'll bet anything that you just picked up a shipment of drugs from Rusty. Boy, this is turning out to be a day of revelation for me." Josh murmured.

Josh picked up the photographs, thanked the attendant and walked out of the pharmacy to see that Matt had already pulled away. He glanced at Rusty's restaurant and contemplated on whether he should approach Rusty and try to get some information from him, but on second thoughts, he let that pass.

"I've got more important things to do—Rusty can wait," he told himself. Josh got inside his car and reviewed the photographs—they had come out as well as he had expected.

"You guys are toast," murmured Josh as he rewound the tape and started playing the conversation that he had recorded in the morning. He looked at his watch—it was ten minutes past five. "Lance should be driving in any time now, I better hurry and get back to Brant," thought Josh and he started his car and headed back to the hotel.

Brant appeared to have regained some of his composure by then, at least he did not have his head buried in his hands any longer—however, he still looked shaken.

"Here you go," said Josh as he handed over a bottle of chilled beer to Brant and sat down opposite to him, so he could watch the doorway of the hotel, "this should get you refreshed. Let me file a report with the LAPD about your loss. Can you please describe the lost briefcase for me so that I can file a proper report?"

Brant's expression started to cloud again. He took the bottle from Josh, drank up almost half of the contents and said in resigned tone, "I don't think it would help by reporting the loss to the LAPD—there are probably a million briefcases that match the description. Please don't worry about it; I have copies of all documents in that briefcase. I don't want to report it."

"Sure you don't," Josh thought. Aloud he asked, "Are you sure?"

Brant nodded.

Josh looked towards the open doorway to see Lance come through the driveway in Brant's car and drive into the parking lot. "Well, if you are feeling better, let's head out for San Diego then, shall we?" Josh asked.

Brant nodded, "Thanks for helping me out in this situation, Officer Timmons."

Josh smiled and shrugged dismissively.

Lance had just parked the car near to the hotel front entrance and exited the vehicle when Josh and Brant approached him. Lance had a surprised expression on his face as he saw the two men walking towards him.

He started to speak when Josh cut him off, "Hey, how's it going, boy?" he asked and quickly glanced over to see Brant's expression.

Brant was in a dilemma again—his car was here, but he could not pick it up because he had already given Josh a different story. He could not just leave the car there, because soon it would be discovered as being unclaimed and Alejandro will be questioned, that could lead the investigation back to him. Moreover the stupid valet had taken his car out for a spin, without authority and can easily testify the fact that Brant was indeed driving the car.

"It would be better if I just tagged along with Timmons to San Diego and then took the train back to LA to pick the car up later," Brant thought. "I am going to wring that bloody son-of-a-bitch valet's neck when I come back, or maybe I will have Rusty take care of the dirty work."

Josh was loving every moment as he watched Brant's pursed lips and furrowed brows—the sight of a man fatigued and distressed and cornered— this cat and mouse game was becoming more interesting by the moment and he really had Brant by his tail now. "Anything the matter, Mr. Sawyer?" Josh toyed with Brant in a concerned voice.

"No, nothing, it is just the events of the past few hours that have me worried, that's all," replied Brant hurriedly.

They entered the car and sat in silence for a while—Brant appeared far away as Josh kept staring at him with a wry smile in his face. Brant realized that they had been sitting in the car for quite a while and Josh had no intention of leaving. He turned to look at Josh and caught that stop-lying-and-stop-hiding-I-know-it-all expression in his face.

"You find my state of distress amusing, Officer Timmons? One man's loss is another man's gain, huh?" Brant said in a sarcastic voice.

Josh said nothing. He just maintained the same expression that made Brant even more uncomfortable. After a while Josh burst out laughing and said, "Care for a soda, Mr. Sawyer? I have a cooler here," as he reached behind and picked out a can for Brant.

Brant took the soda and cracked it open—the cold liquid was refreshing. Josh picked out one for himself and said, "Well, well, Mr. Sawyer, we finally get to meet and talk. So you took the train down from San Diego today, huh?" He had that taunting tone in his voice that made Brant feel weak. What did Josh know—he could not have known a thing.

Brant hurriedly said, "Yes, of course, my car broke down and I did not feel like driving the other one. Are we waiting for somebody here?" Brant was getting impatient to leave.

Josh acted as if he did not even hear Brant's statement about the train ride in the morning and said, "I don't know, you see I have been keeping tabs on this guy Alejandro Garcia in National City for a while now and I see his car parked right there in front of us. I wonder what he is up to. We suspect he is involved with drug trafficking, but have not been able to prove anything yet."

Josh looked at Brant to see his face had drained of all color, beads of sweat had appeared on his forehead, Brant had the soda can up to his lips, but his hands were shaking uncontrollably. The legendary Brant Sawyer brand of confidence and swagger had disappeared a few hours ago and now, he had that appearance of a man beaten, shattered and cornered, probably for the first time in his life.

Brant felt afraid, very afraid—afraid that his supposedly clandestine dealings have been discovered and the consequences would be very unpleasant indeed. However, it appeared that Josh had his tabs on Alejandro, so there was a fair chance that Brant was in the clear. However, he knew that would not be for long.

"I will have to play this carefully and disappear for a while. With all the money that I have been sending to my Swiss account, I've got to go abroad for a while till this blows over," Brant thought.

Josh was speaking again, "Say Mr. Sawyer, you have not been taking on narcotics related cases for a while now, though you had a successful string of success on such cases, right? Why is this sudden loss of interest?" Josh paused as if waiting for an answer then continued in an earnest voice, "How do you really catch these guys?"

"Well Officer, first of all, I think it is better that we settle down on first name terms from now on—we've known each other for quite a while now, don't you think?" Brant appeared to be recovering from his shock, "Evidence is all, you know," Brant really was getting back on his turf. "Gather and present strong evidence in court and you will get your guy behind bars."

"Yes, but when you talk about evidence, what kind of evidence are you talking about?" Josh was releasing some loose rope for Brant, who appeared to be gaining a grip on himself.

Brant was the expert in command and in the spotlight and he was showing his knowledge off, "They must have taught you all of that in the Academy, didn't they?" Brant asked without really looking for an answer. "Well we are talking evidence from eye-witnesses who can prove that they were actually present in the scene of the crime, hand-in-the-pot kind of evidence, you know? Photographs showing irrevocable evidence that the suspect is guilty are great—you would need close shots of the suspect in the act to make a good case out of photographs. Tape recordings are usually not permissible as evidence in court, since you could manipulate those if you wanted to, but you could swing a jury your way if the recording is substantial proof of guilt. Circumstantial and location evidence is extremely important. No lawyer can work around hard evidence—if we lawyers are defending, we will try to wiggle our way through the evidence presented—sometimes we get by, sometimes we don't. Sorry, I didn't mean to lecture you on this," Brant was obviously breathing easier now.

He turned to look at Josh, who had the same prankster smile on his face that puzzled Brant. Josh broke into a short laughter and said, "Boy that is what I call education. Evidence is all, you are absolutely right. You see, I've been following this guy Alejandro for a while now and have been collecting evidence exactly like you said—photographs, circumstantial evidence and the works," Josh caught Brant stiffening again. "Like I said, that is his car right in front of us, but no Alejandro around. I wonder what this guy is up to—maybe someone else is driving his car," Brant was sweating again as he sipped his drink. "Who do you think that could be?" Josh asked.

"You've got me there, Josh, I don't know your man," Brant hurriedly replied.

"I did not expect you to know him, I was just thinking aloud," Josh paused. "Say what do you think about this evidence that I have collected—give me an honest opinion, I am asking an expert here," Josh said as he pulled out the envelope and handed it over to Brant.

Brant set his drink down on the cup holder in the car and pulled out the photographs from the envelope.

The draining of color from his face was almost instantaneous as Josh looked squarely at Brant—he turned a bright red, then a tinge of pink then almost ashen. Josh thought that Brant would faint as he slowly and silently flipped over from photograph to photograph.

Apart from the photograph that showed Alejandro getting into Brant's car, all the others were close shots of Brant getting into Alejandro's car, getting out of Alejandro's car, handing the keys over to the valet, Rusty and Brant talking to each other in obviously congenial terms, they were shaking hands and Brant carrying a briefcase that he claimed to have been stolen in the train.

"So how much money was in that briefcase?" Josh asked with a firm voice.

"I don't know what you are talking about," Brant whispered, "this proves nothing Officer."

"Officer? Whatever happened to the first name terms, my man?" Josh was hauling in the rope now. "Does not prove anything, huh? Well, how about this?" Josh asked as he switched on his cassette player where he had recorded the entire conversation between Brant, Rusty and the other lawyer in Rusty's room.

"Recognize those voices, Mr. Sawyer? They are yours and of your friends in high places."

Brant smiled a wry smile and said in a quivering voice as he tore the photographs apart in desperation, "I told you, Officer—tape recorded evidence can be doctored and is not really considered as conclusive evidence in a court of law."

"Oh yeah? How about this?" Josh sounded irritated as he pulled his jacket from the backseat to reveal Brant's briefcase lying underneath, "That one will provide a generous supply of fingerprints of both you and Rusty, We're not talking cheap stuff here, I reckon about half a million dollars in cold hard cash in there and I did not even count. By the way, do you really think I am so stupid as to give you the only copy of the photographs to you? In case you did not know, I have the negative and a second copy as well. You are busted, my friend—even the great Brant Sawyer cannot save himself and his partners in crime now. By the way, I know that Rusty is running a drug trafficking ring under the cover of a restaurant down the street—does that surprise you? I think not. I also know that you and Alejandro trade vehicles in San Diego at different locations when you have to make these trips to Los Angeles. You can run my friend, but hide you cannot—evidence is all you had said, right? Well, that is one thing that I have in plentiful numbers."

Josh finished, impressed with himself in the manner in which he handled Brant. He had inflicted a receding and advancing wave of comfort and discomfort in such rapid succession that Brant was unable to fully recover his balance at any time.

He smiled to himself—Brant was sitting with his head in his hands—the sight of a man beaten and broken, one who had reached the end of the road.

Brant was caught, there were no two ways about it. Josh had every evidence that he was just lectured on and there really was no way out. Josh was a very competent Officer as he had proved. Brant was finished—this was the dead end. He had taken every precaution, he had planned every move with meticulous care, he had successfully avoided detection so far and now his cover was blown wide open.

Brant could not think any longer, he was tired, his mind was clogged up. He pulled the backrest release lever of the car seat, leaned back to an almost horizontal position and closed his eyes.

Josh let him be in that position for a while and they spent a few minutes in silence—minutes that seemed like hours to Brant. He was not thinking anymore, he wanted to shower and sleep, he was visibly drained of all his strength.

Josh casually glanced around, primarily due to lack of anything else to do. He noticed a brown pickup truck parked at the far back corner of the parking lot. There was a person in the driver's seat and appeared to be asleep given the open mouth and the head slumped sideways on the headrest. From the distance Josh reckoned the man to be in his late fifties or early sixties, given the thin grey hair and the wrinkled skin. Although he had not paid attention before, he thought that truck had pulled into the parking lot shortly after he had come in. But Josh could not be sure. "It's not important," Josh thought, "the guy is taking his late afternoon siesta probably and is waiting for someone."

Josh turned his attention back to Brant who was speaking to him, "So Officer Timmons, where do we go from here?"

Josh looked at him in silence, his face showing no emotion, that unnerved Brant even more. "You tell me. I know where I am going," Josh paused, "With all your experience with the law, I am sure you know where you are going."

Again a long pregnant silence and Brant said almost in a low murmur, "I could make you rich, Officer. What does a cop get paid these days? Let me guess—I'd say about twenty five or thirty thousand a year at your level. I can help you make five times that figure in a month, starting with half of what is in that briefcase back there."

It was all falling into place, Josh smiled to himself, rip open the stash and rake in the cash. Aloud he said in a surprised voice, "Are you trying to bribe a police officer, Mr. Sawyer? You know the penalties for that, I'm sure. You have enough against you, and you still want more?"

Brant looked away from Josh and focused in a far away place and almost whispered, "No Officer, I am not trying to bribe you. You have me on a noose, you really do and for the first time in my life I admit being caught with my pants down. I am just trying to buy my passage out of this. I want to stay free and offer you a handsome payoff as well. All that money will be for you and there will be more to come, of course in exchange of your silence."

"Clutching at straws Mr. Sawyer?" Josh laughed, "You've got guts, you know. I have been following you for the last three years as you have noticed—I was in every trial that you defended and watched you, studied your style and have always admired your guts. I'd say that you have a gift," he paused for effect. "I accept your offer," Josh said in a flat monotone that made Brant sharply turn towards Josh in sheer incredulity. Josh was grinning at him.

"Did I hear you say that you will accept my offer?" Brant asked in a surprised voice.

"Yes, you did. I guess we can really be in first name terms from now on, since we are partners from this moment forward," Josh replied in a soothing voice.

Brant broke into a smile and said, "I still don't believe it—you are not setting me up again, are you?"

"Oh no, I think we are past that stage—it is strictly business from now on," Josh replied and offered to shake his hands.

The tension had eased as Brant hesitatingly shook Josh's hand and, "Well can we destroy all that evidence now that we are partners?"

Josh laughed and suddenly turned serious, "Now that we are partners, let's get a few things cleared out. I am a straight-shooter Brant, so pardon me for my candor. Every business needs insurance, you know—you never know what happens. Your insurance policy is the money that you are going to send my way, doing what you have been doing. My insurance policy is all that evidence on you that I will keep safely tucked away, just in case you have a change of heart, my friend. If you ever attempt to bring me down, you will come with me. Now that we have laid our cards on the table, I think we should celebrate our union."

"I see," Brant looked away and said softly, "you will never have to use that evidence Josh, this partnership is for real, trust me."

"I do, I really do trust you Brant—I have not spent the last three years of my life following you for nothing. What kind of business survives without the partners trusting each other? " Josh was earnest.

He continued, "Well, I guess both of us have had a really busy day today. Why don't you get back to your car—I mean Alejandro's car and drive back home? By the way, I had asked the valet to drive your car away for a while and bring it back as he did, it was not his fault. That kid was carrying out orders from a law enforcement officer."

Brant looked away.

Josh continued, "I have a business plan that I want to discuss with you and some of my trusted friends. We will come over to your house next Saturday to talk it over. When's your next rendezvous with Rusty and Company?"

"Nothing in the next week, but tentatively I will have to make another trip the week after," Brant replied, still shaken by the turn of events.

"Perfect, that will give us time to discuss things over. In the meantime, don't talk about our meeting today and the events of the day to anyone, and especially not to your friends out here. So it is of utmost importance that you and I and of course my friends gel together and work together. We will be playing with fire, so we will have to watch out for each other in the true sense of partnership. Is that ok with you Brant?" Josh asked.

Brant nodded and asked, "I have no idea what plan it is that you are talking about, but I'm sure it will be well thought out with you at the helm. These friends of yours—are they cops too?"

Josh laughed and said, "No they are not, but they come from a diverse background and have very special skills that are key to our success as you will see next Saturday. As I have said, this is strictly confidential and I trust you will keep it that way. What you have been doing so far, my friend with these guys out here, is not a guarantee of your own safety or a guarantee of a steady cash flow. That well could dry up pretty soon and you will be left high and dry—we will need to add more value to your friends and make things more lucrative for them."

Brant stared at the road ahead and said, "I still don't know what you are up to, but yes, I am interested to listen to what you have to say," Brant paused, "well, I'd better get going then."

Josh nodded and casually glanced over to the briefcase lying in the back seat.

"Oh yes, how can I forget that?" hurried Brant.

He pulled up the briefcase and was about to open it when Josh stopped him. He quickly surveyed the parking lot. Apart from that truck where the old man was still fast asleep he could not see anyone else around, but then Josh was always cautious.

"Leave it for now—this is too much in the open. Take that home with you. I will pick up my share when we meet on Saturday next," Josh smiled, "I trust you Brant, I know you will not deny my share. Just to be safe, there is a duffel bag in the back seat. Why don't you empty the contents of the briefcase in that bag and leave the briefcase behind? Just a precaution—never get seen twice with the same stuff in your person, it is something they teach in surveillance class."

"All right Josh. So long and thanks for the new lease of my life. For a moment I thought I had bought it. You did well today," Brant was genuinely complimentary of Josh.

"One more thing, my friend Dave Reynolds will call you on Friday evening and let you know at what time we will come by to meet you at your home. This is just an added precaution, do you understand?" Josh asked.

Brant nodded in approval.

"Good, the name, once again is Dave Reynolds," Josh repeated. They shook hands as Brant transferred the contents of the briefcase in the bag, walked over to the valet stand, picked up his keys and returned back to Alejandro's car.

The driver in the pickup truck parked in the corner of the parking lot finished snapping close pictures of Brant and Josh and their cars, put his camera down and dropped his head sideways and returned to his apparent slumber.

Brant drove out of the parking lot and Josh smiled and murmured to himself, "You just left me a fresh set of your prints on the briefcase my friend—more evidence against you."

As Brant hit the freeway in heavy traffic he mulled over the events of the day and cursed himself repeatedly and wondered how Josh could pull this off in the manner that he did. Josh was smart, he was a thinker and he was very good at what he did, but he was a crooked cop after all. Brant wondered if he could get anything on Josh that will help him get the upper edge, but he saw nothing and then realization struck him.

He just left a whole set of his own fingerprints on the briefcase with Josh and he had not even realized what he was doing at that time. Brant literally slapped himself for that, but it was too late to remedy the situation.

"I'll tag along with him and see what he has to say and take it from there," Brant thought.

Josh waited a while and assessed the situation and appeared pleased at the developments of the afternoon. He drove out of the hotel's parking lot and back into Rusty's restaurant.

"I'm back again," Josh said in a jocular tone.

"Yes, so I see. What can I get for you?" Rusty asked.

"An order of your excellent chicken fingers again and this time, can you please make it to go?" Josh said.

Rusty nodded and turned away to prepare the order. Josh handed over a small sandwich box and said, "I'll be driving all the way to San Diego. Do you mind putting those fingers in this box, they will stay warm and fresh in there."

"Sure thing Sir, no problem," Rusty picked up the box and turned towards a back counter to fill it with chicken fingers.

Josh nodded at the kitchen and said casually, "So what else do you specialize in there apart from these excellent fingers?"

Rusty looked at him for a while trying to find some hidden meaning in that question and said, "Chicken fingers are all that we sell Sir—we have a very loyal customer base here."

"I'm sure you do, see you later then," Josh paid Rusty and walked back to his car.

He placed the box in a plastic bag and murmured, "Thanks for the fresh set of your fingerprints, Rusty. Like Brant had said, evidence is all."

Josh started his car and headed out towards San Diego. He was so content with the way things turned out that day, he failed to notice the pickup truck that he had seen in the parking lot was now on his tail. The wig and the white bushy moustache had come off and the wrinkles were all miraculously gone. The man in his mid-thirties wore a baseball cap and sunglasses. The truck's plates showed that the vehicle was registered in Arizona.

His radio telephone rang and he whipped it up immediately.

"Honey, my water has just broken and I am in labor. How soon can you come home?" the voice sounded distressed and in some pain.

Instinctively, the accelerator floored and the truck leaped ahead, "Oh my dear Joan. I am coming in from LA and should be home in an hour—sooner if I can. Can you hang in there for me or should I send someone to get you to the hospital?" the usually calm Bill McMillan was frantic and nervous.

"I think I can wait for an hour Bill. The contractions have just started and they are still within bearable limits. So don't kill yourself, just get here as soon as you can safely. Darling, it is finally happening, we are going to have the baby. I know you won't agree with me, but I think it is a boy. I love you," Joan sounded peaceful and happy.

"I love you more than life itself, Joan. We are so blessed. I just pray that you and the baby are safe and healthy. God give you both the strength to go through this. I will be home as soon as I can, my love. You know what to do about the water break and breathing through the contractions. I am calling the hospital right away to give them a heads up. We'll leave for the hospital right away as soon as I arrive. Hang in there darling. By the way, I know it is a girl, I can just feel her cuddling up in my arms," Bill laughed and said in a soothing voice.

Bill hung up and peered ahead. The traffic was light enough and he was making good speed. Josh was a few cars ahead of him but then Josh could wait. Bill changed lanes, passed Josh and sped away south towards San Diego.

18

Since the day Bill received his commission as a Supercop he had immersed himself in research. He studied the personal files and career record of every officer in the narcotics department serving in the different precincts in San Diego County. It was an impressive list of highly accomplished officers with several arrests and convictions on record.

The name of a lawyer by the name of Brant Sawyer had come up several times in drug related cases a few years back but there was no mention of this lawyer on narcotics related convictions for the last two years, it was as if he had practically disappeared from the courtroom. Brant took occasional homicide related cases, but they were few and far between. Apparently Brant was responsible for acquittals and mistrials in several narcotics related cases and was having a rather successful career before he decided to move on. Through an unknown instinct, Bill had found the pattern rather interesting, so he penciled in a note to research on Brant Sawyer, not really knowing what he expected to find.

Officer Josh Timmons was born and raised in San Diego and had decent enough academic career from UCSD. He joined the ranks of San Diego's finest about three years ago and had a pretty impressive record in homicide. Recently he had applied for training as an undercover narcotics agent and had been serving in the narcotics department for the last two months.

Bill was tired with all the reading and was about to put the file away, when he realized that he had accidentally skipped a page earlier—for some reason he had turned over two sheets at a time. Bill sat upright as he read the contents of the page that he had skipped. It contained an outline of a homicide case that Josh had worked on and had also been in court to make a statement on behalf of his supervisor. It was a mistrial and the lawyer defending was Brant Sawyer. The judge had ordered further investigation into the matter, after he had released the defendant on grounds of insufficient proof of guilt.

"Interesting connection", Bill murmured, "for some reason, this Sawyer guy is bugging me, though it is probably none of my business." Bill put the file away, packed up for the day and headed home.

It had suddenly struck him that although the judge had ordered further investigation into the matter, there was no documentation on what further investigation was actually done. The case was still "open", but no activity was recorded—Bill found that odd as his brows furrowed and he pondered what might have happened. "Maybe, it is because Josh is no longer with homicide, nobody took care to close the case after all. Anyway, homicide is none of my business anymore," Bill pondered.

Years of experience had taught Bill that his instincts never let him down, so he decided to do some research on Brant and find out where that took him. Bill had set up surveillance near Brant's house, at times, masquerading as a morning jogger, sometimes as an old man enjoying his evening stroll, sometimes as a tourist enjoying the afternoon sun.

He had also seen Brant swap cars with another man, who turned out to be a certain Alejandro Garcia with a National City address. Bill had followed Brant on several trips to Los Angeles. Brant visited a different hotel every time—the common factor in every visit was that Brant would carry a briefcase into the hotel and would come out with a briefcase that appeared to be the same one that he had carried in. He would spend about three or four hours inside the hotel on every visit and met the same person, a Rusty Jones, every time. He would drive back to San Diego the same day, exchange cars at different places with Alejandro and retire for the night.

Brant would also fly out of Los Angeles usually on the last Sunday evening of the month and be gone for almost a week. He appeared to be frequent patron of a Swiss airline and Zurich was the destination all the time. Bill found this routine very intriguing.

Bill was at lunch with another officer one day and heard him complain that the surveillance van was not available for him that day because it was reserved by a Josh Timmons in the narcotics department.

"Man, this is so frustrating," the Officer had complained, "I know he has his duty to perform, but then I do too, you know. I don't understand why the City cannot afford a few more of these vehicles for us to use. Our friends on the other side have a bad habit of not waiting for us to be ready first before they strike," the officer shook is head in disgust.

The name 'Josh Timmons', had grabbed Bill's attention. He found out that the surveillance was being done on a certain Alejandro Garcia. "This is too good to be a coincidence," Bill had thought.

"Surveillance is serious business and an officer would not usually do that unless he was reasonably certain of something," Bill thought. "I wonder why Josh is trying to tap Alejandro. Josh is in narcotics and I know Alejandro and Brant swap cars every time Brant makes a trip to Los Angeles. So did Josh know about the car swap as well?" Bill pondered and decided to tag along with the lead.

Bill had checked out an unmarked pickup truck from the police yard, put on the disguise of an old man to follow Brant that morning to Los Angeles. To his total surprise, he found that Josh was also on Brant's tail. Bill maintained a discrete distance from both of them.

Bill had witnessed almost everything that happened that day in the hotel's parking lot. He knew Josh was up to something, but he decided to wait and watch from a distance. When Brant and Josh had walked into Josh's car, Bill would have literally given his right arm to hear the conversation, but that was not to happen. He had seen Josh glance over towards him a couple of times, but had lost interest to see a sleeping old man in a pickup truck. Bill had been faking, but Josh has no way of knowing that.

Bill could make out an animated conversation going on between the men, where most of the time, Brant had held his head in his hands—the picture of a man who was distraught, while Josh seemed to enjoy every moment of the conversation. "So Josh appears to be on to Brant's game, whatever that is," Bill thought. "But why did he let Brant leave. Darn it, I wish I could hear their conversation," Bill was frustrated.

What surprised Bill the most was the discovery that Rusty Jones also operated a restaurant a block down the street from the hotel. He found it odd for a famous lawyer from San Diego to have some deals going on with a restaurant owner in Los Angeles.

"It seems that Josh has his finger on the pulse here," Bill thought as he feigned to be asleep in his truck, "A narcotics cop, keeping tabs on a guy like Alejandro and following Brant all the way to Los Angeles, making contact with the man who Brant was meeting almost every time, makes me think that this has got something to do with drugs after all. Who are you really Josh," Bill murmured, "a good cop or a crooked cop or is it all plain and simple coincidence? This however is too bloody suspicious to be a coincidence. I'll be watching you guys, and you can count on it."

He kept on Josh's tail until Joan called to say that she was in labor. Nothing else mattered to Bill anymore—his sole concern was to get Joan to the hospital as quickly as he possibly could.

19

"How are you doing George?" Josh asked. Without pausing for a reply he continued, "Hey I was wondering if we can meet socially sometime. Nothing fancy, just a little chit chat with Dave and I. Are you up to it?"

He listened on the phone and said, "Very well then. I know you don't have the opportunity to get out of the bar too often. We will meet you at your house at around six and have dinner afterwards—we're buying. How does that sound?"

He listened and said, "Great, that's all fixed up. What is your home address?" Josh listened as George gave his address. But he did not bother to write it down—he already knew where George lived.

"I got it George. We'll see you at six tomorrow evening," they hung up.

Josh called ahead to meet Dave at his home that evening. "Be there Dave, this is important. I'll bring in dinner for both of us," Josh said emphatically.

Josh knocked on Dave's door at nine o'clock and Dave answered almost immediately—he had been waiting impatiently.

"Well, are you going to tell me what's so important?" Dave was anxious.

Josh laughed and said, "Brant Sawyer is working for us now."

"You've got to be kidding me," Dave could not believe his ears. "You mean the lawyer Brant Sawyer?"

Josh laughed again, "How many Brant Sawyers do you know, Dave? The one and only Brant Sawyer. I'm starving. Let's eat and I'll tell you all about it.

Over dinner, Josh gave a vivid account of the day. When he finished he noticed that Dave had hardly touched his food. "Aren't you hungry?" Josh asked.

Dave snapped out of his trance and said, "You are a genius, Josh. Hats off to you buddy! Man, you're very good. If it was someone else telling me that story, I wouldn't have believed any of this."

Josh laughed, "Well, I guess I was lucky. You might want to get back to your food Dave, there is something else I want to talk about."

Dave was still shaking his head in disbelief and said, "Oh you're not done yet, huh? Let me guess, we've got to line up George now."

Josh smiled, "You're getting better at this every day. Yes, we've got to show George the ropes. The cash will start to come in now, but we need someone like George right away in our team. I have already arranged our meeting with George tomorrow. You and I are going to meet him at his apartment at six o'clock in the evening. I don't think he suspects anything and thinks this is simply a social call."

"Are we really in a hurry to get George into the fold Josh?" Dave said over a mouthful of food.

"Well I always believe is striking when the iron is hot. I want to get George lined up before we meet Brant next Saturday. No time's better than the present, Dave."

20

Dave knocked on the door promptly at six in the evening. After the second knock George came to the door and held it open with a wide grin on his face.

"Welcome to my humble home, guys," George pumped Dave and Josh's hands. He did have huge hands as Josh realized.

"Thanks for having us George," Josh sounded polite.

He looked around. George lived modestly—with a bartender's salary and tips, living in downtown San Diego could not be very easy. It was one bedroom apartment with a small kitchen and dining area. The living room had an old sofa, probably purchased from a flea market. The carpet was old but not worn out yet. The paint was starting to peel from the walls. There was a small breakfast table with two chairs in the dining room area—it also looked like a flea market purchase. The bedroom was visible from the living room and had all the evidence that George lived alone.

"Well this is a surprise guys. As you can see I have rather modest accommodations. So what's this all about?" George sounded genial.

"Oh we just wanted to get to know you a little better. You seemed very friendly to us at the bar so we thought we might look you up socially as well," Josh said calmly.

"Great," George was pleased at the attention—clearly he was a loner. "I never asked you before, but what do you guys do for a living?"

"You go first, Dave," Josh offered.

"Well I work for the SDFD—you know, the San Diego Fire Department. I guess you can say that I get to play with fire from time to time," Dave said.

George stared at Dave, trying to catch some hidden meaning and said, "No kidding! Oh my, that is wonderful."

"How long have you been working at that bar, George?" Josh already knew the answer.

"About two years now," George said truthfully.

"Did you do the same thing earlier as well?" Josh looked pointedly at George.

George hesitated and said, "Well, I have been moving from job to job, tried pretty much everything from a stevedore in the docks to a garage mechanic. But I didn't like any of that. So I decided to get into something quieter."

"You lying bastard. Before that you were serving jail time," Josh mused. Aloud he said, "That's quite a career change, I guess."

"Well, I learn quickly, so it wasn't much of a problem," George said.

"How about you Josh, what do you do for a living?"

Josh laughed and said, as if he never heard George's question, "I was wondering if you have some beer in the refrigerator there. I can't imagine a bartender staying dry at home. Aren't you going to offer us something to drink or what?"

George sounded truly embarrassed, "Of course, how remiss of me. You see, I live alone, so some of these social gestures don't cross my mind so readily."

As George walked up to the refrigerator, Josh and Dave exchanged glances. Josh stood up from the couch and removed his jacket to reveal the service badge stuck to his belt. He turned around as if to admire a picture hanging from the wall. The scenery was beautifully painted and the picture seemed way out of place given George's modest living standards.

"Here you go guys," George returned with two bottles. He handed one bottle to Dave and saw Josh admiring the picture with his back turned to George.

"I found that at a garage sale. It sure looks out of place in here," George laughed and handed the bottle to Josh. "So where were we? Oh yes, what do you do for a living Josh?"

Josh turned around slowly to face George—the gleaming badge from his belt instantly caught George's attention. Josh looked intently as George's face clouded and the wide grin disappeared to give way to a furrowed forehead. Josh knew he had caught George completely off guard with the badge. The reactions were a sure giveaway that George had something to hide and was about to have a nervous breakdown.

Pretending that he was unaware of the badge that showed from his belt Josh put his right hand on his hip next to the badge and said calmly, "Oh me? I am an Officer for the SDPD."

It was a comfortable sixty five degrees, but beads of perspiration glistened on George's forehead and color was draining from his face. Both Dave and Josh noticed the change in appearance and knew they had George by his tail.

"Are you ok George?" Josh asked nonchalantly, "You don't look too good."

"Yes, I just had a little headache," George sat down and gulped down a full glass of water. Dave and Josh exchanged glances and smiled briefly at each other.

"Phew, I guess I've got to see a doctor tomorrow—maybe my blood pressure is acting up again," George said softly.

They spent a few minutes in silence and George appeared to have recovered. He smiled and said, "Sorry about that, guys. It is not everyday that officers from the SDFD and the SDPD honor my humble apartment. Anyway, I am feeling better now."

"Good. Actually I almost had one of those headaches yesterday. It has been very stressful for the past two weeks," Josh sat down and massaged his temples. He continued, "I have not had a decent sleep for a while you see. I am following a court order to find a killer who has been absconding for a while now and that has taken a lot out of me."

"Do you have any leads yet?" George was cautious.

Josh looked directly into George's eyes and held his glare for a while that made George shift in his seat trying to find a more comfortable spot.

"Actually I have," Josh said softly, "as a matter of fact, I am about to close the case. I am sure you have read about it in the papers," Josh paused for effect closely watching George's expression, "the murder of Mark Sommers."

Beads of sweat were beginning to appear in George's forehead once again and he slumped back in his seat trying hard to keep his composure.

"You don't look too well George. Dave, can you please get George some more water please. I think he needs it," Josh had concern in his voice.

"You would not happen to know anything about this would you George?" Josh asked.

George shook his head in confused denial and stammered, "H-How would I know anything about it? I just work at a bar and mind my own business." He gulped down the water that Dave brought over and made an attempt to smile.

Josh wasn't amused and kept a thoughtful expression on his face, "You see George, this is a very interesting case. This guy—Sommers was a paraplegic and had been that way for seventeen long years. Apparently he used to have a normal life before a car accident forced him into a wheelchair. The court had ruled against the defendant who supposedly caused the accident on purpose and to top it off gave a false testimony to the police. The defendant was thrown in prison for a fifteen year term and his assets were liquidated and handed over to Sommers and his family. I'm told that the settlement amount was pretty substantial after the defendant's inheritance was liquidated. This would have left the defendant penniless by the time he was released from prison, which in fact brings us to the motivation behind the murder."

Josh paused to analyze George's reaction. He was telling George what he already knew and it was obvious that George was not at all comfortable in that room.

"Interestingly enough," Josh continued, "the defendant became a free man two years ago and I believe his only aim in life was to have his revenge, which was to kill the man who took it all away from him. It should not have been very tough tracing Sommers—a quick check in the telephone book would have easily provided a list and then through the usual method of elimination the correct Mark Sommers would have been located."

George was staring at the floor. He understood where all of this was going. He was sure that the only reason Josh was discussing the case was because he knew that George was the killer. It did not make sense otherwise—cops don't usually discuss their cases with strangers. He wondered what would happen if he knocked Josh down right away and killed him. He could easily overpower Josh, strangle him and leave the dead body in the desert. But then Josh was a cop and moreover Dave was there too. There was no way George could handle two men at the same time without any weapon handy. He quickly glanced at the kitchen cabinet where he kept his gun. It was quite a distance away and moreover it was not loaded. It was really the end of the road for him—the electric chair was waiting, or maybe lethal injection instead.

Dave and Josh exchanged glances and Dave nodded in agreement that George was indeed getting the drift of things. "So you worked as a stevedore in the docks and as a garage mechanic before you became a bartender, eh George?" Dave asked and George nodded in agreement.

Josh said in a serious tone, "George, I know that this is a needle in a haystack, but on the night of the murder, there were some witnesses who saw the killer enter and exit Sommers' house. Those descriptions from three different witnesses are uncannily very similar. What is even more uncanny is the fact that those descriptions match you my friend."

"In the interests of due diligence, I have to ask you a few questions," Josh was going to continue tightening the screws till George snapped. "Where were you between the hours of eight and ten o'clock at night on June sixteenth George?" Josh was relentless.

"This is ridiculous. You come to my house and try to insinuate that I am a killer?" George sounded insulted and irritated.

"I checked with your manager at the bar," Josh completely ignored George's question, "and he said that you had left at around seven o'clock on the sixteenth , saying that you were not feeling well. He also mentioned that there were some complaints from some of the customers that evening about poor service. Apparently something was bugging you—you served a Long Island to a customer who had asked for a Bloody Mary instead. You were not your efficient self that evening, my friend. This just makes me wonder what exactly was bugging you."

"I wasn't feeling well that day. I came back home, took some aspirin and dropped off to sleep," George was trying hard to cook up a story.

"I am sure you will say that there were no witnesses who can vouch for what you just said, right?" Josh already knew the answer.

"I live alone and nobody saw me get back home," the rug was rapidly being pulled away from George's feet and he fought to gain some traction.

"I already knew that answer George—that is exactly what they all say. I hope you understand how bad things look for you—no witnesses and it is only your word we have to go with. Try to hold that up in a court of law," Josh said softly.

"You can't prove anything, Officer. All you have is suspicion and that never held up in any court of law," George sounded menacing.

"It is good to see that after seventeen years, you still remember what does and does not hold up in a court of law, right George?" Josh had George almost over the edge.

"I don't know what you are talking about," George was clutching at straws.

"What's this—a sudden loss of memory, huh George?" Josh said sarcastically, "Can I see your driver's license, George?"

"I-I don't have one," George stammered.

"Sure you don't George. The Judge took it away from you permanently seventeen years ago in that courtroom, correct George Briggs?" Josh was stern.

George was silent, knowing that he was done for. His mind was racing and he was more desperate than ever. Josh knew everything and there was no escape. He furtively glanced at the kitchen cabinet again. The gun would be there and so would the bullets. He could pretend that he needed a glass of water, go to the kitchen, load the gun and kill both Josh and Dave. They were not too big, so he should not have any problems getting rid of them. He borrowed his manager's truck from time to time, so he could use it to dump the bodies in the desert.

"So you finally had your revenge, right George? You did well to hide your tracks, but I guess life has a funny way of getting back at you. It will either be life imprisonment or an execution order, my friend. They will not show you any mercy, you can take my word for it," Josh kicked up another notch.

"I still don't know what you are talking about, but I like your story. You should try out Hollywood, they may be interested," George got up and headed towards the kitchen.

Josh and Dave exchanged knowing glances. Josh grinned and said calmly, "You really think that you will have the time to find your gun and use it against us, George?"

George stopped mid-step in his tracks. Josh was reading his mind, though he could not figure out how.

He turned around slowly realizing that he was indeed outsmarted. Dave was standing beside Josh who had his right foot on the coffee table and was hunched forward. The ankle holster had a gun in it in clear view. Josh was ready to draw if he had to.

The situation was helpless for George, he was done for and there weren't two ways about it now. His shoulders drooped and he literally collapsed in the sofa and closed his eyes. His temples were throbbing—the strain was too much to bear.

They spent a few minutes in silence. Dave and Josh looked intently, giving George the time to recover. George stirred after a while, sat up. "He destroyed my life and ripped me of all my assets," George sounded crestfallen and beaten. "I had nothing to look forward to. There was nothing else I thought about when I was serving my time. Fifteen years and I thought of nothing else. Everything was going according to my plan, but I expected to find him alone. I thought it would work to my advantage to frame the other guy. So I knocked him off and planted my gun in his hands before killing Sommers and making my escape. I had to have my revenge and bloody hell that was exactly what I did. I have no remorse about that."

Another minute passed in silence and George said, "Well, what's next Officer? I guess my time is up."

Josh winked at Dave and motioned him to silence. George looked up at Josh expectantly.

"Well George, whether your time is up or not depends entirely on you," Josh said.

"What was that?" George was visibly surprised.

Josh repeated and continued, "You can either surrender right now or you can cooperate with us and we can help you get out of this untouched. So it's either the electric chair or life for you George, what's it going to be?" He already knew the answer.

"Are you kidding me? How can I help you?" George was incredulous.

Josh put his foot down from the coffee table, put his hands in his pockets and nodded at the wall clock. "Gosh it's late, let's all go get some dinner."

21

Joan McMillan delivered a baby girl after a long eighteen hours in labor. The baby was alert right from the time she was born. The loud cry and the wide open gorgeous blue eyes announced her arrival.

"Oh my God, she is beautiful. You made it my love," Bill kissed Joan's forehead and pressed her forearm in reassurance.

Joan laughed in relief, "We all made it, thank you God. I'm fine. You go to her Bill—she needs you more than I do."

"Are you sure? God I wish I could clone myself right now. I don't want to leave either of you alone," Bill was anxious.

"You're nuts. One Bill McMillan is already too much for me to handle," Joan said jokingly, "you go on, dear. Go to our daughter. They are going to take her to the nursery for a while."

"Are all her vital signs stable doctor?" Bill motioned at Joan and asked the obstetrician.

"Oh yes, Mom is doing just fine. If I were you, I'd be with the baby right now," the doctor was jovial.

Bill followed the nurse out of the delivery room. The nurse was carrying the baby wrapped in a blanket. She lay the baby on a weighing scale and declared, "Seven pounds Sir, you have a very healthy baby."

The nurse placed the baby on a small crib and she kicked up her voice a few more pitches. Bill kneeled down beside, held her hand and softly murmured in the baby's ear, "Welcome to our world my little darling. Mom and I love you very much." The wailing stopped.

"I think she has connected with you," the nurse laughed.

"I am sure she has," Bill said, "I used to talk to her every night when she was in Mom's womb. She seems to recognize my voice."

The deep large blue eyes were staring at Bill. He bent down kissed the baby on her forehead and murmured, "Hello sweetheart, this is Daddy. We've waited so long for you to come into our lives. I dedicate my life to you, my precious baby."

"What's her name Dad?" the nurse asked. She was getting ready to give the baby her first bath.

"Anita, this is our Anita McMillan," Bill said and kissed the baby again.

The nurse picked the baby and gave her a bath, wrapped her up in a blanket and offered her to Bill, "Here you go Daddy, and she's all yours now."

Bill was trembling with excitement as he held little Anita in his arms for the first time. She looked up at him curiously with her deep blue eyes and yawned.

"Oh my precious, you truly make my life worth living and fighting for," Bill was weeping—overcome with emotion, "Let's go see Mommy." He placed little Anita in her crib.

22

Dave had called Brant to set up an appointment at his house after sundown on Saturday. Josh had his binoculars pinned on Brant's home all afternoon, but there was no unusual activity. Dave and George had joined him shortly after the sun disappeared below the Pacific and the three knocked on Brant's door.

Josh surveyed Brant's living room and remarked, "Jeez, you are doing pretty well for yourself, Brant. Interesting to see how you can keep things so neat without a woman in the house."

Brant smiled knowingly, "Well I am not taking too many clients these days."

"Why work when you don't need to," Josh said in a telltale voice. "This is Dave Reynolds, we don't have any secrets."

Dave and Brant shook hands. "Nice to meet you Dave," Brant had a welcome smile. Dave returned the greeting.

"This is George Briggs, he likes to call himself George though," Josh introduced as George held out his huge hands at Brant.

"George Briggs," Brant looked intently at George and said, "I have seen you before," he paused, "though I can't remember where."

Josh was surprised, "You know each other?"

"Now I remember. It was quite a while, let me see," Brant paused to think, "I'd say about seventeen years ago. You were being tried for on some traffic accident case—the plaintiff got the verdict and you were given fifteen years."

"That's the story of most of my life, Brant. I see that you and Josh have already talked," George said with a deadpan expression in his face.

Josh looked at Brant, "Actually we haven't yet. How did you know George?"

Brant laughed, "Well I was a law student at that time and I was in court on the day of George's trial. You are still well built, George, they must have taken care of you in prison."

"You have a pretty sharp memory, Brant. I'm impressed," Dave sounded genuine.

Brant had a faraway look and apparently didn't hear Dave. He looked back at George, then at Josh with a bewildered expression. "You've got to be kidding me!" he exclaimed. "If I remember right, the plaintiff in that case was Mark Sommers. The same Mark Sommers who was killed last month and you Josh were placed in charge of finding the real killer," he paused. "George is the killer we are looking for, right Josh?"

Josh was smiling, "Man you are impressive, and I mean it. Yes, George was," he stressed on the 'was', "our man. But that is the past Brant. George has agreed to play with us. I will let the case stay open for a while and then it will be closed. We will keep George clear of the ropes. All of us can do much better and lead fuller lives as free men," Josh seated himself in a plush sofa. He ran his hands over the smooth leather and said, "Why dig for dirt in jail when there is so much of gold outside begging to be yours?"

"So we are hunting for gold, are we?" Brant motioned Dave and George to be seated, pulled open a cooler and passed around bottles of beer. "Something tells me you have a plan, my friend."

"Patience my friend," Josh said, "is a virtue. Sit down guys, let's talk."

The four men sank themselves in the comfortable seats and George remarked, "Quite a change from the seating arrangements in my apartment, huh Dave?"

"Yes, but that is only transient, your day to enjoy the luxuries of life is not too far off," Dave assured.

"For the record, what you are going to hear is not happenstance—this is a carefully laid out plan that Dave and I had cooked up four years ago," Josh was speaking. "Shortly before you started to notice me in the courtroom during your trials, Brant and long before I enrolled for the Police Academy, the plans were already made. We were looking for a lawyer who would have an impeccable track record in fighting narcotics related cases. You were the answer to that search, Brant. You were amazing in court, even when I thought you knew that your client was guilty, you still managed to get him off the hook. I followed your style, that cool swagger of confidence and conviction that you had in your voice as you argued for your client. Your string of successes meant that you had already established a favorable rapport and strong links with that group of people, who would pay you anything you wanted just to get their freedom back."

Josh paused to wet his throat and continued, "You had the links to the dealers and the knowledge of the law. However, we needed enough protection from the law and inside information, so that your links could be used to our mutual advantage. This was why I enrolled in the Academy. I spent over three years in homicide and had worked very hard before I changed course to pick up the career of a narcotics cop only recently. I did this on purpose to remove any suspicion from the minds of anyone as to what my actual intent was—to them, it was simply a change of specialization."

"Now I have access to inside information about almost all the major drug rings operating in San Diego. I know who all are on the watch list. Just so you know, Brant and it may surprise you that almost every client that you helped to set free from a drug related charge are in the watch list. We all know that we have tightened up security and screening on our borders down South, but controlled substances still keep flowing in. For a moment we thought that there were some clandestine labs operating in the County, but so far we do not have evidence about that. I do have a theory though, but there are missing links that I will discuss with you. Let us hold off on that for a while. But just to jog you on a bit, I am convinced that you, my friend are involved heavily into it."

Josh poured some more of the fine beer down his throat and watched Brant squirm in his seat—moving from a comfortable position to a defensive posture with crossed legs and folded hands.

Josh smiled, "Not to worry my friend, nothing leaves this room. So as I was saying, I know that drugs enter through our borders and find their way all the way into Los Angeles," Josh paused again. "I have a fair reason to believe that your buddy Alejandro Garcia is the conduit from across the border into the country and you, Brant, are the courier for Rusty in Los Angeles. How am I doing so far?" Josh asked without expecting an answer from Brant.

"Now that is just one theory I have," he continued, "but I am sure Alejandro is not the only person involved. There are others too, given the sheer volume of drugs we have confiscated from different areas up and down Southern California. Brant, we know that you have established relationships with these operations in San Diego and in Los Angeles, which is very good."

"I'm just curious, Josh, but since how long did you know about my side business?" Brant was already impressed with how methodical Josh had been.

Josh laughed, "Long enough my friend and I admire your *modus operandi.*"

"Well here's my plan, Brant," Josh chuckled and said, "or should I say our plan. We will approach Rusty in Los Angeles and Alejandro in San Diego with a business proposition. We will help to eliminate all competition for Rusty and for Alejandro—they will be the only ones in business in Los Angeles and San Diego respectively, we will bust all other drug rings. I will use information about the competition from Rusty and Alejandro to work undercover and organize arrests and a complete shut down of the competition. That will help establish my credibility with the Department and will get me on the road to promotion. The higher I rise in the ranks, the easier it will be to clear the field. You, Brant will help me convict these guys and put them away. After a string of convictions, you will gain all the fame that you can possibly dream of and nobody will suspect any of us. Are you with me so far?

Brant nodded in approval.

"Very good," Josh continued, "This will clear the field for Rusty and Alejandro in exchange for a handsome fee. They will be protected as long as they continue to work with us. They cannot afford to do anything stupid with us, because they will be exposed if they do. If they try to bring us down, we won't hesitate to return the favor. It will be foolish for any party to do any back-stabbing, so there is no reason for anyone to get jumpy and do something rash. They have nothing to lose by this partnership and everything to gain. You and I will protect them from the law and they can flourish, which in turn makes us flourish as well. Immunity from the law and a clear field to operate as they wish for a price—I think that is a fair bargain," Josh paused again and looked around the room.

Brant smiled, "Brilliant!" he exclaimed with a boyish twinkle in his eyes.

George had heard something on these lines, but not as detailed as Josh had described. He was goggle-eyed but like Brant, he was also curious to know exactly what role Josh had in mind for him.

Josh apparently read their minds. He continued, "You must be wondering where Dave and George fits in. You and I will need extra hands to make this work. I have known Dave for a long time—as a matter of fact, he shares the credits for this plan as much as I do. He and I have worked on this together long before we met George and came to know about you. Dave appears to be the silent one but he is really the thinker and his brain works faster than anyone that I have known. He has proven himself to be an accomplished member in the SDFD, you must have read about him several times in the Union Tribune."

"As you know, if you can be a competent fire-fighter," Josh stressed, "you can also be a competent fire-starter. Dave has specialized in arson and has now moved on to more detecting work than actual firefighting. He helps investigate the reasons for the fire, which often brings the SDPD into the picture. You must have read about the case where a failing business started a fire on their own premises so that they could get insurance to pay for the damages. Dave was responsible to investigate the case and bring the owners to justice. They got thirty years in the care of taxpayer dollars, for insurance fraud and intentional destruction of property in a public place. Dave's skill will come in very handy when we start clearing the competition for our friends Alejandro and Rusty. It might be easier to simply burn up the competition, literally, rather than to run them through the justice system—that just slows things down."

Dave looked at George and then at Brant, who was listening intently. He broke out into a grin when Brant nodded in approval yet again.

"George's bulk is his asset," Josh continued. "Size really matters when it comes to him. It is important to have muscle power if we have to operate in the manner that I have described. You know that George has a police record and that we are shielding him from the Sommers murder now," Josh paused to let his statement sink into George.

"He currently works at a bar downtown and has been living a normal life ever since—at least that's the official record," Josh smiled and looked at George. He had been waiting anxiously to hear what Josh had to say. Josh took another swig at this bottle and continued, "We might need muscle power while we try to clear the field—George is your man for that. His recent flare up with Sommers proves that he still has that intensity in him even after fifteen years in jail. Remember that it is also difficult to hide a man of George's size, so if we engage him on anything we have to be absolutely sure that we have strong alibis in his favor."

Josh put his empty bottle on a side table and said, "So that is it, my friends, I have laid all my cards on the table. We are in a position to exploit an untapped market," Josh smiled sarcastically, "where it is a win-win situation for all of us. I believe in equality, since that is what a true partnership is all about. I suggest that we split the take equally among us."

"All I can say is that I am intrigued by all of this. What guarantee do I have that I can trust you and this is not another of your tricks to catch me on the wrong foot?" Brant asked cautiously.

"Guarantee?" Josh laughed out loud—a little irritated by the directness of the question, "You are looking for a guarantee? You my friend, are in no position to ask for a guarantee for anything. However, since we are going to become equal partners, let us let the bygones be bygones and start with a clean slate. All of us can be more profitable that way. I promise to destroy all evidence that I have collected on you and George. Your guarantee is your continued fulfillment of our partnership."

Silently he thought, "Like hell I would, you idiot, all that evidence is my life insurance."

Josh continued, "No Brant, this is not a trick—I am coming clean to you on this one. I want to make lots of money, we all want to make lots of money. You are in a position to help us make that money through your contacts, we are in a position to help you make that money. Symbiotic co-existence my friend, is the key—as long as we continue to support each other, we will be rolling in riches. Failure of any one of us could bring down everyone else."

A pregnant silence descended in the room, everybody was trying to measure the situation in his own terms. Brant got up, went behind the bar and returned with a bottle of Jack Daniels. "Let's celebrate the beginning of our enterprise with my friend Jack," he declared as he poured out generous portions for everybody. Every man raised their glass to a toast and shook hands with each other. "Cheers to our partnership," they echoed.

"Good, but the next important step is still ahead of us, I'm sure you all understand that," Josh said as the laughter ended.

Brant, sharp as ever, nodded and said, "Yes, you are right, the most important step is ahead of us. I am going to meet Rusty again next week and will speak to him about our plan. I am sure he will simply love to run the monopoly in the Los Angeles area. He keeps talking from time to time on how his service area, so to speak, is getting smaller by the day due to the proliferation of other dealers up north. Rusty is a smart guy and I'm sure he will see the value we bring to him."

"Good, you do that, Brant. Tell him that in order to prove that we mean business, we will give him a demonstration on what we can do for him," Josh picked up the conversation again. "Ask him to give you information on any one of his competitors, we are looking for names, photographs if available, addresses where we can conduct an operation to bust these guys. I will organize an undercover operation with my counterparts in Los Angeles and get this guy arrested with sufficient proof that would take him out of circulation. That will be one less for Rusty to worry about. This we will do free of charge for Rusty, after which I am sure he will want to meet with us and establish more equitable relationships."

Brant nodded, "I see, you think of everything, Josh."

Josh smiled, "Who doesn't like a trial period? I really wish I did think of everything. Does Alejandro work alone or does he have a puppet master?"

The sudden switch of conversation to Alejandro surprised Brant, "No Alejandro works alone, he has peddlers through whom he distributes to the general public. He works very closely with Rusty and supplies him exclusively. I don't know how Alejandro gets all the stuff from and I never asked him. He believes in the need-to-know-principle and does not entertain such discussions."

"We'll see about that need-to-know principle. He'll tell us all we need to know once we show him the cheese," Josh said confidently.

"You're probably right," Brant agreed.

Dave and George took their leave and Brant let them out. He returned to Josh and asked, "I still don't get George. Why are you protecting that man? He can be easily identifiable—a man his size cannot mingle in the crowd you know."

Josh laughed, "We will need to have somebody who would do the dirty laundry from time to time, my friend. Dave, yourself or I would risk a lot if we were to do everything on our own. Despite his bulk, George is pretty resourceful. You have seen how he was able to commit murder and evade discovery. I admit that I got to know his little secret completely by chance and for that I give George a lot of credit. Relax Brant, you'll see soon how George proves his worth—trust me on this."

Brant led Josh outside and walked him to his car. "I am excited Josh. I think I have finally found the right company."

Josh laughed and clapped Brant on his shoulder, "You're not half as excited as I am. Let me know how your meeting with Rusty and Alejandro turns out."

Brant nodded and walked back inside his house.

Bill lowered his night vision binoculars and placed them on the passenger seat in his car. He was parked about two hundred yards away from Brant's driveway—he had been there for the last four hours shortly before Josh and the others arrived. Josh seemed rather friendly with Brant—they certainly seemed to be collaborating with each other. Bill's forehead furrowed and he started his engine. Joan and Anita were waiting for him to come home.

23

"I just don't care much for cops, Brant," Rusty sounded concerned. "How do you know he is not using you as bait?"

"I thought about it, but I think this guy is seriously not inclined to bring us down. He wants to make money and has been planning this entire thing for several years now. He is looking for a partnership. I'd recommend that you give him a chance to prove that he means business. Besides, he is aware of your dealings and your links with Alejandro—in fact he is completely into our game," Brant was earnest. "I'm sorry to have brought you into this Rusty, I had never even suspected that someone was on my tail. However the past cannot be reversed, so I'd say we look ahead from this point onwards."

"You make a good point. I have a lot of faith in your judgment Brant," Rusty paused, "regardless of the fact that you led the bear to my camp. Let's give our crooked cop a chance."

"Very well Rusty. I will make arrangements right away. Your competition is up for a shock," Brant raised his glass, "Cheers!"

Within a week, Josh proved that he was good to his word. He had contacted his counterparts in Los Angeles and provided the necessary information. He was invited for the stakeout and sure enough, Rusty's information proved correct. The police confiscated a decent haul of narcotics, unlicensed firearms from a residence and arrested six people in the process. Lieutenant Carter at the LAPD was elated and called Josh to thank him personally.

Bill read the story in the Los Angeles Times and frowned. At first glance it was great news, but yet something bothered him. He called Lieutenant Carter and obtained a more detailed account of the operation. Things appeared to have happened too smoothly—the police knew exactly where to look. Although that was not unusual, but there was still something that seemed wrong and Bill could not figure out what it was.

He had run a search on the two men who had left Brant's home that night before Josh did and had come up with Dave Reynolds and George Briggs. Bill's research led him to learn that Dave was in the SDFD, while George had a police record and had also served fifteen years in the care of taxpayers. "A lawyer, a cop, a fireman and an ex-felon who is now a bartender—what a motley crew," Bill pondered, "I wonder what you guys are up to."

Rusty was satisfied—Josh had proved his case without a doubt. Brant organized a meeting and they all drove up to Riverside to meet in a converted warehouse.

"Officer Timmons, it's a pleasure to meet you. I'm thoroughly impressed with your work. You are as good as your word," Rusty was beaming and Alejandro rose to shake hands with Josh.

"I can tell you that you aren't the first one to be impressed with my talents," Josh sounded confidently pompous. "Actually Josh will suit me fine—there is no need for any formality among friends."

Rusty laughed and shook hands with Dave and George. "Nice meeting you gentlemen. I see great things lie ahead of us."

"Planning is everything and with a little luck, we'll do very well," Josh assured. "We've got some cleaning to do first. Rusty and Alejandro, as you must have already heard from Brant, I need information about your competition operating in Los Angeles all the way down to San Diego. We will have to come up with a strategy on how we are going to take them out of business and open the playing field for you. Dave, Brant, George and I will clear the way for you guys—all you have to do is expand your reach. How does that sound?"

"That's just great Josh. But both you and I know that you are not the only narcotics cop in all of Southern California. There are others who could be on our tail. What can you do to protect us from them?" Rusty was sharp—there was no love lost in business.

"I will tell you how to cover your tracks from the police so that you can operate freely. Just follow my advice and you'll be able to steer clear of the law. If I find anything amiss, I will give you prior warning as required," Josh said reassuringly. "In exchange we want forty percent of your profits that we will share among the four of us. With your wide coverage, you will be making a lot of money my friend. I hope you understand that this is a reasonable compensation to ask for all the value that we will provide to you," Josh paused. "Are we still in business?"

Rusty's expression clouded momentarily but he quickly recovered. He looked at Alejandro who shrugged and nodded in approval. Rusty smiled broadly and held out his hand, "You bet, we are definitely still in business."

"Very well then, let's get some information from the two of you and we'll get down to work," Josh sounded happy and content.

They spent a better part of two hours together and came up with a detailed list of names and addresses along with information about the sources of drugs that find their way into the region.

At the end Dave asked, "How do you guys know so much about these people and their modus operandi?"

Alejandro exchanged knowing glances with Rusty and said, "You've got to know your turf before you can play, my man. They know about us and we know about them—nothing's secret between us. We stay away from each other, because stepping on anyone's toes helps nobody. Everyone has their niche market, just like we do. We are all as vulnerable as the next guy. On this occasion we are fortunate that we have the law working with us," Alejandro and Rusty laughed out aloud.

Josh was amused, "That's a nice way to say it. We'll take your leave today and work on our strategy to bring these guys down and protect ourselves at the same time. We'll keep you posted in about a week. Let's all leave separately now. George," Josh was the man in command, "I know you came here with Dave, but I want Alejandro to take you back to San Diego. No particular reason, but it might be wise to bring in some variation the way we move around now. You never know who's watching."

Someone indeed was watching. Bill's camera picked up everybody leaving the warehouse. He was going to research on Rusty and Alejandro. A suspicion that he had for months now, did not seem baseless anymore. There was something clandestine going on and he wished he could listen in. Josh was into something unlawful and that conviction became stronger by the day in Bill's mind. But he had no tangible proof to substantiate his suspicion.

He followed Josh at a discrete distance on the way towards San Diego. Trained as an undercover cop, Josh had the habit of checking his rearview mirror more frequently than usual. Josh had been watching Bill's car at a distance for a while and something made him uncomfortable, though there was nothing extraordinary about the car behind him. He slowed down and sped up a few times and Bill reciprocated, before he realized that Josh might have suspected his presence and was varying his speed on purpose. He slowed down and veered into the off-ramp of an exit.

Josh watched Bill take the exit and smiled, "Boy am I getting jittery or what? That must have been sheer coincidence the way that guy was driving." He watched the on-ramp intently as he continued southwards, but could not see the car anymore. He leaned back, relaxed and wondered how he was going to organize his master plan.

24

"You are developing crow's feet on your forehead dear," Joan was concerned, "I don't think it's your age. So something's bothering you a lot these days. What is it Bill?"

Bill held Joan and little Anita in his arms and whispered, "Nothing escapes your scrutiny, does it sweetheart?"

Joan looked at him quizzically and said, "Nothing as evident as your furrowed forehead escapes my attention."

Bill bent down and kissed Anita on her pink cheeks and said, "You have a smart Mommy, did you know that little darling?" Surprisingly Anita returned a toothless smile that made Bill feel like a million dollars.

"Well?" Joan was not going to give up.

"I can't tell you, my dear. You know how it is. But you are right, something is bothering me. I hate to bring my work into our home—I know we talked about it. But I am only human, Joan. Please bear with me, okay?" Bill sounded disturbed.

His research on Alejandro returned nothing of much significance other than a period of rehab as a teenager. Alejandro was raised at an orphanage and had become an addict in his younger years. He once had to be taken to emergency to save his life from an episode of drug overdose. He was sent to rehab for a period of six months and had since then managed to steer clear of drug abuse. Apart from that one blemish, he did not have any record.

Rusty however had a more colorful profile. He was born in a small town in Wyoming and came to California with his parents when he was twelve. His father owned a restaurant and Rusty helped out. He got involved in a local gang and was arrested twice on charges of theft and assault. He served two years in jail and came home to find his father in his deathbed. His mother succumbed to the grief of her husband's death a year later, which left Rusty alone in the world. Rusty had taken charge of the restaurant and has been running the place ever since. The LAPD had suspected Rusty had some connections with the drug rings operating in Los Angeles, but have never been able to pin anything on him.

Dave's personal or employment records had turned up nothing out of the ordinary. Apparently he decided to turn over a new leaf and became a firefighter and had been doing rather well at his job ever since.

It did not take long for Bill to dig out George's past. He had caused no trouble during the fifteen years in the care of the law. He had kept to himself and nobody bothered him. At the time of his arrest all he had in his possession was a hundred and six dollars and some change, which was returned back to him at the time of his release. He had since then been working as a bartender in National City. Bill had actually visited George at the bar and had found him to be rather friendly despite his huge figure. Whatever George did to cover his past, he did well.

Bill found his research on Josh rather interesting, especially the fact that he and Dave had worked with the same security company in the past and that he had joined the SDPD at about the same time that Dave joined the SDFD. Josh's service record had been impeccable—as a matter of fact he had proven himself to be a rather competent officer. Just before he joined narcotics however, he had investigated a homicide of a certain Mark Sommers and apparently that case was still open. Bill was surprised that nobody picked up the case. The standard procedure was for the investigating officer to initiate such transfers to someone else, but the case files still showed Josh as the officer in charge. Bill thought that was rather odd and made a mental note to check it out a little further.

Brant had a rather modest upbringing. His parents divorced when he was four and his father remarried. His mother died of lung cancer two years later and Brant was brought up by his uncle. Brant had joined the Army Reserves after graduation and served for about two years before leaving his commission and taking up study in law. He was the brightest student in his class and had turned out to be an extremely successful lawyer. He had a unique style of presenting his case in court and was featured several times on newspaper articles. Apart from just one verdict against his client Brant had a rather impressive record for the last ten years. He had been extremely successful representing clients on narcotics charges, but had literally disappeared from the courtroom for the past couple of years, picking up a few cases here and there, but he appeared to have practically retired.

Bill had spent days trying to piece things together from different angles, but none of it made much sense. He could understand a lawyer, a fireman and a cop moving in the same circles, but he could not draw the connection with George, Alejandro and Rusty. His instincts said that there was more to it than what he saw and he wished he had more to go on.

The car swapping between Alejandro and Brant was the most suspicious thing of all—that just did not seem right. Moreover, he had seen Brant with Rusty come out of the hotel in Los Angeles each carrying rather large briefcases. Then Josh had confronted Brant and what followed was most unusual. Bill had noticed movements inside Josh's car the other day that suggested a heated conversation between the two. Bill was convinced that he was onto something hot, but just did not have enough facts to support his suspicions.

He decided to lie low and wait till something came up—for some reason he knew he would not have to wait too long. He was right.

There was a massive fire in a warehouse in Lemon Grove and the police found the charred remains of three adults—curiously enough two of them had their necks broken before they got fried and the other was found handcuffed to a steel pillar. Apparently this person had a rather violent death. Forensic analysis confirmed the presence of large amounts of methamphetamine and cocaine all over the warehouse. The bodies were identified and all had police records of drug related arrests.

Someone had killed on purpose and had torched the warehouse afterwards. Bill personally went to visit the site and learned that whoever committed the murders and burnt down the warehouse did a rather good job of covering their tracks—the police were practically clueless on what had happened. The smoldering embers still reeked of gasoline. Although the fire was massive, there was no damage to the buildings on either side of the warehouse. Whoever started the fire knew exactly how to contain the destruction—it was clearly the mark of an expert arsonist.

The warehouse had been a mechanic shop and was owned by a certain Curtis Small. The police had to kick down the door to Curtis' home after he had failed to answer the door. They found the man lying dead on the floor. There was no sign of any struggle and not even one drop of blood anywhere. Only Curtis had his head turned at an impossible angle that left no doubt in anybody's mind that his neck had been broken first and his body was then lowered to the floor. Curtis had been dead for almost eighteen hours, which happened to be at least four hours before his warehouse was torched.

25

Alejandro was grinning broadly—the picture of a man evidently content with himself. The morning newspaper carried a rather detailed account of the warehouse fire and the murder of four men, who were actually distributors of prohibited narcotics operating under cover of a mechanic shop.

His telephone rang and Alejandro leisurely picked it up.

"The fog appears to be clearing down there in your neck of the woods, huh?" Rusty was in a jovial mood.

"Yep, the forecast says that the weather is going to start clearing from now on in these parts," Alejandro was cautious.

"Good for you. See if you can send some of that nice weather my way," Rusty said.

"I'll do what I can. Happy tidings will be on their way today," Alejandro hung up.

Bill replaced his headphones on the passenger seat and pursed his lips. He had tapped Alejandro's phone and just heard the entire conversation. He was convinced that it wasn't the weather that the two were talking about. Neither used any names and 'happy tidings'—what could they be.

He was hoping that Alejandro would leave sometime and was pleasantly surprised to see him leave at around ten o'clock in his familiar car. Bill looked up and down the street—it was deserted. He walked up to the back of the house and used his trustworthy skeleton keys to pick the lock to the only door on the back wall of the house.

Alejandro was clearly a bachelor who did not care much for cleanliness. Bill moved around the house, pulled open drawers with his gloved hands, peered inside, frowned and pushed them back in place. Closets, cabinets and cupboards revealed nothing out of the ordinary. Bill walked into a room that looked like an office. He leaned against the wall and surveyed the room—a desk with drawers and a comfortable looking chair was all there was in the room. The hardwood floor was curiously well maintained, compared to the rest of the house.

Bill walked around the room taking in whatever detail there was to notice and frowned again. He tried to pull the drawers open and found them locked. He dropped on all fours and peered underneath the desk to see if there was a way to open the drawers. He tried his skeleton keys, but the drawers refused to open.

He stood up and lowered himself into the revolving chair, rocked himself sideways a couple of times and surveyed the room again. The drawers were bugging him—he needed to look inside, but he did not want to break them open. He looked at the floor beneath the desk with unseeing eyes, deep in thought about when he was going to do next.

Then he saw it—a few ants were coming out between two floorboards beneath the desk. At first Bill did not pay much attention, but the ants kept coming out, while some disappeared back between the floorboards. Bill dropped into his knees again and tapped the floorboards. It was hollow. He tapped the floor elsewhere and they sounded more solid.

He stood up and tried to push the desk aside. To his surprise the rich mahogany desk moved rather easily—it appeared to be on rollers. There was a three by two feet floorboard with a small groove on either edge—enough to insert a finger. Bill held the floor board and tugged. The board came off easily into Bill's hands to reveal a small set of stairs descending into the darkness below.

Bill whipped out a flashlight and peered down the hole. He looked up and took note of his bearings—he was facing west towards the street in front of the house. Bill gingerly lowered himself into the hole, descended the steps and stood on firm ground again. It was pitch black all around apart from the area lit up by his flashlight. He looked up at the surface and wondered if he should try and put the floorboard back in place, in case Alejandro returned. He reasoned that even if he did replace the floorboard in its place, he could never get the desk back in its place without getting back into the room above anyway. He decided to finish his investigation and get out as quickly as possible.

He had thought that the air inside will be foul and be devoid of much oxygen. To his surprise, the air was fresh enough and he was breathing normally. Bill moved his flashlight around to take a better look at the place. It was a ten by eight feet room with a set of long and narrow cabinets on the wall to the north. The dimensions of the cabinets were such that it would be possible to be lowered through the floor above.

Bill slowly opened the door of one cabinet and opened his mouth aghast at what he saw. There were stacks of small polythene packets with a white powdery substance in them. He opened the next cabinet and the next and the one after that. The contents were all the same. The last cabinet contained rolls of clear polythene sheets, four battery-operated portable fluorescent lights and a polythene sheet sealer. "Tools of the trade," Bill thought. On the bottom shelf of this cabinet was a tough quality white plastic bag that could easily have accommodated about 30 pounds of that powdery substance and then some. Beside the bag were smaller polythene packets ready to be filled.

Bill took a small packet, scooped out some of the powder and dropped it in the packet. He carefully closed the mouth of the packet and placed it in the inside pocket of his jacket. He closed the doors of all cabinets and moved the flashlight around.

There was a small door on the wall to the south, enough to let one person stoop down and pass. Bill grabbed the handle and pulled it open. The door creaked open to reveal a long dark tunnel. It was wide enough for a short person to comfortably walk. Bill crouched down and walked into the tunnel. After one left turn Bill knew that he was headed east. He walked about fifty paces and saw daylight coming into the tunnel. Encouraged, Bill kept walking for another hundred paces till he came to the place where he had seen daylight coming through.

He climbed the step ladder placed against the wall and peered through the grilled opening—the grille was padlocked from the outside. Beyond the grille were some overgrown shrubs. Bill realized that he was looking at a backyard of another house. He looked around to get a better idea of where exactly the house was located. Interestingly all the neighboring houses looked exactly the same. However the billboard on the street to the right of the house served as a perfect marker for Bill.

The sound of screeching tires tore through his thoughts and Bill knew he had seen enough for the day and had to make his way back. He descended into the tunnel once again and made his way back to the room below Alejandro's office. He listened intently at sounds overhead and heard nothing unusual— the house still appeared to be deserted. Cautiously Bill came up to the office, put the floorboards back in place and pushed the table exactly where it was before. He checked around quickly for any telltale signs that he might have left and was satisfied to see that the place seemed exactly as it was before he had walked in. He went out the back door and locked it using his skeleton keys.

Cautiously he looked around and listened for any unusual signs. Satisfied, he emerged from the back of the house. He looked up and down the street to see if anybody cared for his presence and headed back to his unmarked car, content that his little adventure was extremely fruitful. He was certain that the powdery substance in his possession was narcotics of some form and that Alejandro was involved with drug trafficking in collusion with his neighbor. He was excited—finally he was getting somewhere. He had found a lead and just had to piece things together. But first he had to know for sure that the sample that he took from that chamber below Alejandro's office was indeed narcotics.

Bill's mind was racing as he started the car and pulled away. Never did he notice that about a hundred yards away, George had been watching him from an old jalopy since the time he emerged from the back of the house. He could almost reach out and touch Bill through the high powered police issue binoculars that Josh had given him.

Alejandro's house was always to be watched as Josh had instructed, especially when Alejandro was out running his clandestine errands. When George was not busy breaking people's necks or working at the bar, he was to stand watch on Alejandro's house and report anything unusual back to Josh.

George made a mental note to report what he saw. He never saw the man before so it will be difficult to provide too many details. "Josh hates half-baked information, so it would be better to keep it quiet I guess," George thought, "the man looked harmless anyway, so I think it will be fine not to mention it."

He wished he had a camera, but he thought he could easily remember the man's face and appearance. He glanced at the binoculars and wondered how much it would be worth—it was a pretty useful gadget and heavy too. He could actually use it as a blunt weapon to knock people unconscious if he used it properly—that way it would be easier to break their necks. George grinned at the thought.

26

"Switzerland is too far away for me Brant. I'd like somewhere nearer," Josh mumbled over a mouthful of Rusty's famous chicken fingers.

"Well anything in the United States will be difficult for you to hide, my man," Brant said. "You will make a lot of people raise their eyebrows if they learn about your assets. The rate at which Rusty is feeding us, we're already looking like a bunch of fat cows."

"More where they came from, guys. Just keep clearing my way and the cheese will keep flowing," Rusty laughed out loudly. "Why don't you try out in Mexico, Josh? That is right in your backyard, and you can build your dream oceanfront mansion dirt cheap. Moreover, nobody will even blink at you there. Alejandro has contacts he can hook you up with and I am sure he will be happy to."

"Of course, I'll be happy to help Josh," Alejandro echoed Rusty. "The Cabo San Lucas area is simply gorgeous. I have a lot of friends there who will take good care of you. That place gets a lot of American tourists, so you might even start a business there to cater to Americans."

"Not a bad idea Rusty. I think I will take you up on that offer Alejandro. I'd like to go and check it out first though. You're right—it is getting more and more difficult to store all that cash at home. Mexico will be a nice place to invest in," Josh said.

"Count me in too," George chimed in. "The risks are becoming higher every day out here for me. So far we have been successful, but then you never know what happens. I need a life too, you know?"

"Absolutely George," Josh said. "As long as you don't knock on my door in the middle of the night, I won't mind having you as my neighbor in Cabo."

"Sounds like a plan gentlemen," Brant pitched in. "You guys must visit my chateau one of these days in the foothills of the Alps in Switzerland—that is one of the most gorgeous places you will ever see. I just built an indoor heated competition length swimming pool out there—it is simply wonderful all year round."

"It is wonderful to see how all of you have prospered," Rusty had a far-away look on his face. "I'm looking back six months when you first approached me, Josh. We've all come a long way together. Quite candidly I did not believe you the first time and had even thought about backing out. But then something told me that you really did have some substance in your plans, so I decided to tag along. Today, I can say that I am happy that I took that decision."

"I have been saying all along to all of you that there is a lot we can achieve outside as free men than we can do in custody. Why rot in jail when you can blossom in Switzerland or Mexico? It is the long term goal we should have in mind and that is all that matters," Josh was enjoying his role as the prime architect and executioner of a successful plan.

"I couldn't have said that any better," Brant said.

"Well, the time to sit on our laurels has not come yet. We still have a fair amount of cleaning to do," Josh said looking at the list in his hand. "We've cleaned out the smaller players and nobody has a clue of what is going on. We have your competition confused, Rusty. It's time to move into the major league now."

"I agree," Rusty nodded. "The road ahead will be tougher. We are talking about some pretty well organized groups and the arson and neck-breaking will not work anymore. You guys will be in the danger zone—a hint of suspicion would make them fold up and hide below the rocks. The smallest mistake could put your lives in danger, so you will require meticulous planning and exercise extreme caution."

"Are you trying to scare us?" after seven successful hits George's ego was hurt.

"Stay scared and stay alive my friend," Josh pitched in. "Rusty is absolutely right. Over-confidence is the last thing we need. You and Dave have done a wonderful job of clearing our way so far—seven shutdowns in six months is excellent by any standards. We have not only been able to confuse the enemy, for lack of a better word, we also have the police scratching their heads for explanations. However, I think we are up against groups that will require a larger scale operation. We've got to use the reach of the law to grab these guys and bring them down. What are your thoughts, Brant?"

Brant leaned against the wall and looking outside the glass window watching the rush hour traffic crawling on the Interstate. "I couldn't agree with you any more, Josh," he said. "We've discussed this before. Josh is a trained undercover narcotics cop as you all know. With the information you provide, Rusty, we will come up with a plan to penetrate the first group on the list. Josh will coordinate the bust operations once he infiltrates the ranks. Chances are that there will be arrests and the justice system will be involved. That is where I will come in to represent the prosecution and seal them in."

"Wow, that sounds risky for you Josh," Dave was concerned.

"No risk, no gain, my friend," Josh smiled. "Don't worry, I am trained in these things and I will not be alone. Since this is going to be an official operation, I will get all the help I want. Nobody messes with a cop, you know."

"All right Rusty, let's get to work," Brant was anxious to get started. "Give us the details about," he consulted a sheet of paper, "the Desert Hounds. Gosh, where on earth did they get a name like that?"

"Search me, but they are one of the larger groups operating all the way down to Tijuana. While you cannot touch the Mexican operations for obvious reasons, see if you can at least knock them out of business in Southern California. That will open up almost forty percent of the market for us, up from the ten percent that we control today," Rusty sounded desperate.

"Forty percent is a lot, Rusty. For the rewards that await us, it is definitely worth it," Josh was mildly excited. "How do I penetrate this group?"

"Come to Papa, he will try to make it very simple," Rusty said jovially.

27

"Where exactly did you get this stuff Lieutenant?" the chemical analyst at the lab asked looking up from the petridish where he was analyzing the sample that Bill had taken from Alejandro's secret chamber.

"That came from a very interesting location—maybe I'll take you there someday. But why do you ask?" Bill was surprised at the question.

"Well this has a methamphetamine base all right, but also has a fair amount of the substance called hydrocodone in it. The hydrocodone messes with the serotonin—that's a chemical in your brain connected with your sense of happiness. Users can become physiologically and psychically dependent on this and overdose can also be fatal," the analyst explained.

Bill listened intently and asked, "Do you have any idea how much this sells for in the market?"

"You've got me there, Lieutenant, that's a tough one. But I would hazard a guess that it will sell for at least a few hundred bucks for an ounce. The seller can get away with practically any amount, since the addict just cannot do without it."

"Hmmm…thanks a lot," Bill walked away deep in thought. His hunch that Alejandro was a distributor of drugs was right all the time. He would not put that money in the bank for sure, so he had to move it somewhere else and it had to be all cash.

Alejandro's relationship with Rusty must be founded on a narcotics business, Bill reasoned. Such people don't cook up relationships for nothing. Then there was the Brant factor of swapping cars with Alejandro and driving all the way to Los Angeles to meet Rusty. Bill couldn't imagine that a lawyer as distinguished as Brant could be involved in this manner, but then life was full of imponderables.

Bill drove home as his mind wandered all over, trying to find a plausible answer. Almost every time that Bill had seen Josh with the group, he had appeared to be in a jovial mood. Josh was definitely an undercover cop and that might be a reason for his attitude. Maybe Josh was simply playing the field and waiting for the right time to strike. Bill had checked Josh's records and had found that he was not assigned to any case in particular. That made it very odd for Josh to travel all the way to Los Angeles and be working undercover when his department had no record of his movements. Josh had to be working in collusion with Rusty and Alejandro, there could be no other explanation. However, Bill needed proof to substantiate his suspicions.

The presence of Dave and George in the group did not make any sense. Bill suddenly slammed his brakes and pulled over as realization dawned on him. Dave was a fireman and there were five cases of arson in the past few months, none of which were solved. Whoever started the fire was an expert and left no trace. A fireman would be knowledgeable enough to control the extent and impact of the fire. Moreover all of these were related to narcotics and involved people who were killed in similar fashion. Their necks either were broken or their skulls smashed in with a blunt weapon. Someone like George would have the brute strength to commit these murders. Again, it was all theory, Bill had no proof to back up.

The common theme, as Bill realized was narcotics. He was convinced that he was sitting on the biggest case of his life. But he had to be cautious, since the group was formidable enough, especially with a cop and a lawyer in the mix. Bill also realized that he needed solid proof. His suspicions were good for a story but would never hold up in any court. He thought it was time to start creating a log of what he had seen and learnt so far since things would become more complicated in the days to come.

He turned on his radio and melodious smooth jazz soothed his mind. He started his engine and headed home where Joan was waiting with the baby. Anita had started cooing these days and was consciously smiling from time to time. Bill thought she could recognize his voice as she responded by turning towards him looking with those large deep eyes that spoke a million words to Bill. Joan seemed more wonderful than ever before—Bill was content with all that life had offered him.

His thoughts of the two lovely ladies at home, in the backdrop of the soothing music was interrupted by the announcer, "Dear Listeners. We interrupt this program to bring you some very unfortunate news. We just received the confirmed news that at four forty five this evening, our very own, Chief Miller has passed away this afternoon after a sudden heart attack. He leaves behind his wife and two wonderful daughters. We request our listeners to join us to spend a minute of silence in prayer for this most respected public servant of our fine city. May his soul rest in peace!"

Bill slammed his brakes once again—the only person of any significance who knew about his Supercops status was dead and he was all alone. He was going to brief the Chief about his findings and his suspicions in a few days. Now that he was gone, Bill was pretty much on his own. The overcast sky suddenly broke into a torrential downpour and Bill's mind floated like a rudderless ship.

28

The newspapers carried the story for a full two weeks—almost a record in the history of organized sting operations where the law enforcement officers from Los Angeles and San Diego worked in perfect coordination to bust one of the largest drug rings operating in the area.

At the request of the mayors of both San Diego and Los Angeles, the names and pictures of the police officers involved in the historical bust operation were not disclosed to the press. Snooping reporters tried every guile and trick to squeeze the information from different sources, but everyone was tight-lipped.

Huge stockpiles of prohibited drugs were confiscated from different locations and several arrests were made. The operation was carried out with utmost precision and had occurred at the same time in all the locations. The entire ring was caught unawares and had no chance to warn anybody else.

It was only two months since Josh had infiltrated the Desert Hounds and he organized the entire operation as if he had been doing the same thing since childhood. His supervisor had a hard time to fully comprehend the plan that Josh had described. As a matter of fact he did not approve of the plan at all. But Josh was so confident and had provided such tangible proof to substantiate his plan, he had agreed to help Josh organize the operation.

The operation was a resounding success. Josh became the apple of the eye in the department and was promptly promoted to Sergeant.

"Thank you Sir," Josh was appreciative. "But there are more of these gangs out there. We have a lot of ground to cover yet. I really appreciate that you kept our identities out of the press. Names and pictures in the newspapers would have practically put my team out of commission from Narcotics for good. The last thing I want is to be a familiar face to anyone and jeopardize my chances to infiltrate into the next ring in the future."

"I agree Josh, that was sharp thinking," his supervisor Lt. Graham had pride in his voice. "You have made the department very proud. Even the boys in LA are singing your praises."

"Miles to go before I sleep Sir," Josh said calmly. "These guys will try to get out on bail and will definitely defend themselves in court. You can count on that. I suggest that we get a strong and experienced lawyer to be the prosecutor in this one. With due respect to our District Attorney, I don't think he is capable of keeping these guys in for long. We need someone better—someone who has been in the dog pound and has come out unblemished time and again. Moreover, we need someone who is licensed as an attorney to practice in the Los Angeles and Orange counties along with here in San Diego. We have to be consistent in all that we do to follow up on our work."

"That will be a tough one to find, don't you think?" Lt. Graham asked.

"Normally yes, but I have someone in mind, who might just be the right person for the job. I just don't want to give these guys any slack. If they get out, they will stay out—you can take my word for granted," Josh said.

"Well, who do you have in mind, Josh?" with the success that Josh had achieved, Lt. Graham was not going to double guess.

"Do you remember a lawyer called Brant Sawyer?" Josh thought for a while and continued, "His record of fighting narcotics cases is impeccable. Granted that he had always represented the defendant on every occasion in the past, but he had the verdict go his way every single time. Apparently he has not been taking narcotics related cases at present, but maybe we can convince him to take on this one—only this time he works for us—there is too much at stake here and I want the best we have."

"You seem to have researched his profile already. Since you have been so successful in this operation, I would not want to do anything that reverses all your hard work. I will see to it that Brant Sawyer is contacted by my office with an offer to play with us," Lt. Graham shook hands with Josh and excused himself.

Lt. Graham called Josh late in the afternoon to say that Brant had reluctantly agreed to represent the prosecution. "Are you sure you want this guy, Josh?" he sounded unsure. "Apparently Brant Sawyer was not interested at first, but then we convinced him saying that he was highly recommended by various people."

"Well, money is not something someone like Sawyer will be after, Sir. He knows his job like the back of his hand, maybe he was just being modest," Josh said.

"Good job Brant," Josh thought in amusement. "Play it cold at first and then agree to tag along. That way nobody will ever suspect anything."

"I hope you are right, Josh," Lt Graham said and hung up.

The press covered the trials in San Diego and Los Angeles in vivid detail at times to the extent of cautious exaggeration. Brant Sawyer was back in the news and with a bang. He had no shortage of evidence, some of which caught the defense completely on the wrong foot. As before, names of the police officers involved in the operation were kept out of the press.

Josh however, was present in court, dressed in plain civilian clothes and thoroughly enjoyed Brant's performance. "A leopard never loses his spots," Josh thought.

One of the largest drug rings in the area was decisively put out of commission. Brant was the hero and the press even ran articles that suggested Brant be invited to take up the office of the District Attorney in the near future.

Bill followed the case very closely and he had watched Josh intently from a distance on every court session. Brant and Josh never made any eye contact and were apparently oblivious of each other's presence. Bill was certain that was also pre-planned between Josh and Brant. "Very clever, Josh," Bill mused as he tried to catch any change of emotion on Josh's face. "You're not giving anything away."

Bill knew that both Josh and Brant had scored a major hit in their respective careers. There was no way Josh could have organized such a large scale operation after collecting so much of tangible evidence within only two months of infiltrating into a gang that was so well organized. He must have had inside intelligence to achieve such dramatic results.

"Could Rusty or Alejandro or both have provided Josh with the information?" Bill thought as a definite possibility.

That confused him even more. Josh and Brant obviously had done a huge public service that deserved nothing but overflowing accolades. It was possible that they were friendly with Rusty and Alejandro for the purpose of getting the inside scoop in the narcotics market. Bill found it impossible to believe that Josh did not know that Alejandro was a drug dealer himself. So Josh must have promised protection of Alejandro and Rusty in exchange of information. Bill wondered if public service was the only motivation or if there was more to it than met the eye.

He felt alone after the death of Chief Miller. There was nobody left to discuss things with—he was all by himself and had his own mission. He had spent several days thinking if he should hang up his boots and go back to his regular job or if he should continue on the mission that he was sworn into. Bill had chosen the latter—the oath he had taken was something he was going to live and die for. That is what the Chief would have wanted if he was alive.

Bill decided to play along with Josh and Brant a while longer and see where it took him. Over the years, Bill had learned to trust his gut feelings. However he hoped for the honor and sanctity of his code of service that he was wrong for the first time.

29

"Los Cabos reports clear skies, winds out of the southwest at fifteen miles per hour and a temperature of sixty nine degrees," the pilot paused for effect and continued. "So it looks like a lovely day in this beautiful city. We are just about seventy miles out of the airport so I will turn on the fasten seat belts sign on at this time. Please remain seated for the remainder of the flight. We shall be in on the ground shortly."

Josh set the magazine down, fastened his seat belts and looked down on the blue Pacific below. "I wouldn't miss much of San Diego as far as the weather and the ocean is concerned," he thought, "but it will be safer to put all the money here."

It had been a rough six months since his first highly successful sting operation as a narcotics cop. The dust hadn't settled completely when Josh infiltrated another drug ring and struck for the second time with the same resounding success. He surprised everyone with the quality and accuracy of information he had provided and everything worked like clockwork during the operation. The number of arrests and the amount of narcotics confiscated were even greater than the first time.

The defense had put up a bold show with arguments of the narcotics being used for medicinal purposes, but they were pulverized by Brant's expert counter arguments and undeniable proof of wrong-doing. The verdict also involved three perjury charges being enforced by the judge—lying under oath was not something the court was going to condone.

Josh had been present in court—again dressed in plain clothes. Bill had watched him and Brant from a discrete distance. Even Bill was impressed how Josh and Brant easily avoided contact with each other in the courtroom, despite the fact that they were so close outside. It was almost pre-rehearsed.

After a couple more of such successful operations Josh had applied for some time off. Lt. Graham was actually pleased to sign the paperwork without even reviewing it. Josh was the hot ticket that made the SDPD proud and Lt. Graham never failed to mention that Josh worked for him. However, he made it certain that the press never got to know any details about any officer involved in the operations. He was like a mother bear protecting her precious cubs.

Rusty and Alejandro were on a song these days—Josh and Brant had turned out to be efficient minesweepers while Dave and George occasionally lent their expertise as required. With the field being cleared Rusty and Alejandro expanded their operations where they had never been before. The cash had started to change into a flow from a trickle and they were happy to extend handsome rewards.

Dave followed Brant to Switzerland once and was not impressed at the concept of entrusting his cash with the Swiss. He was sold the moment he saw the pictures of St. Marteen in the Caribbean and spent a week scouting the area. He knew that money will not be a problem and bought a lovely home in a secluded location with almost two hundred and forty degrees of uninterrupted views of the gorgeous waters and white sandy beaches.

George had decided to tag along with Josh and start building a house for himself in Cabo San Lucas. Alejandro had hooked them up with his contacts in the area and they had turned out to be a great help, especially where language was going to become a barrier. They helped Josh and George select two wonderful lots in San Jose del Cabo and Pueblo Bonito. With a little influence from the locals, the lots had cost them about ten percent of what they would have paid in Southern California.

George was rubbing his hands and had lifted Josh up from the ground in a friendly hug after closing the deal. "Josh, I can never thank you enough. If you were a girl I would have kissed you on your lips right now," George was visibly excited.

"Well, I'm as much a man as they come, my friend. Put me down will you?" Josh laughed and said firmly.

Alejandro's friends came in handy once again, when they introduced a reputed building contractor to Josh and George. The plans for the luxury villas were finalized within a week and the construction started shortly afterwards. As a group, Josh had decided to take things easy for a while, so George would have served no purpose back in the United States. Josh suggested that George stay back in Mexico and oversee the constructions and George gladly agreed. He was having too much fun anyway.

Now Josh was flying back to Cabo San Lucas to check out how his villa was coming. George was hard working, but not really the brightest out there, so Josh wanted to visit and check things out. Moreover, the last payment from Rusty had been extremely generous—apparently Rusty was making good money out there almost running a monopoly. Josh had to move the cash out of United States quickly and then there was George's share to deliver.

Josh looked at his watch when the plane smoothly touched the ground. They were five minutes ahead of schedule. George must have already arrived at the airport to pick him up as they had agreed. The prospect of fresh money always served as a big motivator for George.

Josh gave a friendly smile at the flight attendant at the door and walked out of the plane with two travel bags slung across his shoulders. "Boy, these bags are heavy," he thought. He did not have to look for George too long. George was waiting in the visitor's lounge towering above the rest of the crowd.

He grinned and held his hand out to Josh, "Welcome to Mexico, my friend."

"Gracias amigo," Josh laughed. "Why don't you give me a hand with one of these bags—the weight is killing my shoulders."

"Gladly, my friend," George grinned. "That is one weight I will never mind carrying."

They dumped the bags in the car and drove off.

Bill jumped into a waiting taxi and said, *"Senor, siga por favor ese coche rapidamente!"*

He had tailed Josh all the way from San Diego and had been on the same plane. He had shown his badge at the Mexicana check-in counter and the clerk told him that Josh was seated behind the left wing in the plane. Bill had purchased a seat just behind first class. When the boarding started, Bill allowed Josh to board the plane first and followed shortly afterwards. Among all the tourists on the plane it wasn't too difficult to blend in the crowd. When the plane landed in the Los Cabos, Bill had the advantage of getting out before Josh and had taken up a suitable position to watch Josh. When he saw George come to meet Josh at the airport and drive off in the car he became more certain that his suspicions were not completely unfounded.

"I speak English well, Sir. Hang tight, Marco is fastest taxi driver in Cabo and no disappoint you. I follow that car, no problem," the driver said in broken English and caught up with George.

Bill leaned back in his seat and smiled at Marco, "Good man, just don't get too close, ok? I just want to see where they are going."

"Are you police?" Marco inquired.

Bill laughed in dismissal and said, "No Senor, I stay away from the police as much as I can. I am a reporter and the people in that car are very famous artists—you know, they draw pictures. I am trying to write a story on them, but they will not give me an interview. But I am not giving up."

"Ah!" Marco seemed satisfied at the explanation.

30

Brant's rise to fame had been nothing but meteoric over the past few months. The press had been in constant frenzy to fill their front pages with bold headlines proclaiming Brant's success. He had shut down four of the largest drug rings in Southern California and there was no stopping for him. He went from victory to the next victory and then begun where he started.

The press had interviewed him several times and had asked their pet question, "How do you get all that evidence?"

"That is immaterial to the public service I have performed by taking the drugs off the street and keeping our schools and parks safe," it was Brant's standard answer. "I am not at liberty nor am I obligated to disclose the sources of my information. Firstly that will not be a professional thing to do and secondly, there's more from where this scum came from."

Within a few days, the press released the sensational news of San Diego's most famous lawyer in history, Brant Sawyer had been accepting just one dollar as fees for his work. Apparently he had offered his services for free, but when the Mayor insisted that Brant should accept some form of remuneration, a dollar was all he had asked for.

"With God's grace, I have enough to afford four square meals a day. I am a public servant and do not need taxpayers money. You have given me the opportunity to serve and serve I shall," Brant had told the Mayor. "When I see kids smoking pot and fighting for life in a hospital bed, it makes my blood boil. I have started a crusade to make our community drug free and my only reward will be when our schools, parks and our youth are completely free of the evil reach of any narcotics."

"You've got to take something in return Mr. Sawyer," the Mayor had insisted again.

Brant had thought for a while and said, "Very well, I will accept one dollar for every case I fight for the Prosecution and win, not a penny more. Furthermore, as you can understand, with all this press and the exposure that I have, my life is in danger. There is still a lot of garbage out there that we will need to clear. I feel threatened these days about a possible retaliation from them. Can you please arrange police protection for me? I am sure you know Sgt. Josh Timmons. Without his fearless and meticulous work we would not have been able to achieve anything. With due respect to the SDPD, I will be obliged if you can please assign Sgt. Timmons to arrange for my protection."

The Mayor was more than happy to arrange for Brant's protection. After a few phone calls he had been connected to Lt. Graham, who listened intently to the Mayor's request. "Not a problem Sir, we will always protect those who help us stay safe. I will talk to Timmons and get back to you right away."

Lt. Graham called Josh into his office and had relayed the Mayor's request.

Josh had put up a show as if he was considering the pros and cons of the request and said, "Well, what can I say when the Mayor himself has made the request. Please let him know that I will be honored to organize the protection for Mr. Sawyer. I will get started right away. But then, fewer the number of people who know about this the safer he will be. So I don't want to line up too many of our officers on this. Don't worry Sir. Mr. Sawyer will live the full length of his normal life."

Josh picked up Brant's personal security as his own responsibility. He had officially visited Brant in his home with two deputies and introduced himself. "Mr. Sawyer, I bring greetings from the Mayor. Deputy Anderson and Deputy Carson will join me to provide round the clock protection for you from this moment onwards," Josh shook hands with Brant and stepped aside for the two deputies to introduce themselves.

"We're honored to serve you Sir," the deputies echoed.

"Why don't you check out the grounds and the back of the house while I brief Mr. Sawyer on the particulars?" Josh directed the deputies.

When they were out of sight Brant smiled at Josh and said, "Hello my friend, everything is going according to plan. You are a genius, you know?"

"Yes, I've been told that a few times," Josh laughed. "These two deputies are just a front, Brant. They are new and pretty sharp. They also try very hard to impress me, so they will give you the protection you require. When you need to move around, I will be with you. So that should not cramp you up. Moreover, your second job as a courier is no longer required."

"You think of everything Josh. Alejandro and Rusty have been great partners and have been truly forthcoming with the rewards," Brant sounded happy.

"Yes, they have been. But without us they were nothing and they realize that very well," Josh said. "Your one dollar fee has become a hit with the press. It looks like we will make a District Attorney out of you after all!"

"Hey it was your idea, which by the way, have a great habit of turning out to be winner over and over again," Brant laughed.

Bill had watched them from a distance and shook his head. Josh and Brant were clearing out the dirt, which should have had a positive effect on the region. On the contrary, to everybody's surprise the reach of narcotics had started to proliferate faster and deeper in the past few months.

Bill had a fairly good idea of what was going on. He was almost certain that Rusty and Alejandro were handsomely greasing the palms of Josh and Brant. Years of experience would give a cop a fairly reasonable amount of confidence in his suspicions. However, he needed more solid proof before he could act. Both Josh and Brant were heroes now, so if he had to present anything against them, they'd better be indelible proof.

He thoughtfully glanced at the pictures on the passenger seat beside him. They could be used to prove that the six knew each other very well. But just knowing each other well did not imply any wrong-doing. Knowing Josh and Brant, they would easily cook up a very strong story to wiggle themselves free. There was nothing to be gained and everything to lose if Bill played his cards right away. He decided to wait a little while longer and see if something more tangible came along.

Bill did not have to wait too long. Josh applied for a vacation, which was promptly approved without any questions. Bill was certain that it would be worthwhile if he followed Josh wherever he went for this vacation.

He took up surveillance near Josh's house on the first morning of his vacation. At around noon, Josh drove out and to Bill's surprise, headed to the airport. Josh checked in at the Mexicana ticket counter and went past the security.

Bill used his credentials at the ticket counter and learned that Josh was headed for Los Cabos. He thought for a while debating if he should follow Josh. Bill always carried his passport and a travel bag in his car, just in case he needed to travel—this came in handy. He made reservations on the same flight and called home.

"Honey, something came up urgently. I am flying to Mexico on an urgent assignment. I will be back in three days at the most. Sorry about this, but something came up sweetheart," Bill was already feeling homesick. "Give our little doll a big kiss for me and you take care of yourself my love."

31

"George, I have a feeling that we are being followed," Josh said softly with his eye peeled to the side mirror.

"We're being followed?" George was surprised. "Who would follow us here—we're hardly known around here."

"You are probably right and I hope you are," Josh murmured. "But I have been watching that cab behind us for a while. Unless this is sheer coincidence, somebody seems to be rather interested in us."

George glanced at the rearview mirror and said, "This place is a tourist magnet Josh. Moreover, we're not the only ones who live in the neighborhood. Just relax, you're on vacation remember?"

Josh grinned, "You're right. I am on vacation. But a cop never lets his guard down, you know. Why don't you drive into the strip mall coming up to your right? We'll see if our shadow follows us in there."

"Ok, as you wish" George changed lanes, "but I still think you are worrying for nothing."

He turned into the entry of the strip mall with his attention on the rearview mirror. The taxicab behind them changed lanes in preparation for entering the strip mall.

"Darn it, you may be right," George said.

"Just keep going," Josh ordered in a soft but authoritative voice.

The cab kept going past the strip mall and disappeared over the hill. The driver would have turned into the strip mall, but Bill asked him to carry on without stopping. "Please keep going and pull into the next street to your right. We will have to wait there till they come out and we can start following again."

"Ok Senor, you are paying," Marco laughed and complied with Bill's directions. "Which newspaper do you work for Senor?"

"I am a freelance reporter Marco. I just write up the story and sell it to whichever newspaper pays the better price," Bill said levelly.

"Well, looks like you were right, George," Josh said. "We were not being tailed after all. I am satisfied now. Let's get out of here and back on the road. Why don't you let me drive?"

"Be my guest," George said and swapped seats. Josh eased back into the main road and headed towards Pueblo Bonito.

Bill saw them pass and asked Marco to start following again. "This time, stay at least two or three cars behind them. I don't want them to know that we are following them," Bill said.

"Is this reporting business lot of fun for you?" Marco asked and took up the chase again.

"I get to laugh from time to time," Bill prayed that Marco would shut up some time.

Josh kept checking the road ahead and his rearview mirror frequently but there were quite a few taxis on the road that looked no different from the next one. He decided to let go, since nobody knew him in Mexico. Shortly afterwards he drove into the driveway of his property in Pueblo Bonito and parked under the covered patio of his newly finished house.

"Now that looks just great, doesn't it?" Josh had satisfaction and excitement in his voice.

"You bet, Alejandro's friends have excellent skills I must say. Not to mention your great taste in architecture," George agreed.

"Let's go in. I've got some goodies for you," Josh said. "Why don't you get one bag while I open the place up?"

Josh went into the house and rushed upstairs. He unzipped his bag open, removed his binoculars and peered through the blinds towards the road. Traffic was flowing smoothly except that a taxicab was stopped on the road just outside the entrance to his driveway. The driver and the passenger were both looking towards the house. The passenger had a camera with a telephoto lens in his hands and was obviously taking pictures of the villa and the grounds.

"Where are you Josh?" George called out from downstairs. "Boy these bags are really heavy. I'm getting impatient to meet all the Presidents, you know," he referred to the dollars in the bags.

"I'll be there in a minute. Hang on!" Josh shouted back.

Josh could not make out much about the passenger or the driver. He wished he had brought some more powerful binoculars along, but then he wasn't expecting being followed. The passenger motioned to the driver and the cab pulled away as Josh followed them till they disappeared among the trees.

Josh was about to move away from the window when on a hunch he picked up his glasses again. He almost expected that the cab would show up again and it did. This time, the cab had turned around towards the direction that they came earlier and stopped about twenty yards away from the entrance. The foliage concealed the cab almost completely, but Josh could see enough.

George watched Josh descend the stairs and grinned broadly, "Do you like your house? They did quite a fine job, I see."

Josh did not seem to have heard the question. "Is my car ready to go?" he asked with a thoughtful expression.

George turned serious and said, "Sure, it is in your garage and the keys should be in the car. Is everything ok?"

"That's what I want to find out," Josh said looking towards the entrance to his villa. "Why don't you head back towards home now? I want you to drive into that big mall near your house, park your car and get a table in the Italian restaurant there. I should be able to join you within half an hour. If I don't, I want you to come back to my house."

"Wow, you don't sound too good Josh. What's the problem?" George was concerned.

"I still think we are being followed," Josh said with a faraway look. "There's a cab waiting on the road near to my entrance. I have a strong feeling that this was the same cab that I suspected to be tailing us on our way here. I just want to make sure that we are in the clear and nobody is taking any undue interest in us. So I want you to head out now and see if you get tailed. I will wait a while and follow you."

"Jeez, I hope you are wrong Josh," George said and picked up his keys.

"I do to, George. Pull away on my signal, ok?" Josh asked and opened his garage.

He stood in his garage and saw George waiting in his car. Josh nodded and George pulled away. Almost immediately after George turned into the main road, Josh heard the sound of an automobile engine starting and knew his hunch was right. He poked his head towards the entrance and saw the taxi-cab pass beyond the gates in the direction that George left. Josh jumped in his car, started the engine and took up the chase. He had to get to the bottom of the situation right away.

32

"I have family in Los Angeles, Senor," Marco glanced quickly at the rearview mirror to check if Bill was paying attention.

"Good for you Marco. Do you visit them often?" Bill tried to hide his lack of interest in Marco's personal life.

"No Senor. America very expensive—not like Mexico," Marco laughed.

"How much do you think a villa like that will cost?" Bill asked.

"That one we stopped at, Senor?" Marco made certain. "Very nice villa, big house and has own beach. I think it cost five million pesos."

So that was about half a million US dollars, Bill thought. Mexico was a safe haven for Josh to hide the kickbacks from Alejandro and Rusty. It would not be too hard to confirm that Josh owned the villa—the local registrar should have the information.

Bill had seen George leave alone, which meant that Josh stayed back at home. It was important so see where George went—did he have his own place or was he just the errand boy for Josh. He could make a fair guess, but he had to find out as tangible proof.

Bill knew that he was very close to solve a major case of police corruption as the late Chief had suspected all along. It was such a pity that the Chief was not alive to see the results of his effort come to fruition. He had the foresight to initiate the Supercops program and Bill wished he was still around. He would have made the Chief proud of what he had achieved.

"That car will turn in shopping center, Senor," Marco's voice broke Bill out of his thoughts, "I follow?"

"Yes, please. Do you know a hotel I can stay here, Marco?" Bill said.

"Yes, Senor, behind shops is a good hotel—no expensive, but very good. My amigo, Carlos work there. I make reservation for you?" Marco offered.

"That will be very helpful Marco. I think I have seen enough today and I feel very tired and hungry. You can drop me in the mall," Bill said watching George park his car, exit the vehicle and enter an Italian restaurant.

"Ok Senor, you want me pick you tomorrow?" Marco parked his car and said.

"That will be very nice of you Marco, yes," Marco talked a lot, but Bill thought he was a useful guy to have around. "I'm sorry I do not have any Mexican money, will you take American dollars?"

"Yes Senor. Good exchange rate!" Marco grinned.

Marco looked at the two hundred dollar bills and said, "Too much money, Senor. I have no change."

"That's all right Marco, you have been with me for over five hours today and I greatly appreciate it," Bill was genuinely grateful.

"Gracias Senor, muchas gracias. Call Marco anytime," Marco handed over a business card.

Josh was ready with his camera and got busy when Bill emerged from the vehicle. His brows furrowed even more when Marco opened the trunk and Bill pulled out a fair sized travel bag. The passenger was definitely American and had been traveling. Josh wondered if the man had traveled with him on the same flight as himself. The telephoto lens was powerful enough, and the man's face was in clear view several times. Josh jogged his mind feverishly trying to remember if he had ever seen the man before and came up with a negative.

The man showed no signs to suggest that he suspected Josh was following him. He waved the driver goodbye and walked up to the restaurant. Josh could see George sitting at the bar with a drink, with his back towards the door. The man sat himself at a table sideways from George and placed his order.

Josh locked his car and walked around the restaurant to a side entrance. When he entered, the man had his back towards Josh. George saw Josh come in and started to rise, but Josh motioned him to remain seated. He caught George's attention and nodded towards the man seated at the table sideways from George.

George casually turned around and saw Bill looking outside the window, apparently deep in thought. The man had sandy hair, with an athletic build and would easily be about five and a half feet tall if he stood up. There was a marked confidence in the man's posture and he definitely did not look like any of the locals around. George could only see the side of the man's face and was not sure if he had seen him before.

Shortly, the waitress came by with the order and the man turned to smile. George watched him through the corner of his eye and his brows furrowed. He thought he had seen the man before but he could not remember where. He looked back at Josh and nodded. Josh saw that Bill had already started his meal and motioned George to leave.

George paid the bartender and walked out of the restaurant without a second glance at Bill. Josh watched him stop in the middle of a bite as George walked out before him. From his body language, Josh could make out that the man contemplated following George or finishing his meal. The man apparently decided on the latter.

Josh walked out and saw George walking towards him. In the rapidly gathering darkness, Josh motioned George towards his car.

"Have you ever seen him?" Josh asked.

"I think I may have Josh," George hesitated, "but heck, I can't remember where."

"You are getting me worried, my man. You say you have seen him somewhere. Are you absolutely sure?" Josh asked.

"Well, no not really absolutely sure, but I will work on it," George sounded embarrassed.

"Work on it real fast George. I don't like the smell of this at all," Josh said sternly. "You go on head home. I will get these photos developed, hang around a little longer and see what else I can find out. Come over to my villa in the morning and we'll chat."

"Yes boss," George sulkily walked away, obviously worried about the events of the evening.

Josh walked towards the restaurant and positioned himself behind a pillar, so that he could watch Bill inside. He was worried at what George told him. What did the man know about George or all of them? He was definitely not the regular tourist. If the man's interest was on George only, Josh had to think and act quickly on a solution. He could not risk the entire operation just for George. In any case, George had already served them well enough and may be expendable, if that was the last option he needed to exercise. But Josh fought that thought—maybe he was just being paranoid.

Bill cleared his check, picked up his bag and came out of the restaurant. He glanced around almost as a natural instinct and headed towards the back of the hotel that Marco had mentioned.

Josh followed Bill at a discrete distance. He was certain that Bill did not suspect being followed. Years of experience had taught Josh to make deductions by simply watching a person's body language and he was seldom wrong.

Bill checked into the hotel, grabbed his keys and headed for the stairs. Josh waited for a while and approached the front desk.

"*Ola Senor*!" the clerk greeted him. "How can I help you?"

"Sorry, I don't speak Spanish," Josh gave an embarrassed smile.

"No problem Sir. I speak English. Are you looking for a place to stay?" the clerk asked.

"Actually no," Josh said earnestly. "Is the name of gentleman you just checked in, George Briggs from Seattle in the United States?"

The clerk's eyes narrowed. He glanced at this register and said, "No, why do you ask?"

"Well, George is a friend of mine who was supposed to check in today at this hotel. I am positive it is him. I have been shouting his name all through the parking lot, but could not get his attention," Josh was nagging in his persistence.

The clerk looked at this register again and shook his head in denial, "I'm sorry Senor, his name is not George Briggs, he…"

"Check again please, it must be a mistake," Josh cut him off. "It's got to be George."

"No mistake Senor," the clerk was visibly irritated. He pulled his register, slapped it down on the counter and pointed to the guest list. "You see, the person you talk about is from San Diego and not Seattle and his name is

William McMillan, and not George Briggs. I have also checked his California driver's license, so there is no mistake. Now if you excuse me, I have some work to do." The clerk scowled, pulled the guest register down from the counter and turned away.

"That's impossible," Josh noted the room number where Bill had checked in, threw his hands up in the air in frustration. The clerk had already disappeared into an office behind him. Josh leaned over the counter and picked up a room map of the hotel and left.

He walked into a photography shop and handed his camera to the attendant. "How soon can you get the film developed?"

"You pick up tomorrow morning, Senor," the attendant said—English was not perfect among the locals in Mexico.

"Actually I need it this evening, since I have a flight out of Cabos early tomorrow morning. I am willing to pay you extra," Josh pleaded politely.

The attendant frowned and said, "Come back in one hour. I see what I can do."

Josh thanked the attendant and promised to return back in an hour.

He walked back to the hotel's parking lot and examined the room map of the hotel. William McMillan, whoever he was, had checked in a room on the third floor. Josh looked up and located the room in the hotel. The lights were on and the curtains were partly drawn. He could see the outline of man standing next to the window—he was speaking on the phone.

"Hello sweetheart," Bill blew a loud kiss on the microphone, "guess where I am."

"I don't know," Joan said. "You tell me."

Bill laughed, "I am in Cabos San Lucas."

"No kidding?" Joan was surprised. "What are you doing there? A little vacation or is there someone else that I should know about?" Joan teased.

"Do I smell some jealousy here?" Bill laughed. "No vacation, darling. I am working on a case and had to follow this lead all the way down here. Sorry honey can't say much more. How's our baby doll doing today?"

"Well she's missing Daddy, maybe more than Mommy is," Joan said.

"Give her a big kiss for me," Bill said.

"When can you get back home?" Joan asked.

"I think I should be able to get on a plane tomorrow evening and be home late at night," Bill had seen quite a fair bit of what he wanted to see. He just needed to track down George's whereabouts and review the local registrar's records. He would be done after that with some solid evidence against Josh and George.

"Great, we'll expect you then," Joan said. "I love you, Bill."

"I do too, my love," Bill hung up.

He showered and sat down on a chaise contemplating his next move. He knew where Josh lived, but he had to confirm that Josh really owned the villa.

George was the only person who left the villa, which would prove within reasonable doubt that Josh stayed back home.

The local registrar should be able to provide the information. Marco could help, Bill thought. He was certain that George also owned property in the area. Too bad he could not follow George. However, the proof he had against Josh would be strong enough to initiate some pretty pointed questions. The story of a sworn police officer working in collusion with the underworld to facilitate the spread of narcotics, in the guise of a public servant would be difficult for the press to stay away from.

Bill called Marco's number and he answered promptly.

"Marco, can you please pick me up tomorrow morning around nine?" Bill asked.

"Yes, Senor, gladly," Marco replied.

"I need to know who owns that villa, Marco. How can I find that out?" Bill probed.

"My brother Enrique, work in building department. He can help. I call him tonight and say we come tomorrow to him. I have no address of villa," Marco said.

"I have noted the address, Marco, so that will not be a problem," Bill said, "you are very helpful."

'Gracias, Senor. I come tomorrow at nine to the hotel," Marco hung up.

Bill laid himself down on the comfortable bed and slipped under the sheets. "I think I have this covered well enough."

He never suspected how wrong he was.

33

"Muchas Gracias, Senor," Bill shook hands with Enrique, "you have been very helpful."

"No mention, Senor. I always help my brother's friends," Enrique smiled.

"Can you also check to see if someone called George Briggs owns any property in this area?" Bill asked.

"How do you spell that name, Senor?" Enrique asked.

Bill spelled the name out and Enrique pulled down a thick binder indexed with 'B" and thumbed through the pages. He stopped at the bottom of a page and pointed it out to Bill. "This man you look for?"

Bill craned his neck forward to see the name and there it was—'George Briggs' with an address in Pueblo Bonito. Bill noted the address down, thanked Enrique again and left with Marco.

"Marco, I would like to go to this address," Bill pointed at the address that he had jotted down on the notepaper.

"I know this place. I take you there," Marco started his car.

They weaved through traffic hugging the coastline. The sun was up with a cool breeze coming in from the ocean. Bill rolled the windows down to take in the fresh air. "It is very beautiful here, Marco—you are very fortunate to live here."

"Yes, Senor, it is nice to live here. I have eight brothers and sisters and they love Cabos so everyone lives here," Marco said. "Well, here is the address Senor," Marco pulled up by the curb and stopped.

The hacienda was not as large as Josh's villa, but had an impressive size. The grounds were well maintained with manicured trees and shrubs. The ocean glistened in the morning sun beyond the lot that sloped down to the sandy beach.

"Senor Briggs has beautiful house. It cost two million five hundred pesos, or a little more, I think," Marco answered Bill's question even before he had asked.

Marco was catching on, Bill thought. He clicked away with his camera.

"Artist business is good money in United States?" Marco asked.

"Uh-yes, all good artists make a lot of good money, especially when they are as good as these guys," Josh and George were artists indeed, Bill thought, albeit of a different sort.

"I should learn to be painter. You want to ask for interview?" Marco asked.

"I spoke to my boss at the newspaper last night Marco. He thinks we need to come up with a different strategy to get an interview with these two artists. So I will go back home today afternoon to come up with that plan with my boss. If I come back I will call you again and you can take me around," Bill said.

"Ok senor, you have my number. Should I take you to airport now?" Marco askcd and Bill noddcd.

Josh put the binoculars down as Marco's taxicab disappeared over the bend in the road. "Your faux pas could cost us dearly, George," Josh admonished, "unless we act now. This McMillan guy must be connected to law enforcement in some way—I can just feel it."

34

Josh had waited for almost an hour before the photographs were ready. The attendant had been overwhelmed with orders but had finally come through for Josh.

"All photos of the same person, Senor—a good friend?" the attendant had commented after he handed the photographs and negatives over to Josh.

"No friend, not this man. But he could become a friend if he behaves well," Josh had laughed dismissively.

He had walked back to his car flipping the photographs over and over again hoping that he would be able to recognize the man. However he drew a blank—he did not seem to have seen the man before.

He had called George from a payphone to say that he was coming over to meet George at his home right away. "This is urgent. I have learnt that the guy's name is William McMillan and he lives in San Diego. Does that mean anything to you?"

George had thought for a while and said, "Um-no I don't know of any William McMillan."

"I have some photographs and I want you to take a look at them right now. I am coming over to your house. Hopefully you will remember something," Josh had been persistent.

George had been waiting impatiently for Josh to arrive. "Let me see those photographs,"

He literally snatched the packet from Josh.

Josh poured himself a drink from the wet bar and watched George as he went through the pictures. George could be the weak link in the group and if proven so, he would have to be done with—Josh could not afford to risk the entire operation for the protection of one.

George had looked up from the pictures and his expression was still puzzled. That irritated Josh, "Anything at all?" Josh had hoped the photographs would jog some memory.

"I-I have something to tell you Josh," George had stammered and stared at the floor. His face was ashen.

"I'm all ears George, bring it on," Josh was trying to be patient.

"You're not going to um, like this Josh," memories had started to take shape for George. "About six months ago, I was doing my regular guard dog duty watching over Alejandro's house. I had seen a man come out from behind his house, look up and down the street and then get into his car and drive away."

Josh had reasoned to himself that he needed to stay calm—he already knew where the conversation was headed. He set his drink aside and prompted, "Go on."

"Uh-well, I think that man was this William McMillan," George almost murmured and glanced furtively at Josh.

"How sure are you?" Josh was hoping that George was wrong.

"Yes, I am absolutely sure, Josh. I had those powerful field glasses that you had given me. The moment I saw him today in the restaurant, I knew I had seen him before, but I could not remember. The same height and build, the same hair color, I couldn't be wrong. These photographs leave no room for any doubt," George had hoped that there was a corner in the room he could simply disappear into. He knew that he might have already screwed up big time.

Josh had stared at him for a while and moments had passed in silence, which made George even more uncomfortable.

"I screwed up big time, didn't I Josh?" George finally had to break the ice.

"Why did you not tell me before?" the frustration had almost given way into a menacing tone when Josh spoke.

"I-I completely forgot, Josh," George stammered again. "Oh bloody hell, I completely forgot and moreover, I did not have enough detail anyway. I wanted to tell you but something came up and I somehow got diverted and I never ended up talking to you. My God, what have I done?"

In spite of his anger, Josh somehow had felt sympathetic for George. He had probably made a costly mistake, no doubt, but trying to find a solution had seemed more important at the moment.

"This looks very bad, doesn't it Josh?" George had ventured.

"You think?" Josh was sarcastic. "Let's assess what we have so far. You had seen this man six months ago near Alejandro's house. Although we don't know what he was up to, so let's assume the worst. Let's assume that our William knows about the little packing and distribution operation that Alejandro runs in his basement," Josh twirled the wine in his glass and paused to think.

"This guy shows up here in Mexico and tails us to my house. Now how would he know about my luxurious habitat here? We know he came from San Diego, which adds another interesting dimension to this. He follows you from my house and into the restaurant and then gives up the chase when you left. That could mean that he had learnt enough and needed nothing further. That is disturbing me," Josh was thinking aloud to himself.

"Are we over-reacting Josh?" George ventured.

"Over-reacting?" Josh echoed almost incredulously, "heck I think we haven't even begun to react at all. I'll head back to San Diego tomorrow to get the run down on this guy. I am certainly not comfortable with what has happened."

"Going back already? Josh, you just arrived this morning," George was surprised.

"If this turns out to be what I think it is, the only place you and I will be arriving is in jail. That is if I don't get this taken care of right away. Thanks to your good memory, we've probably lost all the latitude we had all this time," Josh sounded furious. "It's too late to drive back now. I'll spend the night out here and pick this up in the morning."

Josh had a restless night's sleep. He wondered how long George or maybe the entire operation was being monitored and why nobody had acted so far. Probably someone was lying in wait for the most opportune moment or maybe someone was preparing a bait for them. Probably all the man wanted was George and that was all there was to it. If that were true, Josh would have to do away with George quickly before he brought the entire group down with him.

Josh woke up tired and more fatigued than what he was before he had retired for the night. When he came to the kitchen George was up and had breakfast going.

"Sleep well?" George asked.

"Yeah, like a log," Josh said with a sardonic smile. His eyes drifted over to the road outside and suddenly fixed on a spot. There was a taxicab parked right outside George's house. "Oh my goodness, he's here too?" Josh almost wailed.

George whirled around and followed Josh's gaze. He pulled open a drawer and removed a pair of binoculars and handed it over to Josh. "Quick, there is a better view upstairs," George said and ran for the stairs with Josh following.

It was the same taxicab as the day before and the passenger appeared to be the same person. William McMillan had miraculously found where George lived and a chill ran down his spine when Josh confirmed that for a fact.

35

"You're home early," Joan said happily when Bill returned home "You just could not stay away from Anita for too long huh?"

'I could not stay away from either of you," Bill kissed Joan fondly and rushed to Anita's crib. Anita was fast asleep with her little hands spread over her head. She looked like a sweet little angel from heaven and Bill could not turn his eyes away.

Joan came up silently beside him and leaned on his chest, "She's beautiful isn't she?" Joan murmured.

"Gorgeous is what she is. You have created a marvel, my love," Bill whispered.

"How was your trip?" Joan pulled away from Bill and headed for the kitchen.

"It was very successful. I have been following this case for a while now and it seems that I will be able to close on this pretty soon," Bill said.

"Putting some bad people away again, are we?" Joan asked knowingly.

Bill nodded, "Very bad people, right from the devils barn, I'd say. This will be such a major shake-up in the ranks—I'm worried how things will turn out. I have to plan this very carefully. But that's work and no work enters this home," he hugged Joan.

"Go get freshened up and I'll have dinner ready for you," Joan said.

"You're getting prettier by the day, you know? I wonder what you are eating," Bill teased.

"It's just the love in your eyes, my dear. I pray to God that I remain that way for you till death does us part," Joan said softly.

Bill kissed her and headed for the shower.

Josh wasted no time after he landed in Lindbergh field. He drove straight to the precinct and walked into his office.

Lt. Graham knocked and entered the office, "You're back already? You weren't gone even for a day, for crying out loud Josh!"

"The call of duty is too loud to turn a deaf ear to, Lieutenant," Josh grinned looking up from the pile of papers on his desk. "I just remembered something and had to get back."

"Just remember what happens when it's all work and no play, Josh," Lt. Graham said.

"I will, Sir, thanks," Josh laughed.

He logged into the criminal database and searched on 'William McMillan' and came up with no results. "That rules out one possibility," Josh thought.

He reached below his desk and pulled out the telephone directory and found six matches on 'William McMillan' with one showing 'T' as the middle initial. Josh noted all six addresses in his notepad.

He thought for a while and logged into the SDPD officer's database and searched for 'William McMillan'. Josh drummed his fingers on the table as the computer chugged on to generate the results of the search.

The screen returned a single match 'William Theodore McMillan'—Lieutenant. Josh leaned forward in his seat asked for details on the match.

He frowned and slumped back into his chair and stared at the screen—it said—"Access Prohibited by the order of Chief of Police Eustace Miller".

36

"Gentlemen, it is with grave concern that I say that our cover had been blown. A police Lieutenant by the name of William Theodore McMillan has been on our tail and preparing a case against us for almost the past six to seven months now according to my estimates. He is probably ready to make his final move, which is to bring us all down," Josh quickly scanned the faces in the room. There wasn't anyone who appeared relaxed.

"Before he acts, we will have to react and do that now," Josh continued, "I have no idea how much time we have in hand but I can tell you that we don't have any."

"How do you know all this, Josh? I am sure you have done your research, but this just seems impossible," Rusty was trying to comprehend the situation.

"Nothing is impossible for police officers, my friend, especially if we have the motivation," Josh made a valiant attempt to sound relaxed. "Millions of dollars are spent to get us trained. This guy was apparently deployed by Chief Eustace Miller—if you remember, the Chief passed away a few months ago. I just cannot get anything out of his police profile or anything about his commission. What worries me is that even though the Chief is no longer alive, nobody had updated McMillan's profile. This makes me wonder who is giving him directions, or is it that he is simply trying to complete his mission that he was set to do by the late Chief" Josh said thoughtfully.

"McMillan reports to nobody as far as I know. This makes me feel that he runs on his own. Ordinary cops do not do that, there is always an up-line, there is always someone who you report to. I have heard and read stories about McMillan," Josh scanned the faces in the room—everyone was listening intently. "He has a rather distinguished record with a whole bunch of medals and honors to his credit. Apparently he is extremely respected among the ranks. Then suddenly about a year ago, he apparently disappeared from the radar. I strongly believe that he was put in charge of something very special by the late Chief."

"Are you sure he is not only after George?" Alejandro ventured.

Josh gave a wry smile and said, "First of all my friend, McMillan was sighted near your house to begin with. You don't set a high profile cop like McMillan to chase down someone like George—at least a Chief of Police wouldn't do that. There are other detectives for such work. Moreover I have tailed McMillan to Brant's house as well. Enough said. I have no idea how bad the situation is. However, giving the benefit of doubt, I'd say this is pretty bad and that we should take action right away. Does everyone agree?" Josh looked around the room.

"I have always been candid with you Josh. So I believe you guys are responsible for this mess and you should clear this up," Rusty sounded irritated.

"You may be right Rusty and you probably are," Josh was patient. "But the time now is not to point fingers but to seek a remedy. Desperate times need desperate measures and we should pool our resources to find a solution. Regardless of who is at fault, I think all of us have the exposure and should try to work collectively to find a remedy."

After a few moments of silence Rusty finally said, "What do you have in mind Josh?"

"We have to bring him down Rusty, we have to break his backbone so that he does not have the strength to stand up again," Josh said in a monotone.

"We're all ears Josh," Rusty prodded.

"Very well, then. What I have in mind will need cooperation from all of you, since each of you have a role to play," Josh started. "I checked McMillan's office—he has a filing cabinet that is never locked. I had managed to sneak into his office and checked his filing cabinet myself—all he has in there are records of his past cases, there is nothing for the last twelve months or so. That seems extremely odd to me. You can bet a dollar to a donut that he does have evidence against us. But if he is not storing those in the office, where is he keeping them?"

Little did Josh know how correct his assumption was. All that Bill had seen and learned were safely kept in the private locker that he had rented at the local bank. He had felt that it was no longer safe to maintain his records in the precinct, due to the sensitivity of the information. He had decided to rent the private locker instead and use it for safekeeping. Photographs, notes, research papers were all neatly arranged and maintained in the case file that was safely hidden in a private locker.

Josh paused for effect and continued, "We have to get to those records no matter what—we have to get to all that evidence and destroy it if we have a fighting chance. I think he keeps them at home and that is what we need to get to. McMillan has a family—a wife and a baby daughter. We have to get them away for a while so that we can search for that evidence."

Josh looked at the concerned faces and motioned to Dave and Brant to take their seats. "What I am about to tell you is of utmost importance, so listen carefully. Here's my plan."

They talked for over two hours, faces looking grim than ever, thoughtful about the roles that each need to play. Finally Josh said, "All right George, I've spoken a lot today and I'll need that drink now. Let's see how good a bartender you really are."

37

The sun glistened on the turquoise blue Pacific on a typical Southern California summer day. Bill smiled as he watched Joan play with little Anita on the beach. Anita was growing by the day. She was a fast crawler and a happy child. She would try to stand up on her tiny legs then wobble, fall into a sitting position and break into a smile. Joan and Bill reveled at Anita's antics.

"She's growing up so fast Joan," Bill commented, "one day she'll be all grown up and gone to live her own life."

"Hold your horses, Bill," Joan laughed, "we still have quite a few years to enjoy her company. You should try and cherish these moments."

"I guess you are right," Bill said, "Daddy is not too bright is he, darling?" he leaned forward, kissed Anita and asked. Anita broke into a wide smile with her first teeth peeking from her gums.

"I think she just said yes," Joan teased.

Bill laughed and glanced around. The weekend always drew a large crowd of all ages to the Carlsbad beach, especially in these summer days. Surfers rolled over the breaking waves and a beach volleyball game attracted several onlookers. Bill lay down on the mat beside Joan and Anita, pulled his baseball cap over his eyes and mulled over his options to break the public façade and expose Josh along with his cohorts.

He had considered engaging Sgt. Carvey and Lt. Walker on his case, since they were the only survivors from the Supercops program. However that would blow their cover and could also imply potential danger to their lives. Bill wondered if they were also on the verge of a major breakthrough as he was. If that was true, it would be disastrous to their hard work, career and even their lives if they were brought into public focus. Bill would have to do everything alone.

From a distance Josh and Dave watched Bill and his family. Bill had probably dozed off on a slumber, Joan was reading a book and Anita, tired from her antics had also appeared to be asleep in a bouncer.

"That's our man, Dave," Josh said, "I believe he has information against us that can bring us all down. It is frustrating that we don't know how much he knows, but assuming the worst it probably is prudent to assume that our little enterprise is no longer a secret. We've got to act quickly and effectively."

He raised his right arm over his head and held out his fingers on a victory sign. George had been waiting for the signal. He raised his right arm and acknowledged. He reached inside a duffel bag, removed a baseball, took aim and threw it in the air. The ball flew quickly and crashed into the ice cooler next to where Joan was seated. The loud thud startled Joan who screamed out and Bill jerked himself up from his lazy slumber. He was up on his feet on a flash and snatched up Anita in his arms in a reflex action.

"What happened?" Joan appeared visibly shaken.

Bill had picked up the baseball by that time from the sand. He scanned the beach for anyone who might want to claim the ball, but nobody seemed interested. The ball could have come from anywhere. It was unusual for someone to play baseball on a beach, which made Bill frown.

"Someone threw a baseball towards us," Bill said softly still scanning the beach for anyone who may be interested. He drew a blank.

"Why would anyone do that?" Joan stood next to Bill with a concerned look on her face. "Thank God, Anita is ok. It could have struck her."

"That is probably why nobody is interested to claim this ball," Bill was deeply concerned. "Let's pack up and go Joan, sundown is not too far off anyway."

"Right," Joan said and started to collect things together as Bill continued to figure out where the ball might have come from.

"Well, that shook him up," Josh murmured.

"It did no doubt, but how does that help us, Josh," Dave asked.

"You'll see soon, my friend. The intensity of danger to him and his family will only increase from this point forward unless he decides to cooperate. This was a free service, I'll start collecting from the next time onwards," Josh said thoughtfully.

Bill returned to his car with Anita wrapped around him. He placed her in her seat and help Joan load the trunk. He held open the passenger door for Joan to step in and walked over to the driver side. He was about to open the door when he glanced at the front wheel—it was flat. He cursed softly and squatted down beside the front wheel to examine what had caused the leak. A neatly folded piece of paper was sticking out of the inner rim of the wheel. Curiously, Bill reached down, picked up the note and unfolded it.

There was nothing cryptic on the message, "Back off," that was all it said and on the next line it read, "Don't keep what does not belong to you— old tribal saying."

Bill stood up sharply and scanned the parking lot. Except for a few families and young couples heading back from the beach to their vehicles, the lot was deserted.

"What's wrong Bill?" Joan called out.

"Nothing honey, stay in the car," Bill said casually, "I guess we have a flat tire. I'll swap it out with the spare in the trunk you just stay with Anita." The pursed lips and furrowed forehead were clear indications that Bill was worried—the two events in the past half hour appeared to be related. What worried him even more was that the tire was flat not because the tube was somehow pierced—it was because someone had released the valve and let the air out.

"Well done George," Dave patted on his broad shoulders, "I think the message was strong enough."

Josh set his binoculars down and nodded in agreement.

38

"I am just trying to make some money to pay for college ma'am," the young man who had introduced himself as Mark Downey was very cordial. "I will offer you a fifty percent discount for the first time. If you do not like my job, you need not pay anything though every bit of money helps. Hopefully I will be able to work my way trough college and work for the SDPD some day."

Joan considered the proposition. The young man at the door seemed extremely earnest and would not be more than seventeen years of age. The house was in desperate need for some cleaning. With Anita taking up almost all of her time and Bill keeping so busy at work, there was not enough time for keeping the house tidy.

"Mark, since you do not work for a company, do you have any references I can call?" Joan asked transferring Anita's little body over to her left shoulder.

"Sure ma'am," he opened a folder and handed over a sheet of type-written paper, "here you go. I have worked for these wonderful people in the past and I am sure they will give you positive feedback."

"Ok. I will have to call them first before I get you started. I'm sure they will all have good things to say about you," Joan said as she scanned the sheet.

"When do you think you will be able to let me know ma'am," Mark was anxious, "the semester is not too far away and I still have a few bucks to make before they will even consider admitting me."

Joan pursed her lips, thought for a while and made up her mind, "Tell you what—why don't you get started right now, while I make a few calls. If I get even one negative feedback, I will ask you to leave right away."

"You've got it ma'am. You are very kind. I assure you of excellent service—a desperate man always gives his best. I'll get started right away. Let me get my gear and I'll be back," Mark said.

Joan held the door open as Mark dragged in an industrial grade vacuum. "Ma'am this thing is pretty powerful and sucks up everything. It also makes a lot of noise, which may bother your daughter. If you have ear plugs for her, I recommend that you put them on when I start this machine," Mark counseled.

"Well, I don't have earplugs for her," Joan said with concern.

"I see," Mark said, "well, I will close the door when I start this up in a room and you can stay with her in a different room, that way we will be able to lessen some of that sound."

"Ok, I think that will work for us," Joan sighed with relief.

"Very good ma'am," Mark said, "I'll get to work."

Joan observed Mark as he meticulously dusted everything and cleaned every nook and corner of the house, moving furniture as needed, with utmost care and the ease of a professional. When he was done with general cleaning, he would shut the door, start the vacuum and finish the cleaning. Joan was already impressed. She looked at the reference sheet that Mark had handed to her and thought it would be redundant to call anyone. Mark appeared true to his word. He knew his job and was rather thorough as Joan had observed.

She called the first number—after four rings the answering machine kicked in. The machine played the same number that she called and requested that she leave her name and a brief message. Joan left a brief message with her name and phone number and requested a call back.

Joan dialed the second number and a man answered. He gave a glowing reference for Mark when Joan inquired, "Mark's a good kid," the man said, "he is honest and works hard. I like him a lot ma'am. I'm a bachelor, so you can imagine how dirty my apartment gets over time. I hire Mark all the time to whip things back into some sanity."

Joan thanked the man and hung up. She scanned at the list again and put it down—she did not need any more references.

The noise was muffled and did not seem to bother Anita too much. She always peered in the direction of the sound whenever the vacuum started up.

Mark was done in a little over three hours. He stood in the entry way, held his hand in a mock salute at Joan, smiled and asked, "Well, what do you think? Did I earn my bread?"

Joan smiled back and said, "You sure did. Boy you are good and quick. I'm impressed."

"Welcome to my world of satisfied clients, ma'am," Mark said jokingly, "I aim to please. So will you give me a reference to my future clients?"

"I'll be happy to, Mark," Joan wrote out a check and handed it over.

"Wow ma'am, this is much more than what you owe me. With the fifty percent discount I was expecting only sixty dollars," Mark held the check out for Joan to correct.

"I know, that little extra is my token of appreciation for your good work," Joan smiled.

"Well, thanks ma'am, you are very generous. If it is ok with you, I will take my reference sheet—I have only one copy to share with my other clients," Mark said politely.

"No problem Mark, here you go," Joan handed the sheet over.

"If you need my help anytime, just call me and I will be here," Mark sounded genuinely grateful, "God bless your family."

"You too, Mark. Good luck on your pursuits," Joan said and closed the entry door shut behind Mark.

She turned around and surveyed the rooms—they looked so well organized and clean. Joan laughed as she imagined how Bill would react when he returned home in the evening.

Mark put the vacuum in the trunk of his car, started the engine and rolled off. Shortly afterwards he drove into the driveway of a warehouse, stepped out, pulled the shutters up, drove the car in and pulled the shutters down behind him.

Josh and Alejandro were playing cards with Dave and George when Mark entered the room and collapsed on a chair.

"Hello Danny," Josh said, "how did it go?"

"Smooth as silk," Danny smiled, "the toughest thing was to pretend that my name was Mark Downey. I'd say 'mission accomplished and executed' exactly as you had instructed."

"Very good," Josh said and nodded at George who reached behind and pressed a switch. The answering machine played Joan's message that she had supposedly left for a reference check on Mark Downey.

"I figure she checked on me, huh?" Danny chuckled.

Everybody burst into laughter, "She sure did, Danny. I also had the pleasure of speaking to her directly and gave you a great reference," Alejandro was visibly amused. "She did not call anyone else. By the way, she has a very enticing voice."

"Great teamwork, guys. Alejandro, quite candidly I was apprehensive when you introduced Danny to us, I'll admit. I am happy that I was wrong at that time." Josh spoke earnestly. "Danny, I want to thank you—this was a major step for us and without your resourcefulness we would not have been laughing today," he paused. "I think we are ready to make our move now."

"You think this will work Josh?" Alejandro asked.

"No, I don't think it will," Josh smiled, "I know it will," he emphasized. Only a miracle can save Billy Boy now."

39

"I hope you understand what you are saying, Josh," Lt. Graham was astounded. "A decorated officer like Lt. McMillan is involved in drug trafficking?"

"Often a perfect cover, Lieutenant—get a few medals, speak in a few seminars, have the press cover some stories and you are famous. Nobody will even suspect that you have crossed over to the other side," Josh looked at the floor—his face expressionless. "You know how much of cleanup we have done in our jurisdiction and all the way to LA. Despite our efforts drugs have continued to flow into the market, almost snubbing the efforts of my team. I had been contemplating on a theory for a long time and now I have the information to believe that my theory is not too far from the truth."

Lt. Graham shook his head in disbelief and Josh continued, "You checked his record yourself. For the last two years, Lt. McMillan almost vanished from the face of the earth as far as his contribution to the SDPD is concerned. A decorated officer such as he does not just fade away, unless there is a higher incentive for him. Apparently he reported to the departed Chief directly. Access to his records has been restricted and nobody knows how to get access to it. Does that not sound odd to you?"

The Lieutenant pursed his lips, still trying to convince himself about what he was being told by his most competent officer.

Josh walked up to the window, leaned against the frame and said, "The Chief suddenly dies and there is no continuity on who William reports to henceforth. I won't be too far off if the Chief himself was involved in something illegal and wanted to shield William from exposure," Josh was testing the waters.

"Now Josh, that is pure speculation," Lt Graham slammed his desk and stood up, "I knew the Chief personally and he was the most distinguished officer I have ever known. You can't prove any of this about the Chief."

Josh turned to face the Lieutenant and shrugged with a resigned expression, "I agree, that is speculation and I cannot prove anything about the Chief, but I am fairly confident that I can prove my theory on McMillan," Josh said with marked disgust. "You know how I work Sir. I would not do this if I did not have absolutely reliable inside information. I know what this means to the department. I know that if I am wrong, this will have serious repercussions on my career and on our reputation. I have worked hard to get to where I am today. Do you think I will risk all of that on the grounds of pure speculation on something this serious? I know he has dishonored the code—to me he is already just an ordinary citizen."

"Nobody is guilty…" Lt. Graham started.

Josh cut him off, "…unless proved guilty. I know that Lieutenant. That is exactly what I want to do—prove him guilty."

Lt. Graham sighed, "What do you want me to do Josh?"

"Just authorize this search warrant," Josh removed some papers from the inside pocket of his jacket and pushed it towards the Lieutenant, "I want to turn his house upside down."

The Lieutenant glanced at the warrant for a long while, deep in thought. Slowly he picked up his pen and signed the document. "Josh, you'd better be right on this one. Mark my words very carefully," he said clearly. "If this turns out to be a wild goose chase, I'll not only have your badge first, I'll also have your hide."

Josh nodded, picked up the warrant and asked, "What if I am right, Sir?"

"You'd have saved your badge and your hide," Lt. Graham said coldly. "Now get out and don't forget what I just said," he was still not convinced that he did the right thing.

"I'll see you here tomorrow," Josh raised his hand in a salute and walked out of the office and headed purposefully to his desk.

"Listen up people," Josh clapped his hands to get the attention of his team of officers who shared his room, "we have an important mission coming up. I want you all in the war-room in ten minutes."

Josh bit on a half eaten donut, reached for the cup and winced at the bitter taste of coffee that had turned cold. He grabbed some slides for the projector and headed for the meeting room. He inserted the slides in the projector, powered it up and paced the podium. He mentally rehearsed his speech to the group—this one needed to be handled very delicately.

He nodded at everyone in acknowledgement when they entered the meeting room and seated themselves.

"Good, we have a quorum here," Josh started. "What I am about to tell you might surprise you, but knowing you guys, I know this will not be shocking news. I have a theory that explains why our schools and streets are still not drug-free despite the heroic efforts of all of you here. I have done my research and have reason to believe that certain officers of our very own SDPD are playing Jekyll and Hyde with us. My contacts in Orange and LA counties also feel the same way. There is a drug ring operating in Southern California that is being fed with inside information so that they can cover their tracks and throw wool over our eyes."

Josh sat on the edge of a table and sipped from a water bottle as the group exchanged glances with each other and broke into a soft murmur.

Josh continued, "The good news is I don't believe that anyone in this room is the rotten apple that I am referring to—I trust you guys with my life."

He pulled the warrant from his inside jacket pocket and held it up for the group, "Lt. Graham himself signed this search warrant a little while ago. We have been authorized to run a full search on the residence of one of our SDPD officers—a Lieutenant William McMillan. Don't let his rank in the SDPD limit or restrain you from doing your job. In the eyes of the law and under the powers of this warrant, everyone is equal as you know."

The group was silent and rapt in attention as Josh continued. "I'll come along with you but I will stay outside and coordinate the operation while you boys do your stuff. Sgt. Brooks will lead you inside the house," Josh nodded as an officer stood up.

"This is probably the first time you are running a search on an officer's residence, so some of you may be feeling uncomfortable. Please feel free to ask questions now if you have any. I know that this is a very sensitive affair. Trust me, I would not ask you to do this if I was not two hundred percent certain about it. He is a distinguished police officer, so think like a police officer would think. You are looking for anything that is white and powdery and in packets or bags, I want you to confiscate them and run tests on the spot. Does anybody have any questions?"

The group exchanged glances and thumped the table in approval.

"Good," Josh continued, "I have already alerted the canine unit and they will have a sniffer-dog ready for us when we leave the station. Look in every nook and corner, there's got to be something somewhere. I will make sure that the Lieutenant is at home when you boys go in. I have followed his pattern and he is usually home by six in the evening, but I will confirm anyway. You boys should go in right afterwards. Is that understood?"

The group nodded and Sgt. Brooks asked, "Why is that Sir? Can't we just bust in anytime at all, since we are so sure of ourselves?"

Josh smiled, "Good question Sergeant. First of all, we do not, I repeat, do not 'bust in'. The Lieutenant is married and has a baby, so we have to be considerate. I want you to handle this very delicately and with full approval of the Lieutenant. Knock on his door and speak to the Lieutenant calmly and show him this warrant. Have the wife and the baby stay in the family room or somewhere and I want you to take the Lieutenant with you in every room that you boys search. He needs to witness everything that each one of you will be doing. Nobody enters any room unless the Lieutenant is there to observe. So if you do find something, he does not get a chance to say that we planted the stuff ourselves just to implicate him. For a person in his situation, that might as well be a trick that he would play just to throw us off and wiggle free. That is why I want you to handle this so delicately. Does that answer your question, Sergeant?"

Sgt. Brooks nodded, "Got it." He turned to the group and said, "Let's get to work boys."

"Good luck Sergeant," Josh said, "this will be big for all of us. I am sick and tired of chasing our own tails. Hopefully this will finally reap fruit for all our past efforts. I'll meet you guys outside shortly."

Josh went back to his desk and dialed Dave's number and said, "Mount Rainier is about to rumble." He replaced the receiver, stuck his gun in his shoulder holster and walked out towards the waiting group.

40

They had just completed a scrumptious dinner when someone knocked on the door purposefully. Bill and Joan exchanged glances and shrugged—they weren't expecting anybody at that hour.

"I'll get it," Bill said and got up to answer the door.

Sgt. Brooks stood there on the porch in full uniform at a respectful distance and smiled courteously—he was alone.

"Sergeant," Bill was visibly surprised, "what can I do for you?"

"Sgt. Brooks—Narcotics, Lieutenant. This is uncomfortable for me Sir, but I have a search warrant for your house."

"Who's there honey?" Joan called out from the kitchen.

"Just a moment, Joan, I'll be there in a moment," Bill shouted back.

He turned to Sgt Brooks and asked, "You have a search warrant for my house? What are you looking for Sergeant?"

"I'm just following my orders, Sir—you know the drill," Sgt. Brooks handed the warrant to Bill.

Bill scanned the warrant and nodded, "My child is sleeping, Sergeant—can you boys do this as quietly as possible?"

"We'll do our best, Lieutenant. I suggest you have your wife bring the child with her and sit in the sofa right there," Sgt. Brooks motioned at a spot behind Bill in the living room. "My orders are to have you come with us when we search the house. Nobody will go anywhere without you and I accompanying."

Bill frowned, "Why is that Sergeant?"

"Well, we don't want any misunderstandings here, Sir. This is a delicate affair—trust me, I am not enjoying this mission. But those are my orders Lieutenant." Sgt Brooks said. "I'll call the boys in. Let's talk to your wife and have her sit here with the baby."

"What's going on Bill?" Joan's face clouded when Bill entered the kitchen with Sgt. Brooks.

"Nothing honey, Sgt. Brooks here has a search warrant for our house. Apparently his team is looking for drugs in our house. Don't worry this must be some routine they are going through and I was not aware of it," Bill tried to remain as calm as possible. "Why don't you take Anita and go sit in the sofa in the living room? I will accompany the Sergeant as his team performs their duties."

Joan stood motionless at the kitchen sink oblivious of the water running through the faucet.

Bill came around, shut the faucet and shook Joan's shoulders, "Honey, this is only some routine and must be a mistake on somebody's part. The sooner we let the Sergeant finish his search the sooner this will be over. Please get Anita and go to the living room."

Joan nodded silently, glanced at Sgt. Brooks, picked up a sleeping Anita in her arms and went to the living room.

"All right Sergeant, let's get this over and done with," Bill said calmly.

The search did not take long at all. The sniffer dog was quick and effective—two large packets each weighing five pounds were found securely taped below the bed in the guest room downstairs. Another two packets of ten pounds each were found in the attic.

"Things don't look good Lieutenant," Sgt. Brooks commented, "Do you have any idea what you have in these packets?"

"I guess it will be what you came looking for, Sergeant," Bill appeared to be in a trance, his mind was racing in an effort to figure out how the packets got there.

"We'll check it out right away just to be sure," Sgt. Brooks said. He spoke on the radio attached to his shoulder, "Brooks here, I need a test on some samples right away."

"I'm on my way," the speaker crackled.

"Thank you for your thoroughness Sergeant. I can say what they are even without the tests," Bill murmured, 'For whatever it is worth, I have no clue how they got there."

"Hmmm," Sgt. Brooks was sympathetic, "there's nothing I can do, Sir. You know how it is—I will have to arrest you if the tests prove positive, till somebody else sorts this out."

Bill nodded in understanding as the lab technician came in with a portable test kit. He watched in shocked silence as the liquid in the test tubes changed color when the technician added samples from each packet.

"Well Sir, I hope you are satisfied that I have sufficient proof to take you into custody," Sgt. Brooks read Bill his rights. "Five minutes for you to talk to your wife and then we'll have to get going. These things take a long time to clear as you know, so it may be a while before you can come back home again. Again, nothing personal here Sir, I'm just doing my duty. We are not sure whether it is you or your wife who is involved. I know you have a child, so we won't bother your wife for the moment. However, your wife should not leave town without letting us know in advance. Please explain the situation to her. I'll be waiting outside." Sgt. Brooks shut the door behind him.

Bill nodded in resignation—everything was against him and the Sergeant was right on every count.

Bill walked into the living room to an anxiously waiting Joan who held a peacefully sleeping Anita in her arms. He knelt down in front of her, kissed Anita's forehead in deep fondness and held Joan's hand.

"They found some narcotics in the guest room and in the attic upstairs.

I have no idea how they got there—thirty pounds in total, thirty pounds, Joan," Bill repeated. "I am not involved in any of this, my love, do you believe me?"

Joan was sobbing as tears rolled down her cheeks, "I believe you with my life, Bill—you know that. How did this all happen?"

"That is what I am trying to figure out and nothing makes sense," Bill sounded frustrated.

"What happens now?" Joan sounded helpless.

"They are taking me in. You are not to leave town without letting them know, since you are also a potential suspect till they sort this out. I am so sorry to bring this to you and Anita. I'd rather die than to cause such pain to the two most precious people in my life. Please forgive me Joan," Bill could not control his tears anymore as he realized the implications of the evidence that the Sergeant had found..

"Lieutenant, it's almost time Sir," Sgt. Brooks knocked on the door and stepped in.

Bill hugged Joan and Anita, kissed them fondly and said, "Have faith in God, my love. This is a test and we will prevail. You and I know we have done nothing wrong and this too shall pass. Think of this as a nightmare and everything will be normal when you wake up. I love you both more than I care about myself. If all the oceans were one ocean, my love for you is more than that. I promised to protect you in sickness and in health. It breaks my heart that I won't be around for a while to do that."

Joan wiped her tears and attempted a smile, "You'll be back soon, Bill, I know it. We'll be together again even before you know it. We'll be waiting for you here. I love you," she held Bill close and they kissed.

Bill took one last look at Anita, his eyes making the most of the moment. He gave a wry smile to Joan and nodded at Sgt. Brooks, "All right Sergeant, I'm ready."

They were about to go out the door when Bill stopped. "Can I have one more minute with my wife, Sergeant, please? I've got to ask her something."

Sgt. Brooks frowned, thought for a moment and nodded, "A minute is all I can give you."

Bill whirled around and rushed up to a wide-eyed Joan. He grabbed her by her forearms and asked, "Joan, you said there was a cleaner who came by this morning. What was his name?"

"Mark," Joan stammered, "Mark Downey, why do you ask?"

"You said he gave you a reference sheet. Where is it?" Bill was onto something.

"He," Joan stammered again. "He took it away with him—apparently he had only one copy and needed that sheet for his other clients. I called two of the references—I got an answering machine on the first number and the second person spoke very highly of him."

"Were you with him all the time when he was working," Bill was trying to clutch at a straw that he could not find.

"Well no. He had this very powerful vacuum that made a lot of noise. I stayed away with Anita and he shut the door to every room when he was cleaning it," Joan sounded concerned and restless.

Bill sighed as realization dawned on him. It was a plant—someone was trying to frame him and he had a fair idea of what was going on.

He held Joan's hand and said, "Listen very carefully, Joan. I have been framed. I have a strong suspicion that this Mark Downey was no student trying to make some money for college. I think he planted these drugs in our house when he was here and you were not around to supervise. At least I have some idea of what's going on now. I'll get this sorted out right away and be back soon."

"Dear God, I'm sorry Bill. I had no idea…" Joan started.

Bill put a finger on her lips and said, "I don't blame you, Joan. We'll get over this soon. I must go now."

They kissed and Bill followed Sgt. Brooks to the waiting police cruiser.

Josh observed from his car across the street and smiled in satisfaction—everything had transpired exactly as he had planned.

41

"Lieutenant, it's nice to see you. Here, let me take that jewelry off you," Josh unlocked the handcuffs from Bill. They were alone in the back of the van on the way to the station.

"I'm not sure we've met before," Bill said with an expressionless face as the van started to move.

"No?" Josh smiled sarcastically. "You've got to do better than that, honestly."

Bill stared at the probing cold eyes and said, "I still don't know who you are."

"Let's cut to the chase Lieutenant, because I think we are too old and matured for this cat and mouse game," Josh said sternly.

"I'm not having a conversation with you without my lawyer being present," Bill was calm.

"We tried to warn you, my friend and you did not seem to care," Josh looked at his watch. "We have another twenty minutes before we reach the station, twenty minutes that may decide the continued health of your family and your freedom. Work with me and you'll get your life back. Don't cooperate and you will go through misery that you can never even imagine."

"Are you threatening me, Josh?" Bill asked with a wry smile.

"Good, so you do know me," Josh laughed, "I am not threatening you, my friend—I am just trying to counsel you on what is best for you under the circumstances. The charges against you are rather serious and you can be certain of fifteen years—maybe even twenty five years since you are a cop. Can you imagine what will happen to your family in twenty five years?"

"As far as the charges are concerned, someone planted those narcotics in my house and I would hazard a guess that you master-minded this entire thing," Bill stared at the floor.

"Why would I do that Lieutenant? You can never prove that in court, my friend, you know that," Josh laughed in dismissal. "We can also bring in your wife for collaborating with you—can you imagine what will happen to your baby daughter when both her parents are in custody? The state will take over your baby and she will probably end up in an orphanage for all I care."

"So you do admit that you masterminded the plant," Bill asked—the prospect of Anita and Joan being dragged into this matter was frightening at best.

"I admit nothing," Josh laughed again. "All I am saying that you can never substantiate your theory in court, especially not with thirty pounds of crack found in your residence."

"Your friend Brant will take care of everything in court, wouldn't he Josh?" the seriousness of the situation was beginning to dawn on Bill.

"Mr. Sawyer is quite good at what he does, I am sure you will agree," Josh laughed.

"What do you want from me Josh?" Bill asked.

"Now we are talking business," Josh grinned. "I don't know who you are working for and what your marching orders are. I checked your records and they come up as 'restricted access'. Nobody knows how to access your profile. However, I do know you have been tailing us for a while and know about our operations. I believe you have collected and gathered substantial evidence against us. I want you to tell me where you have stored all that evidence and agree to drop this case as if we never existed. I'll arrange to let you have your freedom and we part ways as professionals. You go back to your wonderful family and to your illustrious career and we go our own merry way—that way everybody is happy. This is a small thing I ask for in exchange of your continued well being and that of your family."

"I can't believe that I am talking to a sworn police officer," Bill laughed. "You are nothing but a common thug, Josh. You have tainted that uniform and that badge and violated your oath. You can do whatever you want, that evidence is not going anywhere. I am going to present that in court and bring you all down. Breathe as much fresh air as you can, while you can Josh, soon you are going to crave for that since fresh air will shortly be in rather short supply for you and your friends."

Josh looked at Bill and pursed his lips. He reached inside his jacket and pulled out an envelope. He slowly flipped through each of the photographs and said "I must admit, you have a wonderful family, Bill and a pretty house too," he paused. "Your wife Joan is beautiful—did she ever try her chances at Hollywood? Gosh she is stunning—you've got to protect her, Bill," he glanced at Bill, who held his gaze at the floor. "Your baby daughter, Anita, hmmm…she looks like her Mom, though she appears to have your lips."

Bill still held his gaze at the floor.

"Nope, I admit this is a family to die for, Bill," Josh sounded genuine.

"Don't even think about touching them, Josh. You are testing my patience, but don't push any harder. I will bring you all down. You won't harm them any way," Bill murmured.

"Well, there's only one way to find out," Josh said, "I will get a lawyer assigned to you, if you don't have one already. I leave it up to you on what you will tell him and what you won't. I will give you until tomorrow morning to decide if you will hand that evidence over to me and drop this case or not. If you fail to cooperate, there may be some more bad news coming your way. Again, this is not a threat—just some free advice. I cannot vouch for what my friends, as you call them, will do. They are pissed off with you anyway, so it would not take much for them to take some drastic measures if you don't comply. I will not be responsible for any of that. So be careful of what you decide to reveal to your lawyer and what you decide to do with that evidence."

"This is blackmail," Bill murmured.

"Not unless it is proven in court, my friend," Josh said. "Don't you even try to prove this in court—not when Brant is going to represent the prosecution. Your life and that of your family is in your hands and I cannot stress enough how important it is that you cooperate with me and keep your mouth shut. It will be quite a challenge to offer much protection to your family when you are in prison, you know. Even if I can control myself, I cannot guarantee that my friends will also extend the same favors to your family," Josh said in all seriousness.

Bill felt like he should smash in Josh's face—his sarcastic comments was irritating at best. But Bill fought that down since that would be yet another charge against him. He also realized how helpless his situation was. There were no witnesses to his conversation with Josh, even if he brought it up it will be dismissed as merely his fertile imagination.

He wondered how his cover was blown—he thought that he had taken almost every precaution to stay low, but apparently his best wasn't good enough. Bill was running out of options. Joan and Anita were exposed with serious repercussions if he did not comply. He could ask for police protection of his family, but since Joan was also a suspect, that request would probably be declined. Even if it was offered, Josh would find a way to pierce that veil of protection anyway. He shuddered at the thought about what would happen to Anita if they did bring in Joan, who was as innocent as he was. Anita would be left all alone to fend for herself—probably be turned over to the care of the State. She would be practically orphaned even though her parents were alive.

Bill wondered if circumstances would improve if he did surrender the evidence to Josh. All he had to do was to hand the keys to his bank locker. But then, he would have thrown away years of hard work and sacrifice. He would have gone against his principles and ideals in life. He would have embarrassed the departed Chief. He would have wilted under pressure and the worst of all, he would have broken his oath as a police officer committed to protect and serve the community. He never thought he would ever have to decide between his family and his sworn duties as a police officer. But now that the future of his family and his code of service lay in his hands to choose from, Bill was perplexed.

"I cannot hand over any evidence to you Josh—all of it is in my head. So if you have me in custody you already have all the evidence," Bill ventured.

Josh burst out in laughter, "Come on Bill, you have to do better than that. As cops ourselves, that is not a standard operating procedure, so stop kidding me. You've got to have documented evidence against us. By the way, who have you been working for? You service records have access restricted by the order of the late Chief, so I won't be far off if I assumed that you were drafted on some mission by him. The Chief is no longer there, so who are you working for Bill? All I am asking for is that evidence and we'll call it quits."

"You're smart Josh. You would have been a very good cop and a great public servant, only if you had chosen to uphold the law in its truest sense," Bill shook his head. "But alas, it is unfortunate that you prey on the very same public that you have been empowered and sworn to protect. You…"

"Cut the baloney, Bill—I don't want your lecture," Josh cut him off. "I will ask you one more time—where is the bloody evidence?"

Bill looked at him for a while and made up his story, "Like I said, it is in my head. As far as the documented evidence goes, all I know is that I place all the evidence that I collect in an envelope and lock it in the top drawer of my desk. Someone comes by and picks up the envelope and takes it somewhere that I do not know. I don't know who comes and when the pick up takes place. I was commissioned just to collect the evidence against you and your little enterprise—I don't know and not responsible for anything after that." Bill stopped and prayed that he sounded truthful enough.

Josh narrowed his eyes as he listened. "You expect me to believe that bullshit story?" he almost shouted.

"Let's not talk about what I expect from you, Josh," Bill said sarcastically, "it will be a fairly long list. That is the true story whether you believe it or not."

"So when is the little birdie that you mentioned coming by for the next pickup?" Josh asked with a slight tremble in his voice. He thought he might have acted too soon to make his move, but he hoped the Bill was lying.

"The birdie won't be coming anymore my friend. They already know that my cover has been blown and they will retract into their shell," Bill pressed on. "However they have sufficient evidence to start proceedings against you and your friends. You will be going down Josh, you forced them to show their hand and believe me they will. You have gone too far, my friend, without investigating far enough. Prepare yourself for a deluge that you never faced before," Bill fell silent, hoping the Josh would bite on the bait.

They rode the remainder of the way in silence, eyes locked on each other. When they stopped at the station, Josh opened the rear door and said, "I admire your courage," he gambled, unsure if Bill was lying or not, "you've got six hours to come clean."

42

"You just wouldn't yield, would you Bill?" Josh paced the cell where Bill had been ordered to be placed in solitary confinement. "I am known to be a man with infinite patience, but you have taken me over the limit."

It had not taken long for Josh to figure out that Bill did indeed concoct the story about someone coming to pick up the evidence that he had collected. Bill had just tried to buy some time to think his next move, while he had sent Josh on a wild goose chase. But the more he thought, the more confused he became as to what his priorities were—protecting his young family or upholding the law. He wondered if there was a way he could do both.

Bill's defense attorney had been practically pulverized by Brant's stellar performance in the first two days in court. There was no Mark Downey to be found and the phone numbers that Joan had called turned out to be public payphones—the records from the phone company substantiated that. The check that Joan had used to pay Mark Downey was never cashed.

Joan was called a liar and Brant hinted at her collaborating with Bill in his clandestine moonlighting activities. Bill shook his head in utter despair as he watched Joan sob profusely in court. He felt helpless and responsible—his plea for police protection of his residence was turned down, which left Joan and Anita exposed.

Brant even produced an official deed, forged of course, to a villa in Mazatlan that carried Bill's name as the owner. Brant convinced the jury that Bill had been pouring his riches from his drug-running business to build the villa in a foreign country. Apparently he had planned to flee the United States and settle in Mazatlan when enough money was made. Bill had become over-greedy at the easy money and it was this greed that caused his downfall.

"One can understand when an ordinary person commits such crimes, but we cannot comprehend how a senior decorated public official such as the defendant uses his power to commit such crimes against the same public that he had sworn to protect and serve. Our society cannot tolerate such indulgence and abuse of power. I trust that you ladies and gentlemen of the jury will see to it that the defendant is shown no mercy and handed a stiff sentence so that it becomes an example and a deterrent to anyone in positions of power to even think of straying into any such criminal activity," Brant said in his closing statement.

The judge had adjourned the court and scheduled the verdict in two days.

Joan had picked up Anita in her arms and rushed up to Bill as he was being escorted off the courtroom. "This will soon be over, darling," her voice was trembling, "I have complete faith in you and our love. Keep the faith. I love you with all my heart," she had burst into tears.

"You're the only one who believes me though you have suffered the most. I'll have my justice, I promise you," Bill blew her a kiss and was escorted out through a side door.

Josh had visited Bill in his cell the following morning in a last attempt to squeeze information him. "You are playing a dangerous game Bill, I am not sure you understand that," the frustration showed in his voice.

Bill replied with the same deadpan expression in his face, just like he had done for the past half hour. He did not speak a single word—he simply stared at the same point on the floor all the time.

"Very well then," Josh slapped his knees and stood up, "don't blame me for not giving you a fair chance and I am not going to be responsible for what my friends will be doing next. I came to you today with the hope that you will comply and I can withdraw the charges against you. But alas, you turned out to be more stupid than I ever thought you would be. So long Bill, I won't be seeing you in a while, so enjoy your twenty five years in prison."

"No matter what happens in court tomorrow, the continued safety of my family is your insurance that I will keep my mouth shut," Bill said in a barely audible murmur. "If you hurt a single hair, I repeat, a single hair on Joan or Anita, by God I'll bring you all down—and Josh, don't take this as a threat, but rather some free advice," Bill stressed on every word.

Josh turned around and shuddered sarcastically, "Boo! I am scared."

He called Dave from a payphone and said, "I hear the Towering Inferno is a great movie."

"Really? Well, I guess we are left with no other option but to watch it as soon as possible," Dave commented and hung up.

43

The fire raged through the night and the media coverage was extensive, more so because it was the residence of a prominent police officer of the SDPD who was currently under trial. The newspapers featured the story on the front page. Preliminary reports indicated that the fire started as a result of an electrical short circuit, but the investigation was on to determine the cause of the fire.

The media reported two bodies found charred to the bone among the burning embers—the police identified them to be the parents of Mrs. Joan McMillan who were staying with her while her husband was being held in custody for the trial. The unfortunate victims were burnt to death in their rooms—the position of their bodies indicated that they desperately tried to escape through the window, but failed in the attempt.

The story also carried the news about Fire Marshal Dave Reynolds and his heroic rescue of Joan McMillan from certain death. Mrs. McMillan suffered third degree burns and was admitted to the hospital in critical condition. The doctors were doing their best to save her life.

"My first concern was to get the very brave Mrs. McMillan out of there. She was badly burnt. I was worried about the child too but then I had some unexpected help from a detective from the SDPD," Dave gave his statement to the press as a medic attended to his burns.

The media showered praise on SDPD Detective Josh Timmons for his selfless and heroic effort to rescue the eighteen month old daughter of the McMillans from the hungry flames.

Mrs. McMillan had shielded the little girl from the fire as best as she could before the pain of a thousand flames and the intolerable heat loosened her grip and Anita had fallen out of her arms.

Detective Timmons, who was off duty received the news about the fire on his radio and rushed to the scene. The news reminded readers that Detective Josh Timmons was the officer who was responsible for the arrest of William McMillan

Detective Timmons, the newspapers reported, went beyond the call of duty and burst into the scene without regard for his own safety and rescued the child from certain death. Detective Timmons suffered some minor scalding and is recovering fast.

"I am just happy that the child is doing just fine and has not even a single burn on her," Josh spoke to the hovering microphones and flashing cameras. "I would request you to pray that Mrs. McMillan recovers from her traumatic experience so that she can take care of her child soon enough."

"I'm sorry Lieutenant, I have some bad news," the defense attorney handed over the morning paper to Bill who slowly reached out, trying to read the somber expression in the attorney's face.

He paced the room as Bill read the story in silence. When he was done, Bill ran his fingers through his hair and held his head in his hands. His world was collapsing and there was nothing he could do about it.

"I have already felt that you have been hiding something from me, Lieutenant. I need to know what it is right now if you have any chance of an acquittal at all," the defense attorney was desperate. "You are up for the verdict today and we both know which way it is going—and now this happens to your family. Your stars are not aligned, but I have a feeling that it is not only fate that is working against you. Please, I implore you to let me into what you are trying to conceal."

Bill looked up with tears in his eyes, "It's too late now, Mr. Blake. You have been fighting a losing battle all along and I am indebted to you for that. Can you please do me one last favor?"

"Just say it, Lieutenant," the attorney squatted down.

"Can you please arrange it so that I can visit my wife in the hospital and see my child before the verdict?" Bill clasped his hands as if in prayer.

"You got it, Lieutenant. I think the judge will agree. I'll see what I can do," he rushed off leaving Bill alone to make peace with himself.

"Why me?" he looked up and screamed in despair when he was alone again in his cell. He was convinced that the fire was no accident and the heroic rescue as reported was all pre-planned. Dave had arranged the fire just like he had done several others and then he and Josh set up another smoke screen for the general public through their rescue efforts.

His thoughts were interrupted at the sound of his opening cell door and Josh walked in. He saw the newspaper lying on the floor and said calmly, "I'm sorry at what happened. I tried to warn you about my impatient friends, but you would not listen."

"You lying bastard," Bill yelled out, "what did my in-laws do to you to be burnt to their deaths? What did Joan do to go through this pain and suffering? What did my child do to go through this traumatic experience?"

"Nothing Bill," Josh said calmly with a deadpan expression. "The only mistake they did in life was to be related to someone as stubborn and lead-brained as you. Since you would not reveal where you had stored all the evidence, we were convinced that you had all that evidence stored in some secret place in your home. We searched it thoroughly and could not find anything, but we were convinced that you had it hidden somewhere. So our only option was to burn it down. Drastic, I admit but you have your share to blame for this."

"So you admit to have been part of this?" Bill held his gaze on Josh.

Josh laughed without answering the question, "It was Dave's genius that made it look so much like an accident. I am sure you already figured that out. They will never be able to prove any malicious intent though. George saw to it that nobody left the house while the fire raged. He had secured all doors and windows from outside so they could not be opened from the inside. George had actually wanted to ravage your wife first before the fire was set, and I had to try hard to dissuade him from that. You owe me some gratitude for that, you know?"

Bill clenched his teeth in disgust and desperation. He looked at Josh with bloodshot eyes, shaking his head in disbelief.

"Why do you care anyway Bill?" Josh continued. "You want to have your worthless lawyer put this up in court today? Go ahead, and try it Bill. Not only are people going to laugh at you, but also any arguments will be considered delaying tactics and be overruled. Brant will take care of that. Moreover my friend, how will you ever prove anything?" Josh smirked. "We burnt all your evidence anyway, remember? You little child, Anita—what a lovely child—she is all alone out there to fend for herself!"

"You will rot in hell, Josh," Bill shouted, "all of you."

Josh looked around the extremely modest accommodations in the cell and said, "You my friend, it is you who needs to think about rotting in hell, while I will be living my life as usual, breathing the clean, fresh air. By the way, don't try anything wild in court today—remember that your wife is clinging to her life and your child is probably going to be placed in the state's custody for a while. Just to set the record clear, we never anticipated that your wife will be so seriously burnt—I guess she panicked. For whatever it is worth, I'm sorry for that. But anyway, you, my friend have just a lot of exposure," Josh sounded sinister, held his hands in mock salute and walked out.

Bill sank to his knees in utter despair and sobbed. At least Josh was convinced that all the evidence was burnt down when in fact it was safe in the bank locker. But what good would that be when he could not use it anyway? Joan and Anita were practically at the mercy of the enemy. If Bill showed his hand now Joan and Anita would be subject to more hardship and they certainly did not deserve any of it.

An hour passed when the attorney came back, "Lieutenant, I have good news. The judge approved your visit to see your wife. But you will have to be escorted by your arresting officer during your entire trip outside your cell. I have already informed Detective Timmons and he is on his way."

"I can't thank you enough. Please stop calling me Lieutenant," Bill murmured as Josh walked entered the cell.

"So nice of you to have arranged for this visit," Josh addressed the attorney. "I'll be happy to escort the Lieutenant to the emergency room. I'm ready when you are, Lieutenant. I'll have to cuff you while you are out, my apologies. You know this is standard operating procedure."

Bill looked away from Josh, stood up and held his hands out. Josh promptly cuffed him with a nonchalant expression and led Bill out of the cell. They rode in complete silence—Bill looked outside the window and Josh watched him. To some extent he felt pity for the man, but then, he thought, it's survival of the fittest.

It was embarrassing to be led through the hospital corridor with his hands cuffed behind his back with Josh and two deputies and an attorney following. But embarrassment was the last thing in Bill's mind. His heart just craved to be with Joan.

The doctor and the nurse stepped aside as they entered the ICU room. Josh quickly displayed his badge and mentioned that Bill was the patient's husband.

Bill shivered when he saw Joan. She was in a coma and almost every part of her body was wrapped in bandages, her hair was shaved off, she had tubes running into her nose, her mouth and through her right arm. The heart monitor displayed an erratic pattern and the respirator ballooned and collapsed as Joan fought to breathe through the mask. Josh un-cuffed Bill and winced at the sight. Joan was clearly in bad shape and fighting for her life. Strangely Josh felt sorry for her. He knew the woman was merely a casualty of his war.

Bill suddenly felt a heavy burden on his shoulders and his knees felt weak. Somehow he managed to drag himself to Joan's bedside, stoop down and whispered into Joan's ear, "Hello sweetheart, it's me."

"I'm sorry Sir, she cannot hear you, she is in coma," the doctor said softly.

"You don't understand, she can hear me, I know it," tears rolled down Bill's cheeks. After a while he collected himself and asked, "What are her chances, doctor?"

The doctor glanced at Josh, cleared his throat and said, "Quite candidly, it does not look good, I'm afraid. She has suffered third degree burns, most of her skin on her upper body has been lacerated and the flesh has been exposed. In some places on her left arm the bone is showing. Apparently she took a lot of the burns trying to protect the child. She has also lost a lot of blood which made her even weaker. I had given her pain medication—she would not have been able to bear the pain otherwise. About four hours ago, she became comatose and has been on life support systems ever since. Her heartbeat and breathing has become increasingly irregular, so there's not much we can do. It's up to her how long she lives. It may be twenty minutes or a couple of days," the doctor paused and placed a reassuring hand on Bill's shoulders. "I'm sorry I have not been a bearer of good news."

Bill nodded and sobbed uncontrollably, holding Joan's lifeless hand. "You deserved much better, my love, I never intended this to happen when I first proposed to you," he whispered. "You have suffered for no fault of yours and I am the one to blame. Please forgive me for…"

"We have to go Lieutenant, I'm sorry," Josh cut into Bill's one sided conversation.

Bill clenched his teeth in frustration and anger and glanced sideways at Josh, "Have you no heart Detective?" he screamed in despair, "My wife is dying here and all you are concerned about is getting me to court for the verdict."

Josh kept silent.

Bill embraced Joan's practically lifeless body as best as he could and kissed her on her charred lips and over her closed eyelids, "You are the best thing that happened to me, my love. I will forever cherish you." He slowly stood up and hung his head down in hopeless prayer.

Josh cuffed him again and led Bill back to the waiting van.

"Where is Anita, Mr. Blake?" Bill asked his attorney.

"The judge has ordered that she be placed in the State's custody temporarily till a final decision is made. I visited her today at the Child Care center downtown. She misses her parents, but otherwise she is doing fine. She was playing with the other children when I went to visit her," the attorney said earnestly.

"Thank you again, Mr. Blake. You have been most helpful," Bill murmured.

44

The court had just resumed session when a messenger rushed into the courtroom and handed an envelope to the bailiff—it was addressed, "To the Presiding Judge—Urgent".

The bailiff approached the bench and handed the envelope over to the judge. Everyone had their eyes fixed on the judge as he read the contents. The judge set the letter aside, removed his eyeglasses and leaned back on his chair's backrest with a frown and a thoughtful expression on his face.

He leaned forward and said, "Will the Prosecution and the Defense please approach the bench?"

Brant glanced at the defense attorney and went up to the judge. The defense attorney lightly squeezed Bill's hand and approached the bench as well. The judge handed the paper over to the two attorneys, who read it together and handed it back.

"In light of this development, I would like to postpone the verdict for a later date. Do you have any objections?" the judge asked.

Brant glanced at the defense attorney and said, "No objections from me, Your Honor. I think the State can wait a couple of days more."

The defense attorney nodded and said, "I echo the Prosecutor's statement."

"Very well, then. Mr. Blake you may want to inform your client after I make the announcement," the judge instructed as the two attorneys went back to their seats.

Bill leaned towards the defense attorney and whispered, "What happened there?"

"Umm…" the defense attorney started to speak when the judge's voice boomed in the courtroom.

"Due to an unfortunate situation beyond the control of this courtroom, the verdict is postponed for next Monday at one o'clock in the afternoon—court is adjourned," the judge banged the gavel on his desk.

The surprised jury and the people in the courtroom started to leave as Brant approached Bill. He stopped, looked directly at Bill with an expressionless face, nodded at the defense attorney and left the courtroom without saying a word.

"Are you going to tell me what happened, Mr. Blake?" Bill shook the defense attorney vigorously by his right arm.

"Y-your wife succumbed to her injuries, Lieutenant," the defense attorney was at a loss for words. "The hospital hand delivered the message to the judge, I'm sorry. The judge postponed the verdict on humanitarian grounds to give you enough time to fulfill her last rites."

Bill's grabbed the end of the table for support and collapsed into his seat. The red rose of his life had turned to white. He had mentally prepared for the inevitable, but the finality of the Joan's death broke Bill's heart. He sank to his knees, buried his head in his hands and cried in sheer agony of the loss. His beautiful angel will never be there for him anymore. He had failed her in his promise to protect her in sickness and in health, he had failed her faith and trust that she had in him—Bill felt like dying. Then there was little Anita, alone all by herself in the world. She would not know that mommy will never hold her in her arms anymore, play with her or sing her to sleep. Bill failed her too, as a father. Not only did he snatch away a mother from Anita, he will also not be able to take care of her as she grew up.

Bill was a failure, he thought, his complete life had been a disaster, he failed to see why he should live any longer. He wanted to be with his Joan. He wanted to reveal all the evidence and stop the madness once and for all. But then there was Anita he had to worry about—the unfortunate girl was literally at the mercy of the enemy.

Bill wondered how Anita would feel when she grew up and came to know that her mother was dead and her father was serving time in prison. There will be stories that she will hear without a doubt—all concocted and all exaggerated about her parents. The embarrassment would simply leave the girl distressed—she might be laughed at school and be subject to ridicule and abuse. A girl from a broken home, that's how Anita will be labeled, it added salt to Bill's injury. He had failed his family.

"Sir, I have to take your client back," the guard reminded.

"Yes, I know," the attorney replied and patted Bill's shoulder. "Bill, we need to get you back to your cell. I'm coming with you and we can discuss about how you want Joan's last rites to be performed. I believe they will have to shift her to the morgue for the moment till they hear from you."

Bill nodded and followed the guard to the waiting vehicle.

When they reached the cell, Bill sat down on the edge of his bed and hung his head down. "She was the best thing that ever happened to me, Mr. Blake. I never thought I will live to see this day and I am surprised that I am still breathing when my Joan is no more beside me," Bill sobbed uncontrollably. The attorney kept quiet.

"I know words are useless to comfort anyone in these circumstances, but for whatever it is worth, my heart goes out to you and Anita. The judge and the prosecutor also sent you their condolences," the attorney said.

Bill gritted his teeth at the mention of the prosecutor, since Brant had played an important role in the past few days to ruin his life.

"Before we discuss the late Mrs. McMillan's last rites, I am asking you again, Lieutenant. Is there something you have not told me yet? I am beginning to feel that all of this was not entirely an accident," the defense attorney probed.

"I'd like to have a simple funeral for Joan and want my daughter with me when we bury her mother," Bill apparently never heard the question.

"No problem, I can arrange for that. Any particular place you have in mind for the burial?" the attorney asked.

Bill thought for a while and said with a faraway look, "Yes, the cemetery up north that overlooks the Pacific. Joan loved the ocean, she wanted Anita to grow up and become an oceanographer."

"I'll arrange for that as well. When would you like to have the funeral?" the attorney asked.

"Earlier the better, Joan needs a well deserved rest in peace." Bill murmured.

"I'll see what I can do and I will keep you informed," the attorney left.

The sudden loneliness in the cold and dimly lit cell struck Bill like a thousand knives as fond memories with Joan flooded his mind. Her soft laughter and immense zest for life had been his driving force in life for all the years that he had known Joan. She was a wonderful wife and friend and a loving mother and now she was so prematurely gone for ever.

How unfortunate Anita was to have been born to such a father. He was a father who cannot take care of his own child, a father who cannot share his name with pride, a father whose daughter is practically an orphan even though he was alive. What had Anita done to deserve such suffering even before she learned to understand anything about life? Bill could not answer himself.

Bill lay down in bed, physically and mentally drained from the stress and agony of the past few days and surrendered to the desperate need to sleep.

45

The funeral was indeed a simple affair for the casual onlooker but it was the most intense experience in Bill's life. Bill had insisted that all bandages be removed from Joan's body before the burial despite repeated objections from the doctor who had treated her.

"Her body has been so badly burnt, it will not be a pleasing sight, Lieutenant," the doctor had counseled.

"Joan was the most beautiful woman who walked the face of the earth, doctor, inside and out. Nothing can take her beauty away. I will dress her up for the burial myself and I don't want the bandages to come in the way," Bill had insisted. "By the way, please stop calling me Lieutenant—I am no longer a sworn officer of the SDPD," his voice had drifted away.

The sight was worse than what Bill had anticipated. The stench of the burning flesh from the decaying body was overwhelming. Rigor mortis had started to set in. It was quite a challenge for Bill to dress Joan up in a beautiful white wedding dress. Bill appeared to be in a trance, the stench from exposed flesh and the lacerated skin did not seem to matter. He still imagined Joan as beautiful as long as he had known her, what he saw was simply a mask. "Girl, you're going to need a lot of makeup, you know," he laughed as he imagined what Joan would have said at that remark.

Bill spoke to the corpse as if it were alive, as if Joan still responded to him and laughed her short laugh that always lit up a thousand candles for him. He kissed her lips without inhibition when he was done dressing her up, "All right sweetheart, I'm ready when you are."

The doctor exchanged glances with Josh and the attorney. It was a sight they had never seen before—Bill seemed to have lost his mind.

"Goodbye my love," Bill whispered as he laid her in the casket, "I'll do what is best for Anita. You don't worry your pretty head about her. Be good and keep smiling, sweetheart. I'll be with you soon. I love you more than love itself with all my heart and soul," he paused. "Maybe next time you become the husband and I can be your wife," he laughed, kissed Joan on her lips and closed the casket.

"The Lieutenant appears to be losing it," Josh had commented to the defense attorney as they watched Bill covertly through a glass window.

"Well, he has had his share of trauma, so I would not be surprised if you are right," the attorney agreed. "Apparently he already told the doctor not to address him as Lieutenant any more and that he no longer was an officer with the SDPD."

"Good for him," Josh quipped. "He learns fast. It is a wise man who does not want to fight the inevitable."

A soothing breeze blew in from the Pacific on a gorgeous summer day and Bill held Anita close in his arms as they lowered the casket into the ground. "Mommy is going away for a while, Anita. When you look up at the sky at night, look for the brightest star—that is Mommy smiling at you."

He put some loose soil on Anita's little hands and helped her throw it on the casket that now rested in the grave. He picked some soil, kissed it and threw it on the casket, "K Sera Sera, my love, rest in peace. Fare thee well."

They waited till the grave was filled with earth and the stone was laid with a cross that Bill had chosen. He held Anita close to him, looked into her playful innocent eyes and spoke words to her that she never understood. He played with her just like everything was normal and kissed her when she responded to him with her careless giggles.

Josh stood at a distance watching Bill and Anita and wondered if he could have done it any differently. Things had gone a little too far than he had anticipated. While the fire was justified, Joan's death was not planned. The scare factor would have been enough to keep Bill at bay and Joan need not have burnt to her eventual death.

He felt certain however that the evidence was destroyed in the fire and that he had nothing to worry about anymore. But something in the back of his mind still bugged him. What if the evidence was being held at a different place—he wondered. Bill could still use them against him. However, the continued safety and well being of Anita would help to keep Bill quiet while he served his term. After twenty five years, Bill would not have the juice left in him anyway and a lot can happen in twenty five years. Josh felt safe and thought about the upcoming party in Rusty's ranch in Santa Barbara to celebrate their victory. It was open waters ahead for them now.

"Sir, I think they are done," the voice of one of the deputies broke into Josh's thoughts.

"Yes, prepare to depart shortly," Josh ordered and approached Bill.

"My sincere condolences again," Josh offered. "It is time to go if you are ready."

Bill seemed to have not heard Josh speak. He held a smiling Anita in his outstretched hands and tried to immerse himself into her eyes, he would not be seeing her for a long time, so he tried to make the most of the moment. "You'll be all grown up when I see you again, my love," he murmured to her. "Always remember that Mommy loved you with all her heart and Daddy has nobody else in this world but you. I love you my sweet child, may God protect and guide you through."

He held Anita close in a bear hug until she tried to wiggle free. He kissed her forehead and handed Anita over to the representative from the State-owned child care institution. He turned to his attorney, "I'm ready Mr. Blake," clearly avoiding any eye contact with Josh.

"Yes, the Detective will drive you back and I'll see you tomorrow morning before you leave for the verdict," the attorney replied. "Is there anything else I can do for you?"

"Sure Mr. Blake. You can see that I don't get sentenced tomorrow," Bill said, paused and burst out in laughter. "Just kidding, Mr. Blake, I'm just kidding. The Prosecutor is waiting with the last nail for my coffin," he said sarcastically so that Josh could hear him.

"Detective, can I have a private word with my client?" Josh nodded in approval to the attorney's request.

They walked out of earshot of Josh and the attorney asked, "I have asked you before, Lieutenant, and I will ask you one last time, because after that it will be too late," he paused. "Actually it probably already is."

"Mr. Blake, since there aren't any relatives alive to take care of Anita, it is best that she is placed in the custody of the State," Bill tried to remain as rational as possible, his last pieces of his broken heart were crumbling.

"I agree, Lieutenant," the attorney paused. "As I was saying, if you have kept anything from me that can help me get you out of this mess, please come clean now. I know you are an honest man and I am convinced that you have been framed. So I would like to help you regain your freedom and take care of your daughter. You know how vulnerable she will be without a parent. When you are in jail, she is practically an orphan."

Bill looked towards the blue waters of the Pacific, wondering if he had taken the right decision to remain silent and keep his secret bottled up in himself. Blake was right, Anita was exposed. Even if he did come clean, it will be quite some time before some of the evidence can be analyzed and presented in court. Anita may not have that time, given the desperate measures that Josh had already taken. They might hurt her or even take her innocent life in retaliation while the case was being prepared against them.

"I have told you everything I know, Mr. Blake," Bill finally said softly, "there's nothing more to add. Please see that Anita is properly taken care of. Hopefully she will remember her father when I get out of prison."

The attorney looked crestfallen—it was his last try to help his client.

46

The verdict was no different than what the media had predicted. The jury had decided unanimously.

"It is a slur on the sanctity of the badge and code of the dedicated police officers of our fine city, when one of our very own decides to take advantage of the system and violate the sworn duty to serve and protect," the judge spoke in the courtroom. "While we can sympathize for the recent unfortunate events that happened to the defendant's family, we cannot overlook the damage that he had done to our society and to his code. This jury and the court orders Anita McMillan, daughter of the defendant to be placed in the custody of the State. The court further sentences the defendant to twenty six years in solitary confinement with no possibility of an early pardon. The court also requests the Police Department to terminate the employment of the defendant and that he to be reduced to the status of a regular citizen. He can never be considered for a position in law enforcement in this city or anywhere in the United States," the judge banged his gavel on the desk and left the courtroom.

All throughout the sentencing, Bill's cold eyes were rooted to just one spot in the courtroom—where Josh stood. Josh caught his gaze a few times and had looked away dismissively, but Bill kept his eyes peeled on Josh.

"I'm sorry, Lieutenant," the defense attorney said. "There was nothing I could do for you."

"Just see that Anita is properly taken care of and you would have done everything for me," Bill murmured.

The attorney nodded, shook hands with Bill, gathered his briefcase and left the courtroom.

The guards approached Bill, cuffed him and led him towards the door. He turned around to see Josh and Brant talking to each other—both were smiling, savoring the taste of victory. He saw them look in his direction before the guards escorted him out of the room, through the corridor and into the waiting van.

"Twenty six years," Bill thought, "that is a long time. Anita will be all grown up—I wonder if she will know who her parents were."

His mind drifted off to Joan and the good times they spent together with Anita and smiled as memories kept flooding in to give him company in his loneliness.

They crossed the prison walls and he was led through the corridors of inmates shouting and calling out to him as the freshest meat in town. It was almost customary whenever a new prisoner was brought in. Bill was shown to his cell and the door closed behind him.

Bill sat down on the bed and looked around his new accommodations for the next twenty six years—if he lived that long that is. The low powered light bulb was trying its best to illuminate the room. Apart from the bed there was toilet and a washbasin in the cell. Bill lay down on the bed hands folded behind his back and crossed his legs. Staring at the dark ceiling seemed to mesmerize him and after a while the flood of memories rocked him to sleep.

A few miles away, Josh and Brant knocked on a door, "Hello Mr. Blake, do you have anything for us?" Josh asked.

"Nothing," Bill's attorney stepped aside to allow Josh and Brant to enter his home. "I think you did burn all the evidence he had against you and he had nothing left to go on with. Anybody would break in the face of such hardship that Bill has gone through and would give his right arm to get himself out of prison. Not Bill though. He did not reveal anything which makes me convinced that he had no evidence left to reveal anyway. I honestly think you are all in the clear."

Josh and Brant looked at each other and smiled. "Great job, Mr. Blake, you did well. I am assuming Bill did not suspect that you were working for us all the time, right?" Brant asked.

"No, he did not," the attorney was confident. "He even confided in me about his daughter. He instructed me to ensure that she is properly taken care of while she remained in the State's custody."

Brant nodded and turned to Josh, "I think we all owe Mr. Blake a handsome reward for his excellent service to us."

"Most certainly," Josh hurried. I will have someone come by this evening with your more than handsome reward, Mr. Blake. I hope half a million dollars would be satisfactory. We are extremely grateful for your service."

They shook hands with a broadly grinning attorney and left.

"Do we believe him?" Brant asked.

"Sure," Josh sounded confident. "You picked the right guy to represent Bill. We'll send him his reward."

They laughed and disappeared in the freeway traffic.

The morning papers on the next day reported the death of Mr. Carl Blake, a local attorney, who had represented the ex-Lieutenant William McMillan during his trial. The coroner had confirmed that they found a large concentration of alcohol in the body of the deceased and that his neck was apparently broken from a fall from the second floor into the tiled floor of his living room downstairs.

George read the report and chuckled—he thought he had developed breaking people's necks into some sort of an art.

Part Three

Twenty six years later

1

It was simply pouring down that night. The deafening crack of thunder and brilliant flash of lightning added variety to the deluge of water pouring from the heavens. Carol Mason lay on the ground, absolutely still and completely alert, waiting for the right opportunity to make her move.

She had been there in practically the same position for over two hours lying in wait and trying to blend in with the surroundings. The weather forecast did predict heavy rain, but Carol never thought it would turn out to be a deluge. She wore a black wet suit which gave her the proper camouflage in the darkness, but she felt the black war paint on her face running off in the incessant rain.

The boathouse was dark, but Carol was convinced that her man would show up soon. For over six months now, the man had gone about his own way without leaving a trace. But Carol had discovered a pattern in the mysterious murders. All victims were female university students in their early twenties and were from out of state.

The autopsy report had revealed that all the victims were raped and had consumed some alcohol before death—what was even more interesting was that lethal amounts of the strychnine were found in their bodies. The water content in their lungs was evidence that the victims must have been drowned before the last signs of life escaped their bodies. The killer apparently allured the victims into some sexual act, made them drink alcohol contaminated with strychnine and when they were practically defenseless, they were finally killed by drowning. The similar bacteria content in the water found in the bodies indicated that the drowning had occurred in a river, lake or pond.

Two months and three murders later, Carol had been placed in charge of the investigation. The killer managed to stay one step ahead and managed to thumb his nose at the law. Captain Parks was losing his patience with Carol and the news media made it no easier on him. The department was in considerable pressure and so was Carol.

It was at the scene of the murder of the eighth victim that Carol finally found a clue—traces of grayish brown loamy soil in the woman's hair on the back of her head and a few strands of hair were clenched in her fist. Fishing was a hobby that Carol had picked up from her father as a child. She was well acquainted with the local lakes and ponds. Carol knew exactly where the soil came from.

Her hunch was right when she visited Lake Cuyamaca in the mountains of Julian. The cabin was carefully hidden in a secluded area among the trees. It had caught her attention when she took a boat out on the lake on a reconnaissance mission. The cabin stood just on the lake shore and had a slip for a small boat. The overgrown trees did a good job of hiding the cabin from a clear view—one had to know exactly where the cabin was in order to find it.

Carol had come up quietly and moored her boat away from the slip under the cover of the brush. The front door to the cabin was locked and the curtains were drawn. Clearly nobody was home. She had glanced around and found footprints on the shore just next to the cabin. Someone heavy or carrying something heavy had walked into the water and had come back, dragging something behind. Carol investigated, carefully stepping on the same footsteps as she searched the ground on the lakeshore. The footsteps had to be a man's, who must have been over six feet tall, given the distance between the steps and the size of the feet. Something had caught her eye and she squatted down on the ground to find strands of hair stuck in the loamy soil. She had placed the hair samples in a plastic bag, checked the area and returned back in her boat.

Forensics had confirmed that the strands of hair that she had collected, indeed came from the last victim. Carol heaved a sigh of relief—she had seen the light at the end of the tunnel. The county records showed that the cabin belonged to a Jose Mendes and was passed down as inheritance.

Jose Mendes had no police record, but Carol tracked him down as a final year psychology student at San Diego State University. Apparently Jose had remained in the final year for the past two years, having failed to earn the necessary credits to clear his graduation.

Carol was onto Jose like a shadow—she followed him wherever he went. She even planted a magnetic radio transmitter to the bottom of his car, so that she could keep tabs his whereabouts. Curiously Jose never made a trip anywhere near his cabin.

The man was about six feet four inches tall and rather handsome with his chiseled Hispanic features, auburn colored hair and a friendly smile. He definitely had a way with women—he seemed to attract them like a magnet. He would go out on dates with several women but seemed to favor one particular girl, Cheryl Bowen. Cheryl was from Oregon and a first year student of Computer Science at the UCSD.

When Carol saw them together, she knew in her heart that Cheryl's life was in danger. The girl could have been doing cartwheels when she was with Jose and he enjoyed the extra attention. Carol was certain that Jose was lining up his next victim and unfortunately the girl never suspected it.

It was before the Memorial Day weekend when Carol, sitting in a café, overheard Jose offer to take Cheryl for a little trip away from the hustle and bustle of the city. Carol knew that Cheryl's clock had started ticking—Jose was indeed lining up his next victim.

Captain Parks offered his assistance but Carol turned it down. "I'd like to make this as discrete as possible, the last thing we want is to scare him away and make him suspect that we are on his game," she had countered.

"The girl's life is at risk Carol and I am not going to accept that," Captain Parks was not convinced.

"I am aware of that Captain. The girl will not be harmed, you have my promise. If anything happens to her, you can have my badge and my resignation," Carol had insisted. "Trust me with this one Captain."

"You have never failed me, Inspector, so I am going to tag along with you this time," Captain Parks said reluctantly, "but remember the consequences of failure—this has gone too far and for too long. We cannot afford another murder."

So Carol had taken up her position. She had perched up on a tree near the cabin since the morning of Memorial Day and waited for Jose to show up with Cheryl. Nothing happened all day and Carol was beginning to worry. The clouds came in along with the darkness of the night and the rumble of thunder followed the sharp flashes of lightning. Carol put on her wet suit and waited, concerned that she might have lost her gamble after all.

The crack of thunder almost masked the soft purr of an approaching motorboat as Carol raised herself up on her elbows and peered into the darkness towards the boat slip with her night vision glasses. The searchlight on the motorboat pierced through the darkness as it pulled up against the slip.

Carol's hunch was right, a man helped a woman out of the boat. She clung onto him like vine on a trellis. The man glanced around, opened the door, kissed the woman and carried her over the threshold. The door was shut and Carol saw a light shine through the curtains. The cabin did not have electricity, so it had to be a Coleman that was lit up.

Carol got up on her feet, pulled out her Smith and Wesson, checked the magazine and slowly approached the cabin. She placed her ear on the woodwork trying to listen to the conversation.

"This is so romantic, Jose," the woman was saying, "I'm so glad I found you." Carol recognized Cheryl's voice.

Jose laughed, "Nothing like pleasing my woman. Why don't you change into something dry? I don't want you to catch a cold you know."

Carol heard the sound of glasses and the opening of a champagne bottle—Jose was getting ready.

"You can dry me up, you know? I am feeling lazy," Cheryl said playfully.

Jose laughed, "I have been waiting for this moment all my life, Cheryl. You are the best thing that happened to me. I'd like to see you undress, is that too much to ask?"

"Nothing is too much to ask, my love. I am all yours," Cheryl said seductively.

A minute passed in silence then Carol heard Jose's voice again and his footsteps as he slowly approached Cheryl, "I am speechless, you are so beautiful. You skin shines like a light in the darkness, your eyes are so innocent and your lips are so soft. You are the most gorgeous woman who ever walked on earth," he paused and said, "I could go on serenading you and it would never be enough."

"Oh, Jose, I love you," Carol barely heard Cheryl say.

"Here, let's toast to our everlasting love," Jose said.

Carol kicked the door in, held her Smith and Wesson in her outstretched hands and called out, "Stay where you are and keep your hands where I can see them."

Jose was quicker than Carol has anticipated. He had dropped the two wine glasses, grabbed the girl's naked body and held her close in front of him as a shield so Carol couldn't shoot. He dragged Cheryl into a corner, opened a drawer and pulled out a handgun.

"Who the hell are you?" Jose shouted.

"Inspector Carol Mason, SDPD," Carol shouted, "I want you to release the girl and put your gun down."

"Inspector?" Jose craned his neck to the side for a better look. "I didn't know they hired such pretty whores in the SDPD," he said sarcastically. "If a sexy dish like you is an Inspector, I am the President of the United States," he laughed out aloud. "How's that for an introduction? Let me make this easier for you. Why don't you put your gun down and take it easy? I'll be happy to do both of you."

"Do as I say now," Carol repeated.

"I'll kill her and kill you as well," Jose threatened and pulled the trigger. Cheryl shrieked in sheer fright as the handgun fired near her ears.

The bullet brushed past Carol's upper left arm and she jerked back instinctively. She ignored the burning sensation, regained her position and said, "You are in more trouble than you imagine, Jose Mendes. We know all about you and the murders that you have committed. This place is surrounded by the police, so I suggest you release the girl and put your gun down right now. I won't repeat a second time," her voice was ice cold.

Jose looked towards the door and at the curtained windows, "That's bullshit. There's nobody here but you, bitch. I don't believe you."

"There's only one way to find that out," Carol shifted her glance over Jose's shoulder at a spot behind him and smiled, "what do you say, Sergeant?"

Jose fell for it and twisted around to find the imaginary officer. The Smith and Wesson spat sharply and surely and Jose cried out in sheer agony as the bullet smashed into his exposed right thigh.

He relaxed his grip on Cheryl who released herself and ran away towards Carol. The Smith and Wesson fired again and Jose cried out again as the bullet smashed into his right wrist, which jerked back and sent the handgun flying from his hands.

Carol moved up towards Jose who lay on the ground in obvious pain. Jose picked himself up and lunged towards Carol in a desperate attempt to knock her down. Carol simply stepped aside, grabbed Jose by his belt and used his inertia to send him crashing against the wall. Jose collapsed on the ground dazed by the impact and the pain that sent spasms all over his body.

Carol handcuffed Jose and looked up at a trembling Cheryl, "You might want to get dressed, Ms. Bowen. From the looks of it, the rain won't be stopping anytime soon and we will have to get back."

"What, what is going on?" Cheryl stammered as she struggled to get into her damp clothes.

"You're not hurt, are you?" Carol asked.

"No, I am fine. Can you please tell me what is going on?" Cheryl's voice was trembling.

Carol spoke on her radio and requested reinforcements and a paramedic to be dispatched and turned to Cheryl, "Well you need to be a little more careful while picking your mate, Ms. Bowen. This man is a criminal and to date he had killed nine women not too older than you are. You were going to be his tenth victim, so thank your stars that you are still breathing."

Cheryl was still trembling from the shock as the reinforcements arrived and the paramedics attended to her.

"You shot him up pretty good Sergeant," the paramedic said as he examined Jose's wounds—he was still unconscious. "Looks like our boy here won't have a useful right leg or a right hand anymore. His tibia seems broken and the bullet took out most of the wrist."

"Good, that's the whole point," Carol murmured under her breath and said aloud. "Sorry doc, I've got to work on my aim a little more I guess. When you are done patching him up, can you check my arm as well? I think it got nicked when he shot me."

The paramedics finished their work and Carol stepped out of the cabin with Cheryl. She looked fearfully as the paramedics hauled Jose away strapped to a stretcher. Jose was still writhing in pain despite the painkillers that were injected into him.

"Thank you Sergeant," Cheryl's voice was still shivering from the shock of her experience, "I owe my life to you."

Carol squeezed Cheryl's arm and said reassuringly, "No worries, it's my duty to serve and protect, but next time, pick your boyfriends a little carefully, will you?"

"Paul," Carol addressed the forensics expert, "check that cabinet over there—you should find some strychnine in there. Remove that and record it as evidence. Also, I want you to run this place down for any and all fingerprints that you can find. Once you get back to the lab, I want you to run a match of those prints with what we have on file for the other nine victims—I believe we can finally find an explanation for the murders."

The media was waiting for them at the pier. Carol turned her boat away from the pier when she saw the waiting media vans—she never liked reporters anyway. The rain had stopped, the clouds were clearing and the moon was trying to peek through.

2

"Good morning Sir," the attendant gave a friendly smile at the heavily bearded man who appeared to be in his late sixties. "How can I help you?"

"I am looking for a girl, Anita McMillan. She must be all grown up now, but she was just eighteen months old when she was admitted here," Bill tried to control his anxiety.

"We don't keep children beyond the age of twelve in this facility, so I'm afraid I can't help you," the attendant said with certainty.

"Look," Bill insisted. "This is very important to me. You must have records about her. All I am asking you to do is see if you have any record on what happened to her after she left here."

"You say the child was about eighteen months old when she was admitted and I don't think we ever kept anyone beyond twelve years of age, so she must have left this place at least ten or eleven years ago. We don't have records that old in our computer, I'm still sorry Sir," the attendant shrugged.

"Is there someone else I can talk to ma'am? Anita is my daughter and the only family I have left. I have not seen her for twenty six years," Bill pleaded. "You see it is very important for me to find her."

"Twenty six years?" the attendant was visibly surprised. "If you have not seen her that long, she probably does not even know you exist, Sir."

"Never mind, miss," Bill insisted. "As long as I am alive, I know she is my daughter and I have to get to her."

"Well, I can't help you here," the attendant pulled out a notepad, scribbled an address and handed it over to Bill. "That is where we keep all our records. If there is any record about your daughter, it would still be in paper and they may still have it."

Bill looked at the address and asked, "How do I get there?"

The attendant gave directions and asked, "Just out of curiosity, where were you all these years?"

"I was in prison," Bill hesitated and ignored the reaction. "But I can't thank you enough for this information. God bless you." He left the attendant gaping.

Bill walked over to the building at the address he was given—it was further than he thought it would be. San Diego was so very different from what he knew twenty six years ago. He did not recognize the street names—there were too many of them. The buildings seemed to rise up and kiss the sky and Bill wondered how people built those monstrous structures.

All this time, solitary confinement had taken its toll on Bill both physically and mentally. He was allowed out in the prison compound every now and then and breathing the fresh air was the best entertainment he had for the last twenty six years. He always kept to himself and used his time out side his cell to take a quick jog to work those aging bones and muscles.

As the years passed, Joan became a sweet memory, a dream to cherish and a cause to die for. He spent his years in anticipation of getting together with Anita again. He rehearsed over and over again how he would present himself, what he would say, when he finally caught up with Anita. He wondered if she would know who he was after all these years and how she would react when she knew that she was not an orphan.

Anita would be a mature woman by the time Bill caught up with her. She would be able to understand him and accept him as his father—at least that was what Bill was hoping for. He had so much to say, so much of pain to share—an agony that had broken his heart and shattered his life twenty six years ago. Only by sharing with Anita, would he be able to find solace, soothe his heart and alleviate the pain. But he had to find Anita first in order to find his inner peace.

Bill took the stairs and approached the service window. "Good morning," he started. "I am looking for the whereabouts of my daughter who was admitted to the Child Care facility twenty six years ago. Can you please help me?"

"Twenty six years ago?" the woman behind the tempered glass window echoed, "if she was here, we will have paper records. They haven't digitized them just yet. However, the person who can help you is on personal leave for a month. I'm afraid you will have to come back."

"A month is a long time ma'am," Bill was disappointed. "It may be too late for me. Is there nobody else who can help? I am desperately looking for her."

"Actually no," the woman said. "He is the only person in staff who knows where those records are. You see, that is a lot of paper to wade through to get to records that old and we don't get such requests very often. I'm sorry Sir you will have to come back in a month."

Bill thanked the woman and left—completely crestfallen. He thought if he could wait twenty six years, he should be able to manage another month. He just hoped he will have the luxury to live another month. He had other things to do in the meantime. But visiting Joan in her grave was the next most important in his list.

Bill pushed the button for the elevator and looked up. The lights showed that the elevator was descending from an upper floor. Elevators were so different these days from what he had known twenty six years ago. Time had stood still for him, but not for the world, he reckoned.

The elevator doors parted. There was a fully uniformed police officer standing in the corner. She looked at Bill with a nonchalant expression and nodded at him. Bill walked into the elevator. The light on the panel showed that the next stop would be the street level.

He leaned on the elevator wall and looked at the officer who stood smartly a few paces away from him—feet apart, back ramrod straight, hands clasped in front, her short hair neatly combed and tied into a ponytail. In his younger days, he would have ventured to say that she was a rather attractive woman.

"How are you doing today?" the officer asked without looking at Bill. She knew that Bill had been staring at her from the time he had stepped into the elevator.

Her voice startled Bill, he had indeed been staring for a while although unknowingly. "Very good, officer," Bill stammered, "I have a daughter who would be about the same age as you today."

The officer raised her left eyebrow as she turned her attention to Bill, "Oh really? What does she do?"

"I don't know Officer. I have not seen her for a while, I am actually trying to find her," Bill held his gaze at the officer—he just could not take his eyes away.

The officer looked Bill up and down. She saw a man who was probably in his late sixties with prominent wrinkles on the forehead and crowfeet around the corner of his eyes. The primarily grey hair seemed unkempt and the grey beard practically covered most of his lower face. The man squinted a little—apparently trying to focus his vision. She wondered why he was not wearing his glasses—maybe he lost them or forgotten about them. Old age does things to people.

"They could not help you upstairs?" she asked.

"No," Bill still held his gaze. "They asked me to return after a month."

The woman shrugged.

The elevator stopped at the street level and the doors parted. The officer held the door open for Bill and said, "After you Sir. I hope you find your daughter."

"Yes, thank you," Bill said and stepped out of the elevator.

The officer followed him out and nodded, "Good day to you and good luck." She turned and walked away with confident, quick steps towards the exit.

Bill had the opportunity to read her name badge as she emerged from the elevator. It wasn't the name he had hoped to see—it wasn't McMillan. Bill looked at the receding figure of the officer and shook his head. The woman looked so much like the Joan he remembered, but her name had told a different story.

Bill sighed and walked out of the building. He had to figure out how he would find his way to Joan's grave.

3

"I'll be leaving for the day in a few minutes. Is there anything else you want me to take care of that can't wait till tomorrow Senator?" the assistant asked politely.

Senator Josh Timmons looked up from the document he had been reading and smiled, "No I think I'm good for the day, Katy. You should be done for the day."

"Thank you Senator," the assistant said, "Remember you have a ten o'clock speaking appointment at the Southwestern College tomorrow morning."

"What will I do without you, Katy? Good night!" Josh said appreciatively and went back to his reading.

The assistant pulled the door to Josh's luxurious office behind her and left.

Josh read for a while, dropped the document on his mahogany desk and leaned back on his chair. There were a lot of edits required before the document would be of any valuable use to anyone. The Senate would laugh at his proposal if he presented the bill in its current state, especially with the pain-in-the-neck Senator Banks around.

He got up, poured himself a beverage and walked over to the floor to ceiling glass wall. The Pacific gleamed in a bright orange hue near the setting sun and the scattered clouds painted the sky in a gorgeous combination of pink, orange and white. The view was simply breathtaking. He opened a door, went out on the balcony and lowered himself on a comfortable armchair. The gentle breeze from the ocean felt soothing after a long hard day of work.

Josh set his beverage aside on a side table, crossed his feet, clasped his hands behind his head and settled into a comfortable position. Memories came rushing into his relaxed mind. Never in his wildest dreams had he ever thought that one day he would become a Senator of the United States—an elected official of the nation.

He clearly owed it to Brant—it was Brant who was the first to suggest that Josh should try to gain a place in the Senate. Josh had laughed in dismissal, but Brant wasn't amused. It was the seriousness with which Brant held his ground that made Josh think twice and finally decide to run for the Senate.

"What are you going to do with all this money, Josh?" Brant had argued about fifteen years ago. "It's too much exposure for a cop, you know that. You already have gained a lot of press not only locally, but also statewide. Even national newspapers have carried articles about you. I think you should leverage this public opinion and exposure and aim for a place in the Senate. That is a lot of power to have under your command my friend. Push it a little further and you never know, one day you might even run for President."

That was how it all started, on a paper napkin in a restaurant. The money had been flowing in like water rushing from a broken dam and it was indeed becoming a challenge to keep things under covers. After six months of meticulous planning Josh had a strategy in place.

Three corporations were started in strategic locations in California. The corporation based out of in the San Francisco Bay area specialized in the highly lucrative software technology and home entertainment market. The corporation headquartered in Los Angeles built residential homes and traded commercial real estate, while the corporation that called San Diego its home specialized in export and import.

Josh funded a venture capitalist who in turn poured the money into these corporations and within two years he had broken even on his investment. By the fifth year, the collective net revenue totaled over half a billion dollars.

While nobody could ever link any of that money to Josh, he enjoyed every comfort life had to offer—everything was taken care of. The corporations declared the expense as business development.

By the sixth year Josh had resigned from the SDPD and entered the political scene. He traveled extensively under banner of his party discussing his views in public gatherings. His reputation and work at the SDPD had preceded him and he was recognized everywhere he went. The publicists found it easy to promote Josh—he was popular anyway.

The corporations backed him with effective campaigns and five years later, Josh had outdistanced his nearest rival by a clear majority of over thirty percent. He was ready to run for Senator by the next year.

The campaign was focused and well funded and Josh traveled extensively over the state. He worked tirelessly and covered even the smaller towns visiting companies, factories, power plants, schools, charities. He was a gifted orator and his speeches were well received—the public was motivated, he brought in fresh winds of change and made Californians feel proud to be residents of the Golden State.

The media followed Josh like a hawk and he obliged with interviews and statements. Josh made national headlines as the messiah for California. National television channels and radio stations opened up prime time slots for Josh.

The election was won even before the polls were held. His challenger from Redding in Northern California knew that she was fighting a losing battle, but did her best to attract voters. When the results were declared, Josh had won by a clear majority vote by a whopping fifty five percent in his favor. He was ecstatic.

"I had predicted this, didn't I?" Brant had said when they met after the victory.

"You did, you surely did my friend," Josh had replied with a beaming smile. "I could not have done this without you."

"That's bullshit," Brant had brushed off the compliment. "All I did was to plant the seeds into your brain, you took care of the rest. You worked your tails off on the campaign and I am glad it paid off."

Josh took office after a stirring speech in his swearing-in ceremony and moved quickly to address some of his promises he had made during the campaign. He enjoyed his new role, especially when the Senate was in session. He enjoyed the arguments and counter-arguments and managed to make things go his way on some occasions. The fact that he represented the state with the largest electorate made his voice heard more seriously than ever before. He attracted more enemies in the Senate than friends and he knew who liked him and who didn't. He savored the power that his new position brought along in tow.

His Senator's salary was pocket change for him, most of which he spent on donations and financial support for different groups around the country. He made it sure that his donations were well publicized so that the public was kept well aware of his philanthropic self and his eagerness to help the common man improve their lives.

"It's time you spread your wings beyond California, Josh," Brant had suggested. "Winning the heart of just one State isn't going to make you President some day."

And Josh did exactly that. He sponsored youth education programs, rehabilitation centers and professional training programs for the homeless in the more populous states of the country. He spread out his programs in a bipartisanship manner and made his choices carefully. He rallied public support beyond state lines through these programs and the media was generous with their coverage. His party backed him up as well—they saw a future President emerging and offered him full support.

It had been a heck of a ride, Josh thought. What surprised him was the fact that he achieved all of this under the cover of the law without raising any suspicion of his true background. He smiled to himself as he drank up the remainder of his beverage. "I just love this country."

The ring of the telephone cut through his thoughts. He returned to his desk and answered the call. "Are you free tonight?" the voice asked.

"Sure thing," Josh recognized the voice instantly and laughed. "What's up?"

"Well we haven't met for a while, so I wanted to catch up," the voice said. "Also we have some fresh meat that I am sure you would enjoy very much."

"I can hardly wait," Josh laughed at the word 'fresh meat'—he knew exactly what that meant. "I'll be there in an hour. Save some for me, will you?"

4

Bill collapsed in his seat aghast at what he read in the county records. The address was the same but the name of the owner came as a shock. This was the last thing he had expected and he did not like it at all.

With only two hundred dollars at his disposal, Bill had to make the most of it. The dollars that he had with him twenty six years ago when he was taken into custody were returned back to him when he was released. It did not take him long to find out that the dollar did not stretch as far as it had done twenty six years ago. The cost of living in San Diego had gone beyond his wildest imagination.

The bus had dropped him about a mile away from the cemetery and Bill had walked the way to Joan's grave. She loved red roses when she was alive, so Bill picked up a dozen of them on his way. She lay exactly where he had left her, silent in restful sleep.

Bill had brushed away the dry leaves and twigs that had accumulated, lit a candle and placed the flowers gently on the grave. "Hello sweetheart," Bill said joyfully and bent down to fondly kiss the gravestone, "I'm back."

He had laughed imagining Joan's laughter as she welcomed him.

"You look more beautiful than ever. I am so blessed to have you for my wife," Bill started the conversation. "You are as young as I had seen you all those years ago, but look at me—I'm old and my bones are creaking. But hey, I have such a young wife—all the old timers are jealous of me. Sorry darling, it took me so long to come and see you, they just wouldn't let me get away from work," he laughed.

To a passing onlooker it was someone completely deranged having an animated conversation with a gravestone. But to Bill, he felt completely at peace—he was together with his Joan again. So he would sit down, walk around the grave, squat down beside it, lie on the ground and prop himself up on his side as he talked to Joan all the time. He had so much to catch up on the past twenty six years of their lives.

The hours passed and it seemed like minutes when Bill realized that the sun had set and the darkness was setting in.

"Sweetheart," Bill had said in a level voice, "I am about to embark on the most ambitious mission of my life. They snatched you and Anita away from me, and took away all that we had and cherished. I had said nothing and done nothing out of fear that they might harm Anita. After all these years, although I don't know where Anita is, I feel strongly that she is all grown up and can take care of herself. I am now free to act as I wish and I will. I am going to put an end to this. I had dedicated my life to uphold the law, but those were different times. Now I will dedicate the rest of my life to uphold my love for my family. This was a promise that I had made to myself when they threw me in isolation and that promise had kept me going all these years. Just wait a little longer, my love, I will join you very soon."

He lit a candle, and placed it on the grave. He kneeled down, kissed the gravestone and disappeared into the night.

He changed a few buses and finally approached the street that led to where his house was twenty six years ago. The street name was the same, which helped, but that was about all that had not changed. The residential neighborhood was completely unfamiliar to him. It was as if a storm had come and blown the houses away and new houses were built again on both sides of the street. Curiously all the houses looked similar in design—almost as if someone had taken a cookie cutter and built the houses one after the other.

Bill was confused, he wondered if he was on the right street. He knew that his house had been a quarter of a mile away from the cross street so he trudged his way up the slope. He came up to a house where he thought his house would have been and his jaw fell open in utter surprise.

He had been told that his house had literally been burnt down to the ground. What he saw came as a complete surprise. In contrast to the cookie cutter houses in the neighborhood, the two story house that he saw simply stood out in its magnanimity and splendor. The landscape was professionally done, the most gorgeous Italian-themed fountain stood on the lawn and lights danced to the tune of soft music. The grass was well trimmed and little lights shone like diamonds all over the place. The stone walkway was well lit and it led to the porch. The house itself looked beautiful with the high pillars that supported a balcony. Mahogany double doors in the front of the house beckoned the onlooker to come inside.

Bill glanced at the driveway. The most beautiful car he had ever seen in his life was parked on it. Out of sheer curiosity he walked over the driveway for a closer look. There were actually two of them parked on the driveway. One was a yellow Ferrari and the other a smaller red color Lotus. Bill gawked at the sheer brilliance of the paint and the sleek lines and body style of the cars. He could not imagine how much the cars would be worth, but it was clear that whoever lived in the house was extremely wealthy.

They were right—his house had indeed been completely burnt down, because there was no sign of anything that resembled what he remembered about his happy home. Someone had completely cleaned up the lot and built a new home from the ground up. He wondered who the owner was. Although Bill felt heavy in his heart, he was happy that he did not have to come back to a burnt down home where his dreams and life had perished.

He felt compelled to meet the owner—he had to compliment his excellent taste. Bill started to move towards the front door when the lights to the porch came on and he saw movement behind the tempered glass door. Bill instinctively ducked behind the hedge that bordered the property line when he saw a man open the door, pull it shut behind him and walk over to the Lotus.

Bill frowned and pursed his lips in thoughtful surprise at the sheer irony of fate when he recognized the man. He had a sinking feeling in his heart but he wanted to find out for sure if what he suspected was correct. He had to know for sure who the owner was. The man casually glanced around, got into the Lotus, reversed into the street and screeched away into the night. Bill stood up from his crouching position and looked in the direction of the car.

The flag of the mailbox inside the property line indicated that there was mail inside that had not been retrieved just yet. The owner's name would definitely be on the mail. He looked up and down the street and approached the mailbox. Bill just had to take the chance.

He pulled a pair of gloves on his hands and opened the mailbox. To his dismay, there were a whole bunch of flyers and postcards from local merchants with no specific addressee on them. Bill pulled them all out and quickly examined the contents—still no luck. He was about to put them back when a postcard slipped out from his hands. He put the rest back in the mailbox and bent down to pick the card up. It was some local merchant offering discounts on a haircut.

Bill's eyes opened wide when he flipped the card over and read the name of the addressee. 'George Briggs', Bill read the address again and again and again. After they burnt his dreams, his family and his house to the ground, they had George build a home for himself over the embers.

Memories flooded his mind and tears clouded his eyes as Bill looked at the house—his Joan and his in-laws were brutally murdered right there, for no fault of theirs. How much his Joan suffered, Bill could only imagine. Adding salt to injury, George built a house over the embers with money that could only be sourced through crime.

Bill dropped to his knees and buried his face in his hands, trying in vain to stem the flood of tears. The anguish was unbearable—the harsh twist of fate cut like a thousand knives. He slowly recovered, collected himself and looked at the house once again. His eyes were bloodshot, teeth clenched and Bill was trembling with anger. He knew exactly what needed to be done.

5

Josh parked his car and took the elevator to the lobby of the apartment building. The security guard saw him emerge and nodded, "Good evening Senator. How are you doing?"

"Good evening to you too, James," Josh returned a friendly smile, "I'm doing well, given my age."

"You look fit as a fiddle, Sir," the security guard, "Go on up, you are expected."

"Thank you James," Josh replied and took the elevator to the penthouse.

The door opened inside the luxurious penthouse and Brant walked up to meet Josh. "Hello Senator, good to see you," Brant was grinning broadly.

"Good to see you too, Judge," Josh returned the handshake, "I believe life is treating you rather well."

"Can't complain," Brant laughed and led Josh over to the bar.

After Bill was convicted, Brant's rise to stardom as a trial lawyer was nothing short of mercurial. While Josh directed most of the work his way, Brant picked other cases carefully and made sure that he received ample media coverage. 'Bachelor lawman on a mission to clean up the filth in our fine city' was how the newspapers carried his stories and he basked in the attention.

It was no surprise when he was soon lobbied for the position of District Attorney, which he purposely turned down twice. "I'm not qualified for the job and moreover there's not so much fun in appellate courts," he had said, knowing very well, that there was nobody else in the city who better qualified. Brant just wanted to play things out a little longer. On the third offer, he reluctantly accepted and the media had pounced on the news.

A few years later, Brant was made judge in the San Diego County superior court. The Governor appointed him to the Fourth District Appellate Court shortly thereafter and he was elected to full terms three times in a row.

With all the growing public attention, both Brant and Josh had moved away from their clandestine relationships with Alejandro and Rusty, but they never split ties. Although the drug money stopped coming in, they would meet socially in public and maintained an amicable relationship. All the luxuries and fame in life were at their beck and call anyway and both Brant and Josh rejoiced in their path to success.

However, Brant had already set up a money making machine way before he accepted his appointment as a District Attorney. However, he needed a partner who would run the business as he climbed into public limelight. He had found the perfect partner in Dave.

During his visits to Switzerland, Brant had made contact with Hans Becker, a Dutchman by birth. Hans had mentioned about the lucrative business in Amsterdam where young women from East European and African countries could be enticed to the lure of luxury and grandeur of the free society of the West and willingly take up careers in the flesh trade.

Brant was amazed at the sophistication of the apparently well-oiled machine that operated on a global scale as Hans had described it. Apart from the enormous potential for making money what excited Brant was the degree of secrecy involved in the entire process. The girls had no clue where they would end up and the person making the request never knew and never cared where the girls came from.

Josh had latched onto the idea immediately when Brant had explained the mechanics and both of them knew exactly how they could capitalize on the opportunity. Nevada was the obvious choice due to the liberal laws of prostitution and gambling in the state.

Dave had resigned from his job at the SDFD and opened a limited liability company in Nevada. With generous investments from Brant, Josh and George, they had built a brand new casino just off the Las Vegas Strip. George was appointed as the head of security.

By the time the casino was built and opened to the general public, Brant had already introduced Dave with Hans during one of his trips to Europe and the two had struck a chord right away. They had to find a way to circumvent the strict US immigration laws and operate under the pretence of an honest operation.

The girls were to be brought into the country on student visas to study at the University of Nevada. Josh and Brant set up a scholarship fund that sponsored five students every year. Male applicants were rejected after initial interviews and only girls with the right potential were taken through the process. Hans took care of the interviews and received a commission in exchange.

The girls were free to choose their course of study. They had no idea of what was in store for them when they landed in the United States. They were all excited at the prospect of a sponsored US education and relief from impoverished lives in their native countries.

The girls were allowed their freedom for six months after their arrival in the United States. By that time they had tasted the luxuries of life that only a free society could offer and they had only dreamt about in the past. The pomp and splendor of glamorous Las Vegas added the final enticement to a life of extravagant celebration.

The tides changed after the sixth month when they were brought over to San Diego and housed in an apartment a few floors below Brant's penthouse. The apartment was deeded to a trust of which Dave was the sole trustee.

Dave had indeed created a well-oiled machine for himself and the money kept pouring in. He trained some of the veterans as showgirls and started a show in his casino. It soon became a resounding success and Dave was soon moving in the big league in Las Vegas.

"So there's some fresh meat, huh?" Josh sipped on the tequila and asked.

"Yep," Brant smiled. "Fresh as the morning dew, or so I hear. I'm ready when you are."

"Sorry to keep you waiting my friend," Josh said. "Let's go down."

They took the stairs and approached the apartment. Brant knocked on the door on a pre-arranged sequence and George answered promptly. "So good to see you both," George beamed.

"You too George," Josh replied. "Are they ready for us?"

"Absolutely," George laughed. "All saddled up and ready to gallop."

Josh allowed Brant to enter the apartment and shut the door behind him. They followed George into to the living room and stopped to scan the group. There were three girls sitting together in a sofa. All of them were blonde with lithe and amply endowed bodies. All of them were also blindfolded, so that they could not see Josh or Brant.

Josh and Brant exchanged knowing glances—definitely East European.

"Do all of you speak English?" Brant asked.

The girls silently nodded.

"Very good," Brant said, "ladies we won't take too much of your time. Let's get introduced, shall we?"

One of the girls reached for her blindfold and George was on her instantly. Age apparently did not impede his agility. "I have told you never to remove your blindfolds," George snapped.

The menacing voice was enough to discourage the girl.

"Our faces are not important to you," Josh picked up the conversation. "You simply listen to us and nobody will harm you. My name is Carlos Mendes."

"Hello Mr. Mendes," the girls echoed.

"Very good," Brant pitched in. "My name is Roger Carver. Carlos and I are here to make you all very happy and rich. Or course that is if you listen to us and do what we say."

"Yes, Mr. Carver," the girls reminded Brant of his preschool days when they echoed together again.

"Very good, what is your name?" Josh walked over to the first girl and slowly ran his hand over her bare forearm.

The girl flinched at first and said, "Fayina Petrova."

"You are more beautiful than your name," Josh said, "come with me," he helped the girl to her feet and walked her into another dimly lit room and shut the door.

The girl groped for support and found the bed when Josh led her to it.

"Sit down Fayina, what is the meaning of your name?" Josh asked softly.

The girl giggled and said, "It means the free one."

"How wonderful, you are definitely the free one and you have come to the world of the free," Josh smiled and held the girl's face in both hands. "You are truly beautiful."

"Thank you Mr. Mendes," the heavy Czech accent added to the nervousness as the girl's feminine instincts alerted her that something was amiss.

"Do you want to just study and go back to your country or do you want to stay here in the United States, become rich and enjoy all the luxuries and comfort that life has to offer?" Josh asked gently as he held Fayina's hand and gently patted her thighs. "I have friends in the government and can get you your citizenship very quickly. I also have friends who will give you a very nice job that will make you very rich."

"I stay here, Mr. Mendes," Fayina still needed to work on her English. "I love America very much. I want to become citizen. I have heard America is land of opportunity. I want to become rich. You help me?"

"I will help you if you help me, Fayina," Josh said.

"What do I have to do?" Fayina asked anxiously finding some comfort in Josh's reassuring voice.

"You will not be able to become a citizen or rich by just studying in college," Josh said. "You are very beautiful and have a young and soft body," Josh ran his hands slowly over her thighs and stroked the small of her back.

Fayina felt aroused and confused.

"Las Vegas will make you very rich Fayina," Josh leaned forward and ran his tongue up her neck and behind her ears and felt the girl stiffen. "There are people I know who will give a pretty girl like you a thousand dollars for just making love to you," Josh paused. "Just imagine Fayina, one thousand dollars in just one hour of pure pleasure. Have you ever seen that much money in your life Fayina?"

"No," Fayina shook her head incredulously, "One thousand dollars for just one hour? You joke with me, no?"

"My dear sweet Fayina," Josh laughed. "That is just a start. Once you make them happy they will keep coming to you again and again. You can have two, three, four or any number of clients in just one night. Can you imagine how much money you will make in a month?" Josh was stroking her breast and felt her nipples harden. "You can never make that much money studying in college."

"You very kind, Mr. Mendes," Fayina moaned as the foreplay aroused her.

"Will you do as I say Fayina?" Josh asked and he kissed Fayina full on her lips and stroked both her nipples

"Yes," Fayina was almost bursting as her heart started to pound. "Yes, Mr. Mendes, I will, I will."

"Very good Fayina, you are a very smart girl," Josh said and licked her neck and lightly bit her ear and Fayina moaned. "Let's celebrate with some champagne, Fayina."

George always kept the glasses ready. Josh switched on some light music and handed one glass to Fayina, lightly touched her glass with his and said, "A toast to my sweet Fayina." He put his glass back on the table and watched in silence as Fayina emptied the glass.

"Do you want to make love to me Fayina?" Josh kissed Fayina, kept stroking her breasts and slowly pushed her down on the bed.

"Yes, yes, yes," Fayina desperately needed to relieve the waves of sexual tension that swept through her body.

Josh undressed Fayina slowly to the rhythm of the soft music and kept her waiting. "My God you are so beautiful Fayina," Josh rejoiced at what he saw.

Josh thoroughly enjoyed making love to Fayina and she responded to him like they had been a couple for ever. It was soon after the ecstasy started to subside that Josh felt Fayina's body relax and become limp as the sedative in her drink took effect.

Josh walked over to the bathroom, showered, got dressed and walked back into the living room. George was there alone watching a TV sitcom. He turned around to see Josh. "Looks like you had things under control there, huh?"

Josh laughed, "Yep, you can say that my friend. Dave will be very happy," he walked over to the bar and poured himself a drink. "The girl's a perfect fit for the job."

"I'm glad it worked out there," George said. "I think we have just one bogey this time then."

"How long has Brant been gone?" Josh asked.

"Well the first one did not work out, I guess," George said. "The bitch prefers to continue with her studies, go back and teach in some school in her country," he chuckled. He nodded at a corner room and said, "She's in that room knocked out for another six hours. Brant gave her the larger dose when he figured that she is worthless for us. He's been with the other one for the last half hour, so I think that one will work out just like yours."

"It's a pity," Josh frowned. "She seemed sexy enough. Take care of her will you?"

George chuckled, "I will boss, I sure will. Just like in the past, I have the limo arranged for the two girls. It will be here bright and early tomorrow morning to pick them up and take them to Dave in style. As for that bitch, I will take care of her myself."

"What will we do without you George?" Josh asked. He knew George would first rape the girl over and over again. When he would be spent, he would almost miraculously find some strength to break her neck, smash her face till she could never be recognized anymore. He would then leave her in the Sierras for the coyotes to feast on the dead body.

6

"What can I do for you today, Sir?" the bank teller gave a friendly smile.

"Well, I'd like to access my locker please," Bill replied.

"Sure, do you know the number?" the teller asked.

"I'm afraid not," Bill said, "it had been quite a while since I accessed it, so my memory fails me. But I do have the key," Bill picked out one of the keys from a ring and held it out to the teller. The key ring and a wallet with two hundred dollars was all that he had on his person when he was arrested and that was all he got when they released him.

The teller looked at the key and frowned, "Are you sure this is the right key, Sir? I've never seen a key like that ever since I started working here."

"Yes, ma'am," Bill said emphatically. "That is the right key. I had been a customer of this bank for the last twenty seven years," he paused as the tellers eyed widened in surprise. "Hopefully my account is still active. That was the key to my locker and I had regularly used it in the past."

"Wow!" the teller was surprised. "Thank you for being such a loyal customer. But that was way before my time. Can you please give me one minute? I have to talk to my manager. What is your name Sir?

"William McMillan," Bill said, "my address was twenty eight thirty five Silverado Lane—just three blocks away from here."

"Thank you Sir, I'll be right back," the teller noted the address and disappeared behind a door.

She returned in three minutes with a middle aged woman behind her.

"Mr. McMillan?" the woman greeted Bill, "I am the manager. I checked your account and yes, it is still active with about twenty five thousand dollars in your checking account and about six hundred and seventy six thousand dollars in your investment account. I see some good growth in your investments, Mr. McMillan," she smiled. "There were no transactions to any of these accounts for the last twenty six years apart from interest and dividend credits and annual maintenance fees for your locker," she looked at Bill quizzically.

"Thank you, ma'am" Bill said. "You are very helpful. But I was actually trying to access my locker."

"Yes, Sir, I was coming to that," the manager said. "We upgraded our lockers about twelve years ago and our records show that you did have a locker with us. We had contacted every customer who had a locker in our bank. We had them move their contents to the new lockers and had issued them new keys. Please bear with me while I look up the status of your locker."

She punched a few keys on a computer to read the report. Bill tried to lean over to figure out what she was reading but the screen was not visible to him.

"Well, Sir," the woman seemed to lose some color from her face when she finished reading, "apparently we did try to contact you at your address in Silverado Lane but the mail was returned. Apparently the house there had been destroyed by fire and it was a vacant lot. We put a trace on your forwarding address and found that you were, um…" she hesitated.

"In prison," Bill finished the rest of her statement.

"Y-Yes," the woman hesitated, slightly embarrassed. "Do you have some form of identification Sir?"

Bill dug into his shirt pocket and removed his driving license and his prison release papers and handed them over to the manager.

"This is an expired license Sir," the woman said.

"Yes," Bill tried to maintain his patience. "That was valid twenty six years ago when I was arrested. You can verify the name and address on that license. I know I look different now—age does that to people. So put that and the prison release papers together and you will have my identity verified. I am a free man now and want to get back to my life. I need access to that locker, ma'am."

"We'll have to make some phone calls and keep a copy of these documents for our records. Is that ok with you Sir?" the manager had already dispatched the teller to make the calls and the photocopies.

"Go ahead," Bill nodded. "Now will you please tell me when I can access my locker?"

The woman went back to reading the information on her screen, "It says in our records that since we could not contact you in prison, our branch manager personally authorized and supervised the removal of your box from the locker and had it relocated to our new lockers. I have a signed copy of this relocation in our records and will be happy to print you a copy of it if you wish."

The teller had returned with Bill's license and release papers and handed it over to him.

"So is my locker must still be here, since you are deducting annual maintenance fees," Bill was becoming anxious.

"Yes, Sir, and we are holding the key for you," the manager finished reading.

"Well, can you give it to me and take me to my locker?" Bill was getting increasingly anxious.

"Sure Sir, but you will have to come back tomorrow, since the key is being held at the main branch in downtown San Diego and we'll have to get it for you," the manager said.

"Ma'am, I need to access my locker now. I cannot tell you how important it is to me," Bill insisted.

"Tell you what Sir," the woman looked at Bill for a while and said felt some strange sympathy for him. "Since you have been a customer with us for such a long time, I will expedite things for you. Why don't you come back in the afternoon? I'll send in a messenger and have it brought over. She will be leaving for the main branch a little later today anyway, so I can have her get that key for you. Will that be ok?

"Thank you so much," Bill glanced at the manager's name tag, "Ms. Crowley. I'll be very grateful."

"Sure Sir," the manager said. "Just come back around two o'clock in the afternoon and ask for me at the counter," she handed over her business card to Bill.

"The contents of my box were not removed, correct?" Bill asked with concern.

"By law, we cannot open your box without your permission or without a written directive from a legal authority, so I am sure the contents were not touched," the manager reassured.

"Thank you again Ms. Crowley," Bill gave a wry smile, still unsure if the woman was telling the truth. "I'll be back in the afternoon."

Actually Bill never really left the bank. He did step out for a quick sandwich, returned back to the waiting area. He picked up the newspaper lying on the center table and smiled to himself—it has been quite a while since he read a newspaper. He had so much to catch up.

Bill skimmed the headlines as he flipped the pages—the world had changed dramatically. Russia apparently had adopted democracy and regions had split up into smaller independent governments. The cold war had found its place in the archives. The world seemed to have become a better place, Bill thought.

He had to revise his opinion shortly as he read the news of mass graves being found at Bosnia and the genocide in Africa. Terrorism had turned into a worldwide industry and some people thought they were doing the world a service by taking innocent lives. Bill smiled sarcastically—not much had changed really, it was just the magnitude that had amplified.

It was full page advertisement on one of the pages that caught Bill's attention and he sat upright. A Senator Timmons and a whole bunch of prominent local citizens were apparently endorsing a chain of restaurants in downtown San Diego. 'SunDiegans—the choice of San Diegans in sunny San Diego' was the caption of the advertisement.

"Josh a senator?" Bill mused, "I can't believe this." He stared at the advertisement and reasoned that Timmons was not an uncommon last name. Nevertheless, it was too much of a coincidence and he had to follow up. If his hunch was true, it would not be too difficult to track down Josh.

After the clock struck the second hour in the afternoon, the manager approached Bill with a smile on her face.

"Are you ready Sir?" she asked, "I have your key."

"Wonderful," Bill rose. He hesitated and asked, "Ma'am have you eaten at SunDiegans?"

"Why, of course?" the woman's face lit up. "They are quite upscale, but it's worth every penny you spend there. My husband actually proposed to me in their La Jolla location, but that's a different story."

"Oh, how wonderful," Bill smiled, "Congratulations!"

"Thank you," the woman nodded. "Are you planning to go down there? You'll love it—that I can guarantee."

"I think I will check them out. I'll have to spend all the money that you've been holding for me, you know?" Bill said jokingly.

The woman laughed and led Bill to the locker room.

"Can I ask you a question?" Bill asked on the way.

"Sure Sir, however I'm not sure I can answer it," the manager was friendly.

"You see, I've been away for a while—twenty six years to be correct, so I am completely out of touch with what had been happening in the world" the manager became serious, "I was reading the SunDiegan advertisement in the newspaper. They have a Senator Timmons endorsing their restaurant—is he a local guy?"

The manager looked at Bill as if he was from a different planet, "Can't get more local than that, Mr. McMillan. Senator Timmons was born and raised right here in San Diego. He had a very modest beginning before he became a cop. He served the city for fifteen years," she paused to think, "in the narcotics department I believe, before he entered politics. 'Eraser' was the nickname he earned while he had served as a police officer. Apparently he spearheaded a campaign to make our fine city drug free and was very successful at that. He was a public figure then and is a more prominent public figure now. The city needs more people like him."

Bill listened intently and said, "You know, now that you say it, I remember reading about someone called 'Eraser' many years ago. That's so interesting," Bill paused—he knew he had found the answer to his question. His suspicion was right, but he had to confirm.

"His name is John Timmons if I remember, right?" Bill used a different first name on purpose.

"You're almost there, Sir. His first name is Josh—Josh Timmons," the manager replied.

"Goodness me, it's been such a long time," Bill shook his head.

"Here you go Sir," they had entered a safe room through a steel door and the manager pointed to a locker. "That's your locker and here's your key," she handed a key over to Bill. "As you can see since we could not fit your old locker box in one of our smaller boxes, the manager at that time approved that your box be placed in a larger box at no extra charge to you. That implies that your original box was never opened. We hope you are satisfied with that decision."

"Uh, yes," Bill was indeed relieved. "That was very thoughtful of your manager and it is much appreciated."

"We aim to please our valued customers, Mr. McMillan," the manager laughed. "Please ask for me if you need any help."

"Thank you Ms. Crowley," Bill smiled and watched the manager disappear behind a door.

Bill opened the locker and there it was—the box that was so familiar to him twenty six years ago, lying there in a rather oversized space. Bill removed the box slowly and walked over to a private booth and locked the door behind him. He stared at the box for a while and slowly opened the lid, unsure if the contents were still there as he had last seen it.

7

"Everything ticked and tied, George?" Dave asked when George entered his office.

"Of course, just as usual," George grinned. "I've got to tell you, it is a real pity that I had to do her in. She would have made you proud. She was one of the best that I've ever had and I wish that she had agreed to join us. I would have been a regular client and paid a premium to keep her all for myself," he laughed aloud and then simmered down when he saw that Dave wasn't amused.

"Did you watch the morning news?" Dave had frustration in his voice.

"Uh-no, is anything wrong?" George was puzzled.

"I just hope not, for your sake," Dave was firm. "They found the body and the cops are all over it. Apparently some campers called it in. They saw the lights of your truck last night, saw the driver haul something heavy out of the trunk and roll it over the ravine. Fortunately for you and for us, they were perched on another hill and all they saw was through night vision glasses. One of them got suspicious and pulled in others to investigate. They found the girl's body and realized foul play. That guy promptly called it in but by that time the truck had disappeared."

"Oh God," George was worried, "Any IDs so far?"

"No, you had broken her neck, mutilated her face beyond recognition and had stripped her naked, so they could not ID her right away. They were going to run some DNA tests on her and try to figure out who she was," the frustration continued to show on Dave's voice.

"Well the DNA tests won't do any good, since she has no medical record in this country," George ventured.

"I know. That actually saved your bacon," Dave sneered. "But that's not the point. You were careless and negligent and that is worrying me. Are you losing it man?"

"C'mon Dave, I admit that I screwed up," George looked at the floor in submission. "But everyone makes mistakes and on this one they cannot trace back to anything, you know that."

Dave walked over to George, held his collar and pulled him down till their faces were just a few inches apart. George almost found it difficult to focus.

"Do you understand the implications of such mistakes?" Dave's voice boomed as George blinked. "Do you?" the pitch escalated.

"I'm sorry boss, I'll be more careful next time," George cowered.

"No, don't be just careful," the anger had still not dissipated. "When I ask you to clean things up, I mean exactly that. Do you understand? There may not ever be a next time if this repeats itself."

"Yes, yes," George hurried.

Dave pushed him away and walked back to the large bay window in his office that overlooked the golf course behind his hotel.

He had worked too hard for too long to lose everything and he was not willing to accept such a lax attitude. He owned a casino and an escort service in Las Vegas and was literally minting money, of course he owed everything to Josh and Brant. It was their plan that he had simply executed and he never had to look back. His expansive estate in the Caribbean, exotic cars, high flying lifestyle and of course an ample supply of life's abundant indulgences made Dave a very happy man. Long gone were the days of struggle and stress, he was on cruise control in life and nothing could be better.

"You still mad at me, Dave?" George came around and leaned on the window frame.

"Wouldn't you be if you were in my place?" Dave quipped.

George nodded, "I guess I would be." He paused, "Does Josh know about this?"

"He's a Senator for crying out loud, George," Dave was surprised at the question. "I'm sure he watches the news and I can tell you he will not be very pleased."

Dave paused, looked at George and realized what George was really asking. "You don't really expect Josh to call here and discuss it over, do you?"

George pursed his lips and looked at Dave.

"My God George, what the hell is wrong with you?" Dave almost shouted in frustration. "How can you expect a Senator to call some casino owner in Las Vegas over a public phone line and discuss how someone we know screwed up?"

He walked over to his mini bar to pour himself a drink, "Are you losing it George?"

"I'm just concerned, man," George scowled, "I know what you mean. I'm sorry. I'll be more careful the next time."

"Being sorry never kept anyone out of jail, you know?" Dave gulped down his drink.

George nodded and sighed in resignation, "For whatever it's worth, I am really sorry. It's won't happen again."

"In two weeks, another three girls will be ready to make that trip," Dave appeared to have calmed down. George was a key link in the chain and Dave knew how valuable he was to the entire operation. He poured a drink for George and held it out for him. "This time, bring your payload down here and do your stuff near the Nevada—Arizona border. The terrain is rougher on those mountains and hardly a soul in those parts. So it will be easy to dispose."

"I agree," George nodded, "thanks Dave."

Dave waved a hand in dismissal. "The limo brought over the two girls this morning. Both of them seem to be well tuned into what our expectations are. They can hardly wait to get started," Dave changed the topic.

"I thought they would be," George laughed. "Both Josh and Brant were all smiles after they tested out the merchandise. I've seldom seen two happier men."

"I'll have to check them out myself. It's funny, what the lure of money can do to people," Dave said in a faraway look. "You know, I see these girls and I see us. We're all the same at the end of the day—only our approaches to life are different."

"I didn't know you were a psychoanalyst too, Dave," George said. "What have you been reading these days? Freud?"

Dave laughed, "So how's my apartment in San Diego? Did you get it all cleaned up before you left?'

"Yes, all cleaned and ironed out," George was glad that the tension had passed. He liked Dave since he never minced words and always spoke his mind. Josh and Brant were more secretive in nature and believed in the need-to-know principle. But Dave was different.

"How's your business going in San Diego?" Dave asked.

"Can't complain, Dave," George stretched out on the couch. "Business just keeps growing and growing. I'm thinking of expanding out to Los Angeles and eventually, build a house in Malibu overlooking the ocean with a private beach and a boat slip."

"Oh yeah?" Dave was curious. "What will you do with the house in San Diego?"

"I'll keep it, of course," George said, "I have so many memories of that place. You know, ever since we burned down that cop's house, I had been eyeing that property, primarily because of the expansive views of the ocean at daytime and the glistening diamonds of the city lights at night. Thanks to all three of you for letting me build on it—for that I'll be always grateful."

"You're a good man, George. You have served us well over the years," Dave sat down. "You're right. That is a wonderful lot for a house and quite candidly, I had an eye on it myself. But then you deserved it."

"Thanks Dave," George said. "You know that my doors are always open for you."

Dave nodded, "Talking about that cop—was he not scheduled for release sometime this year? If my math is right, the twenty six years would be up now."

"Hmm," George nodded, "I think you are right. I'll check it out next time I am in San Diego. Don't worry Dave, he won't have any juice left in him after all these years—we broke him up well enough. I'll keep tabs on him. If I find any threat, it won't be difficult to take care of an old man," he paused. "Hey, for all you know those rugged mountains in the Arizona-Nevada border can accommodate the corpse of an ex-cop as well," they both burst out in laughter.

8

"Hello ma'am," Bill greeted the elderly woman behind the desk. "I am looking for some old newspapers, so I was wondering if your library has them."

"How old are we talking about?" the woman asked.

"Oh, say about twenty five, twenty six years ago?" Bill ventured.

"Life was so nice and peaceful then, I was about thirty five and we had our second child," the woman drifted away.

"That's very nice," Bill tried to sound interested.

"Twenty six year old newspapers, huh?" the woman frowned. "We don't keep them in print Sir—they take up too much of space. We simply scan them in and store them in the computer."

"I'm sorry, I don't understand," Bill had no idea what the woman was saying. He was completely oblivious about the rapid leaps of technology while he served his term.

"Well, you see, they decided about ten years ago that it was costing the library too much to store the newspapers in print. Too much of maintenance, the paper quality deteriorates over time and moreover, retrieving and managing them was too much of a hassle," she looked at Bill who was appeared to be more confused than ever. She continued, "So they purchased this computer system that took photographs of the newspapers on a daily basis and stored the images in some database. It took about four full time people that we hired, five years to convert all that paper from the last seventy years into photographs and store them in our computer system. It's quite an archive."

"Wow, that is a huge effort—pretty impressive," Bill thought that statement was pertinent.

"You bet," the woman stressed.

"W-well, how can I access the, um-m photographs?" Bill asked.

"That," the woman was grinning broadly, "my dear Sir, is the most interesting part of our computer system."

Bill looked at the woman quizzically.

"You simply tell the computer what you are trying to find. The computer thinks a bit, and starts to search the database for your information. Then it shows you a list of articles that it found to match your request. It is very smart," the woman said with pride.

"Ma'am, I am intrigued," Bill really was, "can the general public such as I access this computer system?"

"Yes, of course," the woman smiled, "that's the whole point—self service."

"I'm sorry ma'am this is all new to me, do you mind showing me how to use your system?" Bill ventured.

"Surely," the woman motioned to someone to her left and a young man came by.

"Yes Mrs. Jones, what can I do for you today?" the man asked.

"Brad, this gentleman here needs to access some old newspapers. Can you please show him how to use our computer system? He had never used it before," Mrs. Jones turned to Bill, "Brad's our computer genius."

"No problem Mrs. Jones," Brad smiled at the compliment. "Please come with me Sir."

"Thanks Brad and thank you so very much Mrs. Jones," Bill followed.

"What information are you looking for Sir?" Brad asked.

Bill hesitated for a moment and said, "There's a lot I am looking for, but quite candidly I don't know yet. Why don't you show me how it works and I'll take it from there."

Brad looked at the old man doubtfully, "Ok, here's a crash course on how to use our computer system."

Bill watched in awe as Brad took him through the steps to search and retrieve documents and information from the computer. These were completely uncharted waters for him—the world had advanced by leaps and bounds while he served his time tucked away in some forgotten corner.

"What do you think?" Brad looked up at the clock on the wall and asked, "Do you think you can take things from here?"

Bill's mind was racing and he did not seem to hear Brad. There was so much of information he could search in the system—it was almost overwhelming. Maybe he could also find some news on Anita.

"Tell me Brad," Bill asked. "If I have to find the current address of a particular person, can this computer provide me with that information?"

"Well, not this program, Sir," Brad shook his head. "This program only looks into the database where we store the electronic images of all newspapers—believe it or not it goes back seventy years. I actually spend hours reading those old issues—it kind of puts things in perspective for me, you know. Things were so very different then."

He realized that was not the answer Bill was looking for and continued, "But to your point, you could always look up the phonebook to figure out addresses of people if they are local in the San Diego area. All the phonebooks for San Diego County are in that shelf over there if you need them," he nodded at a shelf to his right.

"Well, I don't know if my friend lives in San Diego or not, you see. It has been a while since we last met and I don't know her whereabouts," Bill said.

"Ah, that is where the Internet can be your next best friend," Brad smiled. "Let me show you, what's your friend's name?"

"Blake, Carl Blake, he was an attorney practicing in San Diego," Bill said. Blake had been his lawyer when he faced trial and he would know what happened to Anita. Blake had promised him that he would take care of Anita. Bill could hardly wait to meet him again.

Brad spoke as he started the search, "Well, here's website you can go to," he typed an address on the computer and the content of the screen changed. "Now we click on this link that says, 'search people' and type in the name you want. I'm sorry, what was that name again?"

"Carl Blake, please," Bill prodded.

"Carl Blake," Brad repeated and typed in the name. "You say he was in San Diego, so we'll type that city in here. The state is California and let's search," he smiled.

The computer returned several records with the name Blake, but there was no Carl Blake. Bill was crestfallen.

"You're sure Carl is spelled with a 'C' and not a 'K'?" Brad asked then corrected himself. "Well never mind—this list shows all records with the name 'Blake' and I don't see a Carl with a 'K' here either. Sorry, no record Sir, he either moved or does not have a telephone any more."

Bill sighed, "Well, thank you very much Brad. I think I'll be able to take it from here."

"No problem, Sir," Brad rose from the seat. "If you need anything I'll be right across the room. You see I have an exam coming up in two weeks and I've been taking it easy all the time. I just do this part time."

"You are very smart, Brad. I'm sure you will do well," they shook hands.

Bill glanced around to see if anyone was interested. Nobody appeared to even care that he was there. He sat down in front of the computer and searched for the newspaper on the date when he was arrested. There it was—the front page carried the news of his arrest and a statement from the police department saying that they had no other comment on the arrest other than there was substantial evidence to justify their action.

Bill spent hours reading the news of his trial over and over again. He read about the fire that gutted his house, killed his in-laws and fatally injured Joan and how she had suffered third degree burns in an effort to save her daughter Anita. Unknowingly tears filled his eyes with emotion as memories of the past came rushing in.

Bill searched for 'Anita McMillan' in the phone book and found no record. He wondered if she married and took her husband's last name. In the moments of revitalized grief, the possibility of Anita getting married made Bill smile—he could hardly wait to see her and her family. Maybe she even had a son or a daughter, he didn't know.

Bill searched for Anita in the people search database that Brad showed him. The computer returned eighteen matches and Bill tried to conceal his excitement. He was getting somewhere finally. He noted the address and telephone numbers of every Anita McMillan that the computer reported—all of them were distributed all over the country.

"She must have relocated," Bill thought.

Bill walked up to a telephone booth and called the first number, "Hello is there an Anita McMillan at the number?"

"Yes, this is she," the voice sounded tired.

"Ma'am, this may sound odd to you, but did you live in San Diego before?" Bill asked politely.

"San Diego?" the woman laughed. "I've never been outside Gwinnett County, Georgia in the past forty nine years, Sir. What is this all about anyway? Did I win a lottery or something?" the woman asked in an expectant voice

"Oh, I'm sorry to have bothered you ma'am. I must have got the wrong number," Bill was disappointed—a forty nine year old woman couldn't have been his Anita, "thank you for your time and my apologies again."

Bill went down the list calling each number one by one. By the time he had thanked the person who answered the seventeenth number, his excitement had practically been defused. He was losing hope.

He ran his fingers through his hair, took a deep breath and dialed the last number. The voice of a little girl came on the phone, "Hello!"

"Oh hello my child," Anita has a little daughter, Bill thought, "What is your name?"

"Joan," the girl replied.

Bill's mouth fell open—Anita named her daughter after her Mom. Miracles still happened, Bill thought. "What a pretty name!" Bill recovered himself.

"What is your name?" the girl asked sweetly.

"My name…" Bill started to say when he heard a woman's voice in the background.

"Joan, I told you to call Mommy first before answering the phone," the woman scolded.

"I'm sorry Mommy," the girl said.

"That's all right sweetheart," the woman said and took the phone from the girl's hands. "Why don't you go and play with your brother?"

Anita had a son and a daughter—Bill was overjoyed.

"Ok," the girl said. "Give me a kiss first."

Bill heard the woman kiss her child and smiled. Anita and Joan were back in his life, nothing else mattered. He did not want to know anything else, he felt no remorse and no pain. He was certain that Joan resembled her grandma more than she resembled her Mom. His family was waiting for him.

"Hello there. I'm sorry about that," the voice indicated that she was a young woman.

"Oh, no problem ma'am, you have a very sweet child," Bill tried to contain the excitement in his voice. He felt that his hands were trembling. "Is this Mrs. McMillan?"

"Yes," the woman answered in a suspicious voice. "Look if this is a sales call, I don't need your stuff, whatever you are selling."

Bill laughed. His Joan would react in a similar manner when she received those telemarketing calls. "I can assure you ma'am this is not a sales call," Bill said. "Did you live in San Diego before?"

"Yes, I did actually. I graduated from the San Diego State," the woman said. "Why do you ask?"

Bill was in the seventh cloud—he had finally found his Anita. There could be no mistake.

"Well, it's a surprise ma'am," Bill's voice was trembling. "When can I come and meet you?"

"Come and meet me?" the suspicion grew stronger in the woman's voice. "Who am I speaking with?"

"That's the surprise," Bill laughed.

"Look, if you don't tell me who you are or what this is all about, I think we are both wasting time and I am going to put the phone down," the woman was serious and agitated.

"No wait," Bill hurried. "Do you remember your mother Mrs. McMillan?"

"Remember my mother?" the woman repeated, "What are you talking about? You say like she was no longer alive."

"Yes, ma'am," Bill sighed, "I know it is difficult to accept but that was what I meant. But surely you know that."

"Is this some kind of sick joke?" the woman was agitated. "My parents are visiting us and both of them are sitting right in front of me. They are both alive and well."

"What's wrong Anita," Bill heard the voice of an elderly woman in the background.

"Nothing Mom, it some whacko trying to play some dirty trick," the woman said. She turned back to the phone and almost shouted, "I don't know who you are or what you want. But don't ever call this number again. I will have no option but to report the authorities if you do. Is that understood?" the woman said in a firm voice.

"Y-yes ma'am, I-I'm terribly sorry, I…" Bill could not finish his statement. The sharp click of the phone being disconnected sounded like a thousand explosions to his ears. He collapsed on his knees, completely crestfallen. The wind dislodged the list from his hand and blew it away. He watched the paper disappear in the distance and thought it was hope that disappeared from his life.

Bill collected himself and went back to the computer. He typed in 'Josh Timmons' and waited for the computer to react. After a long minute that seemed like ages to Bill, the computer returned over three thousand matching records.

Bill sighed and picked matching records at random to read the newspaper articles. He was spellbound at the gradual progression of Josh's career from a cop to a political figure to a Senator elected by the people of California. One thing was certain—Josh hadn't been napping all these years. He had shaped his life expertly and had managed to keep his tracks well covered. The general public apparently never knew how Josh had pulled a heavy veil over their eyes. Bill almost commended Josh for that.

It wasn't difficult to find where Josh lived. Not only did some of the articles carry references of his home in La Jolla and office in downtown San Diego, the people search database provided more accurate information. Bill concentrated on the address for a while, closed his eyes and memorized the details.

'Brant Sawyer' was his next search and Bill probably expected what he saw in his subconscious mind. Apart from several articles about his victories in court, Bill read about his appointment as a trial judge by the Governor. Bill pursed his lips and shook his head is disbelief—if a California Governor can be taken for a ride, the general public can surely be influenced to make wrong decisions to favor people such as Josh and Brant. "Whatever happened to background checks?" Bill mused. "But then if they have managed to maintain and promote a clean background, checks would not matter anyway."

Bill was not worried when the phone book had no contact information on Brant. It would not be too difficult to track down a trial judge, he thought.

Dave seemed to have disappeared from the face of the earth. No newspaper articles and no record in any phonebook or in the people search database. Bill wondered if Dave was dead—it would be unfortunate if he was, Bill thought. He had a long conversation planned with Dave—he hated him the most.

Bill walked up to the phone booth and dialed the number for the SDFD.

"I'm looking for an old friend of mine who used to work for the SDFD," Bill started, "can I speak with him?"

"I'm sorry Sir, this is not the correct number to call—this is an emergency line," the operator said. "You may contact our HR department and see if they can assist. I have the number for them if you want."

"Yes, please," Bill noted the number down.

He thanked the operator and dialed the number he was given.

"San Diego Fire Department," the operator said. "How can I help you?"

"I am looking for an old friend of mine who used to work for the SDFD several years ago," Bill said, "Do you have his contact information by any chance?"

"What's his name?" the operator asked.

"Dave Reynolds," Bill said, "I owe him big time, but never had the opportunity to get back to him. I am trying to clear my debt."

Bill heard the operator typing something in the computer. After a brief pause she asked, "What is your name Sir?"

"George," Bill did not hesitate, "George Briggs."

"Well, Mr. Briggs, we are not allowed to reveal names and contact information of our active officers. But I see that Battalion Chief Reynolds left the SDFD fifteen years ago and we don't have a forwarding address or phone number for him in our records. Is there anything else I can help you with today?"

"I desperately need to track him down, ma'am. Is there anybody else who can help me?" Bill asked politely.

"Did you know where he lived?" the operator asked.

"Yes, he used to live in the Sorrento Valley area, but that was," Bill paused as if in thought, "twenty six years ago."

"I'm assuming you have already been to that place, otherwise you would not be calling us, correct?" the operator asked.

"Uh-yes," Bill said.

"The only place I can think of is the county office. If your friend sold his property and moved on, they might have a forwarding address," the operator said.

"Thank you very much for your help ma'am," Bill said graciously. "You have gone beyond your call of duty to assist me."

"Have a good day Sir," the operator laughed and disconnected.

Bill walked over to a water fountain and wet his throat. He splashed cold water in his face—the cool breeze seemed to refresh him. He realized that he had spent almost the entire day in the library and was tired and hungry. He had to find Dave, there was no alternative. He decided to call it a day and catch some rest. He would have to start again tomorrow.

He looked up and down that street and a billboard caught his eye—a family of four was promoting the SunDiegans restaurant. Bill remembered his conversation with the bank manager—she had good things to say about the restaurant chain. He didn't have a good meal for the last twenty six years, so Bill decided to indulge his taste buds.

The billboards, the newspaper advertisements and the bank manager were spot on—the food, the wine and the service were simply outstanding. Bill ate at the bar and watched the Padres play the Angels and the Angels were winning, much to the dislike of the local crowd in the restaurant.

Then the commotion started.

"I can't believe you did that," a woman's voice broke out of the silence.

Bill turned around—there was a young woman in a beautiful white dress almost shouting at a profusely apologetic waiter. The red wine had spilled on her shoulder and ran down her dress. The fabric soaked up the red wine quickly and an ugly stain spread on the dress.

"I'm so sorry ma'am," the waiter said. "I tripped, it was an accident."

"Well, your little accident has spoiled my most favorite evening dress.

This is a special evening for us," she motioned to her date. "You just added some unwanted color to it," the sarcasm in her voice echoed through the room. "This is unacceptable, where's your manager?"

Bill saw a well dressed man hurriedly approach the table, "I'm the manager, ma'am. We are terribly sorry about this. We…"

"Everybody is sorry out here," the sarcasm boomed in the woman's voice. "You guys come straight out of the comic book. This man was giving me flirting looks the moment we took this table and I was feeling uncomfortable", she motioned at the waiter.

Bill looked at the woman with disapproving eyes. She was throwing a fit for a little wine in her dress and for something that must really have been an accident. His eyes widened in surprise at what he saw next.

Two men were having dinner at a table near to the woman. One of them wiped his mouth with a napkin and rose to his feet. He walked over to the woman and motioned the manager and the waiter to leave. They nodded and left the scene.

"Ma'am, I am the owner. I was seated a couple of tables behind you and incidentally, I saw everything that happened. It really was an accident. Please accept my personal apologies. I know you have heard this before, but for whatever it is worth, we're sorry for what happened. While we cannot reverse the past, we can surely control the future. Your dinner today is on the house. You can order anything you want from our menu and it won't cost you a dime. We regret the damage to your very beautiful dress. Please purchase another one for yourself and bring us the bill. We'll reimburse you for that and please don't bother about the cost. Just bring us the check, whatever the amount is and we'll pay you in full. Nobody in my staff will ask you any questions."

"W-well, that's very generous of you, Sir," the woman couldn't believe her ears.

"No problem ma'am. SunDiegans is a culture and not just a restaurant. Nobody leaves here unless they are completely satisfied. For us there is no price for the satisfaction of our customers. That is our standard of service and I hope you will find this arrangement satisfactory," the owner spoke with obvious pride.

"Y-yes, of course and thank you very much," the woman stammered, still in disbelief.

The man turned so he faced Bill and walked over to join his companion at their table. There they were—the two of the men who had burned his family alive and destroyed his life. Dave Reynolds looked up from his plate and smiled as George sat himself down and picked up his wineglass.

9

"Good morning Senator," Brant stood up and held out his hand, "I'm glad you could join me for breakfast this wonderful morning."

"It's always a pleasure to meet you Judge," Josh shook Brant's hands and casually scanned the room.

The restaurant was almost fully occupied with patrons enjoying the cool ocean breeze in the open patio. The patio umbrellas shielded them from the morning sun. The view from the restaurant was breathtaking with the waves breaking into dazzling white crowns before lashing down the sandy beach. The blue skies were punctuated by isolated white clouds that made their way inland.

It was not a daily occurrence that the patrons got the opportunity to have breakfast with their popular Senator and a famous judge. One by one they rose to their feet and started clapping, some even wished them a good morning from their tables. They waved and returned the pleasantries.

Josh winked at Brant and motioned the patrons to take their seats, "Well, I'm not going to make a speech—even a Senator needs a break you know?," he addressed the crowd. "It's jeans, t-shirt and sneakers day for me too." He grinned and waited for the short laughs to settle down.

"I'm just another patron of this most wonderful restaurant just like all of you. We are fortunate to live in America's finest city—just look around you. Mother Nature in her pristine beauty has opened her arms to you beautiful people and each one of us has to do everything we can to keep her that way," he paused to see people nod in approval.

"Well I'm going to shut up now," he laughed. "Please get back to your families and friends. It is a pleasure to break my fast with you today. Be good and God Bless you and yours," Josh sat down to a standing ovation.

"That was very good Josh," Brant said softly.

Josh grinned and waved at the maitre de, "Let's order, I'm starving, man."

"Yep, this coffee is not doing me much good anymore," Brant agreed.

They ordered breakfast and Josh asked, "So how's life treating you these days?"

"Can't complain, Josh," Brant grinned. "I can't complain at all. Did you read the morning papers today?"

Josh sipped on his coffee and shook his head, "No, I didn't get a chance. I woke up late and didn't want to keep you waiting. Why, is there anything special on the papers?"

Brant pushed the papers towards Josh and pointed at an article, "The coast guard confiscated three tons of narcotics from a fishing boat that was making its way into town from Mexico," he sipped on his coffee. "This is really funny. The captain said that they were fishing in the waters and got lost in the fog. Sure enough there was a lot of fish in the boat, but guess what, there was no fishing gear—no nets, no lines nothing."

Josh joined the laughter, "Talk about lying in the teeth. I wonder what these guys think of themselves or for that fact, what they think about our intelligence."

"No kidding," Brant became serious. "You know what this really means, right?" he looked up at Brant over the rim of his eyeglasses.

"I do," Josh paused to allow the server lay down his plate on the table. "I thought we had cleaned up drug running in our city for good Brant—looks like there's some more work to be done," he dug into his plate.

"I know," Brant helped himself to his breakfast. "It's not good for your public image. So what are we going to do?"

"I'm thinking, Brant, I'm thinking," Josh swallowed some of his food and his mind drifted away to his last years as a narcotics cop.

When Brant had suggested that Josh run for Senator both of them knew that Josh had to do something big and something drastic to sway the public image and opinion in his favor. He had to do something dramatic that would provide him with a strong platform for his entry into politics. He had to work his way up after that to run for the highest office in the country.

Josh knew that in his new life, he could not take the risk of being associated with the likes of Rusty and Alejandro. Everybody made mistakes and he could too, but some mistakes had severe and irreversible consequences that could destroy his life and his dreams. He had to split his ties with Rusty and Alejandro as soon as possible. The four of them had amassed enough wealth to last them a few lifetimes. With the three corporations raking in huge profits for all of them, it was time to wrap things up with Rusty and Alejandro.

Josh had met with Brant, George and Dave one evening and outlined his plans. They listened intently and at the end unanimously agreed that the plan was indeed viable and would be very effective to meet the objectives. However, there were considerable risks involved.

Josh had wasted no time to get organized. He knew that he had just one shot at the opportunity and everything had to happen exactly according to plan. He had waited for the right time, which never seemed to come. He knew he could not afford to make any changes to his plans, since there really weren't any alternatives.

Josh was growing impatient by the day. "I'm not growing any younger every day, you know," he had complained to Brant, frustrated at the delay in executing his plans.

"Patience, my friend," Brant had counseled. "The time will come, it always does. You will just have to watch out for the opportunity."

Sure enough, the opportunity finally came by and Josh whipped it up.

Rusty had called Josh to meet him and Alejandro in his Malibu mansion to discuss some important matters and Josh readily accepted.

"Josh, we are about to embark on a large scale operation. My friends from across the border are ready to offload tons and tons of stuff into our hands and we will need your help to ensure a safe passage," Rusty had told Josh. "This is going to be big, Josh, we're going nationwide. I'd like to repeat the same modus operandi in other metros, but before I can convince the groups operating there, I need to prove to them that I have the mechanics completely organized. Otherwise I won't be credible. We have been looking for a channel for years now and with the help of you and your very competent friends, I think we have finally found that channel."

"You know what you are asking for, right?" Josh had said in a thoughtful voice.

"Absolutely," Rusty had laughed. "There are risks involved my friend, I won't downplay that by any means. But the rewards are unimaginable. Fifty percent of the sales are yours my friend, because without your help, we cannot make this happen—you are in the critical path. You will always have a safe passage to Mexico if you ever feel you are in danger. You will be rolling in so much cash that you will want to use the bills as toilet paper," Rusty had played hard on the one weakness that he knew Josh had—wealth.

Josh knew his opportunity had come knocking. He had put up an act for Rusty and Alejandro as if he was weighing the odds and contemplating his options. He had paced the room with his hands on his hips, deep in thought as Alejandro and Rusty exchanged glances knowing that they had set the right wheels in motion.

"It's extremely risky," Josh had paused for effect, poured some Jack Daniels down his throat and said. "But it can be done. I like the fifty percent cut, that is very generous of you, my friends," he had raised his glass and smiled. "What is it that you want me to do?"

"I am hosting a party for all my suppliers from Mexico and my folks out here a month from today," Rusty had briefed Josh. "We'll meet in the villa of one of my most trusted men in Palm Springs. I want you to come and address the group and present your approach to open up that channel across the border. Alejandro will translate in Spanish as required. I want to introduce my suppliers to you since your paths shall cross from time to time. I trust you completely Josh and you have been a boon to our business. Our suppliers want to thank you, not only in words but there will be some very pleasant surprises waiting for you," Rusty smiled.

"So you are giving me a month to work this out, correct?" Josh had confirmed.

"Yep, the date is the twenty ninth of February," Rusty had said. "We'll meet in Palm Springs—the weather is almost perfect there during that time.

You can also brush up on your golf. Josh."

Josh had held out his hands and accepted the assignment—the opportunity he was looking for had finally arrived.

Josh spent the greater part of the month meticulously planning for the big day. He hand picked his team and had sworn them to secrecy. It was the operation of all operations, as he had briefed them. The slightest slip on anybody's part would bring the entire group down. He rehearsed the steps over and over with his team till they operated like a well-oiled machine.

Then the day had arrived. Josh had arrived a little late on purpose and when he did, Rusty was pacing the floor nervously, worried that Josh would not make it. His face had brightened up when he saw Josh drive up to the villa.

"Sorry Rusty," Josh threw his hands up in the air. "This damn traffic slowed me down. Please accept my sincere apologies."

"No problem amigo," Rusty had said cheerfully, "I'm glad you are here."

"That makes two of us," Josh laughed, "I am not the last person to arrive am I?"

Rusty had burst out in laughter, "Actually you are, my friend."

Josh looked embarrassed.

A security guard had approached Josh to check if he carried any weapons. Rusty had watched Josh frown and said, "Sorry Josh, we're doing this for all our attendees just to be sure that we are among friends. No hard feelings, man."

Josh had nodded, stuck his hands inside his jacket and pulled out his gun. He held the gun by the muzzle and handed it over to the security guard. The guard, satisfied had turned around to walk away when Josh had smiled at Rusty and said, "My my, careless aren't we?" He put his right leg up on a bench and pulled out a small handgun from an ankle holster.

The security guard looked surprised, embarrassed at his oversight, "I want them back before I leave," Josh had said casually and turned to see Rusty smiling at him.

"*Pedro, tenga más cuidado la próxima vez,*" he had admonished the security guard who bowed and accepted his mistake.

"I just hope he checked your other guests properly," Josh had said.

"This guy is new. All my other guests were checked in by his supervisor. He had to go to the restroom when you arrived so Pedro was filling in. Don't worry, my friend. I told him to be more careful the next time," Rusty patted Josh on his back and ran his hand down casually and Josh smiled to himself. Rusty was checking to see if Josh carried a weapon on his back beneath his jacket. He had actually anticipated that Rusty would check him out—everything had happened as he had planned.

Josh had given a stirring speech and had described his *modus operandi* in vivid detail, constantly referring to a large map hanging on the wall. When he had finished he had received a standing ovation. The group had a sumptuous lunch and settled back for a short siesta. The moment had come to make his move.

"Alejandro," Josh had frowned at his watch and asked the man seated next to him, "Do you have the time? My watch seems to have stopped."

Josh had been wearing a wire and his conversation was being monitored by the team that he had organized and rehearsed with for the past month. The question about the time was the signal his team was waiting for. He knew that he had five minutes to showdown.

"It's fifteen past three, my friend," Alejandro had smiled, content with all the good food and wine that he had consumed. "You are not leaving, are you?"

"Leaving?" Josh had sounded surprised. "With all that food I can hardly move, my man. That was a great meal—thanks a lot. I think I'll help myself to a margarita."

Josh had risen from his seat and walked over to the bar and ordered a margarita. As the bartender got busy Josh had turned to look at the group. Alejandro and Rusty were in clear view from where he stood. There were six armed guards in the room, but all except one had their weapons in their holsters. He had sensed a growing tension and nervousness in his mind as the five minutes slowly went by and then he heard what he had been waiting for.

The quick and sharp crack of a silenced firearm as it claimed a life was not difficult for Josh to recognize. He knew that the operation had begun. Six uniformed men stormed into the room as the guards reached for their weapons. The crack of silenced gunfire was sharp and effective. The suddenness of the events had taken the group completely by surprise—most of them hadn't even completely woken up from their lazy slumber.

Josh bent down, retrieved a gun from his left ankle holster, aimed and shot Rusty and Alejandro in quick succession. He had allowed them to reach for their own guns first—evidence that he had to shoot in self-defense.

He saw a shocked expression on Rusty's face as the red rose on his forehead grew in size and poured over his eyes.

Alejandro had died almost instantly. The hole in his heart released a pool of blood that soaked the rich fabric of the sofa where he had been sitting.

Josh had achieved a major objective. Rusty and Alejandro knew too much and could not be allowed to stay alive and be taken prisoner. He was glad that they had guns in their hands, it would be easier to substantiate his decision to shoot them.

Josh had sensed that bartender was reaching for a gun beneath the counter. Josh whipped around and pulled the trigger. The bullet caught the bartender square on his chest and most definitely punctured the right lung. Blood gushed out and spread over the white shirt, but not before the bartender had managed to fire his weapon. Josh shrieked out in pain as the bullet fired at close range penetrated the flesh and grazed past the humerus bone of his left arm.

The gunfire stopped and bodies were littered all around the room. Josh had directed them to take no chances, everyone was to be killed if they even blinked. To his surprise, everyone carried guns and had tried to reach for their weapons when the shooting started. That was enough excuse for being shot and killed. Apparently Josh was the only person who had been searched for weapons. Maybe Rusty had suspected something after all or maybe he had been overly cautious. Anyway that did not matter any more.

"Are you hurt, Captain?" the officer leading the group had rushed towards Josh who was sat on a bar stool clutching his forearm in an effort to stem the flow of blood.

"Only my pride, Bob, only my pride," Josh winced at the burning sensation from his forearm, "I've never been shot before. Don't worry, it's not too bad. Is everything clear back there?"

"Yep," Bob had holstered his weapon. "They put up some resistance, but we took care of it—piece of cake, really."

"You guys did great and I mean it," Josh said to the group, "Can you guys ask Mark to come in and take a look at this?"

"I already did," one of the cops called out as a paramedic rushed into the room.

As the paramedic attended to Josh, he asked, "Any useful chatter out there yet Bob?"

"Well we started simultaneously when we got your signal and have not received any updates. Something should come in anytime now," Bob said.

The operation Josh had planned was to take out the entire organization that Rusty and Alejandro had operated. Simultaneous strikes were to take place everywhere they had operations. The element of surprise was critical to the success of the plan and it had worked perfectly.

The media had gone berserk when the visibly proud Police Chief addressed the press conference.

"Ladies and gentlemen," the Chief had started. "In an unprecedented covert operation that involved the police departments from San Diego all the way up to Los Angeles and San Bernardino counties, we have been able to successfully bring down the most organized and extensive drug running chain in Southern California. In simultaneous raids, the different police departments collaborated in an unprecedented operation. They collectively confiscated a total of about a thousand pounds of prohibited drugs intended for illegal distribution in this region. We arrested over sixty men and thirteen women and in the process of our operation. Twenty three men were killed when they resisted arrest. Apart from one heroic officer who suffered some injuries, the police suffered no casualties."

After the usual questions from the media, the Chief had silenced the group and announced, "Now, ladies and gentlemen, I want to introduce to you the pride of the SDPD and an asset of our beautiful city. It was through years of hard work, dedication and commitment to make our cities safe and drug free that this officer of our very own SDPD made all of this become a reality. What he has done does not have a parallel in history, anywhere in the United States. It was through his organization and meticulous planning that involved so many police departments across Southern California that we were able to conduct our operation so flawlessly. He is an asset to the SDPD and an asset to our city," he had paused at the pin drop silence. The media had waited anxiously to finally know the identity of the person who they had come to nickname as 'Eraser'.

"Ladies and gentlemen," the Chief continued. "On behalf of the SDPD it is my pride and honor to present to you my colleague and friend, someone who had been nicknamed the 'Eraser' by the media for years now. Now that we have gained control over the drug running business and put them away for good, it is my pleasure to reveal to you, the person who made this all happen—Captain Josh Timmons."

He had stepped aside when Josh entered the room to the blinding flashes of impatient cameras that kept on clicking and the room erupted in a standing ovation. Josh had stood in a respectful salute for a while and shook the Chief's hands. He made every attempt to keep his bandaged left arm in full view of the media, without really making it evident. It was important for him to show that he had taken a bullet during the operation. There was nothing like a wounded hero who had survived the kiss of death.

After a while he had motioned the group to settle down and approached the podium. He smiled at the reporters and asked, "Did you notice that the air was a little cleaner today when you reported for work?"

The group had burst out in laughter with a resounding 'Yes'.

"I'm glad that this is over," Josh smiled. "I was born and raised in this beautiful city and ever since I was offered a free trial pack of cocaine when I was ten years old, I had vowed to someday put an end to this evil in our communities. I have zero tolerance for such crimes, especially when the prime target group is our kids. What the Chief just described was the result of over six years of meticulous planning, infiltration and undercover operations and of course collaboration of effort between police departments all over Southern California. We had known that the plan of action needed to be executed with clockwork precision in order to be effective and successful. It is through the sheer dedication of our officers and their commitment to bring an end to this evil, that today I stand before you to proudly announce the success of our efforts. I am humbled by the competence demonstrated by every police officer involved in this operation and I am proud to be associated with such fine men and women."

"Captain Timmons," a reporter raised her hand, "how's your arm doing? Is that a serious injury?"

Josh smiled—his effort to show off his injured arm paid off, "In the line of duty such things happen from time to time, ma'am. I for one don't worry about that when I go into an operation that is so near and dear to my heart. The bullet did manage to take a piece out of my pride, I'll admit, but it's nothing serious. My doctor however says that I will carry some physical memorabilia on my left arm till the day I die," he said jokingly.

For the next thirty minutes between Josh and the Chief they had answered several questions about the operation. At the end the Chief said, "I have a public announcement to make," the group hushed into silence, "It is my pleasure and honor to announce our new Assistant Chief of Police—Josh Timmons, congratulations my friend."

The group had erupted in a standing ovation again.

Josh had shaken hands with the Chief and said, "I am honored Chief and I am overwhelmed by the support that I have received over the years from my colleagues and the citizens of America's finest city. While I am eternally grateful and thankful to the trust and confidence that you have placed in me, I must politely decline the position," he had paused at the surprised look on the Chief's face and the pin-drop silence that enveloped the room.

"I have served the city in law enforcement for over a decade and a half now. I believe that our city is now in good hands with the excellent team that you have built for us," Josh had continued and addressed the Chief. "I want to dedicate the rest of my life serving not only the citizens of San Diego but also the people of the Golden State of California. I have decided to enter politics and try to run for a high office. Someday, I would like to be the voice of Californians in Washington. I know there is a lot more I can do than what I am doing now. I hope the people of California will support me in the future like they have supported me in the past, for which I will remain humbly indebted."

A few moments had passed in silence as the group tried to digest what they had just heard and Josh continued, "Moreover Chief, I need a break and a vacation—a long one at that."

The Chief had stepped forward and slapped Josh on his back and congratulated him on his decision. That was how it had all started for Josh on his foray into politics. The opposition party had pounced on the opportunity and signed Josh up—his public image and his public support were too strong for them to pass him up. Everything had worked as he had planned—maybe even a little smoother than he had expected.

"Can I get anything else for you Senator Timmons?" the voice of the restaurant manger brought Josh out of his trance. He realized that he had almost finished his breakfast without any conversation, his mind occupied with the events of the past. Brant was looking at him intently.

"Um-no Jamie, the food was great as usual," Josh smiled, "I wouldn't mind a refill of the freshly squeezed orange juice though."

"Certainly, Senator," the manager bowed respectfully. "Orange juice is coming right up."

"Sorry Brant," Josh said apologetically, "I guess I drifted away in the past."

"I could see that," Brant said. "You were eating mechanically. Is everything ok?"

"Everything is not ok, Brant," Josh said. "You remember how we had cleaned up the muck before I entered politics. I thought I had taken care of things for good. Reading the news today, it appears that those bastards are back in business."

"You can't stop that for ever, Josh," Brant said. "It's like a weed and difficult to completely eliminate."

"I can't let this happen, Brant—not on my turf" Josh said. "It was definitely a ladder for us to reach the top once upon a time and times have changed and so have our priorities. It's just bad for my public image. I'll have to get involved to organize a thorough investigation to clean things up again."

"It will be very useful for your public image," Brant agreed.

"Well," Josh leaned forward, "I need to do something that has a nationwide impact. In three years Brant, I want to run for President. People all over America need to know who I am before I can have my party push my ticket," he paused and drank some of the fresh juice that was served at this table. "I also know that I have to really clean up my life on the way forward. No more tasting any of the east-European white meat. You can have them all for yourself, Brant" he burst out in laughter.

Brant grinned and lifted his glass, "I won't charge Dave any overtime, you can bet on it. Cheers to your run for President."

10

"Hello Sir, how may I help you?" the security guard asked.

"I was told Mr. Dave Reynolds lives in this building, is that correct?" Bill asked.

Dave Reynolds was one of his more favorite residents, especially the complimentary room and free coupons that Dave always arranged for him when he visited Vegas. "How do you know Mr. Reynolds, if I may ask?" the security guard was suspicious—apart from George, Judge Sawyer and Senator Timmons, Dave never had any visitors.

The nature of the question confirmed that Dave was indeed a resident in the apartment building. "I was his best friend in school and have been trying to find him for a while. You see my family migrated to Canada and I haven't seen him since I was twelve. Just trying to catch up that's all," Bill said.

"What is your name Sir?" the guard asked.

"You are not going to call him are you?" Bill simply wanted to confirm where Dave lived. He had no intent to meet him—not just yet. "I want to surprise him."

"We have a problem here then Sir," the guard leaned forward on the counter, "Mr. Reynolds does not like surprises."

Bill had hailed a cab and followed Dave and George from his restaurant that evening he was at SunDiegans. Dave had dropped off George at his house and driven to the apartment building where he had lived. It was almost one am in the morning, and Bill was drained from the events of the day. He had decided to call it a night.

However, he returned the next day to confirm where Dave lived. He had so much to converse with Dave. After all it was Dave who had so meticulously planned the fire to make it look like an accident and destroyed all that Bill held dear to his heart.

Bill shrugged, "Brown, my name is Jack Brown. Look, I know you are just doing your job and I respect that. Now does Dave Reynolds live here or not?"

"He does, Mr. Brown, but you can't meet him here," the guard said.

"Why's that?" Bill asked.

"He left for Vegas early this morning," the guard grinned. "Your friend has come up in the world, Sir. He runs a casino in Vegas—I'm sure you knew that."

"Um-no," Bill stammered. "He owns a casino now?"

"You betcha," the guard laughed. "His casino is just off the Strip. The man has struck gold, I mean almost literally."

"How wonderful," Bill said after a moment's pause. "This is very good for him. Does he stay in the casino when he's there or does he have a house there?"

"You'll find him in his casino, Mr. Brown," the guard said. "Why build a house when you can have all the luxuries in your own casino? It is quite a neat place, you should see for yourself."

"Hmm…I'll surprise him in his own turf," Bill grinned. "Does he come back here often?"

"He does come back almost every other Tuesday or Wednesday, stays for a couple of days and heads back to Vegas. The money is obviously good, but I guess he loves to come back to San Diego as well," the guard chuckled.

Bill asked for directions to Dave's casino, thanked the guard and left. He had considered that Dave might be living in a different city but never expected him to live in a populated place such as a casino—that complicated things.

He walked back to his motel—his mind vigorously working to readjust his plan. He desperately needed a vehicle to move around, but with an expired license he knew he could not just walk into a car dealership and buy one. He did not want to renew his license—that just meant added exposure. They would ask him for his residence address and he had none. He did not intend to have one anyway. He had to find another way to find a vehicle that did not attract unnecessary attention.

He picked up a newspaper and a sandwich from a nearby thrift store and walked into the lobby of his motel. The man in the front desk waved at him, "Good afternoon Simon. How's life treating you today?"

"Can't complain Kurt," Bill had registered himself as Simon Parks at the motel. The accommodations were rather modest and the clerk did not ask too many questions, especially to a customer who paid for everything upfront in cash. Low key was what Bill was looking for and the motel suited him well.

He flipped over to the classified section in the newspaper and scanned through the advertisements in the automobiles section. He circled a few of them and finished his sandwich. He ripped out the sheet and walked over to the telephone booth down the street.

He dialed the first number and waited. Someone picked up on the third ring. "Talk to me," the voice started gruffly.

Bill brushed aside his surprise and said, "I'm looking at an ad in the newspaper today in the automobiles section."

"Yeah, what about it?" the person apparently did not care about any pleasantries.

"Well, is it still available for me to come and take a look?" Bill asked patiently.

"Yup, she's still here. When are you coming?" the voice asked.

"How about in an hour from now—will you be around?" Bill asked.

"Boy, you're in a hurry! Yeah, I'm going nowhere," the man chuckled,

"I'm Johnny, who are you?"

"Simon, Simon Parks," Bill said.

"One hour, Mr. Parks," even this man had some politeness, "I'll keep her dressed up for you. Let me give you my address."

Bill had gotten used to the bus lines in the area. He was at the mercy of the bus timings, but they took him where he wanted and the drivers never complained about his company. The buses were empty most of the time anyway, so they welcomed short conversations with Bill. Moreover, he never bothered looking at the route maps—the drivers gave him the right directions anyway. He did not have to wait long at the stop. A bus came along after a few minutes and Bill hopped on.

When the bus dropped him off at the nearest stop to the address, Bill looked around himself. It did not seem to be a very affluent neighborhood. He followed directions and arrived at the address he was given. He walked past a vehicle parked on the driveway with the 'For sale' sign placed on the window. Bill had to knock on the door a few times before he heard footsteps and a man opened the door.

"Johnny?" Bill asked.

"Yeah, are you Simon Parks?" Johnny asked.

"That's me. Did I catch you at a bad time?" Bill asked.

"Don't worry about it," Johnny brushed the question aside. "That's the car I advertised. It runs very well, you will be very happy with it."

"I'm sure I will," Bill parried. "How much exactly are you asking for it?"

"Eight thousand dollars will make me happy. I put in new tires last month and had the brakes replaced. I received several calls this morning from people interested to buy," years of training had taught Bill to detect when a person was lying—Johnny clearly was.

"Looks like a hot item then. How long have you owned it?" Bill asked.

"Let's see," he paused. "Just about six years now," Johnny seemed to be a compulsive liar.

"I'm guessing you have the title paperwork to this vehicle, correct?" Bill asked. "I'll need that to transfer the title over to my name."

"Oh yes, no problem," Johnny's eyes lit up with the hope that he was near to making his sale, since Bill did not flinch at the amount he had asked for. "Do you have the money with you?"

"I don't Johnny, not nearly half as that much" Bill saw the excitement simmer down. "But that is not a problem. I'd like to take it for a drive first. If I like it we can work on the price. Is that ok?"

"I guess," Johnny said. "I won't come down on the price and I need a decision in the next thirty minutes though. I have another interested party lined up to come and check it out. Let me get the keys for you. You have a driver license, I believe?"

"Of course," Bill said confidently, hoping that Johnny will not ask to see his license—it had long expired. "I'll check her out while you get the keys. Oh, by the way, don't forget to bring the title along as well."

Bill walked around the car. It was a nondescript gray in color and had a few scratches on the rear bumper. All four tires looked new as Johnny said—he did seem to speak the truth sometimes. The odometer showed a hundred thousand twenty six miles.

Johnny came by, locked his front door shut and tossed the keys over to Bill, "Here you go, give her a spin."

Bill got in. Johnny slid into the passenger seat and they rolled off. It was the first time in twenty six years that Bill drove a vehicle. The automatic transmission definitely helped in the driving.

"What do you think?" Johnny asked expectantly after they had driven around a while.

"Well, she's got over a hundred thousand miles, the wheel is not aligned properly and the upholstery has stains all over it. I think there is some engine work to do as well. I don't think this is worth the amount you are asking for," Bill said.

"You did not expect a brand new car did you Mr. Parks," Johnny asked.

"No, I didn't," Bill said—actually the car drove well enough for its age and would definitely serve that purpose he wanted it for. "But this isn't worth that kind of money."

"No problem," Johnny was irritated. "Why don't we get back to my place right away? There are several parties who are interested," he wasn't sure if he did the right thing, since the woman and the man who had called in earlier that morning had already passed up on his offer.

"Look, you and I both know there aren't any parties who will be interested or have been interested," Bill glanced at Johnny and took a calculated guess. "So let's stop kidding, ok? Tell you what, I'll pay you cash right away and take this off your hands. Let me drive this to my bank so that I get a better feel of the controls. If I like it, I'll withdraw the money from the bank and pay you five thousand dollars and a little extra for you to catch a cab home. Is that ok with you?"

Johnny considered the prospect. He had been trying to sell the car for over a month now and the creditors were making things more and more difficult for him. The best offer he had got in the past was four thousand dollars. This was a better offer without a doubt. "You are killing me, Mr. Parks. That is three thousand dollars below what I expected. I can't do this," Johnny looked outside the window nervously biting on his nails.

Bill caught the body language and smiled to himself—Johnny will eventually come around, he was certain. "All right, Johnny," Bill said, "I'm not familiar to the neighborhood, can you give me directions to get back to your place?"

Johnny quietly directed Bill through the turns and made up his mind,

"How about another five hundred dollars? I have some backed up bills to pay, so I am in a tight spot, you know?" he sounded defeated.

Bill thought for a while, "Did you say your house was the next turn on the right?" he ignored the offer.

"Yes," Johnny was becoming nervous. "So you can't come up with another five hundred dollars?"

Bill frowned and shook his head, "Sorry, finances are tight with me as well."

"All right," Johnny gave up, "let's get this over and done with. You are getting a very good deal on this vehicle."

"I guess it's mutual and that's why I am still talking to you, my friend," Bill shook hands with Johnny.

The transaction went smoothly as expected. Bill withdrew the money from the bank, walked over to the post office and purchased money orders in various denominations totaling five thousand one hundred dollars.

"You could have just given me a cashier's check from the bank you know?" Johnny was surprised at the manner in which Bill made the payment—it seemed too complicated for him.

"Oh, those guys charge me a lot of money to write cashier's checks—this is much cheaper. There you go, take that to any post office and you'll have your money. I'll register the transfer of the title over to my name right away at the DMV," Bill reviewed the document to ensure that Johnny had signed all the appropriate places for the release of ownership on the title of the vehicle.

Johnny left and Bill got inside the car, shut the door and analyzed the events of the day. He covered his tracks well enough. The bank account will show the amount that he withdrew but there was no record anywhere of what the money was for. He looked at the title and put it away in the glove compartment. He had no intention of transferring the title over to his name.

He had the legal paperwork to substantiate his ownership if needed. If his plates were ever researched it would still come up as registered to Johnny, which will divert the attention away—at least for a while.

Bill drove up to a service station and asked for a complete check up and tuning service for the vehicle. He needed the vehicle to be in top condition. While the mechanics attended to his car, Bill walked over to the adjacent thrift store and picked up a few souvenir California license plates. He was going to need them in the days to come.

He walked over to the phone booth, thumbed through the yellow pages, called a motel and made reservations to stay. He was going to check out of the motel he was staying at and move over to another place. He owned a car now and he had no intention of revealing that to the meddlesome owner of the motel where he had been staying so far. He needed to remain under cover as much as possible, if he had any shot at carrying out his plans. Bill was trying to meticulously cover his tracks.

11

"Most certainly, Jack," Bill wasn't going to let the opportunity pass without taking action. He cleanly caught the keys that his supervisor tossed out to him and picked up the well known duffel bag with the well known initials engraved in gold letters on the outside. He nodded at his supervisor and headed for the parking lot. Finally he was getting somewhere.

He turned around to ensure that nobody was watching, took a small detour, reached above a pillar, removed a small bag and continued towards the space where the boss always parked his car.

He reached the vehicle parked in a space that was clearly marked with red lines. The nearest parking space was about fifty feet away in either direction. The gleaming sports car that was parked there certainly had an attitude.

Bill walked around the vehicle and marveled at the sleek body shape and the perfect lines that flowed gracefully bumper to bumper. Those Italians sure built these toys with passion and there was definitely a market for such cars—exclusively for the richly endowed of course.

He clicked on the button on the keychain and the trunk opened up smoothly with a silent hiss of the hydraulics. Bill peered inside and examined the space—it was larger than he had expected on a luxury sports car. He played around with the trunk door latch, satisfied with what he saw and shut it down.

He walked over to the driver's side and tugged on the door handle. The wing door smoothly opened up, revealing the plush leather interior. Bill sat down on the driver's seat and could not help but grin at the exquisite sophistication of the interior. Controls and dials started on the T-roof and came all the way down to the console beside him—almost like an aircraft. Never in his life had he ever thought that he would ever find himself behind the wheel of such a machine.

Bill sighed and closed his eyes—it was a big day for him. He clasped his hands together and prayed, "My Father in Heaven. You will never forgive me from this day onwards and I know that. You have given me the strength and the courage to stay alive for all these years and for everything I am eternally grateful. However, we must part ways now, because what I am about to start is against your will and I know that—but then I am only human."

He sat there with his head hung down preparing himself for the days to come. It was almost seven weeks since he had arrived in Las Vegas and approached the casino management for a job. Fortunately for Bill, two positions for a janitor and one position for a valet were available. Bill had opted for the valet position.

The forged California license that he presented indicated his name as Daniel Smith living in Tahoe, California. He cooked up a story that his doctor recommended that he needed to relocate to a drier place for health reasons, which was why he moved to Vegas. The management had approved his employment at a little over the permissible minimum wage limit with the provision of a raise in six months if he performed his duties well.

Over the course of the past six weeks Bill had seen Dave several times in the casino, but Dave spent most of his time inside. He lived in the penthouse at the highest floor which could be accessed only though a particular elevator. The penthouse floor was not even marked on the elevator panel. Rather a security swipe card was the only way to make the elevator go up to the penthouse. Every day the cleaning lady would be accompanied by a security guard to the penthouse to complete her job. The security guard accompanied every room service order that was placed from the penthouse. Dave had indeed built a fortress around himself.

Bill had learned that Dave traveled to San Diego every other Tuesday or Wednesday based on his work schedules. He preferred to leave around six o'clock in the evening, so that he could get to his apartment in San Diego before midnight.

The chances of failure of his plans were so high that to the common mind, it would border on insanity. But then Bill had gone way past having a common mind—desperate times needed desperate measures. He rehearsed as best as he could and waited for the opportunity to arrive. He missed out on the last two occasions when all he could do was watch Dave drive away and disappear in the heavy traffic. But that opportunity finally came by and Bill was not going to let it pass.

He picked up his radio and flicked the switch to activate the transmitter, "Jack come in, Jack come in please," he repeated.

"Jack here, is that you Dan?" the radio crackled.

"Yes, Jack, Dan here," Bill hurried, "I have a bit of a problem here, Jack. I am feeling a little light headed and dizzy—I think I will go home right away. I am at the boss' car right now. Can you please come by and drive it to the front? I'm not feeling too confident to drive a beauty like this when I am not sure I'm feeling ok. You wouldn't want me to throw up in his car would you?"

"Heck no," the supervisor's voice boomed. "Hang in there man, I'll send Tom to drive it to the front," the supervisor directed.

"All right, I think I'll rush to the bathroom, I may be throwing up anytime now. I'll leave the keys in the car," Bill had urgency in his voice.

"Wait, don't leave the key in the…" Jack could not finish his sentence. Bill cut him off on purpose and switched the radio off.

He left the keys in the ignition, opened the trunk, climbed in and settled down in as comfortable a position as was possible in that confined space.

He did not have to wait for long. The sound of running footsteps grew louder every moment and Bill heard the unmistakable hiss as the hydraulics eased the door open on the driver side. The healthy sound of the engine starting needed no guesswork about the power beneath the hood and the car eased into reverse gear.

Soon the car stopped and the wing door hissed open again.

"Good evening Sir, her tank's full and she's ready to whisk you away," Bill heard the valet's voice.

"Is my bag in the trunk?" it wasn't difficult to recognize Dave's officious voice.

"I'm sure it is, Sir, let me check it for you anyway," the valet said.

Bill pushed himself as far behind as he could towards the back of the trunk and pushed the duffel bag as far in the front as possible.

The trunk door hissed open and Bill peered outside. It was dark enough and his dark clothing would not be so easily detected, especially since his presence was not expected.

The valet caught sight of the bag when it was less than half open and said, "Yes Sir, it's right here, should I bring it in front for you?"

"No, just leave it there, thanks," Dave called out.

The valet shut the trunk door and Bill heard the engine start with the controlled roar. The driver's side door hissed shut and the car was in motion.

A few turns later, Bill realized that they were on the freeway—the din of evening downtown traffic was unmistakable. He knew he had another thirty minutes at the most before the oxygen in the trunk would run out and in the air would start to become foul. He focused on the situation and hoped that the traffic would start to move faster soon.

Fifteen minutes had passed and Bill realized that the traffic has thinned out. Dave was enjoying his time behind the wheel. He had his stereo on and some band was bringing down the house. It sounded more like cacophony to Bill. The car seemed to handle very well and the suspension made it a little easier on Bill in his cramped position. It wasn't still time to act. Bill took shorter breaths and held it longer before he exhaled. Every bit of oxygen in that trunk was worth his life.

Bill let another fifteen minutes pass and realized from the speed of the vehicle that they were on the open freeway. There wasn't too much traffic to worry about. The air inside was indeed getting foul. He groped for the trunk release lever, found it and pressed it open. The hydraulics kicked in and the trunk door started to open. Bill saw the receding lights of the city of Primm fade away in the distance and realized that Dave must have had a lead foot. The fresh air gushed in and Bill graciously filled his lungs with the cool evening air.

Bill knew that the dashboard would indicate to Dave that the trunk was open and he would stop. But Dave showed no signs of slowing down—maybe he did not notice. It worked in Bill's favor because he wanted to go a little further before taking any further action. He held on to the opening trunk door that had opened just a few inches.

The hydraulics groaned in protest. After some effort Bill managed to pull the door down and heard the click of the latch. However air was still coming in, which meant that the door did not shut completely. He hoped that the dashboard light about the open trunk had turned off—it wasn't time to act just yet.

Bill lay down on the trunk floor and took some deep breaths. He was feeling a little tired in his arms. Soon he felt gravity trying to slide him towards the rear of the trunk, which meant that Dave was climbing the upslope. He did not seem to slow down and the car obliged effortlessly. After another fifteen minutes had passed and Bill realized that they were leveling out. This meant that they would start on the downwards gradient of the freeway very soon. He waited till he felt the tilt of gravity towards the front of the car and clicked the trunk door latch open. This time he let it open all the way up. He knew that would block Dave's rearview mirror and he would have to stop.

Just as he had predicted, Dave started to slow down. Bill checked outside. It was pitch dark and traffic was extremely light. Nobody was going faster than Bill anyway. Everything was going according to plan for Bill.

He reached inside the small bag that he had retrieved from his secret cubbyhole in the casino parking lot and prepared himself to confront Dave. The moment that he had been waiting for all those years had finally arrived.

Dave pulled over the side of the road and engaged his parking brakes. Bill slid out of the trunk and silently moved to the right of the car. He saw the wing doors on Dave's side slide up and Dave stepped outside the vehicle, cursing the valet. The man was definitely irritated at the carelessness of the valet, who apparently did not shut the trunk door properly. Dave came to the back of the car, grabbed the trunk door and almost banged it shut. The cursing did not show any signs of stopping any moment soon.

He was about to get back to his seat when a voice boomed in the silent darkness, "Hello Dave, good to see you again," Bill held a steady voice.

"What the bloody hell? Who is that?" Dave was visibly startled and he whirled around in the direction of the voice. He held his hands up to shield his eyes from the bright glare of the torch that shone directly into them.

"There's a loaded Beretta just below this light Dave and it is ready to taste some rotten blood," Bill's voice was cold. "Shut the engine, close that door and come around slowly to this side. If I were you, I would ask before I even thought about batting my eyelids. No funny moves, Dave. I am pretty good with this gun."

The Beretta had been a friend for the past thirty years. Bill had left that gun along with several magazines in the bank locker along with all his paperwork. He was relieved to find it still there when he finally got access to his locker after this release from prison. Bill had cleaned it up, tested it and was satisfied. It worked just fine, what did not work as well was his aim. Lack of practice and his age had its toll on his shooting skills but as long as he remembered the basics of shooting, he felt that he could still get his target.

"I can't believe this. What's this, robbery on the high roads? Who are you and what the hell do you want?" Dave shouted.

"At the moment, I want you to shut the engine, close the door and come over to this side of the car. I won't repeat this another time," Bill said in a no-nonsense voice.

Dave wondered if the shivers down his spine were from the menacing tone of the voice or the cool desert breeze that came down from the mountains.

Dave walked over to the door and took his chance. He had left the engine running so he felt that he could just make a fast getaway. His movements were too sharp which made it clear to Bill that Dave was in no mood to comply with his instructions.

The Beretta delivered its first payload at twelve hundred feet per second and did not have to travel more than six feet before it found its mark. Dave's yelped out in sheer pain as his right shoulder jerked back and the top of the humerus bone shattered at the impact.

"Next time it is your head, Dave," the voice meant serious business. "Now that your right arm is useless, close that door and walk over to this side like a good boy."

The pain was getting more and more unbearable by the second. Dave shut the driver's side door and stumbled over to the right side of the car. The headlights revealed that he was bleeding profusely. With his torch, Bill motioned Dave to walk down into the ditch beside the freeway and he obeyed reluctantly. Bill opened the passenger door, shut the engine, pocketed the keys and switched the headlights off.

Some headlights showed up in the distance and a few cars whizzed by engulfing them once again in complete darkness in the moonless night. Bill had switched his torch off, so that he wouldn't attract undue attention from the passing vehicles. When he switched his torch back on, Dave wasn't where he was supposed to have been. However the trail of blood gave him away. Dave hoped a miracle would happen and he could stumble his way back to Vegas with his shattered and bleeding arm.

Bill caught up with Dave and pushed him down on the ground. Dave practically collapsed on his knees. He was in obvious pain and bleeding rather profusely. Bill wondered if the bullet had hit the brachial or the axillary artery.

"Please don't hurt me. Who are you and what do you want?" Dave was gasping for breath. "I need medical attention urgently, please help me get to a doctor. I'll give anything you want, just name it," he managed to say between breaths.

"Can you really?" Bill squatted down before him. "Can you really give me anything I want? Who do you think you are? God?" the menace in the voice surely did not help Dave ease his pain.

"Just name it man, just name your price and it's yours," Dave tried to let out a scream that was drowned by the whizzing roar of a passing car on the freeway above.

"Very well then, I want to see Joan McMillan and her parents alive. I want to know where Anita McMillan is and oh, before I forget, I want William McMillan to be reunited with his family. I want his life restored back to what it was twenty six years ago. You know, what I am talking about, don't you Dave?" Bill had the light from his torch on Dave's face. "Give all of that back and I will carry you on my back to the nearest doctor and walk away from your life."

Bill watched the expression on Dave's face change from pain to fear like he had never felt before. Horror showed in Dave's eyes, the worst of his concerns had finally come true and he was all alone to fend for himself. The pain made things worse and the gushing blood was making him weaker by the minute.

"L-Lieutenant McMillan?" Dave managed to stammer.

"No, that guy died twenty six years ago, you and your friends saw to that," Bill said sarcastically. "I am just Simon Parks, or is it Daniel Smith or let me think—maybe I am William McMillan who was released from prison a couple of months back. Tell you what I'll have you look at me and let you decide who I really am."

Bill placed the torch below his chin with the beam shining upwards on his face, "It looks eerie does it not, you son of a bitch? You destroyed my life and all that I held dear to my heart. All these years in prison I had only one goal in my mind and that was to see you and your friends in the situation that I see you now. I wanted to see you helpless, fatally wounded and having a candid conversation with you while life slowly ebbs out of your filthy body."

"It wasn't my fault," Dave ventured in desperation.

"Maybe it wasn't but you know what, its too late, you lying bastard. Do you know why you are bleeding that badly Dave? Your axillary artery has been severed," Bill said softly. "You know, that artery has a direct connection with your heart through the aorta. So every time your heart beats, it pushes more and more blood out of your body. You must be feeling very tired by now, aren't you? Do you feel life slipping away from your body? You are finding it difficult to focus aren't you? My face is blurring with every passing second, is it not Dave? Do you now feel what it means to die slowly? That was exactly how my wife and her parents felt when your artwork slowly took their lives. I want you to suffer like they suffered, Dave. I want you to feel just like they felt."

Bill removed a bottle from his little satchel and sprinkled gasoline over Dave's body and removed a lighter from his pocket.

"Oh God," Dave tried to scream in anticipation of what was coming, "please don't do that."

"Did you care twenty six years ago when you were burning my family alive? Did you?" he repeated. "Wait don't answer me, I already know you didn't. Well, if that was the case, tell me why I should care about a scumbag like you? Goodbye Dave."

The flame from the lighter turned Dave's body into an instant blaze as Bill watched him scream and flail about in a desperate attempt to douse the fire. His movements were sluggish and irregular and eventually he collapsed on the ground and resigned himself to eternal sleep.

Bill calmly sat in a distance and watched the flame burn itself out and darkness enveloped the surroundings once again. The stench from the burning flesh was revolting, but Bill did not seem to care. Tears rolled down his eyes. He imagined Joan making a futile attempt to save herself and Anita from the flames and crying for help that never came on time. Seeing Dave burn alive, he could picture how much Joan had suffered. He wept uncontrollably. It was quite a gory sight to witness.

A few vehicles zoomed by on the freeway above showing no signs of stopping. Maybe they thought that it was a camping party who had lit the fire. Bill wondered if anyone ever cared for anything but themselves anymore.

12

"In a developing story since yesterday afternoon, Mr. Dave Reynolds a prominent businessman and successful casino owner in Las Vegas has been reported missing. The spokesperson from the Las Vegas Metropolitan Police Department stated that his Italian sports car was found abandoned in a parking lot of a shopping mall in Mesquite, a small town north of Las Vegas," the newscaster reported. "Mr. Reynolds who owns a thriving casino just off the famous Las Vegas Strip had been reported missing for the last six days. He was last seen driving away from his casino in his vehicle last Tuesday evening. Casino officials say that Mr. Reynolds was headed for a routine trip to San Diego where he owns an apartment. Nobody has heard from him for the last six days."

Josh and Brant were seated together in Brant's apartment with their eyes glued to the television screen. Dave always got together with Brant at a minimum when he was in town and he was indeed six days overdue. The fact that they both lived in the same apartment building, made it easier to catch up.

"At the request of the casino management team, the LVMPD has authorized our channel to show you a photograph of Mr. Reynolds," the newscaster's image was replaced by the image of a smiling Dave. "If anyone has any information about Mr. Reynolds please dial the toll-free number at the bottom of his photograph. The LVMPD is continuing their search and has been working with the Nevada Highway Patrol and other county law enforcement agencies in an effort to determine the whereabouts of Mr. Reynolds."

"Elsewhere in the world…" Brant muted the television audio and said, "I don't like it at all. That is so unlike Dave to just take off like that. He did not have any trips planned and he was headed back here like he always did. Even if he did go away somewhere, why would he leave his car in Mesquite of all places? I'm worried Josh, I really am. Something just does not smell right!"

Josh listened in silence and the concern in his expression was evident. Brant was right—it was quite unlike Dave. Something was very wrong and it frustrated him. "Let's give it another day and I will start making some calls," Josh was deeply concerned.

"I know this is hard, but quite candidly, I would not rule out the possibility of foul play," Brant said watching the television with unseeing eyes. "We both know he picked up a generous collection of enemies on the way. I wonder if this is some act of revenge."

Josh looked at him thoughtfully for a while and said, "You may be right and I admit I am almost inclined to agree with you. But he was last seen driving away in his car headed for San Diego before he disappeared. If it was an act of revenge, why would his car not have any damage and why on earth would it be found in Mesquite? The Dave Reynolds' of the world never go grocery shopping or casino hopping, my friend. It puzzles me Brant and we must prepare for the worst."

"What if…" Brant cut himself off and hurriedly reached for the remote control when he saw the newsflash on the television. The caption said 'Reynolds disappearance update'. He turned up the volume and the news-caster's voice came on.

"We have just received news that the California Highway Patrol has found the badly charred and disfigured remains of a body on a ditch beside southbound Interstate Fifteen. Whoever it was apparently did not die peace-fully. The CHP thinks that the person might have been burnt alive based on their assessment of the crime scene. We have received pictures from our local correspondent. However due to the graphic nature of these images we will not be showing them to our viewers. The CHP found a gold Rolex watch with the initials DR engraved on the band among the rocks nearby. This leads us to believe it might have been the missing Dave Reynolds. Forensic experts are trying to determine the identity of the person from whatever still remains of the body of the deceased. CHP reports that they found a bullet lodged inside the skeletal remains of the body. This leads the CHP to believe that the man was shot before being torched. At this time, no arrests have been made and the authorities are investigating as we speak. For those viewers who are joining us just now, Mr. Reynolds' Italian sports car was found abandoned in a shopping mall in Mesquite, a small town north of Las Vegas this morning, which is almost a hundred miles away from where the CHP found the charred remains of a human body. Till confirmed otherwise, we must consider that Mr. Reynolds is still alive. He is a prominent businessman in Las Vegas and owns a flourishing casino. We will keep you updated as more information comes into our newsroom."

"I knew it, I just knew it," Brant turned the television off.

"Keep it on Brant, but just keep it in mute," Josh said calmly. "I know how you are feeling and trust me, my friend, I feel no better. Put the television on mute and let's talk."

The video showed up on the screen again and Brant said, "You seem too relaxed Josh."

"When was the last time you saw me flip out in trying situations?" Josh replied calmly. "Unnecessary excitement never did any good to anybody, my friend. The rush of adrenaline like the one you are having now will always overpower your natural rationality and make you do stupid things. So calm down and let's figure this out."

The authority in the voice seemed to take effect. Brant sipped on his martini and pushed himself down into the comfortable recesses of his plush sofa.

"So we know that Dave is probably dead and if he really is, he has been murdered. Burnt alive, they said—that is horrifying," Josh paced the room and analyzed what he had just seen and heard. "I can understand why the killer would choose a spot like that to kill the victim, but what puzzles me is why Dave's car would be found in Mesquite of all places."

"Maybe the killer had no interest in the car—he just wanted to get rid of Dave," Brant ventured.

"Put yourself in the shoes of the killer," Josh said, "how would you get hold of Dave in the first place when he was in his car? You would have to stop him and confront him first, correct? Well, we know about Dave's lead foot especially when he is in that speed demon of a sports car on an open freeway at night. So the killer could possibly not have outmaneuvered Dave. Dave had no reason to go to Mesquite where his car was found with absolutely no damage to it, so the killer could not have confronted Dave in Mesquite. It had to be elsewhere."

"Where are you going with this Josh?" Brant asked anxiously.

"I'm just thinking aloud and trying to make some sense out of all this," Josh paused and frowned. "So if I am the killer, I would have to know Dave very well and be able to predict his movements. I would have to know what Dave did, where he went, what his regular habits were. I would have to study Dave for a while before I could come up with a plan and make my move. I would have watched and waited for the right opportunity and would possibly have had some failed attempts before I finally found the right time to strike."

"You're getting somewhere, Josh," Brant commented, "keep going."

"Dave had left his casino at the same time that he always did when he used to make his San Diego trip," Josh was unknowingly speaking in the past tense and did not seem to have heard Brant speak. "He could have had a prior appointment before his trip. But then it takes five hours to get here and we know Dave hates to stay awake beyond midnight. So he could not have had a prior appointment way north in Mesquite and then turned around for his trip down here. Essentially I don't think he ever went to Mesquite."

"A leopard never loses his spots," Brant remarked at the manner in which Josh was analyzing the facts in hand. He used to do this for a living when he served the SDPD.

"What was that?" Josh was surprised at Brant's apparently unrelated comment.

"I was referring to you, Josh," Brant gave a wry smile. "Once a cop, always a cop is what I really meant. You still have not lost your analytical skills on such matters even after all these years. That is commendable."

Josh grinned at the comment, "So I am the killer and I need to force Dave to stop on an open freeway what would I be doing? I would have to create a situation where Dave would have no option but to either go somewhere else where I wanted him to go or to pull over from the freeway so that I could have a private conversation with him. That leaves me, the killer, only one option. I have to be in Dave's car and with him all the time right when he left the casino."

"But his car was a two-seater so it is impossible for someone to sneak in beside Dave without his knowledge. He always had his tank filled before he made this trip, so he could not have stopped for gas either," Brant caught on with Josh in the line of questioning.

"Exactly," Josh agreed. "So I, the killer had to be with him right when he got into his car at his casino entrance. That means that Dave would know me very well and would have invited me to accompany him to San Diego."

"Right, so all we have to do is figure out who was with him when he left the casino," Brant seemed to have found daylight in the darkness.

"You should stick to the courtroom my friend," Josh laughed. "If I was the killer, do you think I would be so stupid to get in the car with Dave when the whole world was watching in front of his own casino? I would have a hundred witnesses lined up on my door the next morning after the cops found the dead body. Are you following me?"

"I-I guess, you are right," Brant looked crestfallen.

"So, I, the killer could not have been in the car beside Dave when he left the casino," Josh continued to pace in front of the muted television. "But I know I have to be in the car in order to force Dave to stop on the way. Now I know that Dave has a two-seater—that leaves me only one possible place to hide—the trunk."

"Hide in the trunk?" Brant repeated. "Sports cars don't have much space in their trunks."

"Exactly, although you'd be surprised at the generous space in the trunk of Dave's sports car—it is quite a clever design," Josh was on a roll. "So if I had to hide in the trunk I would not be a person the size of our George. I would have to be a short enough person who could squeeze towards the front of the car and hope to remain undetected. I would be wearing dark clothes, knowing very well that by the time Dave left the casino, night would have fallen. Unless someone was over cautious, I would not even be noticed," he paused. "Actually I remember opening Dave's trunk on one occasion, there is a recessed space where a five feet tall person can easily get in and hide."

"Oh my goodness!" Brant exclaimed.

"So I'm in the trunk now and Dave is tearing the freeway apart," Josh continued. "I know that my oxygen would eventually run out in the confined space, and I am relieved that Dave was driving fast. This works well for me because I know that I would be able to quickly get to a point, where traffic would be light. I would have to do something to force Dave to pull over. When he did stop, I could spring a surprise and catch Dave off guard. Now there are two important things for me consider. First, how would I know that I have reached a suitable spot to spring my surprise on Dave? Second, what would I do that would leave no other option for Dave but to pull over?"

"I have a feeling you are going to tell me," Brant encouraged.

"I don't know Brant, this is where it fades off a little," Josh picked up his glass and flushed some martini down his throat. "I could be smart enough to make an educated guess on how fast Dave was driving, look at my watch, figure out how long I was on the road and calculate the distance that I had traveled so far. I know the freeway and the terrain it passes through. I know how empty and lifeless the surroundings are after it goes beyond Primm. When I know I have traveled far enough, and the air in the trunk started to become foul, I would realize that I will have to act. But what can I do to force Dave to stop when I am locked out in the trunk?"

"You would pop the trunk from the inside. Not only would the trunk open lid pop up, Dave's rear view would be blocked by the open trunk and he would have to stop to shut it back down," Brant did not bother to contain his excitement.

"My friend, there is still some hope for you," Josh grinned and almost instantly became serious. "So I make Dave pull over, spring my surprise on Dave, who would definitely be taken off guard. I would probably have a little chit chat with him and then do him in. That is how I would have done it, Brant, if of course I was the killer," Josh emptied his glass.

"If I did not know you any better, I would have thought you really were the killer," Brant nodded slowly with a faraway look, "I think it happened exactly as you described. But who do you think will be so desperate and brutal to kill a man that way? Of course we did not know everyone that Dave interacted with in his life, but he may have told you something about his enemies."

"I was thinking the same, Brant," Josh pondered. "A man in his position would have enemies no doubt, but I can't think of anyone who would take such drastic measures."

"What do we do now, Josh?" Brant asked.

"Stay tuned on the television for a while and see if they come up with a forensics report. Then we'll be sure if there is positive ID or not and take it from there," Josh said picking up his jacket. "I'll head back home now and retire for the night. Too much of excitement for one day, I guess. Let's get together tomorrow and figure out what we can do about this. See you later Brant," he opened and shut the entry door behind him.

He pushed the elevator call button and waited. Josh felt tired and he was increasingly beginning to believe that it was indeed Dave's remains that the CHP had found. There was too much coincidence in the circumstances. He looked up to check where the elevator was—the light was illuminated at the fifteenth floor. It still had a few more floors to come up to the twenty sixth where Brant had his penthouse.

He leaned on the opposite wall and watched the lights change from floor to floor and then he became instantly alert. He stared at the number twenty-six and realized what that meant. He suddenly knew it, everything seemed to fall in place and he was certain that there could be no other explanation for Dave's disappearance.

He rushed back to Brant's door and knocked urgently. After four knocks Brant opened the door and asked jokingly, "Did you forget your car keys in here or something?"

Josh brushed past him and pushed the door shut leaving a bewildered Brant gaping. Josh grabbed the telephone and dialed a number. He waited for someone to receive his call and said, "I would like to speak to George Briggs urgently. This is Senator Timmons speaking."

He listened for a while and asked, "Are you sure he returned back from his trip to Mexico today?"

He listened again and asked, "I see. Do you know if he went straight home or not?"

He nodded, thanked the person on the other side and replaced the receiver. He dialed another number and waited—the voicemail responded. He waited patiently for the recording to end and spoke, "Hello Mr. Briggs, this is Senator Timmons. I am sorry to call you at home. I called your restaurant and they gave me your number. I urgently need to host a party in your restaurant this coming Sunday, which is two days from now. I would like to discuss the details over with you as soon as possible. Can you please come to my office first thing tomorrow morning? Please treat this as extremely urgent, Mr. Briggs and I cannot stress enough," he disconnected, sat down on Brant's couch and buried his head in his hands.

Brant had heard the conversations and waited patiently for Josh to explain. "This really isn't about some party, correct?" he asked.

"Brant, do you know what month and year this is?" Josh asked.

"Y-yes, of course, what kind of a question is that?" Brant was trying to solve the riddle.

"Twenty six years have passed, since we put away William McMillan. Are you still with me?" Josh asked.

Realization dawned on Brant and his eyes opened wide, "Oh my God? You think it is him?"

"What do you think?" Josh asked. "I can't believe the possibility never came to our minds. Twenty six years ago we had decided to deal with him conclusively when he would be released from prison. I'll check it out in the morning, but our carelessness might have cost us Dave's life. I told you about the controlled hatred I had seen in the man's eyes when I saw him last. If he is out, he is going to seek his revenge and I think he just claimed his first victim very successfully."

"What does that mean for us Josh?" Brant asked nervously, "Can't you hunt him down? With your resources and connections it should not be too difficult to track him. Why don't you call the prison and ask about McMillan right away?"

"Call the prison warden at twelve am in the morning and ask about a prisoner that I put away twenty six years ago?" Josh was astonished at the request, "Can you even imagine how weird that sounds? A nightmare wakes a Senator up in the middle of the night and he has to find out right away if his worst enemy has been released from prison or not? Is that my story? Brant, you disappoint me," Josh ran his fingers through his hair.

"I'm nervous," Brant never really had been able to manage stress in his entire life—especially when his personal well-being was at risk.

"Times have changed, my friend and I am a public figure. I have to watch my step so that I don't get burnt in any way. Let me think about this and figure out a plan. For the moment, we need to be on our guard. I wanted to warn George as well right away. As you can understand we have to stay alert and watch what we are doing and where we are going."

"This is not good, Josh. I think we screwed up big time," Brant sounded depressed.

"I just hope I am wrong in my hypothesis. Come to think of it, Brant— I said earlier that the killer must have been hiding in Dave's trunk? Well, that would mean that the killer would also be slightly built and have a flexible enough body to squeeze into that crawlspace and still manage to be out of sight."

"Yes, that's how you analyzed it," Brant agreed.

"Well, if you remember, McMillan was just a little over five feet tall and was rather athletic in his days. Given that twenty six years have passed and age would have taken its toll on his physical flexibility, it would not have much of an effect on his size. Moreover age would have not have affected his sharp mind. As a matter of fact he could have become smarter over those years. I can't think of anything else that makes sense Brant. Six days have passed since he supposedly murdered Brant in such a gruesome manner and we knew nothing about it. I wonder what he has been up to for these days. The three of us need to be extra careful. If it is indeed him, he will be planning to strike again. You can bet on that."

Brant was about to answer when the subdued audio of the television indicated that there was another update on the Reynolds disappearance. He turned up the volume and the newscaster's voice came loud and clear, "In the developing story about the disappearance of Dave Reynolds, a prominent businessman in Las Vegas, CHP has just confirmed that the remains found earlier this evening alongside southbound Interstate fifteen was indeed those of Mr. Reynolds. Forensic tests performed on the charred remains of his body. Mr. Reynolds leaves behind a thriving casino in Las Vegas and has no heirs on record. We will update you on any other information that comes to our desk."

"He was a good friend," Josh murmured as memories of the past wandered into his mind. "Funny that a fireman should go this way—burnt alive in the middle of nowhere. We burnt McMillan's family alive and he is returning us the favor. All signs convince me that McMillan is responsible."

"I agree too that it is McMillan," Brant stared at the muted television. "If I was him who had lost everything that life had to offer and I knew who were responsible for my loss, I would come back for my revenge. Then if I had to choose where to strike first among the four of us, I'd choose Dave since it was his artwork that burnt most of my family and my house into ashes."

"Uh-huh," Josh nodded, "and if you were McMillan, you would continue to go to extreme lengths and take desperate measures to make peace with yourself by having your revenge against the three of the survivors."

"We screwed up man, we just got sloppy and fat on our comfortable lives," Brant made no effort to hide the frustration in his voice. "We should have tailed him the moment he was released from prison. If my calculations are right, he was released about two months ago," Brant sighed. "We have to tie this up right now, Josh. It could be any one of us any time. You know how resourceful he was in his heydays. If he did manage to get rid of Dave in the manner that you described, I think the three of us are living in a delusion of safety."

Josh nodded and stood up to leave, "Brant, I want you to stay home at least for the next couple of days. Cancel your hearings or whatever appointments you have. Whatever you do, don't leave your apartment and don't open the door to anyone. We are all in danger like you said, so don't take any chances. Is that clear?"

Brant nodded in agreement—he was visibly worried.

"I'll make some calls in the morning to get to the bottom of this. I wish I could get police protection for all of us, but that could trigger unnecessary attention," Josh said. "I may manage protection for myself and maybe for you as well, if I present my case properly. But I cannot do anything for George. I mean he is just a public citizen. Unless there is a proven threat, he cannot get police protection even if he owns fifteen restaurants in the area. He will have to get a personal bodyguard for himself. I'll talk to him when I see him tomorrow. Hang in there, we'll figure something out," Josh took his leave.

"You watch out for yourself, Josh," Brant said. "Are you sure you want to drive back home alone at this time of the night?"

Josh smiled, "Yeah, I think I'll manage. Lock this door and stay put for a while. I'll keep you posted on what I find out tomorrow."

He walked back to the elevator and pushed the button. He felt safe for the moment. He had figured out that he was not yet at risk from Bill. If his suspicions were correct, the next one in line would be George. It was George who had battened down all exits from Bill's house when it was burnt down. Josh had told that to Bill himself in his prison cell, not knowing at that time the true significance of that statement. Now that Dave was eliminated, George would be next in line.

The elevator came up and Josh got in. Playing the criminal mind had earned Josh many successes in the past and he never lost the skill. But he could not be sure who would be the next one in line—Brant or himself. They were both equally responsible for what had happened to Bill's life, so it could go either way.

Josh nodded at the security guard who snapped into attention when he emerged from the elevator. Josh had never seen the guard before and he instantly stiffened. He had the same height and build as Bill when Josh had seen him last. The hat that the guard wore hid most of his features. He gave Josh a friendly smile and said, "I am a big fan of yours Senator. You should run for President this time. Have a good night!"

Josh tried to smile and left the lobby for the stairs that went down to the underground parking lot. He had just set foot on the parking lot floor when the lights flickered and went out. It enveloped the space in pitch black darkness. Josh quickly pushed himself against the wall and listened intently for any sound. The drop of a pin would have sounded like a distant explosion in that confined space.

A chill ran down his spine as Josh feared the worst. He thought that his theory was completely incorrect. It wasn't George that Bill was after next. It was himself. He wondered from where the attack would come. He could see nothing and he could hear nothing. Senators never carried weapons, it frustrated Josh as he waited and listened.

The stairwell door above opened above and clanged shut and Josh heard the sound of steps that rushed down the stairs. The beam of a flashlight provided some illumination for Josh and he stepped behind the stairs to hide himself away from the view of the person descending the stairs.

"Senator? Senator Timmons, are you there?" the guard called out as the sound of steps grew louder and the flashlight grew brighter.

Josh stayed silent. He was right about the security guard, it was Bill trying to lure him out. Josh felt helpless—the rush of adrenaline made his heart beat faster.

The guard ran down the stairs and rushed towards a power panel. Josh could see that he opened the panel and inspected the circuit breakers. He reset the switch and the parking lot was flooded with light again.

"Senator?" the guard called out again and looked around the lot.

Josh slowly emerged from behind the stairs and stood behind the guard. He eventually turned around and saw Josh standing with his hands in his pockets.

"I'm sorry about that Senator," the guard had removed his hat so Josh could see his features. "We had the same problem twice this morning. Something's wrong with the circuit breaker, I think. The electrician can come only in the morning tomorrow. Can I get your car for you, Senator?"

"No, it's just there," Josh could feel the warmth returning to his palms. "Thanks for coming down to bring some light in here—the blackout got me worried."

He stepped into his car and glanced around to see the guard watching him from a distance. Josh did not know if it was paranoia or not, but the guard made him uneasy. Twenty six years could do a lot to a man's features. He wondered if there was a bomb planted in his car that would go off when he switched on the ignition. He groped beneath the dashboard trying to feel for anything unusual. There was nothing out of the ordinary. He popped the hood, stepped out of his car and lifted the hood all the way up. The insides looked perfectly normal. He pushed the hood shut and saw the guard standing about fifteen feet away from him.

"Is there a problem Senator?" the guard asked.

"I don't know," Josh shrugged. "The car would not start."

"Do you mind if I try?" the guard offered.

"Sure, here you go," Josh readily accepted the offer. If the bomb went off, it would kill the guard first. He tossed the keys over to the guard and walked back a few paces behind a couple of cars. If there was an explosion, Josh could easily duck for cover.

The guard got into the driver's seat and turned the ignition on. The engine responded instantly and settled down to a healthy hum. He pulled the car out of its space and reversed near to where Josh was standing. He got out of the car and held the door open for Josh, "There you go Senator, I think she's just fine," he handed the keys over.

"Well thank you very much," Josh smiled, "I'll have the battery checked tomorrow—the car should have started when I was trying a little while ago. Oh, well, thanks anyway. Good night to you."

"Good night Senator," the guard went back for the stairs.

Josh emerged from the parking lot and into the street—it was deserted at that time of the night. He headed for the freeway and contemplated on what just happened. Almost unknowingly he had been terrified for the first time in his life—the fear that he might be killed in the parking lot had gripped him like a vice and had affected his logical mind. In reality nothing unpleasant had happened, however he had acted as if something was indeed amiss. He thought that was stupid of him and quite unlike himself to react in the manner that he did.

If Bill was indeed out and had started his killing spree, he already had started to win the battle, even though on a psychological plane—this concerned Josh.

13

It was a long and tiring day for George. He was not an early riser, but he had to get up early in his oceanfront villa in Puerta Vallarta that morning. The direct flights to San Diego were booked to capacity all day and he was assured by the airline agent that there would be no cancellations. There was just that one seat left in business class in the first flight out of Ordaz International. He would have to stop over at Mexico City first, then into San Francisco before he could be connected to the final leg into San Diego.

The American news channel he had been watching the night before carried the news about Dave's disappearance and that bothered him. He remembered the last time he had met Dave in Las Vegas and how he was admonished for his carelessness. He knew that he had relaxed his guard and thought that Dave's reaction was justified. Dave was a good friend. He had always been more helpful and amicable than Josh or Brant ever was. Over the years he had begun to almost respect Dave.

Josh had strict directions that George should never call him or Brant for that matter from international numbers, which frustrated George to no end. Whenever George was out in Mexico, he was really out of touch from Josh and Brant. Josh was meticulous and at times paranoid about things. This was just one of the many instances where he had strictly forbidden George to make calls to his or Brant's office or home from Mexico.

George was desperate to know what happened to Dave when he learned about the disappearance and he knew that the only way he could know anything was to get back to San Diego. The cursing and irritation in his voice did not help George at all with the airline agent and he had reluctantly agreed to the circuitous route to get back home.

Storms in Mexico City and a baggage handling incident in San Francisco caused delays in the connecting flights. When he finally set foot on Lindbergh field around ten o'clock at night he was almost five hours behind the scheduled arrival time. George was practically at his wits' end. He picked up his car from the parking lot and was homebound within minutes.

He stopped over at his downtown restaurant much to the surprise of his staff, ordered a quick meal and headed home. The strong and hot coffee kept him from falling asleep at the wheel. He heaved a sigh of relief when he finally pulled up inside his garage. He disarmed the security system, collected his bags from the trunk of his car and shut the garage door.

George fumbled for his keys and opened the door that led into the house. He passed through and let the door shut behind him. The motion activated lights came on and he saw that his answering machine had eight messages waiting for him. He groaned, dropped his bags on the floor and trudged upstairs for his bedroom. He then realized that he could have a message from Josh or Brant in his machine. They never called him at home. This was another directive from Josh, but Dave's disappearance was not an everyday event.

He cursed out loud, trudged back to his answering machine and played the messages. The first seven messages were from telemarketers trying to sell him free vacations and credit cards. The fatigue was overwhelming and George cursed loudly. When the eighth message played, George snapped into attention.

Josh had left a message for him about fifteen minutes ago as the answering machine confirmed. He played it back several times, trying to figure out any hidden message on what Josh said. He had to meet Josh at this office in the morning to supposedly discuss a party in his restaurant in two days. That sounded unusual to George. If that really was the intention, Josh would have called his restaurant directly and would have been taken care of. His manager knew Josh very well as he was a frequent and a very important customer.

The urgency in the voice indicated that Josh had something more important to discuss rather than some party. George wondered if he should call Josh at home, but then decided against it. Contacts at home were strictly forbidden, but then Josh himself left a message for George at his home number. Something did not make sense to George, but then his body was still complaining about the fatigue. George decided to take it up in the morning.

He went upstairs, turned on the water for the Jacuzzi in his bathroom, undressed and poured himself a drink. He stepped into the Jacuzzi and let the warm swirling water soothe his aching body. He sipped on his drink, closed his eyes and stretched his hands out on the rim of the tub. Nothing like home, he thought and let the water perform its magic.

"Hello George," he never heard the voice at first, the swirling water was taking George to a different world and he was definitely falling asleep it the hot tub.

"Hello George," the voice repeated and George opened his eyes this time. Someone had switched off the main overhead light in the bathroom—only a low powered bulb from the shower cubicle offered a soothing ambience to the room.

"Who's there?" George was startled and in a reflex action his body stiffened. He peered into the semi-darkness in the direction of the voice.

"I see you are enjoying yourself in that hot tub of yours," the voice did not seem to have heard him. "I must commend you on your taste. I never knew you had such qualities. Those cars you have parked in your garage—they must have cost you a fortune. I walked around your house. It's very nice and you have decked it up very well."

"Just who the hell are you?" George shouted in the direction of the voice, "Why are the lights off?"

He started to get up from the tub but the cold urgency in the voice discouraged George, "If I were you I would stay exactly where you are. There's a hungry and loaded Beretta aimed straight at your head and trust me. I shoot well," George instinctively collapsed back into the Jacuzzi.

George knew he was in a very disadvantaged situation in the confined position that he was. He had no weapon handy and he knew that he could not move fast enough to beat a Beretta if it really was there.

"You lying bastard," George summoned some courage. "Get the lights on. Let me see who you are, bloody coward!"

The click of a switch illuminated the bathroom and George blinked at the sudden brightness. Indeed there was a man standing directly in front of him and he wasn't kidding—the Beretta did look menacing in his hands. He was a little over five feet tall with an average build. Long grey and black hair and a thick graying beard concealed most of his features. The man would be in his late sixties, as George guessed.

"Remember me George?" Bill said softly.

"Remember me—what are you talking about? I have never seen you old man. This must be a mistake and you've got the wrong guy, I'm afraid," George still wasn't thinking straight enough. He just wanted to get out of the hot tub and collapse in his bed.

"Wow, you have a very short memory then," Bill said sarcastically. "Especially when you built this house over the same rubble that you helped to create with your fireman friend," he watched color draining rapidly from George's face.

Bill had been waiting patiently for that day. After he had watched Dave die a violent death, he had driven his car back into Mesquite, a town north of Las Vegas near the Nevada-Arizona border. He had been careful not to leave any prints behind when he left the car that morning. He had felt a sense of accomplishment as the fresh morning breeze soothed his mind. Revenge or not, it was a gruesome experience to see a man being burnt alive, but Bill had felt no remorse. Visions of his beloved Joan desperately fighting a losing battle with the hungry flames kept coming back. It made Bill clench his teeth in anger.

He had boarded a bus and arrived at Las Vegas in the afternoon. He had walked the way to his apartment, packed his belongings and drove back in his car to San Diego to plan his next move—George was the next one in his list.

When he had called the downtown branch of Sun Diegans he was told that George was on vacation in Mexico and they had no information when he would be back. Bill was disappointed and worried at the same time.

He had known that Dave's body will eventually be found and that he was already living on borrowed time. Though it might take a while for the cops to figure it out, he was certain that Josh would be smart enough to figure out what happened. Josh would put the two and two together and come up with the inevitable four like he always did. Josh would leverage his political connections to organize a search for Bill, of course for some reason unrelated to Dave's death. So Bill knew that of all things, time was not on his side.

When he heard the news about Dave's disappearance on television, Bill was anxious. He had been calling every day at the restaurant for George, but there was always the same answer. However when he saw the report being broadcasted through the television networks, he knew that his luck might turn around.

He was right on his analysis. When he called the restaurant that morning, the girl said that George would be flying into town that evening. "You have been so persistent to meet him Mr. Parks I am sure he will be grateful for your patronage. I will give him your name when he comes in," the girl had told Bill.

Bill had waited in the shadows behind the bushes for over six long hours. He had almost given up for the night when George had turned into the driveway, opened the garage door and parked his car inside. Bill was in his toes, ready to move when the time was right. George had removed his bags from the trunk of this car, disabled the alarm system and entered the house through the garage entry door. When the garage door started to roll down, Bill had quietly slipped inside, taking care not to intersect the infra-red sensor at the bottom of the garage door frame.

He hid behind the two cars parked in the garage and waited for the overhead light to turn off. From his position, he could hear the messages as George had played them back on his answering machine. Bill had frowned when he heard the message that Josh had left for George. Just as he had predicted, Josh did suspect who had killed Dave. The urgency in his voice and the choice of cryptic words in the message left no doubt that Josh was on his trail.

Bill knew that he had almost run out of time and had to act quickly. He had listened intently for any sound coming from inside the house and he had heard nothing. He had silently crept up to the garage entry door and tried to turn the handle. It was locked. It did not take more than a couple of minutes for George to pick the lock and enter the house.

It felt strange to Bill. He was standing there on the same ground where most of his mortal family had perished, but he did not recognize the house. Joan would have not approved the aggressive look and feel of the interiors. There was lust and greed written in every nook and corner of the house. Nowhere was there any of the love that Bill had once shared with Joan and Anita.

He had heard the sound of running water from upstairs and a whirring sound to indicate that George was preparing for a bath. Bill had double-checked his Beretta and had tiptoed upstairs with the gun held out in front of him. It was cocked and ready to fire. Bill had ignored all the rooms alongside the corridor and walked in the direction of the whirring sound. When he arrived near the bathroom, he sank to his stomach and quickly peeked around the corner.

George was in the Jacuzzi with his eyes closed. From the relaxed expression in his face, Bill guessed that George must have dozed off in the tub. He had got up on his feet and turned the main light off. George had not responded as the darkness had enveloped the room and the low powered bulb above the shower cubicle provided a soothing illumination to the room. Bill had watched George for a while and had then called out his name.

"McMillan?" George knew there could not be any other answer. He kicked himself mentally for not following up on Dave's instructions in Las Vegas. Dave had asked him to set up a trace on Bill after his release from prison, but George had forgotten all about it. He had underestimated Bill, given the fact that Bill would be touching his sixties by the time he was released. Moreover the long years in jail would have killed his spirit anyway.

"So you do know me, huh?" Bill grinned.

"Look whatever happened before was a long time ago. I am a changed man now," George ventured to strike up a conversation with Bill and distract his attention. If only he could get his hands on Bill, he thought, it would not be too difficult to break the neck—he was a quite a specialist at that.

"I can see that you are a changed man. Quite honestly, I have changed too as you can see," Bill said in a monotone. "I have lost all my patience and restraints. Come to think if it, there I was a compassionate husband and a loving father twenty six years ago. Just about a week ago, I shot Dave and burned him alive right before my eyes," the nonchalance in his voice was menacing. "I felt no remorse about it."

George felt a sudden dryness in his mouth.

"I actually watched him burn, you know—right in front of me," Bill repeated. "For some strange reason, I felt no compassion at the pain that Dave was going through as the hungry flames devoured his body one tissue at a time. He shrieked out in sheer agony, threw himself on the ground a couple of times in a futile effort to douse the flames. But I guess the fire just fell in love with him and did not stop until it completely consumed him. He burned for almost half an hour, I was actually timing him. Thirty minutes of horrified screaming for help and begging me to douse the flames. George—I just sat there and watched him die. Now that I think about it, I think I enjoyed it very much and wouldn't mind doing it again."

The prospects did not seem too bright for George as he weighed his options. There was none that came to his mind which had curiously become very alert for the last ten minutes.

"Yes George, you can say that I am a changed man just like you are," Bill finished.

"I—I cannot reverse the past, McMillan," George stammered, "I was young and stupid and yes, I did some bad things in my days. But these are different times and I have a different life now. I am clean now and own the most flourishing restaurant chain in the county. I will give you any amount of money that you want, just name it."

"How many people have you killed in your life George?" Bill edged closer—George had his knees folded up to his chest. "Tell me the truth and I will let you go, I promise."

"I don't know, there were too many to keep a count," George realized that was not the answer Bill was looking for. He hurried, "about thirty or forty maybe."

"Wrong answer," Bill's voice was drowned in the sharp crack of the silenced Beretta as the left knee broke into a hundred pieces and the swirling water turned red in the Jacuzzi.

The shock gave way to intense pain as the stunned George grabbed his left knee and stared at the mess of blood, flesh and bones. He shrieked out in pain as the realization struck him that he would never use his left leg again if he ever survived.

He looked up and the horror in his eyes was something that Bill had always wanted to see and pondered about. "How many people have you killed in your life, George, I won't be so patient the next time!" Bill's voice was ominous.

"Oh God, I don't know," George managed to say.

"Wrong answer again," Bill said calmly and pulled the trigger again. The exposed right knee shattered almost instantaneously as the bullet struck at close range.

George's body jerked up in reflex action and his screams touched a new high.

"Let me help you answer that question, George. As far as I am concerned, you killed just one person," Bill said with a deadpan expression. "You killed the one person who had once given me a meaning to life—the one person who had taught me to live and love. You killed just one person George. She was my wife, Joan. She was the most compassionate and the most wonderful person who ever walked this earth and had never hurt anyone. Yet you and your friends killed her for no reason. You burned her so badly that she suffered in the most extreme agony for three long days before she succumbed to her injuries. You've never felt physical agony in your life, have you George? How does it feel now with both your legs decommissioned for life? You'll be restricted to a wheelchair all your life, you know? Of course if you survive after I'm done with you."

"I was just following orders," George still believed in miracles. "It was Josh and Brant who had planned the entire operation. They thought you will be forced to hand over the evidence that you had collected," George gasped for breath as spasms of pain shot all over his body. "We were supposed to kidnap your wife and daughter first before setting your house on fire, but Dave did not agree. He wanted them to be in the house when the fire started. He thought it would scare you enough to make you talk. But things got out of hand and he could not get to them on time. We were all very sorry for what had happened, trust me."

The Beretta fired again and this time it was George's right shoulder that took the direct hit. With three limbs destroyed beyond repair and his voice hoarse from the screams of agony, George let out a little more than a whimper. The water grew redder by the second as blood gushed out of his body. George reached out with this left arm and tapped on a switch that shut the Jacuzzi off.

"You were sorry for what you did?" Bill asked with feigned incredulity, "Boy, I'm impressed. Tell you what, George, I cannot reciprocate that feeling. Do you want to know why? You destroyed innocent lives, lives that were precious to me—I can understand why you would be feeling sorry. But you are a criminal who has evaded the law for decades and hoodwinked the public with your masks of righteousness. All of that stops right now. I am your judge, George—how do you plead?"

"Guilty, I plead guilty. Oh Lord! Please, please help me. I am losing blood and my vision is blurring," George squealed.

"Tell me George, when you guys set the fire, why could my family not get out of the house? I have always wondered about how they died, so tell me George, help me unravel this mystery," Bill asked a rhetorical question, but he wanted to hear it from George.

"I-I had battened down the doors and windows, so they could not come out," George was breathing faster and the breaths were becoming more shallow every minute. "Please help me. I'll confess everything in court, I promise. I will testify against Josh and Brant if that is what you want. But please help me get medical attention."

"Why did you build this house over the house that you burnt down?" Bill tapped lightly on the shattered right knee with the Beretta and George yelped out in a newly found source of pain that made him feel nauseous.

"Because," George gasped for air, "because I wanted to build my dreams on your destruction."

When the Beretta delivered the bullet to the left shoulder, George's body arched backwards momentarily as he found some hidden strength in his legs and his body ejected from the Jacuzzi and crashed down on the bathroom floor.

"You saw to it that my family could not get out of the house as it burned around them," Bill said with a deadpan expression. "Well, I am going to return your favor, George. Your limbs are all useless, as you can see. Do you notice that you don't feel as much pain now? That is because your body has reached the limit to how much pain it can bear. You must have lost at least half of your blood by now, your vision is blurring, and your body feels numb, does it not?

It is a pretty warm day today, but I'll bet that you are feeling cold, aren't you George? You must be feeling nauseous too, aren't you George? Do you know why George? You are dying, my man, life is slowly escaping your body. Gosh it must be really painful to die like this. You must…"

"Stop, please stop it," George screamed and cut Bill off.

Bill stepped aside, picked up a body length mirror and brought it over for George to see his reflection. What George saw horrified him—he had blood all over his naked body and there was blood on the floor. The visual confirmation of his physical pain further aggravated his agony as he lay there helpless and gasping for breath.

"So long George—all your victims have been waiting for you all these years. Finally their wait will be over. I still have a few more errands to run before I join you in hell," Bill drenched a helpless George with the gasoline from the five gallon jerry can that he had hauled along with him and sprinkled some on the floor around his limp body. He lit a matchstick, looked into the bloodshot and terrified eyes that anticipated the inevitable, and dropped it on the floor.

The gasoline ignited instantly and hungry flames sprinted towards George and engulfed him from all sides. He screamed like there was no tomorrow—literally. Bill rushed out of the bathroom and emptied the remainder of the gasoline on the carpet down the hallway and down the stairs and into the carpet on the first floor. He lit a match stick and set a stack of newspapers on fire and set them on the carpet in the dining room. He rushed into the adjoining kitchen and turned on all the six gas burners all the way up. The unmistakable smell of un-ignited cooking gas filled the air. Bill quickly left through the garage entry door into the garage. He opened the side door, jumped the low picket fence and sprinted through the trees to his waiting car.

He had thrown the empty jerry can in his trunk and had just started the ignition when he heard the explosion. A blinding yellow ball of fire rose up in the night sky and disappeared into the darkness. The mounting pressure inside the house had been too much for the house to contain within the walls and it erupted in an explosive inferno.

Bill sat behind the wheel, looked at the burning flames, hung his head and wept. His innocent family had perished in the flames and that destroyed his life. He wept because he knew that whatever he did could never bring his family back to him again. But he had to go on and complete his mission. Maybe that was his salvation and that was probably why he was still alive.

He wept because he realized how evil and ruthless he had become. He had rejoiced at the agony that he saw before him when Dave and George died. What he had done were against the basic principles that he had grown up with. He had shot people before but that was always under the power of the law— that too only for the purpose of containment of the threat. He had never killed anyone before. Now he was in effect committing murder, without giving the victims their right to a trial. He wept because he had become a merciless killing machine, who would not stop until the last target was achieved.

Bill wondered how much Joan had suffered and how helpless and desperate she must have felt when the fire had engulfed her house. Seeing the agony and horror in the eyes of Dave and George as their bodies slowly gave up the fight for survival among those flames painted a vague picture of how Joan must have suffered in that inferno. Bill did not weep anymore. He took a deep breath and drove away.

14

The television came on exactly as programmed at thirty minutes past six in the morning. Josh always wanted to be informed about the latest greatest in the world when he woke up. He had actually intended to disable the timer when he went to bed at around two o'clock that morning. The events of the day had exhausted Josh both physically and mentally.

When he left Brant's apartment around midnight, he thought that he would be able to arrange for police protection for himself and Brant. However, more he thought about it, he realized how difficult it would be for him to substantiate that with the Chief of Police. There was no imminent threat to him or to Brant—at least none that he could prove in public. His request might not be considered as top priority. Such matters required special approvals and funding and such matters never happened overnight.

Josh had analyzed various angles and had come up with dead ends every time. By two o'clock he was completely spent and had literally collapsed in his bed. He was in the arms of Hypnos within seconds and had completely forgotten to disable the television timer. He had no intention of waking up that early in the morning.

When the television came on, the voice of the newscaster woke Josh up. He fumbled for the remote control on the side table, but it wasn't there. Josh groaned, dragged himself out of his bed and stumbled towards the television.

"This morning, the SDFD spokesperson said that the fire was under control at this time but not completely out just yet. They are still trying to douse the last embers," the newscaster's voice came in the background and the video showed the remains of a practically gutted structure of a house with flames still trying to feed on the open air.

Josh turned the television off and went back to his bed and slipped under the covers. His body craved for more sleep. In his subconscious mind, the images of the scene he saw on television played back and Josh was instantly awake. He sat bolt upright in his bed and ran to the switch the television back on.

"The SDFD are yet to confirm how the accident happened," the newscaster continued. "Charred body parts were found among the embers, which we believe were from Mr. George Briggs, who owned the popular restaurant chain—SunDiegans in the San Diego area. The explosion fatally wounded Mr. Briggs and literally tore his body apart. Incidentally, Mr. Briggs did get into trouble with the law about forty years ago. However he had clearly turned over a new leaf after his release from prison. He had been a model citizen ever since and was engaged in several philanthropic activities all over San Diego county. The gas company has shut off the gas supply to all homes in the neighborhood. They intend to keep it that way until they are satisfied that the accident was not caused by any problem in their supply lines."

Josh groped around for the sofa and slumped back on the plush cushions. Just the night before he had predicted that George would be next and it had already come true. It was much sooner than he had expected. There was no doubt in his mind anymore that it was indeed Bill who was on the rampage. Surely there was no proof that he could hold up in court, but his instincts had never failed him in his entire life. Moreover no other explanation made any sense.

He wondered how a person of the size as Bill would be able to incapacitate a man of the size of George—it must not have been easy. Bill must have caught George in a disadvantaged situation and taken advantage of it. He ruled out the possibility of a blunt or a sharp instrument being used to put George out of commission. The man was too strong to be put down that way. Moreover Bill was smart enough to even try it. It could have been poisoning, but that was also a remote possibility. That left just one option—George must have been shot inside his house before it was set on fire.

Josh reached out for the telephone and called Brant. After four rings, Brant's tired voice came on the line, "Good morning Senator," they were always formal on public telephone lines.

"Good morning to you Judge Sawyer," Josh said. "Did I wake you up?"

"I guess I overslept, I am not feeling too well this morning, so I think I will give it a rest for a few days," Brant said.

"Good for you, let me know if I can help," Josh said. "What's happening in our fine city, Judge?"

"What do you mean?" Brant sensed something was amiss, especially because it was unusual for Josh to call him so early in the morning.

"Apparently there was a big fire that broke out last night in a residential neighborhood. The television report says that the owner of the Sun Diegans restaurant chain was killed in that fire," Josh tried to keep his voice under control.

Brant sat bolt upright in his bed and switched the television on. Josh could hear the same news channel on the other end carrying the same information about the fire.

"Have they figured out how this happened?" the tremor in Brant's voice was not too hard to discern.

"Not yet, but I am sure we'll learn something very soon," Josh said, "I'll make some calls and see what's going on. If this is not an accident, we should get to the bottom of this. I will not tolerate such acts in my city."

"They seem to be certain that the deceased was indeed Mr. Briggs—he was a good friend and a changed man ever since he was released from prison," Brant spoke without really meaning to say anything.

"So you say you're not feeling too well, is that right Judge?" Josh asked.

"Yeah, maybe I've caught a virus or something," Brant said.

"Well, stay put for a few days then," Josh said hoping that Brant would read between the lines. "You don't want spreading your germs all over my fine city. I already have some clean up work to organize," he laughed.

"Yes, I'll let this virus get under control first. Till later Senator," Brant knew exactly what Josh had implied.

Josh moved mechanically that morning—even breakfast was a quick affair. He did everything he always did every morning, but his mind was elsewhere. He had to come up with a plan to protect himself and eliminate the threat to his career and to his life. He still felt that the next attack would be on Brant, if Bill was not stopped earlier. He thought he could use Brant as bait and lure Bill out in the open—that way he could be easily taken out.

Offering Brant as the proverbial sacrificial lamb would not be difficult. What would be difficult was to present the case to the Chief of Police that ex-convict William McMillan was indeed the man they were after. He had no evidence to back up his theory.

George had no direct official or recorded connection with Bill. That would make it more challenging to substantiate a plausible motive without raising any suspicions. Moreover, official records indicated that Dave had actually risked his own life to save Anita McMillan from a certain and gruesome death. There was no way that such a noble deed can be substantiated as a motive for Bill to commit murder. Josh had to be careful. Otherwise the worms from the open can could soon be all over him.

Josh wondered if he could use insanity as an explanation for Bill's behavior, and say that the killings were completely random without any tangible motive. But then he would never be able to put up a plausible argument on why he suspected Bill to be the killer.

Josh was at his wits' end. Bill practically had him and Brant on a vice. With his current political status and position the smallest hint of a scandal would completely destroy his career. Josh just could not afford the exposure. The press was watching his every move ever since the word leaked out that his party was considering the prospect to present him as a candidate to run for President.

Josh needed someone else to go after Bill. Someone who would have the passion and the drive to persistently stay on Bill's trail and eliminate the threat conclusively. Knowing how resourceful Bill was, Josh was certain that he needed to engage someone competent enough to anticipate Bill's next plan of action and remain one step ahead of him.

He checked his watch and dialed a number.

"Chief Baxter's office, how may I help you?" a feminine voice responded.

"Good morning, is that Myra?" Josh asked politely.

"Yes, this is she," the secretary said.

"Hello Myra, this is Senator Timmons," Josh said with a short laugh.

"Senator Timmons," Myra said. "What a pleasant surprise! Do you have a cold? I did not recognize your voice."

"I cannot hide from you can I?" Josh joked. "Is the Chief in the office yet?"

"Yes, I will patch you through," Myra always had a friendly attitude, "Enjoy your day Senator. I can't wait to hear you running for President."

"Thank you Myra, you are very kind," Josh said and waited as he got transferred.

"Senator Timmons," the Chief came on the line, "Good morning to you Sir. How may I be of service to you today?"

"Hello Chief," Josh started, "I wish I could greet you in a similar fashion, but it is not a good morning for me I'm afraid."

"I'm sorry to hear that Senator—what's bugging you?" the Chief sat upright.

"Chief, San Diego is my home town as you know. I was born and raised here and spent years of my life, enforcing the law to keep this squeaky clean—none of this is a secret," Josh started ambiguously on purpose. "However the events of the past week have disturbed me very much. Dave Reynolds was ruthlessly burnt alive in the high desert within California borders. This morning, I have this news about another fine citizen of this city being killed by fire that completely gutted his house last night. Both men were from this city and had served well in their lifetime. What on earth is going on here Chief?" Josh asked with grave concern.

It wasn't every day that a Senator and a potential candidate for President called the Chief of Police to complain about criminal activity in the city. "It concerns me too, Senator. Trust me, I have been on yesterday's incident since last night. As soon as the SDFD gives us the clearance I'll have someone check things out. There are still some small fires burning out there and a lot of unstable rubble. I cannot risk the safety of my people by going in right now—we have to follow protocol as you know."

"I want to know if it was arson or an accident, Chief. I hope it was the latter—otherwise, we will have to start a thorough investigation and get to the bottom of this," Josh was firm even in his politeness. "Such events are not good for my political image, Chief. How can I protect a nation when I cannot even protect my own town? I hope you understand this."

"I surely do, Senator," the Chief said.

"What is the status of the investigation on the death of Dave Reynolds?" Josh asked. "Is the SDPD taking over the investigation?"

"Well the incident happened in San Bernardino County as you know, so we do not have jurisdiction there," Chief Baxter said. "I think it is still in the hands of the CHP at the moment. The last bit of news I heard was that Baker police has asked for help from the SBPD who will take over the investigation from the CHP. They are getting organized on the paperwork."

"Mr. Reynolds was born and raised in San Diego as you know. Do you also know that he had served this city as a fireman for the SDFD?" Josh asked.

"I-I did not know that Senator, but please go on," the Chief's interest was piqued.

"Well, check his record—you'll find it quite impressive. He retired as a Battalion Chief with the SDFD," Josh said. "Anyway, what I am trying to say is the SDPD should take charge of the investigation. I'll make a few calls after I hang up here and pull some strings. It is important for people to know that I will do everything possible to take care of my town. Is that ok with you?"

"We will have to work very closely with several agencies to get to the bottom of this Senator and that takes time as you know. But I see how important this is to you," the political motivation was clear to the Chief.

"I want the best man you have to lead the investigation. Whoever is running around with the intent to torch people alive, is clearly evil and a sadist. This person should be ruthlessly hunted down and brought to justice," Josh spoke with authority. "Who's the best you have in the SDPD, Chief? I don't care how busy this person is, I want him dedicated to this case."

"I have the perfect officer for the job Senator," the Chief thought for a while and said. "However there is a slight difference from what you are asking for."

"What's that?" Josh asked.

"As the name suggests, Sergeant Carol Mason is a woman," the Chief let out a short laugh. "Don't let her hear that I told this to you. Quite honestly Senator, she is the best the SDPD has had for over a decade now. She truly embodies the spirit to serve and protect. She is something that every officer strives to achieve throughout their lives, but seldom succeed to live up to it. If you trust my judgment I would strongly recommend that she be assigned to lead this investigation. You will see over time that the choice is a good one."

"I see," Josh pursed his lips. "You understand that what we may have here is a person who must be completely deranged to kill someone so ruthlessly. Will she have the balls, for lack of a better word, to be up to the challenge?"

"I don't want to preach to the choir here, Senator, but you need steel to cut through steel," the confidence was evident in the Chief's voice. "Sergeant Mason is that steel that you are looking for. She works quietly and she prefers to work alone. Till this date she has a hundred percent success rate in all investigations that were assigned to her. The men here say, 'when the going gets tough Carol gets rolling'. That is saying a lot about Sergeant Mason when it comes even from some of our more accomplished officers."

"I'm beginning to like her," Josh said.

"She has one little problem though—if of course it can be called a problem in the first place," the Chief said at length.

"I'm listening," Josh patiently waited for the Chief to continue.

"She hates the press and would do anything to stay away from the cameras," the Chief laughed. "It makes it difficult for us to keep the reporters off her tail, but she prefers it that way. It's not that she is shy or anything, it's just that she does not like the public limelight."

"I like her even more," Josh said, "how long has she been at the SDPD?"

"That should be another surprise for you Senator. Sergeant Mason is just twenty eight years old and joined us three years ago. Her family is from Ohio. She was here to study at the University, fell in love with the city and decided to settle down here."

"Twenty eight and she is already a Sergeant?" Josh was surprised. "That is impressive, without a doubt. Does she have a family?"

"No boyfriends and no girlfriends either if you get my drift," the Chief laughed. "She keeps to herself most of the time."

"Interesting," Josh murmured. "Hopefully I will meet her someday. In the meantime, looks like she is the best we've got."

"I agree. I will give her a heads up," the Chief promised. "As soon as you do what you have to do to make the SBPD transfer the investigation to us, we'll take over and Sergeant Mason will be assigned. You have my word."

"Very good Chief," Josh said. "I'll watch the news and see how the George Briggs case turns out. I just hope it really was an accident."

"I do too. You take care of yourself Senator. As promised, Sergeant Mason will be on the job as soon as I receive clearance from Chief Browning of the SBPD," Chief Baxter hung up and mulled over the conversation he just had.

He wondered why a Senator would be so keen about an investigation regarding an ex-fireman and a casino owner in Las Vegas. They must have been long time friends, but the Chief found it unusual that the Senator mentioned nothing about their relationship. He knew that the Senator's campaigns were financed by several large companies. Dave Reynolds could have been one of such people who financially supported the Senator's campaign.

Chief Baxter somehow felt reasonably certain that there was some relationship between the Senator and Dave Reynolds—something that he was unaware of. He pressed the intercom for this secretary, "Myra, can you please put out a page for Sergeant Carol Mason? I need her to report to my office at her earliest convenience."

"Sure Chief," Myra replied. "Actually there is a call waiting for you from the Captain Brown on the other line, should I patch it through?"

"Yeah, put him through," the Chief said.

"Hello Chief," the Captain said. "I've some news for you."

"Go ahead Captain," the Chief prodded.

"Chief, the SDFD just pulled the stops and have given us their clearance to look around the scene of the fire down here," the officer continued. "I was talking to the Fire Captain in charge and he indicated that from the looks of it, apparently gasoline may have been used to start the fire. There was no gas leak. This raises some doubts on the possibility of an accident—it could be arson."

"I see," the Chief frowned. "I want you to secure the area and ask your boys to stay off the property for the moment. Tell the Fire Captain to keep a lid on it for the moment. The press will pounce on the SDFD and on us if they know it was arson. Ask him to hold them off as long as he can—say that it is pending investigation or something. The last thing we want is panic in this city. Do you copy?"

"Yes Chief, I'm on it," Captain Brown confirmed.

"What about the body parts? Any positive ID yet?" the Chief asked.

"The explosion must have been pretty strong—whoever it was had his body practically ripped apart," Captain Brown was well accustomed to the manner in which the Chief asked for reports—detailed information supported by evidence was key. "We have reason to believe that it was indeed George Briggs. We called his restaurant a little while ago and they said that he had returned from a trip to Mexico yesterday and had his dinner at the downtown location before telling the manager that he was going home. They have tried to reach him but are unable to get through. From the size of the body parts it does seem to have belonged to Mr. Briggs after all, although we have not done the forensics yet."

"Thank you Captain, that was a comprehensive report," the Chief sounded worried. "Just lock the place down and leave everything exactly where they are for the moment. I'm going to engage Sergeant Mason on this one and she should be down there sometime soon to take over. I want her to take a look at things first before we do anything else."

"Roger that Chief—a very good choice," the Captain was satisfied that the most competent officer in his team was being deployed.

Chief Baxter replaced the receiver on its cradle and leaned back on his chair. The two fire-related incidents in the past week that concerned two San Diegans troubled him. They seemed to have a remote similarity with each other. He felt frustrated that he did not know enough and realized that there was only one way to find out. He needed to initiate a thorough investigation and he needed to act quickly.

He pressed the intercom and spoke, "Myra, any word from Sergeant Mason yet?"

"Yes," Myra said. "She called in to say that you can expect her within the half hour. I'll send her in when she arrives."

"You do that," the Chief released the intercom button, leaned back on his chair again and closed his eyes in deep thought.

15

"Do you have the bullet that you had removed from the body?" Carol asked the coroner.

"I knew someone would ask me for that," the coroner replied and opened a drawer beneath his desk. He removed a plastic pouch and pushed it towards Carol.

Carol picked the small pouch and examined the bullet. She frowned, ran her fingers through her hair and dropped the pouch in her jacket pocket. It was the same type of bullet that was found on George Briggs' remains. Ballistics had confirmed that the bullets found on the corpse were fired from at least a twenty five year old Beretta.

"How certain are you about the age of the Beretta?" Carol had asked the ballistics expert.

"As certain as the fact that tomorrow, the sun will again rise in the east," was the reply.

"Anything wrong Sergeant?" the coroner caught the expression on Carol's face and asked.

"No, nothing special," Carol replied. "Is there anything else important that I need to know about your observations?"

"Well, I think the victim was shot at an angle to his right. I know that from the orientation of the bullet lodged between the bones of the chest cavity," the coroner was confident of his analysis, "It had to have either completely severed the axillary artery or would have taken out a good portion of it when it struck. The victim would have died due to the loss of blood. Each time the heart pumped it would have pushed out more and more blood from his body. Whoever torched the victim really did not have to do anything more. Reynolds would have died anyway slowly and painfully. That tells me that the killer is a vicious and ruthless person and likes to watch people die in agony. You are looking for a whacko, quite honestly."

"Or the killer is someone who did not know that he had actually struck a major artery and wanted to make sure that his goal was achieved no matter what," Carol added.

"I don't want to put words in your mouth Sergeant, but one thing about that theory bothers me," the coroner continued. "If I am the killer armed with a no-nonsense firearm such as a Beretta and I don't know if I have already done the damage that would be necessary to kill the victim, why would I not shoot a few more into the helpless man and get it over and done with? It was dark and the freeway was almost deserted. Nobody would ever notice until maybe the next morning. Why would I go to such lengths as to torch the victim alive?"

"I see where you are going," Carol murmured as she listened intently.

"So if I was the killer, the reason I would torch my victim alive was because I wanted to watch him die in agony as the hungry flames tore into every tissue of the victim's body," the coroner reasoned. "The question is, what motivation would I have to plan and do something that drastic? Again, I think you are looking for a complete whacko, Sergeant. Beretta has stopped manufacturing magazines for those bullets twenty five years ago. Those magazines are no longer available—even in the black market. That's how I estimated the age of the gun used in this murder. You are looking for someone who is probably in his sixties or someone younger who has access to grandpa's collection."

Carol looked at the coroner as he summed up his hypothesis and smiled, "Did you ever think about a career change? I'm impressed at your analysis."

The coroner laughed, "Oh no! What you guys do is too much excitement for me. My heart couldn't take all of that adrenaline rush. However I do like to make sense of what I do for a living—keeps my mind well tuned."

Carol took her leave and got into her vehicle. She dialed a number that the Chief had given her before she left San Diego. She waited for someone to pick up and said, "Hello this is Sergeant Carol Mason of the SDPD. I was asked to call this number to get in touch with Patrolman Paul Whittaker. Can you please patch me through to him?"

Shortly he heard a man's voice on phone, "Hello Sergeant this is Patrolman Whittaker."

"Hello there, I was asked to call you about the Reynolds case," she started.

"Ah, yes," Whittaker said, "I believe the SDPD has taken over the investigation and you are looking for some more information. I thought we had filed a rather comprehensive report."

"Yes and I have read it, thank you," Carol said, "I would however like to visit the crime scene for myself just to get an idea of how things happened."

"No problem Sergeant," Whittaker said. "We have left a marker there that should be easy to spot. Keep going north on Interstate Fifteen towards Las Vegas. You should be able to see the orange flag about twenty five miles north of Wheaton Springs. At the moment I am on a different assignment, so I cannot come with you—my apologies."

"No problem. I think I can find the place," Carol replied, "I'll call you if I need anything."

She started her vehicle, found her way into the Interstate Fifteen and headed north. The freeway was rather empty and Carol put the vehicle on cruise and mulled over the events of the past three days.

Although she knew how much Chief Baxter held her in regard, she also knew that the Chief seldom showed it in her presence. When she had walked into the Chief's office three days ago, he had wasted no time to get right to the point. He had directed her to take charge of the George Briggs case right away. He had informed her of what might also be placed under her wing if Senator Timmons had his way.

"Any resources that you need to get to the bottom of this will be made available to you, Sergeant," the Chief had committed. "You will be given unrestricted access to all the relevant information that we have on file."

"As you wish, Chief, but you do realize that I am working on the Ortega homicide at the moment and that is taking a fair amount of my time," Carol referred to the case that she had been assigned to investigate.

"Consider yourself re-assigned from this moment onwards. I will figure out who the right person is to pick things up from here. You will have to transfer the files over that's all," the Chief had said.

As Carol rose to take her leave, the Chief said, "I have a daughter who is your age—she is a school teacher. Sergeant, if I have never told you before, I am glad you are with the SDPD. Thank you for your commitment and dedication to the Department."

Carol had smiled—that was the closest the Chief ever came to saying how good and valuable she really was to the department.

When she had arrived at the scene, she was taken by surprise. She had seen video footage on television, but she never realized how extensive the damage was to the building that was once the residence of George Briggs. The explosion must have been strong enough. Pieces of glass had been thrown as far as the adjacent park and on the street in front of the house. However, none of the neighbors were affected by the flying debris when the explosion occurred. Those double-paned windows must have held on to the mounting pressure inside the house for a long time before they gave up the fight.

The fire had been almost completely controlled though there were some pieces of wood that were still smoldering. Carol had stepped into the embers as members of the SDPD waited outside the cordoned off area. She had groaned in disgust when she had seen some reporters in the crowd waiting patiently with their cameras ready.

She had found some of the charred body parts that once allegedly belonged to George Briggs. The left arm and the right leg had been ripped off the body. They were definitely missing from the skeleton that lay a few yards away. The size of the skeleton and the hand that still had some raw flesh on it, left no doubt that the deceased was a well-built and strong man. It must not have been easy to incapacitate such a person without a fight. The hand towel that she held on her nose did not help much to ward off the stench from the charred flesh.

She had removed some debris and inspected the remains of the body. After she had thoroughly examined the body parts, she had squatted down and frowned at what she had found. The deceased was shot on all four appendages and that must have happened before the fire was set. One bullet was still lodged on the left knee—the patella must have shattered on impact. Carol had removed the bullet and dropped it on a plastic bag. She had wondered what kind of gun was used.

Being shot on all four appendages would incapacitate any human and Carol realized why the killer would do that for a person as heavily built as the deceased. He would have tried to defend himself if any arm or leg was still functioning. That had also told Carol that the killer must not have even chanced a physical contact with the deceased. The killer might not have been physically capable or strong enough for a close physical encounter with the victim.

An examination of the skeleton revealed where the bullets had struck, but Carol had found just one bullet—the others must have done the damage and passed right through the body. The accuracy of the location of where the bullets had struck the body implied that the killer was either a very good marksman or must have shot the deceased at practically point blank range.

She had looked around the smoldering embers, turning over pieces of debris and had found the remaining three bullets roughly in the same area where she had found the major portion of the skeletal remains. She had placed all of them in the same plastic bag. She had paused a while to visually examine the bullets. As far as she could tell, she had never seen shells like that before. It was difficult for her to figure out what kind of a weapon might have been used.

The Chief had told her that gasoline might have been used to start the fire. So Carol had picked up some of the debris and sniffed it. The odor of gasoline was indeed unmistakable.

She had looked around and walked over to an area that appeared to have been the kitchen. The granite countertop did not show much damage but its weight had collapsed the burning wooden cabinets that had once supported it. She examined the destroyed stovetop and had found that all the six burners were in the open position. The plastic knobs had melted away in the intense heat, but the metallic spindles were still intact. They were turned all the way up. This could not have happened during the explosion. Someone had turned the burners completely open.

She had reckoned that the killer was either a complete psychological mess or a cold blooded maniac, who could go to such extreme lengths to kill a human being so mercilessly. She wondered what motivation drove the killer to commit such a complete and conclusive destruction of life and property. Carol knew that she would have to research the records of George Briggs when she got back to the precinct, but at the moment she had no lead on who she was looking for.

She had heard the news of the murder of Dave Reynolds, who apparently was also shot before being burnt alive. She had not paid much attention to that incident primarily because it was outside her jurisdiction and she had her hands full on the Ortega homicide case. Things changed when the Chief had indicated that she might have to take over the investigation of the Reynolds murder as well if Senator Timmons could have his way.

Carol had wondered if the two incidents were linked to each other in any manner. If they were, she knew that she had a major investigation in her hands. She had to act quickly because there was no way to know if the killer would strike again or when and where the next attack would come.

Carol had stepped over the debris and covered most of the area when she found a small house safe hidden beneath the rubble. She had motioned to an officer standing nearby for assistance and together they had pushed the rubble aside away from the safe. It had appeared to be strongly built and the fire had done practically no damage to the safe. She had tugged on the handle and found that the safe was securely locked.

She had thought there could be something concealed inside the safe that might prove important to the investigation. Having seen all that she had to see, she stepped outside the secured perimeter and asked the waiting forensic experts to start their analysis. She had the safe placed in the trunk of her car and was about to enter her vehicle when the waiting reporters rushed towards her.

"Sergeant Mason, do you have a statement to make on this incident?" one of the reporters had shouted as the cameras furiously started clicking.

Carol groaned in her mind and had said, "I don't have a statement yet. Hopefully the evidence that we have collected would throw some light into this," she wondered if the press would buy her false statement. She knew very well it was a deliberate act of homicide and arson, but she did not want the press to know that just yet—the Chief had been very particular on that matter.

"Since the press has always helped the SDPD in investigations in the past, the SDPD would be grateful if you do not publish any speculative content in your upcoming editions," she had continued. "It is too premature to make a statement on how this happened. We'll keep you informed as things develop."

"Was this an accident or…" one of the reporters shouted. He was cut off when Carol got inside her car and had driven away.

She had gone directly into the ballistics lab and requested a report on the bullets that she had retrieved from the crime scene. She then had the safe brought over and requested the combination lock to be opened. Within ten minutes the technician had succeeded to get the right combination of numbers that unlocked the safe. When Carol returned back from a quick snack, the technician already had the safe open and ready for her.

Carol had found several legal documents inside the safe. They were property deeds from several coastal towns in Mexico. Carol had dropped the documents in a large manila envelope, thanked the technician and walked over to her office. When she got behind her desk she found another envelope on the seat of her chair. The ballistics and the forensics reports had already come in.

She had tossed the manila envelope she was carrying on her desk, opened the envelope and retrieved the ballistics report. The report had indicated that the bullets were indeed fired from a very close range just like she had anticipated.

The specification of the bullets proved that could have been fired only from a Beretta. What Carol had found most interesting was a comment at the bottom of the report. It indicated that the type of bullets used must have been at least twenty five years old because the manufacturer had discontinued producing them twenty five years ago.

The forensics report had confirmed that the victim was indeed George Briggs. He had been shot four times on his hands and legs in places that would have incapacitated anyone completely. He must have lost a lot of blood, since the bullets would have taken out a piece from some of the major arteries in the body.

She had set the ballistics report aside and reviewed the property deeds from Mexico. The deceased had quite an empire of real estate in Mexico. She wondered if the restaurant business would generate that kind of revenue for someone to hold such expensive assets. She had scanned through every document for possible clues. But they all seemed standard legal jargon. At least her limited knowledge of Spanish did not reveal anything unusual.

She had set all the paperwork aside, pushed her chair back and stared at the documents on her desk with unseeing eyes. On a hunch, she had examined the property deeds a second time. Only one deed was recorded twenty seven years ago.

The bullets were manufactured twenty five years ago. The deed indicated that George had purchased the property two years earlier. Carol had wondered if there was a link hidden somewhere—she needed to do a background check on the victim.

A search on the computer had revealed several links to information about George Briggs. Carol had spent most of the day reading the material. It was late at night that she had got back to her car to go home for the day. The deceased certainly did not have a glorious past although he appeared to have turned over a new leaf over the past couple of decades of his life. She was left with little doubt that the motive had to be some sort of a personal vendetta that someone waited for at least twenty five years to fulfill.

The facts had Carol confused. The viciousness of the murder clearly implied a deep rooted hatred in the killer's mind. She had wondered why someone would wait that long to have the revenge if the killer hated George that much. The Beretta and the magazine that contained the bullets used to maim the victim would probably only remain in someone's personal collection or in a museum in the present day. It had frustrated Carol because none of the fragmented pieces of information connected to make much sense.

She had returned home, showered and prepared her dinner. The Chief had called in to say that she was also being placed in charge of the Dave Reynolds murder. Senator Timmons had apparently pulled the proper strings to have the case assigned to the SDPD.

"No problem Chief," Carol had said. "I will drive down there tomorrow and check things out. We may have to get the remains transferred over here if I am not satisfied with the reports that those guys have filed."

"It's your case Sergeant," the Chief had said. "Do it the way you want. Any leads on the George Briggs case?" he had asked.

Carol briefed the Chief who listened attentively.

"I know it is frustrating, but Sergeant, this is your first day in the case," the Chief had encouraged Carol. "Nobody expects you to solve these things in a day!"

"Thank you Chief," Carol had said, "I'll do my best."

"I know you will," the Chief was genuinely confident of his most brilliant prodigy. "Keep me posted if you find any connection between the two murders."

"I will Chief, good night!" Carol had gone back to her steak.

When Carol passed the exit to Wheaton Springs, she knew that she had almost reached her destination where Patrolman Whittaker had told her. He was right—there was an orange colored flag clearly visible from the freeway that marked the crime scene.

Carol parked her vehicle on the shoulder and followed the markers to the place where the remains of the body were found. She scanned the surroundings. Inadvertently or not, the killer had found a very convenient place to commit the murder. The area where the victim was murdered was actually a ridge with a short overpass for the freeway traffic. Unless someone stopped to look, nobody would ever notice what was happening under the overpass. There was nothing in that area to really stop and look anyway. Just rocks, a few scattered cactus trees and a barren landscape were all that met the eye.

There were several footprints around the area, but that meant nothing to Carol. Too many people had already trampled upon the place. The shrubs nearby were signed and appeared to have been crushed. This indicated that the victim probably had thrashed himself into the ground in a desperate attempt to douse the flames that had engulfed his body. But if he was so fatally wounded like the coroner had explained, he would have felt weaker and weaker by the minute. The flames would have just made matters worse for the victim.

She slowly walked around the area and picked up a trail of what she thought to be dried up blood. The harsh conditions in the area had almost obliterated the trail. However Carol was able to pick up the dark gray patches that almost went right up to the freeway. So the victim must have been shot near the freeway and he had somehow managed to stumble over the area under the overpass where the killer set him on fire.

Carol looked up and down the freeway and wondered what could have made the victim to stop in the middle of nowhere. If he was shot inside his car, the killer would have been either inside the vehicle along with the victim or in a different vehicle and somehow shot the victim.

But that did not make any sense to Carol either. The report indicated that the victim's vehicle was found without any damage far away in Mesquite. Nothing about any blood stains were reported either. Moreover it would have been almost impossible to shoot someone from a moving vehicle at the angle at which the victim was shot. That ruled out both possibilities of the victim being shot inside the vehicle or from another passing vehicle.

Having seen enough, Carol got into her vehicle and headed towards Las Vegas. She had to interview some people in the casino. There was little doubt that the Reynolds and Briggs murders were related given the similarity of the manner in which both men were killed. She knew she was looking for a desperate and vicious killer who liked to see people burn alive after being fatally shot. She wondered what sort of motivation caused such hatred and drove a human being to take those extreme measures. What worried her was that she had no clue if the killer was going to strike again. Moreover, if that happened where the killer would strike and who the next victim would be were also open for conjecture.

She remembered the coroner's comments about the age of the killer. Someone in his sixties or someone younger with access to very old weapons was the profile Carol needed to search for. Both of these profiles made sense, but that narrowed the number of people possible to a few million..

She had been told that Dave Reynolds was an ex-fireman of the SDFD. It was ironic that a fireman would be burnt to death when he had retired from active duty several years ago. Carol wondered if it really was the same killer in both incidents. She thought there was some connection between the killer and the victims but she had no clue about what motivation had forced the killer to commit those gruesome murders. Carol needed more information on Dave Reynolds. An ex-fireman and a casino tycoon did not seem to be the most common career transition path.

16

"Good morning ma'am," Bill took his hat off and bowed slightly.

"Good morning to you," the woman who appeared to be in her mid-sixties smiled. "How can I help you?"

"I am trying to move into the area and want to learn a little more about this community. Your neighbors told me that your family has lived here for decades. So I thought that if anyone knows anything about this neighborhood it will be you," Bill gave a warm smile.

The woman laughed, "It's true that my family has lived in this house for the past forty years, ever since my ex-husband and I got married. I do know a lot about this area, but there is so much that I don't. That's what makes it interesting to live here. You'll like it here in Bay Village."

"Wow, I am already sold," Bill laughed.

"Where are you moving in from?" the woman asked.

"Palm Springs, California ma'am," Bill said. "I guess the desert is getting to me."

"I have a daughter who lives in California," the woman said. "We miss her a lot. Would you like to come in? I just started a fresh pot of coffee" she said in an inviting tone.

"Most gracious of you ma'am—I'll be obliged. By the way, my name is Adam Jones," Bill held out his hand.

"Hello Mr. Jones, please come in. I am Carla McIntyre," the woman introduced herself. Bill already knew who she was. "Why don't you make yourself comfortable, while I go get my husband from the backyard?"

"Thank you very much ma'am it will be a pleasure to meet him," Bill sat himself down on a couch and looked around.

The house was old but very warmly decorated. The large bay windows overlooked the glistening blue waters of Lake Erie that disappeared over the horizon. The McIntyres seemed to be friendly people. Bill had found all the locals to be very friendly in the little Ohio town. He smiled to himself—the world still had some hope as long as people such as the McIntyres lived in it.

Bill had visited the child care facility where Anita had been admitted when he was arrested. The person who could provide him with the information had finally returned from his vacation. At Bill's request the man had asked him to wait while he had searched the old archives. After an anxious hour of waiting, the agent had beckoned Bill over to his window and showed him Anita's file.

Unknowingly to Bill, tears had rolled down his eyes when he saw a picture of little Anita on the first page with all her details. The attendant had seen how disturbed Bill was and had come around and helped Bill to a seat and brought him a glass of water. Bill had thanked him read the contents of the file. He learned that after about a year of her admission, a couple had visited the facility and had offered to adopt Anita. They wasted no time to initiate the adoption proceedings and Anita was gone with them within four weeks of the application.

Bill had noted the address of the couple and was on a plane within hours. The four hour flight had seemed too short for Bill. He was excited at the prospect to finally meet Anita. At the same time he was apprehensive about how he would approach her when he met her. Twenty six years was a long time. He did not expect her to remember anything about him. Who knew how she turned out to be. But Bill had crushed those pessimistic thoughts in his mind—that way lay defeat. He was not going to rest unless he knew everything for certain.

When the plane touched down on the tarmac of the Cleveland airport, Bill was nervous about what the future held for him when he met Anita. He would have to approach her very delicately. He had to get to know her a little first before explaining who he really was. She was the only family he had left and she was his only hope of redemption. Anita was truly worth dying for.

Bill had taken the rapid transit system to Bay Village and found the address he was looking for. It was an old house with a very well maintained and nicely manicured front yard. Lake Erie was clearly visible in the distance and the Stars and Stripes flapped away merrily in the wind. Just like the other houses in the neighborhood, the house also had the family name engraved on a plaque that stood on the grass.

Bill had been crestfallen when he saw 'McIntyres' engraved on the plaque instead of the name he was expecting to see. So close and yet so far, Bill had suddenly felt tired. He had seen an elderly couple walking towards him on the sidewalk and had approached them.

He learned from them that it was indeed the correct address, but the man of the house had passed away several years ago and the widow had remarried. It had become quite a challenge for the lady to raise the little girl all by herself. Fortunately for her, she met her present husband in a local sailing event. Mr. McIntyre turned out to be an honest and kind gentleman and loved his new family. The little girl who was adopted in California was very close to both parents and it was a happy home.

Bill had thanked the couple and heaved a sigh of relief. He had finally found Anita and it wasn't a wild goose chase after all. He had to prepare to meet her and contain his excitement when he saw her. The moment that he had been waiting for all those lonely and painful years had finally…

"Mr. Jones, good day to you Sir," the warmth in the friendly greeting snapped Bill out of his daydream. He realized that he had inadvertently walked over to the bay window while he recollected the events of past few days. He turned around to see a man almost his age standing behind him with a broad smile in his face.

Bill stepped up and held out his hand, "Adam Jones, I'm glad to meet you Sir."

"Nathan McIntyre," the man said with a genuine warmth in his voice. "My friends call me Nate. Please have a seat and make yourself comfortable Mr. Jones."

"Adam will suit me fine, Nate," Bill laughed and lowed himself on the couch. "You have a beautiful house Sir and a great view of the Lake."

"That's what everyone tells me, Adam," Nate said. "But quite candidly you know what? A major portion of the beauty that you see, comes from the peace and happiness in this family, wouldn't you agree my dear?" Nate asked his wife as she carried in the coffee and some snacks on a tray.

Carla McIntyre laughed, "Yes, Mr. Jones, we're truly blessed. Do you take cream and sugar with your coffee?"

"Two sugars and cream, ma'am, thank you," Bill said.

"Carla tells me that you are looking for property to move down here." Nate said.

"Yes, Palm Springs was nice as long as I was employed," Bill said. "But I retired last month and want to settle down somewhere better. As you know, we have a very high cost of living down there in California. My savings won't take me too far out there."

"What does Mrs. Jones think about the relocation?" Carla asked.

"Actually she passed away twenty six years ago," Bill fought back the memories.

"Oh, I'm so sorry, I did not mean to be so meddlesome," Carla apologized.

"No matter, ma'am," Bill dismissed. "You did not know, so no offense taken. Do you have children?" Bill already knew the answer and he was getting impatient.

Nate glanced at Carla who was seated next to her and held her hand, "Actually we do. We are blessed to have such a wonderful daughter. She does not live with us anymore, but she calls every other night to check on us. We better not forget our medication you see. We are literally scared of the tantrums that she would throw over the phone if we did," they laughed.

"You see, she is miles away but we hardly get to miss her. She is simply an adorable child and loves us very much just like we love her with all our hearts," Carla leaned on Nate shoulder tugged his arm fondly.

"When I first saw her, she was just about six years old. Carla's ex-husband had passed away suddenly and I had met them at a sailing event one day," Nate recalled. "You can say it was love at first sight for me. In this case however, I fell in love with the mother and the daughter simultaneously," he laughed.

"You know, Mr. Jones, I did not give birth to her. Actually I was diagnosed sterile and could never have a baby. My ex-husband and I were on a vacation in California and we visited the Child Care Facility in downtown San Diego without any intent to adopt anyone. When we saw this cute little three year old child, both of us felt an instant connection with her. We knew that God had found us the child that we would want to call our own. We had applied for adoption right away."

"I see," Bill managed to say, "I guess she was an orphan?"

"Actually, they told us that her mother was killed by her father who had been served a death sentence and was in prison waiting for his last moments. I remember the warden saying that she came from a broken home and it could have been the lure of another woman that had estranged the father from his family," Carla recollected. The fallacy of what she said broke Bill's heart yet once again. Nothing could be farther from the truth.

"Well, I'm glad she found a good home with you," Bill smiled—there was indeed a God.

"She was a bundle of joy when she came into our lives and still is even after all these years. When my ex-husband passed away, I was very distraught. Apart from her love, this home and a small savings that he had left me, I had nothing," Carla continued. "I could not go to work because I did not have anyone else to take care of my daughter. Then God sent this wonderful man to my life and he brought back the happiness in this house. Believe it or not, we still talk about my ex-husband."

"You do have a wonderful family," Bill was happy that Anita had found a good home. The McIntyres were obviously proud of their daughter and loved to talk about her. "Where does your daughter live?" he asked casually.

"Just south of you, I guess," Nate laughed. "San Diego. I find it very interesting that she came from San Diego all the way to Ohio and went back to San Diego for her studies. She fell in love with that city and decided to settle down there."

The surprise and the elation came as a booster to Bill's spirits. Anita was right there in San Diego and he never knew about it.

Carla pulled out an album from a shelf and said, "I kept an on-going record as she was growing up and this album is a great companion for us today. She is physically thousands of miles away from us, Mr. Jones, but this album helps to keep her close to us all the time. Would you like to see her pictures?"

"You really should not be imposing on Adam," Nate objected.

"No, no, Nate, she is not imposing at all. I can see the pride and love that you both have for your daughter," it was a great day for Bill, he was being given an opportunity to see how his little Anita grew up over the years and wild horses could not keep him away. "I'd be delighted to see that album."

Carla sat next to Bill and opened the album. She started a commentary on each and every photograph in the album. Her memories of the past were still so vivid in her mind.

Anita's life was visually unfolding before his eyes, and Bill was spellbound as Carla flipped through the pages and explained every picture. Occasionally Bill nodded almost mechanically as Carla went through her commentary, but in reality he was spiritually transported to the scene of the photographs with Anita.

There she was, Anita learning to walk on her own, Anita learning how to swim, Anita winning the gold medal in some track and field event in her school, Anita cutting the cake on her birthday party, Anita smiling as she touched a dolphin in a water park, Anita being honored as the best student in her class, Anita frozen in a karate stance as her opponent lay on the mat, Anita hugging Nate, Anita lying on Carla's lap, Anita making a poker face when she lost some game. It was all there and Bill was there with her in spirit.

Bill fought hard to fight the tears that welled up in his eyes. He was being tormented with the mixed feelings of happiness and the realization of what he had missed out in life.

He wondered how he would ever let the McIntyres know that Anita did not come from a broken home and that her father never ever intentionally left her alone to fend for herself in life. The McIntyres were such a happy family and Anita was happy with them. Bill wondered what right he had over Anita anymore. He was not around when she needed him the most. He did nothing to bring her up while the McIntyres gave her a home and a name and of course a good life.

"Are you still with me, Mr. Jones?" Carla's voice cut into his thoughts.

"Y-yes, of course," Bill stammered. "You have a lovely daughter. I can see why you love her so much—she is indeed a darling. What does the pretty Ms. McIntyre do in San Diego?"

Nate laughed, "Adam, I must warn you. Carla is about to show off now. She just loves to answer that question, don't you my dear?"

Bill smiled and looked at Carla with a puzzled expression not knowing what Nate or Carla had in mind.

Carla smiled, "Nate wanted our daughter to keep the name of my ex-husband even after he married me. He thought that one day she would appreciate being associated to my ex-husband's name and he was right."

"You are an amazing man, Nate!" Bill remarked.

"Mr. Jones, it is my extreme pleasure to introduce you to our beloved daughter," Carla flipped the page of the album and said with obvious pride. "Sergeant Caroline Mason of the San Diego Police Department."

Bill suddenly felt light headed and almost fainted when he heard the name and saw the photograph of a young woman, smartly dressed in a full Sergeant's uniform staring at him from the album.

Although the media never revealed the name of the investigating officer, the newspapers carried her photograph in the George Briggs crime scene and the television channels had also carried some video footage. He had recollected meeting the same officer in the elevator on the first day that he had gone to inquire about Anita in the Child Care facility. He had thought that she was Anita, but her name tag had a different name engraved on it which had misled him.

Bill had known that he had to work around the investigating officer if he had to get to Josh and Brant. He also knew that it was not going to be easy. They didn't engage such young officers to investigate such criminal activity without very good reasons. He did not know how much she knew or how close she was on his trail, but what he did know that he did not have time on his side.

He had always wondered how he would feel when he saw Anita for the first time. Now that he had actually seen the photograph he realized that he had already met her and also had a short conversation with her. The woman in the elevator was indeed his Anita. Although every beat of his heart had told him that the woman was his Anita, his eyes had fooled him—the name tag had misled him. He had always searched for Anita McMillan and then Anita Mason. He never knew that Carla and her ex-husband had changed her name to Caroline Mason.

The most shocking realization dawned on Bill. It was his very own Anita who was trying to hunt him down. She had been engaged to protect the same people who had once destroyed her life, killed her mother and had her father unlawfully sentenced to twenty six years in prison.

In the puzzle of lines and dots, the dots were all finally connected. Bill passed out and slumped down in the couch. The realization of the harsh implications of the facts that he just learned was too much for his nerves.

17

Carol sat up sharply on her bed. The same nightmare that she had since her childhood woke her up again. She was sweating and the sheets were damp from her perspiration. She groaned and looked at the clock by her bedside. The green digits showed that it was a little after three o'clock in the morning. Nothing of what she saw in her nightmare was there. The room was quiet and peaceful and everything was normal.

She pushed the sheets aside and stumbled towards the bathroom groping her way through the dimly lit room. She winced at the bright light when she flicked the switch and looked into the mirror. What she saw was not anything new to her. Her hair was disheveled and beads of perspiration glistened on her upper torso.

"When are you going to finally grow up Carol?" she scolded her image on the mirror and splashed cold water on her face—that refreshed her. She wiped her body dry with a towel, filled a glass with water and gulped it down. She turned off the light and made her way back to bed. She slipped beneath the sheets on the other side of her bed, where it was still dry. She clasped her hands behind her head and looked up at the barely visible ceiling.

All these years she had been trying to figure out why she would have the same nightmare over and over again—there was never a variation. Every time she tried to analyze what her mind saw in her sleep, she would come up to a dead end.

The nightmare was consistent each time. It would start with a woman holding a little baby girl in her arms and she would be walking through a beautiful garden, softly humming a lullaby. The baby would be squealing with joy in her arms as the woman kissed her and played with her. The woman and the baby would cross a doorway and they would suddenly be surrounded by a blazing fire literally out of nowhere. The hungry flames would lash out to them as the woman desperately tried to find a way out of the inferno—she would find none.

The woman would hold the baby close to her chest and cry for help that never came. The baby would also scream out of sheer fright as her immature brain tried to interpret the situation. The fire would close in on them and the woman would collapse on the floor face down with the baby still clenched to her chest. She would scream in agony as the hungry flames licked her body. Carol would see the helpless and frightened expression on the woman as she tried to protect the baby and try to calm her down. Carol would see the woman's lips moving in an effort to say something to the baby. She would then hear an explosion that would snap Carol out of her nightmare. She would wake up panting for breath and sweating all over in the damp sheets.

The nightmare was her private secret. Carol never shared it with anyone, not even with her parents who loved and adored her. Ever since she was a child, she wanted to figure out what the nightmare meant and why it kept coming back to her every now and then. Over the years she had resigned her efforts to find a suitable explanation for her nightmares and accepted it as a part of her life.

Her mind drifted to her trip to Dave's casino in Las Vegas. Nobody could help her with any information regarding potential enemies that Dave might have had. Apparently he stayed aloof from his staff and never discussed anything with them but business.

On a hunch Carol had pulled out a photograph of George and showed it to the security guard on duty and he had instantly made a positive identification. She had learned that George was a rather frequent guest to the casino and that he and Dave had been seen together several times. The security guard also showed Carol a Sun Diegans discount coupon book that George had given him one day as a courtesy.

"He said I could use it any time I visited San Diego, ma'am," the guard had said, "Mr. Briggs was a very friendly man."

Carol had also learned from the casino management that a valet by the name of Daniel Smith was also missing from the same day that Dave had left for San Diego. Carol had obtained a copy of the driver's license from the personnel records. California DMV confirmed that the document was stolen since the owner had requested a new license almost two months ago. A comparison of the two photographs on the license showed two completely different people with the same information. Since the valet was on probation, the management did not have a detailed personnel file on record. Although a local address was listed, a check had revealed that address to be bogus.

She had examined the photocopy of the driver's license that Daniel Smith had provided to the management with the hope that she would search the police records for a match. Although one could see the overall features of the person on the image, it was apparently photocopied with a darker setting. This made it rather difficult to know how the man really looked like. The human resources clerk mentioned that Daniel Smith had voluntarily photocopied the license himself when he had applied his probationary employment. Carol had wondered if the darkness in the photocopy was intentional.

There was a signature on file on a pay slip, but Carol knew it would be worthless as well. The original Daniel Smith had a very simple signature. That closely matched the signature on the personnel records of the valet—however the forgery was evident to the trained eye.

Carol lay in bed and wondered if it was sheer coincidence that two persons would go missing on the same day. In her heart she knew that the two were related in some way, but she had no evidence to prove that they were. She was convinced that she needed to find the missing valet. The forgery made him a criminal regardless of whether he was involved in the Dave Reynolds murder or not. What she did not know was how she could ever find the missing valet. It would be nothing short of searching for a needle in a haystack.

Analyzing the similarity in the manner in which the two men had died, she had always suspected that there was some connection between the two. The statement from the security guard in the casino confirmed that theory. She was fairly confident that the same killer was involved in both murders. Hence Dave and George must have had a common enemy. She knew that she had to dig into their backgrounds in more detail with the hope of finding something of any substance to the case.

George Briggs's life seemed to be an open book for Carol. His prison record had surprised her. Not because he had one, but because of the sudden transformation in his life. "More people should be sent to prison, if all the felons transformed their lives to follow the footsteps of George Briggs," she had told herself. George was a real life personification of the adage 'from rags to riches'.

A further research provided the explanation that Carol needed for George's elevation to society. Years ago, she learned, District Attorney Brant Sawyer and Captain Josh Timmons of the SDPD had sponsored a pilot program to assist ex-felons get a fresh start in life after their release from prison. George Briggs was apparently the only one who had the determination and tenacity to take advantage of the program and make it big in life. After a couple of years, the DA became a Judge. The program was discontinued citing reasons that it did not have enough funding and that was not as successful as expected. George had of course taken off like a rocket and established the most profitable upscale restaurant chain in San Diego County.

Dave Reynolds' life was a checkered flag. He had an immensely successful career as a fireman for the SDFD. He had risen to the ranks of Battalion Chief before he gave everything up on grounds of ill health and started a casino business. Somehow he had approached three separate corporations and managed to convince them to invest in the casino business in Las Vegas. With their sponsorship, Dave had built a highly profitable business in Las Vegas and managed it rather well.

Carol was intrigued with what she had uncovered. There seemed to have been a distant relationship between Judge Sawyer, Senator Timmons and George Briggs. There is an even remote relationship between Senator Timmons and Dave Reynolds. George and Dave had known each other and it appeared that the Senator and the Judge were well acquainted too.

She had begun to trace a connection between the four names that she had come across in her research but there were too many missing links and the different possibilities did not make much sense to her. Moreover she had found nothing that could lead her to the ruthless killer that she was after.

Carol yawned, sunk deeper beneath the sheets and closed her eyes. Carol knew she had to catch some sleep. It was almost five in the morning and she had a long day ahead. The killer was still out there and who knew where the next strike would come.

18

"Send her in, please," Josh spoke on the intercom and adjusted his tie.

The door opened and Carol walked in with her hat under her arms. Josh tried hard to contain his surprise. The woman was dressed in full uniform, but looked nothing like a cop. Cops should not be so pretty to look at, Josh told himself. They could kill a suspect just by those stunning looks. He hurried out of his chair and went around his mahogany desk with his hand outstretched.

"I'm glad to meet you, Sergeant" Josh looked Carol up and down wishing she wasn't a cop. A couple of dates and he would have had her in bed in no time otherwise.

"The pleasure is all mine, Senator Timmons," Carol shook hands with Josh and gave a professional smile, "I'm Sergeant Caroline Mason from the San Diego PD."

"My secretary tells me that you had some questions for me that could not wait," Josh looked into her eyes, trying to catch a weakness. People usually adopted a submissive attitude when they interacted with Josh. A Senator automatically commanded a level of respect. Apart from the professional smile, Josh could detect no hint of submission in Carol.

"Yes Senator, I do," Carol said. "This will not take too much of your time. Pardon me for the urgency, but there's a killer out there and he has us on the run, quite frankly."

"I'm not sure how I can help, but I'll do what I can," Josh walked back to his chair behind the desk and motioned at Carol. "Please sit down Sergeant and tell me what's in your mind."

Carol took a seat at the desk and laid down her hat on the polished surface. "What I am about to tell you is not something I would normally discuss with a Senator. You served the SDPD once and did so gloriously. I think you will appreciate the nature of my questions. If I come in too strongly, please pardon me, as an ex-cop I'm sure you will understand the reason for my questions."

"Sure thing, Sergeant," Josh was impressed at the professional attitude in the young officer—maybe there was some submissive attitude after all. He continued, "Let's hear what you have to say."

"Very well, Sir," Carol paused to collect her thoughts. "The Chief told me that you had a special interest in Mr. Dave Reynolds. You arranged for the case to be handed over to the SDPD although the incident happened in San Bernardino county. May I ask the nature of your interest in the late Mr. Reynolds?"

Josh laughed, "Sure Sergeant Mason. The late Mr. Reynolds was one of the major sponsors for my campaign. He was a San Diegan and I knew him since the days he was with the SDFD. This is a loss of a good friend and the manner in which he died was rather shocking. I felt obligated to do everything I can to get to the bottom of this. I owe a lot to Mr. Reynolds."

"Working for the SDFD doesn't help raise the kind the capital one will need to start a casino business. Do you happen to know who financed Mr. Reynolds' business when he started?"

"We never discussed this, but I believe there were some venture capitalists who poured some capital into Reynolds's hands," Josh wondered how much research Carol had done on Dave.

"Actually Sir," Carol said casually, "There were three California corporations that I have been able to draw links to. The first one is from San Francisco, the second from Los Angeles and the third from right here in San Diego that provided Mr. Reynolds with the financial support that he needed. Apparently he had paid them back and much more in a very short period of time when his casino business had taken off like a rocket."

"I see," Josh was testing the waters. Carol had indeed done her research.

"What interests me Senator is the fact that all of these three corporations are now funding your campaign," Carol folded her arms and leaned forward on her seat.

"Every political party and candidate needs funding. That isn't illegal, is it Sergeant?" Josh looked away from Carol. "However I did not know that those corporations funded Dave Reynolds. We never discussed it," Josh hoped he was convincing enough for the young Sergeant.

Carol found the comment rather unusual. The Senator seemed to know exactly which corporations she was talking about, even though she never mentioned their names.

"Nothing illegal Sir, but I was trying to understand the nature of your relationship with Mr. Reynolds," Carol spoke in a monotone. "How did you come to know about these corporations Sir? Did they approach you or did you approach them for funding your political campaign?"

"I don't quite understand where you are going with this line of questioning, Sergeant, but actually they approached me offering support," Josh appeared irritated.

"I checked the tax records of these corporations, Senator. The founders, who are no longer involved with them, had no financial capital to start their business," Carol remained serious. "Funds apparently just appeared out of nowhere from some venture capitalists. I checked them all. They are all bogus information. The names of the founders are also bogus. I wonder if these corporations or Mr. Reynolds were involved in something illegal and clandestine."

"You've got me there Sergeant," Josh shrugged. "I didn't know Mr. Reynolds that well and I have no idea how the corporations were founded. If there is something illegal, my party and of course I would not condone it.."

"As you know Senator, Mr. Reynolds did not have the most peaceful of deaths. Whoever killed him is either mentally ill or just plain ruthless. You don't get such characters running around the streets every day," Carol reasoned. "You were in narcotics when you served the SDPD, so you know what lengths those criminals will go to in order to achieve their goals. I am just trying to find a lead that's all. At the moment all I have is bits and pieces of information and I don't see a link between them."

"Why don't you tell me what you have gathered so far? Most certainly I have aged since my SDPD days. But once a cop is always cop. Maybe I can help you analyze the facts," Josh had to know how much Carol knew.

Carol looked at Josh, made a quick assessment of what Josh said and replied, "I don't want to bother you with all the gory details Senator, but I appreciate the offer. I don't want to share any half baked facts to you and they are really no better than that."

"No problem Sergeant," Josh was disappointed—the young officer seemed to be a tough cookie. "This is your case, so handle it your way. But if you ever need my help you know where to find me."

Carol nodded in agreement. "Did you know George Briggs?"

"As a matter of fact I did," Josh said. "I was one of his frequent customers. It is a pity that he had to die so prematurely in the accident. He was a good man."

"He wasn't a good man all his life, Senator—surely you know that," Carol said emphatically.

"We all make mistakes in life Sergeant, some get caught and some don't," Josh held Carol's gaze. "Of the people who get caught, some repent their wrong-doing and turn their life around and the others are just plain deadbeats. George Briggs was an ex-felon, but he served his time and seized the opportunity we gave him to turn his life around. We cannot all be God, but we can certainly forgive those who deserve the compassion."

"How well do you know Judge Brant Sawyer?" Carol knew she was asking a rhetorical question. The Senator and the Judge were long time buddies—it was no secret.

"You're asking a rhetorical question, aren't you Sergeant," Josh laughed. "I know Judge Sawyer very well. Together we put away an army of drug runners in the past. I hunted and he did all the cooking. We cleaned up this city of all the filth that roamed our streets and haunted our schools. He's a great lawyer and a very good friend of mine. Together we started a program to rehabilitate ex-felons into society but then had to discontinue when my friend decided to move up in life."

"What can you tell me about this program?" Carol asked.

"Judge Sawyer was a visionary and he still is. He puts people away. But even today, he strongly believes that there is always something in a person that can be leveraged to make them turn around in life. It was with this strong belief that he proposed this program to me and I was excited about it. So together we started the program," Josh paused, "George Briggs was a real life example that the program works."

"What's bugging me Senator is the fact that quite curiously, George Briggs was really the only real life example that was ever successful in the program," Carol remarked.

"Boy you've done your research," Josh observed. "That's very good, Sergeant. Truly, our program was open to the public—we did not hand-pick anybody. It required determination and tenacity for the individual to be successful. The subject had to make an honest effort in the program," he paused. "If you are lazy and expects things to be pre-baked for you, you could not take advantage of the program. George Briggs was the only example where he took the challenge and made it happen. The Judge mentioned to me once that George was indeed repentant about the crime that he had committed years ago. He had vowed to turn his life around, which he did with finesse, I think. It is really unfortunate that such a man was killed in such a gory accident."

Carol listened carefully and said, "Can I hold you in confidence on something Senator Timmons? As an ex-cop you realize the importance of confidentiality."

"Sure Sergeant, my lips are sealed," Josh said anxiously.

"Mr. Briggs did not die in an accident like the press has been reporting," Carol murmured. "He was murdered in cold blood and in the most gruesome manner imaginable. We are keeping this from the press to avoid panic. You know how hungry those guys are for any sensational news that they can print."

""Yes, I know, but are you sure about this Sergeant?" Josh wished Carol would tell him everything she knew.

"As sure as the light of day—no questions about that," Carol was confident. "Mr. Briggs was shot at very close range first before he was torched. I personally inspected the body parts and had forensics check out the remains," she paused. "He was shot on both knees and both shoulders. The killer meant to incapacitate him completely. The bullets that struck his upper body had most probably taken out the axillary arteries. Mr. Briggs would have died from the loss of blood anyway. I believe that the killer was aware of how seriously he had injured his victim. The accuracy of where the bullets were aimed at rules out any theory about random shooting. Despite that knowledge, the killer poured gasoline on Mr. Briggs and torched him alive. Then he proceeded further to burn down the entire house. That was absolutely unnecessary. For some reason, the killer did not want to leave even the most remote chance that the victim could possibly survive his fatal injuries. I think that in addition to ensuring the elimination of Mr. Briggs, the killer was also trying to send a message to someone else. If this is true, I believe that this someone else is alive somewhere today."

"Oh my goodness!" the shock in his voice was genuine. Josh never thought that George would have died so violently. "That is the most gruesome case of homicide I've ever heard." He was also feeling uncomfortable with the deductions that the young Sergeant had arrived at.

Carol nodded, "Mr. Reynolds died in a similar manner. Only that he was shot just once and in the middle of the high desert. Mr. Reynolds was also shot in the area where the axillary artery would be. There is a marked similarity in the manner in which both men died."

"You think it is the same killer was involved in both cases?" Josh wasn't worried about the answer, what worried him was how much Carol had figured out in such a short time. He had to be extra careful with her. She was indeed a very smart cop.

Carol looked into his eyes for a while and said, "What's more sensational Senator is that we found the same type of bullets in both the victims. Ballistics had confirmed that they were fired from a Beretta—a Beretta that is at least twenty five years old. We know that for a fact because the manufacturer had stopped manufacturing those bullets around that time."

Josh leaned forward on his desk, clasped his hands and rested his lips on the tips of his forefingers, "It is the same person then?" Josh was convinced that that the killer was none other than Bill. He had always anticipated that Bill would seek revenge after his release, but he had never anticipated the vehemence of his intent. He did not know how Bill got hold of the Beretta. If he did manage to hide a gun away, it was also possible he had also hidden all the evidence that he had collected before his arrest. Josh had never got his hands on the evidence—he had just hoped that the fire had destroyed it.

"You will have to engage wild horses to tear me away from that theory, Senator," Carol said. "That's the only theory that makes sense to me and I am going to follow it up until I am proved wrong," she paused. "Who could be using a twenty five year old Beretta?"

"Tough question, Sergeant, millions of possibilities," Josh murmured.

"I don't buy that, Senator, sorry," Carol was serious. "In George Briggs' personal safe that we recovered, we found several property deeds registered in Mexico. One of them goes way back twenty seven years. We know for a fact that in those days, Mr. Briggs was still trying to get his head above water after his release from prison. So how could someone with such limited financial resources hold real estate in Mexico? There was no childless and rich aunt who passed away leaving behind a fortune. It seems that he had access to funds that he needed to stash away somewhere safe and outside US jurisdiction."

"Goodness Sergeant, you've made quite some progress on this in a very short time," Josh was truly impressed. "The Chief was right about you." Josh was feeling increasingly uncomfortable.

"So we keep going back to that twenty five year plus timeframe and that is trying to tell me something," Carol did not seem to have heard Josh. "Twenty five years ago, you were quite a phenomenon with the SDPD, Senator," Carol gave a fleeting smile and became serious again. "Can you throw any light on anyone who could have been involved with the two victims in any manner?"

"I-I don't know what to tell you Sergeant," Josh stammered. "George Briggs was never in my radar and Dave Reynolds was busy saving San Diego from annihilation. George could have picked up an enemy in prison or something. Sorry Sergeant, I am not much of help, am I?"

"That's all right, Senator?" Carol said, "I don't expect you to cook something up on the fly. If you don't know anything, that's the way it is," she paused. "I want to be respectful of your time, Sir, so I have one last question."

Josh nodded.

Carol reached into an inner jacket pocket, pulled out a photocopy of a picture and pushed it towards Josh. "I found this on a manila envelope outside my door when I returned home last night. What do you make of it?"

The sudden chill that ran down his spine made Josh shiver inside. On the picture were six men standing on the steps that descended from the front porch of a house. Alejandro, Rusty, and younger versions of Dave and George were clearly visible in the picture. Curiously, the faces of the other two men were blacked out. Josh had no doubt who they were.

Josh was fully aware that Carol was watching him intently and he knew that he had to keep his emotions under control. He had feared and doubted all along that Bill had managed to stow away all the evidence somewhere else and he was right. This was clear evidence that Bill had started to play his cards.

"Well?" Carol asked.

"Looks like the younger days of Dave Reynolds and George Briggs, correct?" Josh did not really need any confirmation.

"Yes, they are indeed. Do you recognize anyone else in the picture?" Carol asked.

"I'm afraid not," Josh hoped that his voice sounded steady. "I wonder why the faces of these two men are blacked out. You say you found this on your doorstep yesterday?"

"Yes," Carol nodded, "it proves that the two victims go back several years in time—they are laughing like they had been buddies all their lives. I believe that this was left for me by the person responsible for the two murders. This person is trying to tell me something. It also proves that this person knows who I am, where I live and what my role is in this investigation," she paused. "You are certain you don't recognize the other two men, can you please look at the picture one more time?"

Josh shook his head in denial, "Why do you think I could possibly know these two men?"

Carol looked directly into Josh's eyes. "Senator, I was down in the labs today and ran an image search on these two men. The man on the extreme left is Alejandro Garcia and the one next to him is Rusty Jones. Surely you remember those names, right?"

Josh frowned and shook his head in denial. He was getting more and more nervous with every passing minute with the young Sergeant.

"They were killed in the large scale sting operation that you had organized when you were working for the SDPD," Carol knew what she was asking.

"I'll be darned," Josh knew he had lost his gamble, "It's been such a long time. My goodness, you are right!" Josh acted surprised and excited.

"Do you think Dave Reynolds and George Briggs were involved in the drug running business?" Carol asked. "We know for a fact that the Garcia and Jones operated almost an empire in these parts."

"I knew Dave very well but I never suspected that he was involved," Josh paused to collect his thoughts. "If he was indeed in cahoots with Alejandro and Rusty, then I guess I did not know Mr. Reynolds well enough. Sorry Sergeant, I don't know what to make of this picture. It is really not conveying much to me."

Carol held her gaze on Josh in silence for a while—it made Josh uneasy. She knew that the Senator was hiding something although he was trying hard not to reveal his emotions. The body language was rather evident. The Senator seemed nervous and from what she had read and heard about him, he was seldom nervous.

She had been baffled the night before when she had found the envelope on her doorstep. The two men with their faces blacked out could have been anybody for all she cared. However it could have meant that the two men were not important or the killer did not want to reveal their identities—at least not just yet. If it was the latter, then their lives could be in danger. When she had determined who the men were in the picture, she had realized that all had some sort of link with the Senator sometime in their lives. She had called his office and requested an appointment.

"Tell you what Senator, why don't you keep that copy for yourself and dwell on it a bit," Carol advised. "If something comes to your mind, please call me and let me know," she got up from her seat and shook hands with Josh. "Thank you very much for your time. I'm sure the campaign is keeping you very busy."

"Yes it is Sergeant," Josh smiled, "But it's worth it. How old do you think this picture is?

"That's easy Senator," Carol said. "If you look very closely at the bottom right corner, you will find a date there. The numbers are so tiny, it could easily escape your attention. I magnified the picture in the lab. The date is a little over twenty six years ago. So long Senator," Carol nodded, tipped her hat and walked out of the room leaving an astounded Josh gaping behind her.

19

"Thank you for the opportunity to meet you Judge Sawyer," Carol extended her hand to Brant. She ignored the very familiar astonished expression in his face as he shook hands with her. She got that a lot from men, who usually found it difficult to relate such a pretty woman to the uniform that she wore.

"My goodness, are you sure you are not a model or an actress?" Brant ventured.

"Too tough for me to handle, Judge," Carol smiled, "I'd rather dodge bullets than cameras in the catwalk."

Brant laughed and motioned her inside his apartment, "Please make yourself comfortable Sergeant Mason. How can I help you?"

Carol lowered herself into the plush leather sofa opposite Brant and said, "I was told you were not feeling well for a while."

"Yes, maybe it's a virus or something that is making me feel very tired these days. I'm sure this will go away," Brant said casually. "Something tells me that you did not come to simply ask about my health, Sergeant."

"Guilty as charged," Carol laughed. "This will not take much time, I promise."

"I'm listening," Brant rested his chin on his folded hands and waited.

Josh had visited Brant the night before and had given him a detailed account of his meeting with Carol. He had predicted that Carol would eventually approach Brant for questions and cautioned him to be extra careful with his answers. Josh had indicated that the pretty Sergeant Mason was extremely sharp with a keen analytical mind. She had reminded Josh of his younger days. "I'll admit to you, Brant that this chick is smarter than I ever was. God only knows why a gorgeous babe like that would end up a cop."

"You must have read and heard about the two gruesome murders of George Briggs and Dave Reynolds," Carol started.

"Yes, those two incidents are all over the news these days," Brant said levelly.

"I won't bore you with all the details, but my investigations have led me to believe that the two cases are related and that it is one person responsible for both murders," the confidence in her voice was unmistakable.

"I see," Brant furrowed his eyebrows.

"Somebody knows that I am investigating both cases and has been trying to communicate with me in a very discrete manner," Carol paused. "The other day I was visiting Senator Timmons and showed him this picture," Carol removed the photocopy from an inside jacket pocket and handed it over to

Brant. "This was left for me on my doorstep the night before in a sealed manila envelope."

Brant looked at the picture and recollected what Josh had told him the night before. There was no doubt that the two men with faces blacked out were Josh and himself. Bill really did have the evidence stored away for all these years.

"I do recognize a younger Mr. Briggs, but I cannot say that I know the other three men," Brant frowned said slowly. "Why are the faces of these two men blacked out?"

"I don't know that yet," Carol shrugged. "Maybe there is a hidden message in there that I am unable to see."

Brant handed the photocopy over to Carol, "Pardon my ignorance Sergeant Mason, but how do I fit into this?"

Carol held her gaze on Brant for a moment and said, "I didn't say you did, Judge. I was wondering if you ever saw the other three men in company of the departed Mr. Briggs."

"Nope, can't say I did," Brant looked at the picture again and set it on the coffee table in front of him.

Carol leaned forward and asked, "You are sure that you have never met Mr. Dave Reynolds? Please look at the picture again."

Brant picked the picked up the picture from the table, looked at it, frowned and set it back down. "Sorry Sergeant, I don't know which one is Mr. Reynolds, if he is one of the men in this picture."

Carol looked at Brant for a brief moment and said, "Hmmm, that's interesting," she leaned back on the couch, "Mr. Reynolds had an apartment in this building a few floors below you. You say you never knew him?"

Brant feigned a surprised look, "No kidding? No, I did not know that. My goodness that really is interesting. Quite candidly Sergeant, I don't socialize too much and keep to myself. I can't remember if Mr. Reynolds and I ever crossed our paths in the past."

"The two men on the left were kingpins of a drug running operation that the ex-SDPD Captain Josh Timmons killed in a sting operation about fifteen years ago," Carol change the topic of discussion. "I'm sure you know Senator Timmons, don't you?"

"Of course," Brant grinned. "We go back several decades. He and I together put away many criminals in the past—we were a good team. We still maintain a healthy relationship with each other."

"You know Judge," Carol started. "In this investigation, all I have so far are mostly isolated incidents and facts and very few links between each other. I'm trying to build some of those links based on what I have, so please bear with my questions. I'm just trying to get to the bottom of this as quickly as I can. Who knows who's next on the killer's hit list? I have reason to believe that we have not yet seen the last of it just yet."

"Sure Sergeant, tell me what's on your mind," Brant shuddered inside. There was Bill out there probably trying to hunt him down. Then there was this Sergeant who appeared sharp enough to put things together and expose both Josh and himself. As Josh had advised, he knew that they were both walking on thin ice. He had to choose his words carefully.

"Did you know where Mr. Briggs lived?" Carol asked what she thought was a rhetorical question, but she had to ask anyway.

"Not the exact address, if that's what you are asking, but I know his residence was somewhere near La Jolla," Brant hoped that the lie was not too evident.

"Yes," Carol said. "That was the only real property he owned in this country. He also owned eight other homes in the most exotic locations in Mexico. Did you know that?"

"No kidding, eight homes in Mexico?" Brant repeated, "I did not know that," he lied again. George had invited him several times to visit him in Mexico and he knew exactly what Carol was saying.

"One of those properties was deeded to him twenty seven years ago," Carol stated. "Here's what puzzles me Judge. George Briggs was nobody twenty seven years ago. He was a bartender in those days. I don't care how much of tips you get, you can't afford such properties in a foreign land. Moreover, I have reason to believe that these killings are some sort of a vendetta that has its roots in the twenty five to twenty eight year period of time."

"Interesting," Brant commented. "There is so little you know about people unless you dig into their past lives."

"So you can understand why it is so vitally important for me to know about the past lives of the two victims. If I can't get to the bottom of this in time, there may be more lives lined up for a very gruesome end," Carol said in all seriousness.

Brant nodded.

"In my research, Judge, I came up with something which may seem very trivial, but the nature of the coincidence caught my attention," Carol continued. "I have learned that the lot where Mr. Briggs had his residence, was left vacant for over a decade and a half. There was another house before that in that same lot. Coincidentally, that house was also completely destroyed in a fire about twenty six years ago," Carol paused and looked at Brant intently. He stiffened instinctively and relaxed when he realized that Carol was watching his reactions very closely.

"I see," Brant prodded.

"Does that ring a distant bell, Judge?" Carol asked.

The bell did ring. It had rung loudly and clearly several days ago. Brant thought a while and shook his head, "I can't say it does, Sergeant," Brant was non-committal.

"Let me help you here," Carol started. "The lot and the house were destroyed by one of the more uncontrollable fires in history of this city twenty six years ago. It was owned by a certain SDPD Lieutenant William McMillan and his wife Joan McMillan. Do you recognize those names?"

Brant furrowed his eyebrows and pursed his lips, hoping that the swelling warmth inside his body did not appear as beads of perspiration on his forehead. "What were the names again?" he asked and Carol repeated.

There was no point in denial and Brant knew that for a fact. The Sergeant was smarter than he thought and she must have done her research. Brant frowned, as if in deep thought and looked away into the distance trying to frame up his reaction.

His expression changed as if he suddenly realized what Carol was talking about, "Ah, yes, I do remember that case. The guy was a crooked cop and was running drugs from his home believe it or not. He even had a little daughter and a beautiful wife—talk about stupidity. When the word got out that his cover was blown, I believe that his gang members burnt his house down. It was rather awful. His wife was killed in the fire, if I remember and his daughter was badly injured, I think. I don't know if she survived or not. We put him away regardless," Brant paused with a faraway look, well aware that Carol was watching him closely. "Gosh Sergeant that was years ago and my memory has faded."

"Yes, it was a long time ago—twenty six years to be exact," Carol said softly.

Brant looked at her for a while and feigned that he just realized what Carol was getting at, "I see. Hence your reference to the twenty six to twenty eight year timeframe, I guess?"

Carol nodded.

"It's probably coincidence, Sergeant," Brant suggested. "Just another unfortunate coincidence that makes the events appear to be related. But pardon me, I don't see enough proof to make a connection."

"You see Judge, that's my problem," Carol got up to leave and picked up her hat from the coffee table. "Too many coincidences are flying around and it is becoming a challenge for me to form a sustainable connection."

"I'm sorry that I could not be of much help Sergeant," Brant rose to show Carol out.

"Here's my contact information," Carol handed a card over to Brant. "You have a very keen and analytical mind. If you think of something I'll be obliged if you can please call me."

Brant took the card from her and nodded, "Definitely Sergeant. It will be my pleasure to assist the SDPD yet again. We have a mutually respectable relationship you know?" he grinned.

"Thank you for your time Judge Sawyer," Carol opened the entry door.

"Sergeant, about this Lieutenant McMillan," Brant ventured, "He is still in prison, right?"

Carol turned around on her heels, "Actually he completed his term and was released as a free man—that was three months ago," she paused and searched for a reaction and found none of much significance. She put her hat on and said, "I hope you feel better soon, Judge. Again, if you think of something, you know where to reach me."

She walked away and replayed her conversation with Brant in her mind. The judge had seemed jittery. For some reason he had been trying to conceal his emotions. It is possible that he had never known Dave Reynolds. With so many residents in the apartment building, it is quite possible that the two never met each other, especially when both had very busy lives.

However the vicious circle of disjointed coincidence came back again in Carol's mind. Through her research, she had come to know that Dave Reynolds was the officer in charge in the William McMillan case. He had even risked his life to save the baby daughter from certain death. He had also managed to extract the wife from the fire but then she had succumbed to her burns a few days later. Brant Sawyer was the attorney who had tried William McMillan case and had sent him to prison. Though possible, it was hard to believe that the Judge never knew Dave Reynolds as he just told her. Both Sawyer and Reynolds lived in the same building and apparently they never knew each other—something did not seem right to Carol.

Carol slid into the driver's seat and shut the door of her car. She sat there for a while with a quizzical expression in her face contemplating what she should do next. There were too many facts to consider and even more missing links, she felt frustrated and stumped.

She was convinced that people were not telling the entire truth or were definitely trying to conceal some facts from her. It was a sixth sense that Carol had developed over the years. Her studies on human psychology, body language and behavior led her to believe that Senator Timmons or Judge Sawyer were not telling her all that she wanted to know. It made her wonder why.

She watched the road ahead with unseeing eyes. A gardener was trying to fix a broken pipe in the lawn of the apartment building. Carol's mind was far away is some distant world as she watched the gardener take a connector, apply glue on the inside, then take a pipe and apply glue on the outside. Then he placed the pipe inside the connector and twisted them together. Then he took another piece of PVC pipe, applied glue to its outside and connected it back to the connector.

Carol sat straight up on her seat, suddenly attentive to what the gardener was doing. That man was building a connection, or rather forcing the two pipes to be connected. She knew instantly what she had to do. She too had to build a connection between what she had gathered so far on the case and see where that took her.

With the lack of evidence, she realized that she had to use her intuition and make assumptions to construct a plausible theory. By the process of elimination she hoped that she could come up with a handful of characters that were really connected to each other and maybe that would take her somewhere.

She ran the names in her mind. There was Senator Timmons, Judge Sawyer, Briggs, Reynolds, Alejandro, Rusty, William McMillan, his dead wife and their daughter Anita. Those were all the characters she had come across in her investigations in that order and were all links to the puzzle in some way, shape or form.

She started the car, glanced at the gardener and smiled. He had unknowingly given her a new avenue to pursue in the case. As she passed him, she rolled her window down, shouted a "Thank you very much" and drove away. The gardener looked up in surprise and wondered what he had done for the woman in the car to deserve the greeting.

20

"Just one last signature right here, Sir," the notary instructed and Bill complied.

"Great we are all done and you are good to go," the notary shook hands with Bill and handed the signed documents over to Bill. "Here's your pour-over will and your living trust."

Bill thanked the notary and left with the fully executed documents which indicated that in the event of his death all his assets would go to Anita McMillan, a.k.a Caroline Mason. It wasn't much that he had for assets, he thought, but the accumulated funds in his investment account would be a nice gift for Anita.

He remembered the last gift he had brought for Anita when she was a little girl—it was an oversized teddy bear. Joan had laughed when Bill had struggled to haul the oversized toy in through the door. Anita had fallen in love with her new companion instantly. She had looked up at Bill, had smiled the sweetest smile, opened her tiny arms and hugged Bill. He remembered how he and Joan had laughed at little Anita's antics.

The warning horn of a passing vehicle snapped Bill back to reality. He walked into the lawyer's office and handed the documents for safe keeping. "Thank you Mr. McMillan," the lawyer reviewed the notarized paperwork. "I will keep this in our custody and per your instructions we will contact your daughter only in the event of your death."

Bill thanked the lawyer and walked out into the street. He felt happy to have taken care of something important that he had intended to do for quite a while. He looked at his watch and hurried towards his car. Joan must have been eagerly waiting for him. It was a special day for both of them.

Bill had been at war with the demons in his mind on his way back from Ohio after he had discovered who Caroline Mason really was. She was none other than his very own Anita. Events in life had given her a different name, but she was his daughter all the same. His blood ran in her body and nothing could ever change that.

However the elation of the discovery had been overshadowed by the fact that it was Anita who had been placed in charge of the investigation to hunt him down. He cursed himself at the wicked twist of fate. He had hoped to find solace in his daughter after all those years of anguish and pain in prison. He realized however that it would continue to remain his hope and probably never become a reality in his lifetime.

She was a law enforcement officer and he had definitely broken the law by taking matters into his own hands with the two murders. In his mind the law was literally in a blindfold. He could not afford to wait for a fair trail even if he produced the evidence. Even if there was trial, in his mind it would not be fair. No verdict in the world would give his life back to him or undo the injustice that was enforced on him.

He knew he had to complete his mission all by himself and to hope that Anita was still a few paces behind him. His time was running out fast. He had to act quickly and stay away from Anita until such time when he finally confronted her. He wondered how she would react when she knew who she really was and what motive drove him to commit such brutal murders.

She would be torn in her mind between her obligations as a police officer and her duties as a daughter. He did not want to place the burden of the harsh reality on Anita's shoulders—he loved her too much. His career was finished and probably his life was on the same path. But Anita's career and life had just begun—he could not take that away from her.

He was happy that Anita had turned out to be a fine young woman with a noble purpose in life and had grown up to be an honest citizen. God had been gracious to him and he humbly acknowledged that. With his last will taken care of, a huge burden had lifted from his mind. He felt relieved and content. He could not wait to share his feelings with Joan and it was good day for that long conversation before his final onslaught on Josh and Brant.

He parked his car on the curbside near the mortuary. He purchased a dozen white roses and some candles from the flower shop nearby and hastened towards Joan's grave. It was beautiful day and he was happy and excited to be with Joan. He had so much to share with her.

He reached the grave and called out, "Hello sweetheart, I'm home!" He sank to his knees, placed the flowers on the gravestone and bent down to kiss the grave, "I love you my darling. My heart beats only for you."

He was about to brush the fallen dry leaves away from the grave when he heard the sound of a twig cracking behind him. He started to turn around to check and stopped. Every drop of his blood and every sense echoed the same note in unison.

"Wouldn't you come and sit down with me?" he said even without looking. "This wonderful lady who lies in this grave was taken from this world twenty six years ago on this date and," he paused. "This is the first time I am with her on this day after twenty six years. I am so ashamed of myself."

He heard cautious and hesitant footsteps behind him and waited. The footsteps stopped close to him. He looked up and smiled, "Hello my sweet little Anita!" He turned to the grave and said, "Just look at our daughter, Joan. She is all grown up and so very beautiful. I must admit she is prettier than you," he gave a short laugh. "She is an honorable and a very accomplished police officer with the SDPD you know? You see, my love—our daughter has found us."

He looked up to see Carol still standing with a perplexed expression in her face. Bill smiled and beckoned, "Come here Anita, sit with me by your mother's grave. Let's celebrate her life together today."

"Y-you are a suspect in…" Carol stammered.

"Sergeant Mason," Bill cut her off. "All of that can wait for a while I'm sure. Your mother is waiting for us. After these twenty six years she has found her family together again—it is a miracle. Please don't hurt her feelings. For a few minutes try to pretend that you are not Sergeant Carol Mason, just a few minutes is all I ask. Just be the daughter we love so very much. The hope of being able to meet you again had kept me going all these years. Now that we are together again, your mother and I would like you to set our differences aside for a while and just be the family we were always meant to be. Can you please grant us a few minutes?"

Carol hesitated and slowly sank to her knees beside Bill. "Welcome home Anita," Bill smiled, "Both your mother and I are so very pleased to have you with us. Wouldn't you greet her, Anita?"

"Hello M- Mom," Carol murmured as the realization of her true identity finally sank into her. There was no longer any doubt about who she really was. The seemingly crazy theory that she had groomed in her mind had finally come true. Unknowingly tears rolled down her cheeks and fell on the grave as she leaned forward to brush the dry leaves away from the gravestone. "I miss you," she managed to say without an attempt to fight back her tears.

After she had met with Brant, Carol had made up her mind that she had to make some assumptions if she was ever to tie the disjointed bits and pieces of information together. She spent several days in her research based on these assumptions and almost everything led to that one event twenty six years ago. The highly accomplished and respected Lieutenant William McMillan of the SDPD was convicted of running drugs in the guise of a police officer. The SDPD led by top narcotics cop Josh Timmons had found substantial quantities of prohibited drugs in his own house. While he was in prison, his house had been destroyed in a fire that was recorded as an accident.

His wife had succumbed to her burns in an attempt to save her baby daughter, who was ultimately rescued unharmed. Josh Timmons had apparently risked his life to rescue the child from certain death. Furthermore, Dave Reynolds from the SDFD had also risked his life in an attempt to save the life of Joan McMillan. However, she had succumbed to her third degree burns a few days later.

Shortly after McMillan was sentenced to twenty six years in prison his attorney passed away. The records indicated he had been drinking. He had lost his balance and fallen from the second floor, landing into the marble floor below. The impact cracked his skull and took his life. Brant Sawyer was the lawyer responsible to send McMillan to prison. These facts intrigued Carol— there was too much coincidence to ignore.

She had made the connection between the fallen Lieutenant McMillan,

Dave Reynolds, Josh Timmons and Brant Sawyer, but her only lead into George Briggs was the photograph that was left on her doorstep.

Her research on the missing Anita McMillan led her through the same channels that Bill had gone through. To her utmost astonishment, she had realized who Anita McMillan was. It took a while for her to come to terms with reality. Suddenly she had realized the implications of her nightmares that had become a part and parcel of her life. It all made sense to her. The woman in her nightmares could be none other than her mother who had died in an effort to save her life.

She had taken a couple of days off to visit her family in Ohio and had a candid conversation with the two people she had known to be her parents. She had learned everything about her past. Her adopted parents also mentioned how a very friendly man by the name of Adam Jones had visited them. He had passed out right before their eyes when they had shown him her album.

Carol had not slept peacefully ever since. She knew in her heart what the answer to the mystery murders were all about. But there was no evidence to substantiate her theory and that frustrated her. William McMillan could be none other than her own birth father and for some reason he was out on a mission of vengeance.

However if the motive was really revenge, Carol was stumped. Josh and Brant were responsible to put the irons on him. So if anyone else, they would be the prime targets for revenge. But they were still alive. Dave, who had saved her from certain death, had been killed in the most ruthless manner. Nothing in George Briggs' record indicated any link to William McMillan. But Carol knew in her heart there must be something that she could not see just yet.

If her father was truly responsible for the death of George and Dave, she knew there was a very good reason. In her heart she felt that her father was probably wrongfully accused and had been framed. It was possible that the fire that killed her mother and destroyed all that she had was no accident, but a deliberate act of arson. The records could very well have been doctored to hide the facts. That complicated matters even further. Her father had an unblemished and immaculate record and had been an accomplished police officer. Though not uncommon for cops with such profiles to have a second life, Carol had found the transformation of her father hard to believe.

Theory, theory and then more theory was all Carol had—no evidence. It was a predicament that she had never been faced with before. Carol was torn between opposing obligations—one towards her practically decimated family and the other towards the code of her profession that she was sworn to uphold.

If there was any true evidence to substantiate her suspicions, Carol felt that Bill would have it. If her theory about her father was correct, Carol knew without a doubt that it was none other than he who had left the photograph of George and Dave on her doorstep. She could also hazard a guess about the identity of the other two men with the faces blacked out.

It was not difficult for someone who watched television to figure out that she had been assigned to the investigation of the two murders, so her professional identity was not a secret. Moreover Bill had already figured out who Carol really was after his visit to her parents in Ohio. The fact that he left evidence for her to follow through indicated that her father was trying to send her a message. She was just not able to read it properly just yet.

If her hunch was right, those two men were Josh Timmons and Brant Sawyer. In fact someone would have to bring in wild horses to take her away from that theory. That implied that the lives of those two men were in danger. She had sensed a guarded discomfort in both men when she had met them and the name of William McMillan had come up by way of conversation. She had not paid much attention at that time. But now that Carol had constructed a plausible theory, the pieces of the jigsaw puzzle had begun to fall in place.

She knew that she had to track down her father. He was the only person who could tell her the real truth and maybe even lead her to some evidence. She wondered how she would react when she first saw him. She did not remember what he looked like. The question was how she could track him down. He had been a cop in his active life, so he would know how to cover his tracks. Carol had to beat him at his own game but she did not know how.

Then it struck her as she stared at the old newspaper clipping that reported the fire that destroyed the house where she once lived with her parents. If her father really was on a mission of vengeance, his motivation could be his love for her mother. Carol knew that her father had sought her out in Ohio. Chances were that part of the reason for vengeance could also be the fact that he had not come to terms with being prematurely estranged from his daughter. If she was right, her father would come to visit her mother's grave on the upcoming anniversary of her death. It was a long shot, but Carol thought that it would be worth checking out.

After a few phone calls to the county registrar's office Carol knew where her mother was buried. She wasted no time to visit the cemetery and identify the grave where her mother had been lying for twenty six years. She observed her bearings and decided to come back later to set up surveillance near the grave. She was fairly certain that the man who she thought to be her birth father would show up.

Very early that day, just after the first rays of a gorgeous orange sun appeared over the mountains, Carol had arrived at the cemetery. She had taken her position about a hundred yards away from the grave behind a giant poplar tree and had waited patiently. After five anxious hours, her heart skipped a beat when she watched an old man walk up to the grave and lay down a bunch of roses on the gravestone.

In her heart she knew who that man was and was ecstatic that her theory was right. But she also knew she had to control her emotions. If her father was the killer, he was a criminal in the eyes of the law and she could not afford to let him escape.

She had tiptoed towards the grave without noticing the broken twig on the ground and had unknowingly stepped on it. She had seen the man who was kneeling at the grave was beginning to turn at the sound of the broken twig and then stopped. Then he called out to her by a name that she never knew she ever had. It appeared that he knew about her presence all along. He then invited her to sit beside him by the grave.

Bill reached out to Carol and fondly ran his right hand over her neatly tied down hair, "Don't cry my dear. You found both of us, so this is a day your mother and I will both cherish forever. Can you hear your mother calling out to you, Anita? She loves you very much and always talks to me about you," Bill referred to his fertile imagination.

Carol turned to find Bill smiling. His deprived heart was trying to capture every moment. Her eyes were filled with tears and she was speechless with emotion. She loved and admired her adopted family but she was with her real family now, with her parents who had brought her into the world.

"Here you go Anita," Bill reached into his jacket pocket. "Light this candle and place it on your mother's grave."

Carol took the candle and the lighter from Bill's hands in silence. They looked into each other's eyes, soothing each other in an effort to wash away the agony that they both felt.

She lighted the candle and placed it on the grave as Bill smiled. "There you go my love, aren't you simply thrilled today?" he spoke to an imaginary Joan. He listened intently and told Carol, "Your mother says that the day is brighter and more beautiful than she had ever known. She fondly sends you a big hug and lots of kisses."

Carol sobbed silently.

"Hey Joan, I know you always wish me the best and always pray for me. But I am on my home stretch now. I have plenty of your good wishes and prayers stored up to last me a lifetime or whatever is left of it," Bill chuckled. "Give all your love and your blessings to Anita, my dear. She will need them in the days to come."

Carol glanced sideways at the last comment, searching Bill's face for the implications of what he really meant. She watched in amazement as Bill conversed with the grave as if his wife was sitting right there in person. He laughed and talked, made references to his beloved daughter—it was surreal. Then he realized that his wife was not alive anymore and he wept profusely. Carol watched him and realized how much he loved her mother. His love for her mother so intense, that such a man could kill and die for.

"I met your adopted parents, Anita," Bill said softly, "I liked them very much. You are very fortunate to have them as the only parents you know. I can tell you that they are very proud of you. I'm so sorry darling. All these years,

I could not take care of you—they did. I have no right to call you my daughter. I have done nothing for you all your life. But trust me none of this should have happened to your mother, to you or to me. I have been wronged, Anita. All that you may have seen or heard is just a veil that covers the truth. There was nothing I could do without endangering your life. Your mother and I are so glad you turned out to be a noble human being. There's nothing more that we could ever ask for."

Carol looked at him in silence.

"You haven't spoken a single word since you came and sat beside me, Anita," Bill observed.

"This isn't easy for me, you know?" Carol murmured with a quivering voice. She stooped down to kiss the grave. She got up on her feet, avoided eye contact with Bill, walked back a few paces and waited.

Bill watched her body language and smiled. The little family get together was over and now it would be business. He remembered how professional and committed he had been to his code of service in his younger days. Anita had turned out to be his mirror image or maybe better than that. It was amazing how she had found him. He had left no trace so she could not have found any leads to find him. Bill knew that Anita must have done a substantial amount of research and made rational assumptions to finally catch up with him. He felt proud of her. She had very sharp powers of deduction. She had the ability to peek beneath the rocks and a keen eye to observe and analyze. She was much like himself or maybe even better than he ever was. She was his blood—there was no doubt about that.

He kissed the grave, arranged the flowers neatly around the candle. The flame flickered in the light breeze but revived again. He stood back, hung his head down and clasped his hands in a silent prayer. "Joan, my love, I will probably not see you in this mortal world again," he murmured. "The law knows about my visits here. So even if I manage to escape today, they will make sure that there is surveillance around here. I have a job to finish my love and you know it. I just cannot afford the luxury of being arrested again. You have always been and will always be in my heart nevertheless. I'll see you in the afterlife. Goodbye for now darling. Keep the fire burning and I will be with you very soon."

Carol watched him and realized that it was time to leave. She prayed for her mother who she never remembered, apart from the woman who kept coming back to her in her nightmares. She was excited to be closer to the truth than she ever was. However a true professional that she was, she contained her emotions and waited. She silently cursed herself to have let her emotions show when she learned without a doubt who she really was. She was only human and for a brief moment the police officer in her had taken a backseat. The sudden confirmation of her loss and confirmation about her true identity had overpowered her rationality and brought her into tears. But she had recovered and the officer in her was back in control.

At length, Bill turned and walked towards Carol. "Can you spare this old forgotten father of yours a few moments Anita?"

She nodded and said softly, "Sergeant Mason will suit me fine, Mr. McMillan."

He tried to take her by her forearm and lead her through the winding path. Carol gently released herself from his grip. Bill smiled, his daughter was a police officer and they were both past their private moments. Now it would be business.

"Well Sergeant," Bill started, "I'm sorry I cut you off back there. You were saying something about me being a suspect for something?"

Carol glanced at Bill and said, "I am sure you know that I am investigating the murders of Dave Reynolds and George Briggs."

Bill smiled, "You look better in person than on the television."

Carol wasn't amused at the comment, "I have reason to believe that you are involved with those murders."

"You have reason to believe?" Bill laughed. "Let me correct you there officer. You have theories," he stressed, "to believe what you just said. You have no evidence to support what you just said. You are a pretty high ranking officer of the SDPD for your age. They don't promote people that quickly unless there are very good reasons. So you know what holds up in court and what doesn't. So pardon me for preaching to the choir, but your statement is not evidence in a court of law. You have no evidence Sergeant and I know it."

"How do you know that, may I ask?" Carol asked.

"Because Sergeant," Bill laughed out aloud. "Firstly, if you had the evidence we would not be having this conversation. Secondly, the murderer made sure that he left no evidence in the first place. He is a thoroughbred, isn't he? I'm sure you figured that out."

"So you say a man and not a woman is involved in these murders?" Carol asked.

"You do have the habit of asking rhetorical questions, Sergeant, don't you?" Bill toyed, "An accomplished police officer is asking an ordinary civilian for help?" he laughed. "I'm not saying anything—that's your job to figure out."

Carol glanced sideways and asked, "How did Mrs. McMillan die?"

"You address her as Mrs. McMillan? Anita, you disappoint me," Bill said with a marked bitterness in his voice. "You addressed me as Mr. McMillan. That surprised me, but I ignored it. As an officer I know you are trying to do your job. But that is not how you refer to your birth mother, child," Bill admonished. "If you have the intelligence and the analytical acumen to find us, it will be foolish of me to believe that you don't know how she died," Bill sparred with Carol. "You are asking rhetorical questions again Sergeant."

Anita stepped in front of Bill and stopped him in his tracks. She looked up at his eyes and said, "I need to know, I have the right to know what happened, if you are truly my parents. I have been working on this case for weeks now and all I have is disjointed facts that lead to nowhere. I am trying to string the pieces together and I'm getting nowhere. I admit, all I have is theory. But that theory is based on the fact that the death of my mother is somehow connected with these murders. I need help, Sir, is there anything you can tell me?"

"Who's asking for help—Anita McMillan or Sergeant Carol Mason?" Bill looked straight into her eyes searching for the daughter he missed growing old with.

"Your daughter, Dad," Anita murmured.

"Say that again," Bill's eyes welled up with emotion.

"Dad," Anita repeated. "Please help me so that I can help you and Mom. I know in my heart what this is all about, but I need to know how this all started. Can you trust me? I am the only living family you have, please talk to me, Dad. I really need to know about you and Mom."

Bill reached out to hold Anita in his hands and slowly held her close. Anita let her defenses down and closed her eyes as she rested her head on her father's chest. Bill kissed her on her head and wished that the moment would never end. He held her close in a warm hug. Father and daughter were together again after what seemed to be a lifetime.

"Come Anita, let's find a place to sit and chat," Bill held Anita by her shoulders and led her towards a nearby seating area.

He spoke for hours with Anita listening intently without interruption. The past could not be changed and there was nothing Anita could do about it. It intrigued her to learn about her father's past life. She learned how he had been framed for a crime he never committed. She heard how he had been blackmailed into silence and forced into prison.

Anita realized how passionately he loved her mother and how desperate he was to find his daughter. She felt strangely compassionate with Bill and it angered her even more to know how Josh Timmons and Brant Sawyer had misled the general public all along. The pieces of the puzzle had fallen in place. The mystery that had eluded her so long was solved. She finally understood the story behind her nightmares. It was a brutal memory of her childhood that was etched in her mind and had stayed with her all along. She wasn't afraid anymore—it all made sense.

She was in a quandary on what she should do next. She knew Bill was responsible for the two murders and Josh and Brant were in the line next. She had to stop her father and use the power of the law to expose the two men who had taken advantage of the law to conceal their true identities. They had also framed an innocent man, blackmailed him and destroyed his life and his family. Anita felt a sudden hatred in her heart. It was something she had never felt before. She had to bring them down and hope to redeem her family's pride.

"Dad, I want all that evidence you have to bring those two men down,"

Anita finally said. "I want that evidence now. Help me redeem your name and bring peace to the mother I don't remember"

Bill laughed, "I'm sorry Anita. I cannot give that to you."

"Excuse me?" Anita was surprised, "What do you mean you cannot give that to me?"

"Well, Anita," Bill grinned. "If you were not a police officer, I might have considered giving it to you. But since you are, I can't do that. Not that I don't trust you, but it is because I trust you. Once I hand that evidence to you, I know you will file a case against Josh and Brant and present them in court. They will be found guilty without a doubt and will be probably be sentenced for life. They will also find that I had taken law into my hands and had committed two of the most gruesome murders in the history of this State. I will have no chance of a pardon. Whatever the reason, my dear, I did take the law into my hands. It will be a miracle if I don't get a life sentence myself. I am not worried about that Anita. What I will be worried about and will agonize about would be the fact that I was not able to complete my mission. I will die with the sense of failure that I was not able to avenge the brutal murder of my innocent wife and the complete destruction of everything that I once held dear to my life."

Anita listened speechlessly

"I have to go through with my mission and kill them myself Anita. I am tired and not getting any younger by the day," Bill paused. "Nothing short of an agonizing death is the real verdict for that Senator and that Judge. I will take their lives first and then hand the evidence over to you, of course if I am still alive. My redemption, Anita, cannot be achieved by throwing those two men in prison. I will not rest in peace even after the public embarrassment, ridicule and wrath that they will face when you expose their true identities. My redemption is in a conclusive termination of their miserable lives in my own hands. The same hands that they chained up twenty six years ago, burnt my innocent wife to her death, estranged my baby daughter, incinerated my house and extinguished the fire in my life. I don't know how much longer I have to live. Every day is critically important for me especially with the SDPD hot on my tail," he smiled. "So you see, Anita, I just cannot have the luxury of a trial. I don't have time on my side. I just want to be with your mother. I have waited too long for this."

"I understand your feelings, but I want to redeem your name Dad," Anita pleaded. "Can you please give your daughter a chance?"

"When I came to know about you and who you have become, my name was already redeemed, my dear," Bill gave a wry smile, fondly ruffled Anita's hair and kissed her forehead. "The very fact that you turned out to be a law abiding and honest citizen of this country is a miracle that I never expected. You have already redeemed my name, Anita. But there are just a few more obligations I have to complete before I can rest. I promise you that once I complete my mission, I will surrender to you all the evidence that I had collected about these scumbags of society. Too bad the law will not be able to get to them first, because I will. But at least people will know who they were and the reasons why I committed those murders. Hopefully then you will be able to redeem my name in the way you want to."

"I just cannot sit here and watch you commit those murders Dad," Anita said, "I am an officer of the SDPD for crying out loud. I have a code of service to uphold, just like you had to, Dad. I have to follow the dictates of the law, I don't have to preach you any of that. There are channels we need to go through to do what's right. I…"

"What channels are you talking about Anita?" Bill cut her off, "Those channels can be doctored my dear, don't I know that? Those are influential people—a Judge and a Senator. God only knows what connections they have to manipulate the system. They have done so successfully thus far and the public has no clue about who they really are."

"I trust you Anita, but I don't trust them," Bill continued. "You have the best of intentions, but not everyone follows your lead. Once they know that you have all the evidence and are going to use it against them, your life my dear will be in danger. Let alone the fact that an army will be released on my tail. Being a father I cannot afford to expose you in harm's way. You have no idea how ruthless these men are. I have taken two of them out, sure, but they were the easy ones—the low hanging fruit. The remaining two are the true masterminds and it will not be easy on the way forward. Sorry Anita, I cannot comply."

"I am not worried about my life, Dad," Anita was not giving up. "If I did not know anything about this, it would have been a different story. But Dad, I am aware of the gory details, just like I am aware of what you wish to do. As a police officer I cannot let that happen. It's my duty to uphold the law, not to fool the system or knowingly allow anyone to take it in his own hands. We live in a civilized world, Dad and there are protocols."

"This conversation is over, Anita," Bill stamped his feet and got up from the bench. "The evidence stays with me till I am done. My life has come almost full circle Anita. I need to complete it and go home to your mother. I've got to leave now. Meeting you, knowing you, holding you in my arms and talking to you has soothed my heart and soul to a degree that I cannot even begin to explain. I wish we could spend some time together, but I've got a mission to complete. Good luck Anita, till we meet again." Bill smiled and turned around to leave.

He had not walked more than a few paces, when he stopped at the sound of safety catch being released on a gun behind him. He turned around to see his daughter standing in a steady position, ready to fire her weapon.

"Mr. McMillan, I am arresting you on the charge of murder of George Briggs and Dave Reynolds," she said clearly and extracted a small voice recorder from an inner jacket pocket. "I have our entire conversation on tape. You are a criminal and you have admitted your crimes yourself. Please do not move because I will not hesitate to use this weapon. So please do not provoke me. Clasp your hands behind your head and sink to your knees very slowly right where you are standing. I don't have to tell you that I shoot very well. It would not be the first time that I have used it against a criminal."

"Anita, don't you understand, they will…" Bill was cut off.

"Sergeant Carol Mason to you, Mr. McMillan," Carol said sternly, "I really do understand everything by the way. So do exactly as I say, clasp your hands behind your head and sink to your knees right where you are standing."

Bill looked around the cemetery—it was deserted. He quickly checked the position of the sun, casually turned his back towards it and away from Carol and started to sink to his knees.

"No I want you to face me and the sun all the time," Carol stopped him midway, the Smith and Wesson steady in her hands. "No tricks Mr. McMillan—I don't like playing with criminals."

Bill smiled to himself. Anita truly was a pretty smart cop and had the experience in dealing with such situations. She was evidently going to cuff him with his hands behind his back. She did not want him to see her shadow when she came up behind him. If he was facing away from the sun like he had intended, he would have seen her shadow behind him when she came up to cuff him. He had planned to surprise her when she was closer, but apparently she saw through him.

He obliged and followed Carol's orders. It was going to be difficult to get out of the situation and he knew it. It wasn't his daughter before him any more. It was indeed a police officer with a drawn weapon that he will have to deal with.

"Stay there very still Sir," Carol cautioned. "Any movement will be considered a threat and I will not hesitate to use this weapon in self-defense."

Bill watched in silence as Carol circled around behind him with her weapon trained on him. With the corner of his eye he saw her reach behind her back and remove a pair of handcuffs. The cemetery was still deserted and the sun was full in his face. He could see nothing behind him, so he waited and listened intently. He had to do something very quickly if he was going to get out of the situation. He hoped Carol will not call for reinforcements.

"All right Mr. McMillan, hold your position and stay very still," Carol called out. "I will have to cuff you. Remember what I told you—no tricks and I will not hesitate to shoot."

Bill heard cautious footsteps behind him. When he sensed that Carol was directly behind him, he knew it was time to act. In a sudden move, he bent down sharply to prop himself up on his hands. In the same motion his legs forcibly kicked out sharply behind him. Carol fired and the bullet grazed Bill's right cheek and lodged itself on the ground. But Bill had already made contact. His kick hit Carol in her midriff which knocked the wind out of her. Her gun went flying from her hands. She collapsed on the ground with a thud and was gasping desperately for breath—she was in obvious pain.

Bill whipped himself up, grabbed the handcuffs from the ground, put one on Carol's right wrist and dragged her body to the pack bench. He placed the other cuff on the iron legs of the bench and stood back to see what he had done. His heart cried out in distress not because of the burning sensation on his right cheek where the bullet had grazed it, but because he had hurt his daughter so viciously. He hoped he could do things differently but he had been left with no option. If Anita had her way, everything would be over and his mission would have remained unaccomplished. That was a luxury he simply could not afford.

He wanted to rush up to Anita and help her, but he knew that would not be prudent. Anita was right in what she was doing. Every police officer is sworn to serve and protect every citizen equally regardless of any personal prejudice. She was following that code and instead of being disappointed in Anita, Bill felt proud of her. She had the courage to set aside the emotional bonding with her long lost father and maintain the honor and integrity of her duty as a police officer. He felt no remorse, he was happy that Anita had indeed grown up to be a fine young woman who valued her principles more than her own emotions.

"Mr. McMillan, you are charged with murder and with assault on a police officer in active duty," Carol winced as she tried to sit up. She was on her way to recovery and managed to speak between short breaths. "Don't make matters worse for yourself than it already is. Take these cuffs off right away—the key is in left pocket of my trousers. I won't repeat myself, Mr. McMillan."

"You are in no position to demand anything officer," Bill glanced around to see if the gunshot created any interest in the cemetery. He still could not see anybody around. He pulled a pair of gloves and walked over to Carol's weapon "So you use a Smith and Wesson, huh? I prefer my Beretta any day."

He removed the magazine and dropped it in his pocket and laid the gun on the bench out of Carol's reach. "Well Sergeant, I will take your leave now. Someone will eventually come around and help you get those cuffs off. Thank you for those wonderful moments when you were my daughter, Anita. But I guess those moments are over and you are a cop after a criminal."

He stooped down to pick up the voice recorder that was lying beside the walkway. "So how do these gadgets work, Sergeant?" he flipped the switches, pressed the levers, hoping for a cassette to drop out. "Well Sergeant, looks like you will have to place yet another charge on me—theft of police property. I cannot leave this behind with you as you can imagine," he dropped the recorder in his pocket. "My apologies for striking you down, but you left me with no other option. Goodbye Sergeant and God bless you," he turned to leave.

"I am faced with the most confusing predicament at these crossroads of my life, Mr. McMillan," Carol called out after him. "On one hand I am concerned about my father and want to protect him and on the other hand I want to uphold the law that I have been sworn into. What should I do," Carol paused, "Dad? Please help me."

Bill stopped and turned around and walked towards her. He squatted down near to where she lay on the ground. "Anita, you have asked for my help and I am telling you this as a father. If you had asked me the question as a police officer, I would have just walked away from here," he paused. "Do your duty Anita and I will have to do mine, that's all the advice I can give you. Without the evidence, whatever you have learned today is only theory and you cannot hold that up in court. I have told you before that I will not give you that evidence, my dear. That makes me a common criminal in the eyes of the law and you need to use all resources at your disposal to hunt me down."

Carol simply stared at Bill.

"I will not make it easy for you," Bill continued. "But your duty is to come after me and protect those two men that you now know to be in my sights. Without the evidence, they are not guilty even if you know in your heart they are—they deserve the protection of the law. Always be true to your code Anita and protect the innocent. Personal relationships should never cloud your judgment. Like I said before, you can have all the evidence after my mission is complete. It is your mission now to prevent me from completing mine. I am on my home stretch Anita and your life has just begun," he patted Anita on her outstretched legs. "I just cannot afford to be taken into custody just yet, my dear. Goodbye and good luck."

A car had pulled up in the parking lot in the distance, so Bill hurried away. He could not afford to be seen with a handcuffed cop on a park bench in a cemetery, which could complicate matters for him.

Carol watched him disappear beneath the hill and leaned back against the bench. She knew in her heart how much she admired her father and his love for his wife. She looked up at the heavens and cried, "Mom, you are so unfortunate to have a daughter like me who does not hesitate to shoot her own father. I have wronged you and I have wronged him. But you are very fortunate to have a husband like him who loves you so dearly and is willing to die for your love. I will follow his advice, Mom, because that was the only advice I ever have received from him. His words are like Gospel for me. It may result in his death in my hands, for which I will never be able to forgive myself. But he literally swore me to my code of service once again and asked me to do my duty as a police officer. I admire him, Mom, I wish things could be different for all of us. I am my own prisoner, Mom, just like Dad has been for all these years. Please forgive this ungrateful daughter if you can."

She sobbed silently for a while before she collected herself. There were people walking through the cemetery and it would be embarrassing to have them see her in that state. She propped herself up, managed to remove the key from her trousers and freed herself. She collected the gun from the bench and walked back towards her car.

There was a lot she had to do in a very short time. Bill was right. Without the evidence both Josh and Brant were innocent of any crime. She had to protect them even though she despised them and was tempted to just let her father have his way. She called the Chief and mentioned that she was coming over. She had to discuss the matter with him and arrange protection for the Senator and the Judge.

She also had to set a trace out for Bill. Every police officer at her disposal needed a description and a picture. They took photos of the subject at prison prior to release. That photograph can be obtained and distributed. They needed to search every motel, hotel—every place where a man could possibly stay temporarily.

It would have been helpful if the media was alerted, but she hated them like the plague. Almost always they distorted the facts and added their own color to influence public opinion simply to boost their sales. She could not afford to have doctored information being published—matters were too delicate. Moreover, panic was something she just could not be held responsible for.

There was this bad taste in her mouth about the whole affair, but she fought it away. She knew that she was indeed a prisoner of her own principles and to her sworn code of service.

21

"Senator," the voice of his secretary came over the intercom, "I have someone on the phone asking for you. He says he is an old friend Willy, calling from Cabos San Lucas in Mexico. Do you want me to patch him through?"

Josh sat up straight in his chair in astonishment and stared at the phone, "Willy from Mexico?" he knew exactly who it was although he didn't want to believe his ears. He cursed himself silently for his instinctive reaction. He did not really want to say the name out aloud in front of Sergeant Mason. She was seated right in front of him and watching him very closely. Ever since she had walked in his office that morning, he just did not feel comfortable with her body language. There was something in her mind that she had been trying to conceal. "Tell him that I am busy right now and cannot take his call," Josh picked up the receiver so that Carol could not hear the conversation.

"I tried that already Senator, but he insists. He mentioned something about a package that is being delivered to you and he wants to give you a heads up," the secretary said.

"All right," Josh resigned. "Patch him through," he waited and Carol watched him in rapt attention. She knew who Willy was—her father had already started to engage.

"Hello this is Senator Timmons," Josh waited for the caller to respond. There was silence.

He repeated and still there was silence.

"Look, I am a busy man and don't have time for games. Who's this?" Josh sounded irritated.

All he heard was heavy breathing on the other end.

"Trouble Senator?" Carol whispered.

Josh quickly glanced at her and shook his head in denial, "Listen, whoever you are, if you don't want to talk stop calling my office and…"

"A Senator should always remain calm and hide his emotions. Especially a Senator with a record of prematurely terminating people's lives," the voice cut him off.

"What are you talking about?" Josh asked nervously.

"You know exactly what I am talking about Senator," the voice continued. "I had never seen a man being burnt alive before you know? He would have died anyway very slowly from a continuous loss of blood that could not be stopped no matter how hard one tried. Seeing Dave burn alive was quite a revelation for me on how someone suffers when the searing heat of the hungry flames cuts through the flesh and digs through the bones. No you don't want to experience such agony, trust me. Being shot between the eyes at point blank is a more humane way to die."

Josh listened silently. Beads of perspiration had begun to show on his forehead but he never realized it. His mind was racing. The presence of Sergeant Mason complicated matters for him. He could not react in the manner that he would have reacted otherwise.

"What happened here Senator? Did the cat get your tongue?" Bill said sarcastically. "Oh you should have seen how George yelped in pain when I shot him in both knee caps and then through this shoulders. That man that size and strength just could not move. He simply shrieked out in the most hellish pain that a man can ever endure. This Beretta can really incapacitate a monster," Bill gave a short laugh.

Josh was searching for words that did not come.

"That pool of blood in his Jacuzzi," Bill continued with an expressionless voice. "My goodness it just swirled round and round his disabled body as he begged for mercy. I think he was begging for mercy. Yes, I do believe he was begging for mercy," Bill repeated.

"You know, quite candidly he was screaming so loudly, the agony actually slurred his speech, so I cannot be sure. But I think he must have been begging for mercy. You should have seen the terror in his eyes when the hungry flames crawled on the ground and ran towards him. He did not know which to fear the most. Was it the pain from four bullets fired at close range that devastated his body? Was it from the loss of blood draining out of his paralyzed body? Or was it the flames that licked on his naked skin and ate into his raw flesh? Quite candidly I could not tell," Bill paused momentarily.

"Have you ever imagined the pain when fire slowly digs into your bones through an open and bleeding bullet wound? I never knew what it could feel like until I saw George in that situation. You know," Bill laughed, "I never knew George was a religious man, but he kept calling for God to help him. I guess hopelessness does that to people."

Josh was feeling suddenly light-headed. He leaned back on the backrest of his chair and stole a furtive glance at Carol. She did not seem to blink and simply stared at Josh.

"Is this some kind of a joke? Who's this?" Josh feigned ignorance.

"I'll skip the pleasantries, but you know very well who I am, you little piece of shit," Bill started casually and ended with a menacing tone. "You think this is a joke? Well, my wife and her parents did not think it was a joke when you and those maggots of yours burnt them alive. My daughter didn't think it was a joke when you estranged her from me. Do you know what happened to her, Josh? Is she dead or is she still alive? Do you care at all? I for one do not think this is a joke at all".

"You destroyed my life, Josh and I cannot let you continue to hoodwink the public and live in peace. You still think this is a joke, huh?" he paused.

"Wait a minute, I get it. Maybe you are trying to put up that upright-citizen public image in front of that police officer sitting in front of you, aren't you, you faggot?"

Josh stiffened. He could not figure out how on earth Bill knew Sergeant Mason was with him. Instinctively he looked up sharply at the Sergeant and then kicked himself mentally for his reaction. She continued to remain transfixed on him.

"Got you worried, huh Josh?" Bill asked with a deadpan voice. "Worried how I know about that officer in your office? I have my tabs on you, you son-of-a-bitch. I know who you are meeting, who you are talking to, where you are going and when you are going," Bill had no emotion or excitement in his voice. "You cannot trust anybody anymore, Josh. Not even that sniveling two-faced attorney friend of yours. I can't believe they made you a Senator and that sniveling rat a Judge. You did well in the masquerade party so long, Josh, but party time is over for you."

The door to his office opened and his secretary walked in with a manila envelope. "This came for you Senator. It was hand-delivered to my desk. It has 'urgent' written all over it. So I thought you might want to see this right away, Senator."

"Hang on," Josh spoke into the mouthpiece and covered it. He looked suspiciously at his secretary. Bill had said he could not trust anybody and he knew everything about him. He wondered if his secretary was in cahoots with Bill. She was an old woman nearing retirement and not even in his wildest imaginations could he believe that she would be working behind his back. He took the envelope from her. "Thank you," he said and motioned her to leave the room.

He cradled the phone between his head and his left shoulder and opened the envelope to remove the contents. There really was just one sheet of paper inside. It was a photocopy of the same picture that the Sergeant had showed him a few days back, however there was a difference. The faces of Dave and George were blacked out on this one. Brant was clearly visible. However his own face had a circle around it with a plus sign smack in the center of his forehead. The sign represented crosshairs of a gun-sight.

His heart rate kicked up and he could feel a sudden heat around his ears as anxiety escalated his blood pressure. He broke out into a cold sweat and fought to contain his emotions before the Sergeant. His theory was wrong all along. It wasn't Brant who was up next in Bill's list, it was him. Bill was coming after him next. Josh suddenly needed fresh air.

"So Senator," Josh could hear Bill spit with distaste. "Heck that word Senator for a maggot like you does taste like decaying Swiss cheese," he paused. "How do you like your picture? You did not look too bad in your younger days, you know?"

Josh froze. He could not figure out how Bill knew about what he was doing. He placed the photocopy inside his envelope and asked, "Willy, where are you?"

"Closer to you than you can think," Bill said. "Look outside your window across the street."

Josh got up from his chair and walked over to the window and looked down across the street. There was a public telephone booth on the sidewalk and Josh could see someone inside. He motioned to Carol to come over to the window and pointed at the booth. He covered the mouthpiece and whispered, "Sergeant, I don't have time to explain. I need you to arrest that man in that telephone booth? He is on the phone with me and appears to be a terrorist. He is threatening me on the phone. He is saying he has this building all wired to blow up. I think he is lying. I'll try to keep him on the line as long as I can. If he tries to escape, shoot him down. Please hurry."

Carol rushed out.

"I am looking outside the window and I don't see you," Josh said.

"It's not your fault Josh, age does that to people," Bill sounded sarcastically concerned. "Your eyesight deteriorates but then someone else's gun sights pick you up."

"Look Bill," Josh looked outside. Carol was still on her way, so he had to keep talking and give her some time to reach the booth. "Whatever happened, it was long time ago. I have repented the death of your wife and her parents. That is not how we had planned things to be. We were supposed to get your family out of the house before the fire got to them. Dave got delayed on his way. There was an accident that had backed up traffic so badly that his fire truck could not get through on time. We were all very sorry about how things had turned out. All we wanted to do was scare you." Another minute longer and the Sergeant would be there.

"Liar, Josh," Bill said with disgust, "you have lied all your life. You have lied your way into public life and I hear that you are now trying to lie your way into the White House," Bill showed no emotion in his voice. "For whatever it is worth, I still have faith in this country and still honor its constitution. I shudder inside at the very thought of seeing a piece of garbage like you become the President of this country. But then you won't get there Josh. I'm going to hunt you down like a mad dog. Run as far as you can Josh, but you cannot hide."

Josh could see Carol sprinting across the street as cars screeched to a halt in an effort to avoid a collision with her. "I think it is you who should run, my friend, now would be a good time," Josh sneered. "Your days are over you bastard."

Carol yanked the door open, grabbed the person inside and threw him face down on the pavement. She un-holstered her gun and held it steadily in her hands pointing downwards at the prostrate body.

Josh laughed, "I told you to run, Bill. You see now you have messed it up again. Don't you ever learn? Why don't you ever listen to me? You think you know it all, don't you hotshot? You are nothing but a failure, a has-been."

"I think it's you who messed up, yet again Josh," Bill was cold. "You just sent the pretty Sergeant on a wild goose chase."

Josh did not expect an answer from the other end. He thought he was speaking to an open line, since Carol had already pulled the person out from the booth. He looked down on the street. Carol was apologizing profusely to a Chinese woman as she helped her to her feet and led her to a bench.

"Damn you Bill," Josh murmured as he realized that he had been taken for a ride.

"Well I'm not Chinese," Bill laughed sarcastically, "and I am definitely not a woman."

"What do you want?" Josh asked.

"Nothing, just nothing," Bill started. "You guys never got to all the evidence that you thought you had destroyed, Josh. I had it stored safely all the time. I am going to start releasing it to the media one by one. I have pictures, audio tapes, documents and all kinds of interesting collateral that will reveal your true identity. I had already sent the Sergeant my first installment. It is the same sheet of paper that was just delivered to you a little while ago in your office. It's just a different version—you may have already seen it. Anyway, I will start off with an un-edited version to the media. They just love such stuff, as you know. Nothing like a political scandal—that will grab the headlines for weeks. Also, I am going to start sending copies to your opposition party office and of course to your own party office," Bill paused.

Josh clenched his teeth in anticipation for the worst.

"Everyone needs to know how pretty you look without that mask, Josh," Bill had a tone of finality in his voice. "You're finished, Josh, it's just a matter of time. Don't worry, you won't have to live much longer, I'm a compassionate man. If you want, I'll end your life before the public disgrace kills your soul," he paused. "On second thoughts, I think I'll spare your life and let you face a trial. It would be great if we can get your Judge friend preside over your case. That will be an interesting trial to observe. Yep, that's what I think I will do, Josh. Let me think about it and I will get back to you very soon."

"I'm going to hunt you down, you son-of-a-bitch. You are trying to blackmail a Senator. You cannot even begin to imagine what consequences that imply for you," Josh let down all his politeness. "Better watch your back Billy boy, the SDPD will be breathing down your hole any moment now. They will have orders to kill on sight. You are already being labeled as a terrorist. You know how they treat terrorists these days."

"I'm laughing Josh," Bill laughed out aloud. "That was good show. You think the SDPD will get to me? Sure they have pretty Sergeants, but that is all they have Josh. All beauty and no brains—that's the SDPD for you. Want some advice? Get the SDPD out of the way and bring in the FBI, pretty

Sergeants cannot protect you, you filthy bastard."

Bill hoped that Josh would be able to pull the necessary strings to get Anita to stand down. He did not want another confrontation with her. He did not want her in his line of fire.

"You think I really care if I live or not anymore?" Bill continued. "Heck you killed me the day you took me into custody, you cannot kill me again. Bring in an army if you want, nobody will be able to save you. I will pick you whenever I choose to, wherever I choose to. You don't believe me at all do you? Watch your head Senator."

The window pane above Bill's head shattered into pieces and drenched Josh with broken glass. He threw himself on the floor in a reflex action and the phone fell from his hands.

"Anytime and anywhere, Josh, anytime and anywhere. Your time's up." he could hear Bill's voice on the phone and then it went dead.

Josh picked himself up as his secretary rushed in, "Oh my God, are you ok, Senator? What happened here?"

Josh was literally covered in small pieces of broken glass.

"Yes, I'm ok Mrs. Buxton, nothing to panic about. Can you get someone to clean this up and fix that window pane? Looks like a bird flew right into it. These things happen, you know?"

"Y-yes, if you say so, Senator," Mrs. Buxton almost mechanically replaced the telephone on his desk, but could not figure out what species of bird that lived in the area could shatter an industrial grade glass window.

Josh grabbed the manila envelope and tossed it inside a drawer. He hurried into the men's room. He was shivering and sweating profusely. He just survived an attempt on his life. He never expected to be shot at—that too in his own office. He wondered if Bill had missed him on purpose as a warning message or whether he had actually aimed and missed. He splashed cold water on his face and around his neck but his heart was still pounding.

He realized that Bill literally had him over the blade of a guillotine. His career would be finished if Bill actually did what he threatened to do. The public disgrace will destroy all that he worked so hard for. He would be tried in court and despite his connections he would be exposed. He wondered if it would be easier to just take his own life. That might be easier than to face the wrath and disgrace from the public and the harsh verdict of the law. Even if Bill did not expose him, he could kill him anytime and anywhere he wanted, just like he had said and demonstrated.

Josh held on to the washbasin and hung his head in utter despair. Bill really had him cornered and he was out of options. In fact he had no cards left to play anymore. He wondered if he should take up on Bill's advice and call in the FBI. But then he would have to substantiate his reasons for that action. With Bill out there, poised and ready to release all the evidence he had on him, it might as well be a moot point. In fact he was certain that if he did manage to engage the FBI, he could in fact force Bill's hand to release the evidence prematurely, just like he had mentioned.

He had gambled all his life, so Josh decided to gamble one last time. He was going to let the SDPD continue the investigation and hope they would be able to catch up with Bill on time. There might just be that slim chance that Bill would hold off on that evidence for a little longer—long enough for the SDPD to catch up with him. Josh was clutching at straws and he knew it. He splashed some cold water again on his face, hoping it would wash away his worries.

He wiped his face with a paper towel and came out of the restroom to see Sergeant Mason pacing the floor outside.

"Are you ok Senator?" she asked, "Mrs. Buxton told me what happened. A bird hit? You've got to be kidding me. An impact that strong will kill any bird let alone shatter an industrial grade glass window. There's no dead bird," she paused. "Somebody just made an attempt at your life, isn't it Sir?"

Josh looked at her with a worried expression and frowned. He was about to roll the dice on probably the last gamble in his life and he wasn't sure if the odds were in his favor at all. "Let's go back to my office Sergeant, we have to talk," his voice was a shade over a whisper.

"In your office? I don't think that is safe, Senator. The person who shot at you may still be watching and try again," Carol cautioned.

"I don't think so, Sergeant," Josh sounded certain. "You don't shoot at a Senator and stick around to enjoy the party. Our bird has already flown by now."

"We'll know very soon about that. I have already called in reinforcements," she listened intently, "I can hear the sirens. Gosh I wish they would shut those damn things off. We're going to comb the three buildings across the street from where the bullet might have been fired. I found the bullet in your room, Senator. It struck the opposite wall, which gives me some idea on the trajectory," she paused and searched for some emotion—there was none. "At least the sirens will scare him off. Just to be safe Senator, let's go to another room and chat about this."

They entered another office and Josh motioned everyone to leave. He sat down and sighed. The media would be swarming his office any moment now. The news about a Senator being shot at was too juicy for the newspapers to stay away from. Most certainly the tabloids will cook up their own concoction.

Carol sat opposite to Josh and waited. Her father did well, she thought. It was very well calculated. She too had fallen for it with the hope that it was him in the telephone booth. She could not figure out how she should feel. Should she be elated that it wasn't her father or disappointed that she had been sent on a wild goose chase. He had set up the decoy perfectly to get her out of the way before he took his shot at Josh. She was convinced that Bill simply wanted to scare Josh, without the intent of killing him just yet. He wanted Josh to experience the terror of living with the constant fear of death that may come at any moment and completely unannounced.

Carol was confused about something that Bill had hinted on when they had spoken in the cemetery. Bill had indicated that he would be going after Brant next and save Josh for last. But his first attack was on Josh instead. Carol wondered if Bill had changed his plans. It was a possibility, since Bill knew that he had already disclosed his intentions about Brant to her.

Carol knew that she had to get to her father first before he got to Josh or Brant. She just could not see more murders on her father's record. It would be increasingly difficult to save him from a certain death penalty if she failed.

She had told everything to the Chief after her meeting with Bill at the cemetery. The Chief was not only intrigued when he heard the story he was also concerned about Carol. "I think I should re-assign you to another job, Sergeant. If this man is serious, your life may be in danger. I cannot expose you this way. I know that you will do your duty and protect the Senator and the Judge. But this man has already demonstrated how ruthless he can be. He will stop at nothing unless we stop him first. You will be in the line of fire Carol and I cannot afford to lose you."

Carol held her gaze on a spot on the floor and had listened intently.

"She is your father for goodness sake," the Chief was genuinely concerned. "You may hesitate to take your shot if you had the chance and those seconds could cost you your life. If he is desperate, he won't hesitate shooting you to get to this ultimate goal. Even if you did manage to take his life in an encounter, you will never be able to forgive yourself. You are a very good police officer, Sergeant. You're probably the best I have worked with. But you are also human and a daughter. He has already demonstrated that he would not consider you as his daughter if you became an obstacle in his mission. No, Carol, I cannot let you continue in this case, you have to excuse me. I will have to reassign this case to someone else."

Carol had smiled, "Chief, I honor and respect you for who you are and what you do for all of us. This is the biggest case in my career, Chief. This is not only a test for my duties as a law enforcement officer it is also a test of my duties as a daughter. I cannot have more blood in the hands of my father. Chief, that man is not a born killer. We killed his soul and never cared to listen to him. We should also be tried in court for our ignorance of the facts. I need to protect him and I need to protect the law. Without the evidence, my father is just a common criminal and the Senator and the Judge are innocent. US Law 101, Chief, nobody is guilty unless proven guilty. Nobody knows it better than you do Chief and you know how committed I am to uphold the law. Believe me, Chief, I will not waver if I have to take a shot and take him down. I may repent it for the rest of my life, but I am sworn to my code, Chief. Please, I implore you not to re-assign me. I won't let you down."

The Chief had held his gaze on her for a while, then patted her on her shoulder and reluctantly agreed. "Are you going to tell the Senator and the Judge about this?"

"Not yet, Chief, not jut yet" Carol had said. "I want to play this out a little further and see if they come up with something on their own accord. They are under a lot of pressure and I could feel the tension and apprehension when I met them. I have a feeling that they will buckle under their mental conflicts eventually. This is turning into a mind-game and I just need to stretch it out a little more. However, I need round the clock protection for both of them without letting them know about our presence. I want to pick a team of officers who will have to be sworn to secrecy. I will brief them personally and they will report to me. All they will know is who they are protecting and who they are protecting them from. My relationship to William McMillan is not important for them to know. Rumors in the ranks can cloud one's judgment. That's all, Chief. I need your support."

The Chief had approved and Carol eventually had her team in place.

She had held her gaze on Josh, allowing him the time to align his thoughts. The mastermind behind the death of her mother and the destruction of her family was sitting right in front of her. There was nothing she could do about it without the evidence. She had felt an almost overpowering urge to empty her gun on the man, but she fought it down. There must be another way under the power of the law to deal with Josh. She found it difficult to convince herself why she should protect someone who brutally murdered her own mother and got off scot-free. She reasoned that by protecting Josh she was actually protecting her father from committing another crime. She was also protecting his soul. It would be interesting, she thought, on how Josh would cook up his side of the story.

"Sergeant, I have a confession to make," Josh sighed, staring at a spot on the floor.

"I'm not a priest Senator, but I'm listening," Carol reached into her pocket, removed a voice recorder, switched it to recording mode and placed it on the table. Josh saw the recorder and looked up at Carol. "I'm ready when you are Senator," she prodded.

"That was no terrorist who wanted to blow up this building," Josh started, "I'm sorry I lied to you at that time. I could not think of anything else and I had to send you after him. I apologize for having misled you and for sending you on a wild goose chase, Sergeant. I was so certain that he was calling from the telephone booth—I'm sorry."

"That's all right Senator, I understand," Carol said. "The fact that I had to go and check out the telephone booth does not bother me. What bothers me is you are not forthcoming with who called you and why you reacted in that manner."

Josh looked at Carol without seeing her—he had to cook up a plausible story. "I think I know who it is, Sergeant."

Carol remained silent, waiting for Josh to continue.

"I think an event in my life twenty six years ago has come to haunt me again," Josh started. "We talked about this briefly in the past Sergeant. The more I think about this, the more convinced I am that my suspicions are correct."

He paused to collect his thoughts again.

"Twenty six years ago, I had arrested Lieutenant William McMillan from his house on charges of harboring and trafficking prohibited drugs. We had a search warrant with us and we found large quantities of narcotics concealed all over his house. We had been keeping tabs on him for sometime and we finally caught up with him," Josh paused. "When he was in prison awaiting his trial, his house accidentally caught fire and was completely burnt down. His in-laws who had moved in with his wife and baby daughter were burnt alive. His wife succumbed to her third degree burns a few days later and his daughter was placed in custody of the State. Eventually he got convicted and was sentenced to twenty six years."

"I have done that research, Senator," Carol clenched her teeth to contain her emotions—Josh was effortlessly lying in his teeth. "What has this got to do with what happened here a little while ago?"

"Then you must already know that McMillan was released a few months ago," Josh asked without really expecting an answer. "He's seeking revenge."

"Why would he be seeking revenge?" Carol said nonchalantly. "He was proved guilty, correct? Are you saying that he did not agree with the verdict?

"Look, I don't know what's in his head," Josh said nervously. "He thinks I am to blame for what happened to him and his family. Well I arrested him and testified against him in court, but I was just doing my job. That man was dealing drugs working under cover of the law, so I had to stop him. I had nothing to do with the fire that destroyed his house or killed his family, Sergeant." If Carol did not know better she would have been convinced. The earnestness in Josh's voice was rather compelling.

"So with that theory, I guess what you are saying is that McMillan will also be after the Judge who read the verdict and his attorney who failed to get him acquitted, correct?" Carol wanted to see how Josh reacted to such an outlandish possibility.

"Well, Judge Smith passed away a few years ago, so McMillan couldn't reach him even if he wanted to. As far as his attorney is concerned, he can't reach him either. That man fell from his balcony and smashed his head on the stone floor right after the trial was over. The impact killed him. The records say that he had consumed a substantial amount of alcohol prior to his death and must have lost his balance," Josh paused. It was he who had ordered George to kill Blake. "So I guess if they were alive, a madman such as McMillan would have gone after them as well."

Carol's jaw stiffened and relaxed—Josh was quite a consummate liar.

Somehow she knew that Bill's attorney was pushed—he did not fall to his death. "How can you be so sure that it's McMillan trying to kill you?" she prodded.

"Curiously, McMillan did not say much during the trials. He knew he was guilty, so there wasn't much he could say anyway," Josh tried to sound convincing again. Carol shifted in her seat and crossed her legs, trying to fight the welling disgust in her mind. Listening to Josh lie his way through so effortlessly made her blood boil.

"The last time I saw him in prison, was the only time that he spoke to me," Josh continued on his story. "He had threatened me to watch out for him after his release. I had ignored him at that time thinking he was just venting his frustration. I thought after twenty six years he won't have the juice to do anything anyway. Empty threats from criminals were not uncommon and so I just ignored him. I guess he is trying to follow up on his threat."

"So you think this Willy from Mexico is really William McMillan?" Carol asked.

"Yes, I have very sharp memory Sergeant. I remember people's faces and voices very well. I know it is McMillan and nobody else," Josh was certain.

"Where's the Mexico connection coming from?" Carol pushed.

"That I have no idea, Sergeant," Josh lied again. "That fooled me the first time as well."

Carol looked at Josh in a manner that made him uncomfortable. He wondered if Carol was seeing through his lies. He thought he was convincing enough, but the Sergeant was a sharp one to contend with.

"Let's tag along with your theory Senator and say that you are right," Carol picked up the conversation, "Who was the Prosecutor in that McMillan case?"

"You already know the answer, Sergeant, I'm sure. It was Brant Sawyer, he called me to say that you had met him and had been asking questions," Josh was slowly getting back on his feet again.

"I am talking to you now, aren't I," Carol sounded irritated, "I asked you a direct question, if you would please answer it."

"It was Brant Sawyer all right," Josh cowered a bit.

"I'd say that in that case, Judge Sawyer is also at risk, wouldn't you think?" Carol asked. "I mean he was also responsible to throw McMillan in prison, right? So McMillan will be after him as well, don't you think?"

"Well, there was nothing much for Sawyer to do, really. I had lined up all the evidence against him and we really did not need anyone of Sawyer's caliber to try this case. McMillan's fate was sealed even before he set foot inside the court," Josh scowled.

"Let me ask you a question Senator," Carol looked straight into his eyes. "Do you think McMillan was responsible for the murder of Dave Reynolds and George Briggs?"

Josh desperately needed a glass of water to drink, "Why do you ask Sergeant?"

"Quite candidly I don't know. Call it coincidence if you will, but we found bullets on each victim's body from probably the same Beretta. Ballistics confirmed that the bullets in both cases were manufactured at least twenty five years ago—apparently the manufacturer stopped making those during that time."

"Are you telling me that McMillan stored his old service weapon somewhere secret and retrieved it after his release from prison?" Josh leaned forward.

"Well, I don't know if it is a service weapon or not, but those bullets don't fit any other gun, that's for sure," Carol held her gaze.

If Bill did manage to store a weapon somewhere safe, then he truly could also have stored the evidence along with it. That meant that his threat about releasing the evidence to the media might not be an empty one. Josh was sweating again.

"What about the bullet you found in my room, Sergeant?" Josh asked, "Was the same gun used again?"

"I don't think so," Carol said as she pulled out the spent piece of metal from her jacket pocket. "This looks like it was fired from a rifle—probably one with telescopic sights. So what do you think about the possibility of Dave Reynolds and George Briggs being murdered by McMillan?"

"It's a possibility, Sergeant," Josh said at length.

"Really?" Carol widened her eyes. "How's that? The Chief told me that you and the late Mr. Reynolds were friends from your past lives. You and Reynolds actually risked your lives to rescue McMillan's wife and daughter, right? So McMillan should be grateful to both of you, don't you think?"

"McMillan's a madman, Sergeant," Josh was emphatic. "Nobody can be more desperate and deranged than a crooked cop—that's McMillan for you," Carol gritted her teeth in disgust again. "You see Sergeant, McMillan may be under the impression that Dave purposely arrived late with his crew and hence was responsible for the third degree burns on his wife, which eventually killed her. He may be thinking that his family could have survived if Dave was there on time. The man's insane, Sergeant—you can never predict what such a man could think."

"Why could he have killed George Briggs then?" Carol asked. "Was there ever a connection between them?"

"None that I know of," Josh chose a faraway point in the ceiling to gaze at. "The only thing that I can think of is after his release, McMillan must have found his way to where his house was, expecting nothing but rubble. Instead he found that somebody had built a luxurious mansion over what was once his own house. Granted that it is just stupid to even think of something like that after twenty six years, but then McMillan is not in his right frame of mind, you know. So he finds this luxurious mansion where his house once stood and that infuriates him. He thinks that someone has built their dreams over the embers of his house. He blows his top and decides to take out the owner. Complete whacky, Sergeant, but that's McMillan for you."

Carol was amazed at how convincingly Josh could instinctively talk his way through situations. No wonder he was able to cover his tracks and paint his public image.

"Well Senator, if what you say is right, then we have a big problem here," Carol maintained a level tone. "The court will be lenient to someone who is mentally unstable. At the most he will get life, but in a mental asylum. That's if we catch him. If we don't, he will strike again and he will make sure that he does not miss."

Josh broke into a cold sweat again. "So what is the SDPD going to do about this?" he could not contain the nervousness in his voice.

"We cannot risk your life, Senator. I'll arrange for round the clock protection for you. They'll follow you wherever you go. Know who they are and make them your allies. If your theory is correct, they actually stand between your life and McMillan. Don't go anywhere without letting them know, is that understood?" Carol asked without really expecting an answer.

Josh nodded.

"Good, don't make any statements to the media under any circumstances and tell your staff to maintain complete silence as well," Carol continued. "The last thing this city wants is a mass panic and some concocted version of the true facts. Moreover, we don't want to force McMillan's hand if we can help it. We'll set taps on your phone line so that we can monitor all calls made to you. Are you ok with that?"

Josh reluctantly nodded approval.

"Sergeant Mason?" her radio crackled.

Carol flicked the switch to receive, "Mason here, go ahead, over."

"Officer Dunn here, Sergeant. We combed all the buildings Sergeant," the voice reported. "They're all clean. However we did find that the lock to the door to the roof on the west side building was broken—probably with a sledgehammer, over."

Carol stole a quick glance at Josh who was staring at her radio.

"Looks like our bird has flown," Carol commented. "Look around that roof to see if you find anything interesting—anything at all that you think is unusual. Officer, I know the press is probably swarming the place by now. Tell your guys not to make any comment to anyone, that's an order, Mason out," Carol tucked her radio in her waist belt.

"They wouldn't have found anybody," Josh murmured.

"I know that, moreover an ex-cop will know the standard procedures. If it was McMillan, he would have taken that shot and made his escape before we got there. So where were we with your protection?" Carol switched topics.

"You were talking about staying away from the press," Josh said. "You don't care much for them do you, Sergeant?"

"No I don't. All they look for is gravy to fill their pages. I don't think they care about the social consequences of their reports," Carol waved her hand in dismissal. "Anyway, like I was saying, keep it together and work from home for a while till this thing blows over. I am going to set up a trace on McMillan and see if we can track his movements. Unless he disappears into thin air every time we come near to him, we should be able to find him. Are you ok, Senator?"

"When you find him, shoot to kill, Sergeant," Josh summoned up courage. He was certain that he had convinced Carol about the seriousness of the situation.

"With due respect, I don't need instructions from you on what I have to do, Senator," Carol was cold. "The SDPD does not make Sergeants without brains and proper judgment, I am sure you know that."

"Sorry Sergeant," Josh apologized, realizing that he might have overstepped the line. "I was just trying to warn you about this madman."

"Thanks for the warning," Carol said, "We don't know if he is a madman, just yet. He may be perfectly sane and has a perfectly valid motive, something in his mind that we don't know about. So don't jump to conclusions just yet. Nobody is guilty unless proved likewise. That's US Law 101 for you Senator, in case you are remiss," Carol was not in any mood for levity.

"Thanks for listening to me and doing what you do," Josh brought himself back on track.

"Sure thing," Carol said. "Keep your head down and please follow my instructions. I'll send officers to come a get you from your office."

"Thank you again, Sergeant," Josh extended his hand to shake with Carol, "I feel relieved talking to you."

"I'll shake hands with you after this thing blows over," Carol ignored the gesture. "By the way, McMillan's wife was killed, as we know. What happened to his daughter?"

"Well, the last time I saw her, she was placed in an foster home managed by the State," Josh said, "I don't know what happened to her afterwards. Sorry."

Of course you didn't, Carol thought. Aloud she said, "I'll try to track her down as well. She's a grown up woman by now, if she is alive of course. McMillan may be staying with her for all you know," she looked into the puzzled eyes and loathed every moment with Josh. "She may be able to shed some light on this, although I have my doubts. So long Senator."

Carol left the room. She shook her head in disgust at all the lies that Josh had told her. Again she felt frustrated that she had no evidence in hand to prove that Josh was lying all along. She hoped Bill would cooperate, but she knew that was not something she could expect.

Josh assessed his situation. He felt he was convincing enough for the Sergeant. There was no factual evidence that he gave up, only theories that should be enough to put the Sergeant on Bill's tail. She was going to arrange for his security anyway, which was what he had wanted all along.

He looked at the open window in his office. The shattered pieces of glass were cleared away and the cool breeze seemed to refresh him. He hoped that Carol would follow his theory and get to Bill before he got to him. Working from home did not seem to be a bad idea, but that was bad for his public image. A Senator trying to save his skin from a common terrorist would be just fodder for the press. He could not afford the public to believe that he was running scared. Moreover he had to keep it quiet from the press—just like Carol had said. He did not want to force Bill into any immediate reaction.

Josh reached out for his intercom, "Mrs. Buxton, can you connect me to the California Department of Social Services right away?"

"Certainly, Senator," she paused and sounded confused, "The Sergeant mentioned that this line will be tapped so that they can monitor all calls on this line. She said she already spoke to you about it."

"Yes, I know, can you get the connection to me right away, Mrs. Buxton?" Josh had urgency in his voice. He flicked the switch and drummed his fingers on the table. The taps would take a few hours to be placed, but he wanted to find something out before they clipped his wings.

The telephone rang and Josh picked it up. "I have Mary from the Department on the line, Senator, is this a good time to talk?

"Yes, please put her through, thanks Mrs. Buxton," Bill waited.

"Hello Senator Timmons, this is Mary from the California Department of Social Services. I am a big fan of yours, Senator. This is indeed a pleasure to have the opportunity to talk to you. How can we help you Sir?" the voice of a young woman came through.

"Good afternoon to you, Mary. I hope you and yours are all doing well," Josh started. "If I had to know the whereabouts of a child who was placed in the State's custody some twenty six years ago, who would I need to talk to?"

"That will be Marcus Corbin in the Child Care and Rehabilitation department," Mary said. "Are you looking for a particular child?"

"Actually I am," Josh was at his usual best. "A cousin of mine had been divorced about twenty six years ago. She had lost custody of her child to her husband. Well her ex-husband remarried and his new wife did not want to take care of the child who was then placed in the custody of the State. Well, now she wants to reunite with her daughter and she contacted me asking if I could help. I promised her that I would try."

"We adults certainly don't make it easy for the children, do we, Senator?" Mary asked. "Let me give you a number to call," she repeated a phone number that Josh noted down.

Josh replaced the receiver and dialed the number he was given.

"Marcus Corbin speaking, how can I help?" Josh winced and held the earpiece away—the man had a rather loud voice.

"Hello, this is Senator Josh Timmons calling. How are you today, Mr. Corbin?" Josh paused for reaction from the other end.

"Senator Timmons, this isn't a joke, is it?" the voice grew louder.

Josh laughed, "No Mr. Corbin, this is indeed Senator Timmons. I need your help."

"Yes, yes, of course Senator, it will be my pleasure to be of any service that I can be," the voice curiously became softer. "My goodness, my wife will never believe me that I actually spoke to the future President of the United States."

Josh smiled to himself. He did work hard for a popular public image— they just loved and respected him. Now Bill was out there trying to take it all away from him. "Well thank you Mr. Corbin, you are very kind. I need to know the current contact information for a child who was placed in the State's custody twenty six years ago. Her name is Anita McMillan."

"Twenty six years ago, hmm…" Marcus thought a while, "I know we converted the records to electronic form, but I will have to call you back on that one, Senator."

"How soon can you get back to me Mr. Corbin? This is extremely important," Josh could not have had more urgency in his voice.

"Give me a couple of hours, Senator. I should be able to get that information before that, but just in case I hit some snags. I will get on this right away after I hang up and call you back Sir," Marcus promised.

Josh knew he did not have two hours—the taps will already be in place. "Well, I will actually be in an important meeting in a couple of hours, so let me call you back. If not today, then I'll definitely call you tomorrow."

"No problem, Senator," Marcus said. "I will find Anita McMillan for you and have the information ready. You can call me anytime. If you want I can give you my home number, you can call me there too—not a problem. At least then my wife will believe me when I tell her that indeed I spoke to you today. By the way Senator, you can call me Marcus."

Josh laughed, "All right Marcus, if I cannot get you at this number, I will call you at home and maybe even get to chat with your wife a bit."

"She will be absolutely thrilled, Senator," Marcus was overjoyed.

"All right Marcus, thanks for all your help in advance," Josh replaced the receiver.

Carol removed her headphones and pursed her lips. She wondered what Josh would learn from Marcus and how that would influence his attitude towards her. She rewound the tape and listened to the phone call that Josh had received from Bill. The tap on the phone line to Josh's office was already in place even before she had walked into Josh's office in the morning, the Chief had approved it.

Her radio crackled.

"Mason here, over," she responded.

"Sergeant, we're here at the Senator's office and ready to move. He's coming with us in our car as you directed and Officer Cash will drive his car home. The Senator has agreed. Are we all clear there?"

"Yes, Officer, all clear. Like I said, check the parking lot before you get the Senator in there. Mason out," Carol replaced the radio on her shoulder holster.

Carol went back to the recorded conversation between Bill and Josh. The phone company had informed her that the call was made from a cellular phone using a calling card. The phone was registered to a Randall Sparks. The address turned out to be bogus when Carol had checked with the Postal Service. The Senator was nervous, Carol had seen through his façade. Her father had been able to instill fear into Josh's heart. Fear of death and fear of being blackmailed into public disgrace—he had locked Josh into a vice.

She watched an unmarked police vehicle roll out of the underground parking lot with the two officers flanking Josh on either side in the back seat. Another officer followed behind driving Josh's car. As it turned into the street, the front tires of Josh's car blew almost simultaneously. The sound made Josh jerk and twist around in his seat. He asked the officers to stop the car.

"Senator, it's not safe to stop," the officer said, "I'm under strict orders, Sir."

"Well, I'm overruling your orders for the moment, Officer, stop this car," Josh was emphatic and demanding. The car pulled over by the curb.

Carol jumped out of the police van and rushed towards the other side of the street. The officer driving Josh's car was already out on the pavement inspecting the front tires. Carol sprinted towards the other vehicle and pounded on the driver's door. "I specifically told you never to stop, get out of here now," Carol shouted through the window pane. "Go, go, go," she pounded on the roof as the vehicle started to pull off.

The explosion was subdued, but it was an explosion all right that ripped open the trunk lid of Josh's car till it stood vertically upright on its hinges. The officer inspecting the damage to the front tires hit the ground in reflex action.

Josh was horrified as he spun around to see the trunk lid of his car open all the way up. Someone had used a knife to etch a message on the paintwork. It said, "Anytime, Anywhere."

22

"Leave it outside the door. I'll pick it up a little later," Brant yelled from his couch.

"Sorry Sir, I need your signature on this charge slip," from the voice, Brant could tell that it was a middle aged woman at the door trying to deliver the pizza that he had ordered.

"All right, I'm coming," Brant walked over to his door and peered through the peephole. It was a woman carrying a pizza delivery box at the door. He could see that she had blonde hair tied at the back on a ponytail and had her face tilted sideways at an angle. She was a short woman—Josh could only see the top of her head.

He unlocked the door and held it open.

"Hello Judge," the woman appeared taller than what Brant saw through the peephole, "I guess you had been expecting me for a while." She walked in through the door, pushed Josh away and shut the door behind her.

"What kind of a joke is this?" Brant was furious.

"Stop shouting Judge," the woman said calmly, "I just want to complete my delivery. I don't like people shouting at me. This pizza, I can tell you, is no joke," she was still calm. "Let's make you a little comfortable in your couch, shall we?"

"Get out of here, right now, or I'll have to call in sec…" Brant did not get to complete his sentence. The uppercut on his jaw from what seemed like a metal fist was sudden and forceful. It exploded a dozen light bulbs in his head. The flesh in his jaw was cut open at the impact and the jawbone showed through. Blood started to ooze from the open wound. Brant started to slump on the floor. The woman grabbed his almost limp body, carried it over the couch and sent him crashing.

"Let's get you undressed," the woman was coy, "and have some fun." She ripped his shirt off and slid his track pants off his legs till he was down to his boxers. Brant groaned in pain and his head lobbed uncontrollably. He was still groggy from the impact, trying to figure out in his confused mind what was happening.

"There you go, pretty boy," the woman propped him up, grabbed him under his arms and dragged him over to a chair. She opened the pizza delivery box, retrieved a roll of packing tape and trussed him up completely to the chair. She grabbed his hands behind the backrest of the chair and tied them up next. Finally she taped his mouth in a way that the tape ran over the open wound in his jaw.

She walked over to the kitchen and filled a jug with water. Brant was beginning to regain consciousness. She carried the jug over to the Brant, splashed some water on his face and emptied the remaining contents over his head, "Wake up Judge, you have a trial in your hands. I need a verdict right now and I don't have much time," she slapped his face hard on both cheeks.

Brant recovered and almost immediately attempted to cry out in pain from his jaw. The adhesive on tape held on and stretched the skin around the open wound even further. It took him to new levels of agony that he never knew was even possible.

"You must be wondering who this bitch is, aren't you?" the woman sneered. "Well, ask me. Ask me, you son-of-a-bitch," she kicked the chair and Brant almost lost his balance.

He tried to speak, but the tape stretched the skin over his exposed flesh and he yelped out in pain, screwing his eyes shut—only a mumbling noise came out of his throat.

"What was that? I did not hear you," the woman craned her ears to listen.

Brant's eyes opened wide in horror as the woman yanked at her hair and the wig came off. "Hello Brant, is that any better?" Bill asked sarcastically in his normal voice. "Sorry about the voice and the makeup, I had to get past those cops that the pretty Sergeant arranged for you downstairs. Jeez Brant, you must be very important to the SDPD, personal bodyguards and all, huh?

Brant mumbled in an attempt to speak but no words came.

Bill reached out and ripped the tape of in one jerk and Brant shrieked in sheer agony as the strong adhesive took some raw skin and flesh along with it.

"Oops, sorry, should I have been a little gentler?" Bill asked. "I promise I will be the next time. You were trying to say something?"

"McMillan," Brant's worst fears had become reality. He panted to breathe, "Josh was the mastermind behind all of us. Dave, George, myself were all pawns for him. He used us and made us do things that we never wanted to do. I am sorry for what happened to you and to your family, I honestly am sorry. None of us had any other option, but to tag along with his plans. He was blackmailing us. I beg you to forgive me for whatever harm I have caused you."

"So now you tell on your mentor when you are in a tight spot, huh? You sniveling bastard!" Bill glanced at his watch—he did not have much time. Pizza delivery does not take too long. "You are a rational person and I believe you have some pretty sharp brains as well. Just because someone asks you to do what you did, you will just follow?" Bill taped up Brant's mouth again. "All of you made fortunes and enjoyed all the luxuries in this world, courtesy of Josh. I am certain that you never complained about that, did you? All of you framed me and destroyed my family. You doctored your argument and the evidence to implicate me in your court of law. Well, there is nobody else to judge you, so I guess I will have to do the honors."

He reached into the pizza delivery bag and removed some sticks of explosives and taped it to Brant's chest. Brant mumbled in urgent protest. His eyes were wide open with the terror of his impending fate. He moaned and shook his head desperately in an attempt to speak, but no words came.

Bill yanked the tape from his face forcibly once again, and Brant screamed as the tape claimed some more of his open flesh. "All right Brant, your last words?" Bill asked.

"I'm sorry, I am sincerely sorry," Brant said in a quivering voice.

"I am too, more sincerely than you are, Brant," Bill said woefully, "I've been sorry ever since I got to know about scum like you."

"Forgive me McMillan," Brant implored. "Let me go, and I will be a witness for you against Josh. I'll tell them everything."

Bill laughed, "I'm so impressed. I think you are about to say that the moment you disclose all the evidence in court, my wife will magically come back to life. I will magically get the twenty six years of my life back like it was just a bad dream. Also, just out of the blue, my daughter will come and fall asleep in my arms. Will all of that happen, Brant?"

Brant was sobbing profusely, "You know that is impossible."

"Uh-huh," Bill said. "Never thought it would not be, but I was just checking. So long, Brant. When you meet your Maker, you can ask him for forgiveness," Bill taped him up again against vehement protests.

He dragged Brant out to the balcony and fastened the chair to the railing. He then connected the detonator to a timer and set the clock to ten minutes. "They tell me that if you sincerely ask for forgiveness, the good Lord forgives you. He's quite different from the law that we humans have created, don't you think? I am no God, I am only human," Bill murmured.

Brant was wide-eyed and moaned in protest.

"I don't have the luxury of time on my side today, Brant, so forgive me for making this short and quick. Consider yourself fortunate, you won't have to suffer as much as your other friends did. Ten minutes and you will find yourself in a different world. See you in hell," he placed the pizza in front of him. "Just in case you get hungry waiting for your time to come."

Bill started the timer, closed the balcony door behind him and rushed out of the door. He inserted the door key in the keyhole and snapped it at the base, leaving the broken piece of the key inside the lock. That way, one would have to break down the door in order to get inside.

Bill pressed the switch for the elevator and the panel lights above indicated that it was still on the lobby. He pressed it again and still there was no motion. The lights still indicated that the elevator was in the lobby. He looked at his watch. Fifteen minutes had already passed since the guards in the lobby allowed him to come upstairs to deliver. His masquerade had worked wonderfully—the guards thought he was actually a pizza delivery woman.

Bill sensed something was wrong. The elevator showed no intention of coming up, which was unusual.

He was right, something was indeed wrong.

Carol had arrived in the lobby ten minutes after Bill was allowed to get past the guards. Her intuition had told her that the attacks on Josh were merely to distract her attention. It was intended to make her believe that Josh was going to be his first target instead of Brant. In her heart she knew that Bill would strike soon. He knew that an army of police officers would be behind his back after the attack on a Senator. She knew Bill would try to get to Brant and had decided to come down personally to check things out.

The moment she arrived in the lobby of Brant's apartment building, Carol had asked for an update of the situation. She was instantly suspicious about this pizza delivery woman who was apparently upstairs delivering an order to Brant.

"Have you seen this woman before?" she had asked the security guard in the lobby.

"No, ma'am she's new," the security guard had replied.

Carol had turned to one of the officers and asked, "Did you call ahead to Judge Sawyer before letting the woman through?"

"Yes, Sergeant, we called ahead and the Judge said that it was ok for her to come up," the officer had replied confidently, "We also checked her delivery bag. Pizza was all she had in there," he had smiled. Having worked with Carol before he knew what she was looking for. Little did he know that he should have done a more thorough search. Bill had the explosives hidden in a small compartment inside the bag.

"Does the Judge usually order food for delivery often?" Carol was not yet satisfied.

"Not really, ma'am," the security guard had said. "He has not been keeping well for the past three weeks, and has been staying indoors all the time. He had been ordering pizza almost every other night."

"Do you have the number of this pizza place?" Carol had asked. The guard nodded.

"Call this place and ask how long the woman has been working for them," Carol had directed one of the two officers.

"How long has she been gone?" she had turned to the security guard as the officer dialed the number for the restaurant.

"A little over ten minutes," the security guard had glanced at his watch.

"They are saying that the woman's name is Mercy Williams and she was hired as a temporary worker on probation just two days ago," the officer had covered the mouthpiece to inform Carol.

"All right," Carol had stiffened. "Lock the elevator right now," she had turned to the security guard.

The guard had started to protest, "There are other tenants who may need…"

"Now, and I won't repeat this a second time," Carol was in no mood for reasoning. The guard hurried to put the elevator out of service.

"Take the master key from the security guard here. I want the two of you to take the stairs and go up to the Judge's apartment, use your key to enter if he does not open," Carol had rapidly directed the two officers. "If you meet that woman, arrest her. Be careful since she will be armed," she put up her hand to dissuade a comment from one of the officers. "If my hunch is right, the woman is in disguise and is the man we are looking for. Draw your weapons and be very careful. He is dangerous and no I am not kidding. Now hurry, let's just hope for your sake, you are not too late. I'll stay here in the lobby. Now go!"

The two officers, still unsure of what they just heard, pulled out their weapons and ran for the stairwell door.

Bill had started to descend the stairs and had come down eight floors before he heard the sound of running footsteps coming up. He could identify at least two people rushing up the stairs. He knew that his cover was blown. He had spent too much time with Brant. He descended another floor, pulled the door to the stairwell open and pressed himself to the wall. The corridor was thankfully empty.

He listened intently for the footsteps, which grew louder every second and pounded their way up to the higher floors. Bill waited till he could not hear them anymore. He re-entered the stairwell and started his descent again. He wondered if the lobby was swarming with cops already. He was about to open the door that led to the lobby from the stairwell when he heard the distinct crackle of a police radio.

"Sergeant, the Judge is not answering, over", the voice was clear.

"Well, use the master key to enter the apartment. I already told you that, over," the door separated Carol from Bill and he stepped back from the door, looking for a place to hide. There was none, except in the small triangular space behind the stairs.

"We tried, Sergeant, but the key won't go in. There's already a key jammed in the keyhole and broken at the base. We can't take it out, over," the officer reported.

"All right, shoot the lock and force yourself in," Carol shouted in desperation. "You may be already too late. I'll call for backup right away. We're going to seal the building."

"Are these the only stairs down?" Carol shouted at the perplexed security guard, who nodded.

Bill could hear Carol call for backup. He knew he could not wait much longer. He saw the door to the stairwell start to open inwards as Carol started to come in. Bill lurched towards it and banged it shut. The sudden impact of the door on her out-stretched hand took Carol off balance and she fell backwards on the floor—gun and radio flying from her hands. The pain shot through her left wrist and into her upper arm—she reckoned it must have been broken.

Bill saw her fall and knew she was seriously hurt. He cursed himself for hurting Anita but realized that he had no time to waste. Anita was doing her duty and she would recover soon. She would not show any clemency in her line of duty. Furthermore, there were only moments left before Brant would be blown into bits and the place would be swarming with cops any moment.

The security guard was trying to reach for something under his desk and the Beretta recoiled in Bill's hand as he fired a warning shot. The bullet bounced off the granite counter. The guard set his hands up in the air and moved against the wall. Bill sprinted across the lobby towards the exit. "That's what you get for having elevators that don't work. Next time, you won't be so lucky," he yelled and ran through the door.

The bullet caught him on his left upper arm as Carol fired. Bill grabbed his arm in a reflex action. He turned back for a quick glance and saw Anita wince in pain as she tried to recover. He smiled and continued to sprint towards his car. He fired and the front wheel of Anita's car sank to the ground. He got into his car and sped off. His tires screamed in protest as they tried to get a bite on the road.

The sound of wailing sirens from the approaching backup was drowned by the explosion about a hundred feet upwards on the face of the building and debris started to rain down. Bill hoped the officers were not able to get inside on time to save Brant. The mahogany door could not have been easy to break down. He rolled his eyes as the pain in his upper arm started to call for his attention. The bullet must have passed right through his left biceps. The round red spot on the left arm of his shirt was gradually growing in size and soaked his sleeve. He desperately needed medical attention and had to stop the loss of blood.

He closed his eyes momentarily and said a silent prayer for Joan, "Just one more to go my love, then I'm coming home. I am so proud of Anita, you should be too. She thinks like I think. She anticipates my movements and is always so close on my tail. She has indeed turned out to be a fine officer. God bless her."

He rolled his windows down, hoping that the fresh air would help revive him and keep himself from slipping into an overpowering urge to fall to an unconscious slumber.

23

Josh watched the news on television and a chill ran down his spine. Someone had actually videotaped the explosion and sold it to the news channel. The newscaster reported that body parts believed to belong to the late Judge Brant Sawyer were found strewn on the ground below his penthouse apartment.

Josh had always known that he would be the last to survive. However the events of the day with repeated attacks on him and his possessions had actually made him doubt his own theory. Bill had seemed rather committed to take him out regardless of whether he was protected or not. Bill had left no room for conjecture that he could indeed strike at will—anytime and anywhere.

There was some relief that Bill had taken out Brant first, just like he had anticipated. It gave Josh some extra time to secure himself. He knew however that the extended lease on his life would not last much longer, unless Bill was captured.

Marcus Corbin from the Department of Social Services had given Josh the most shocking news of his life when he had called him at home earlier that evening. Anita McMillan was named Caroline Mason by her adopted parents.

The name had come as a complete surprise for Josh and his mind had been racing ever since. He had walked over to the bookstore adjacent to his residence with his bodyguards in tow, and placed a call to the Mason residence in Ohio and learnt that Caroline Mason was indeed the Sergeant Mason he had come to know so well.

Women had always remained open books for Josh all his life, but the Sergeant was different. This was one woman that he could not see through, she saw through him instead. Josh wondered just how much the Sergeant had actually seen through him and how much of the facts she really knew.

Those penetrating eyes saw more than what met the normal eye. However, Josh felt fairly confident that the Sergeant was still far away from learning the truth. She had seemed genuinely concerned about his safety. If she knew the true story, it would be almost a superhuman effort to feign ignorance and conduct herself in the manner that the Sergeant had so far.

According to the news report, the Sergeant had even managed to shoot and injure Bill before he got away after setting Brant up for that brutal murder. No daughter would shoot her own father, if she knew who she was shooting at. He wondered, if she knew Bill after all and missed her mark on purpose. He wondered if everything that she was doing to provide the protection for Josh was only a façade for some ulterior motive that she had. Josh wasn't sure if Bill knew that Carol was actually the same Anita who was estranged from him twenty six years ago.

Josh felt extremely tired. The mental fatigue from incessant tension of embarrassment in public and anticipation of the incumbent threat to his life was becoming too much for him to bear. Under normal circumstances he would have felt safe at home, but little was normal about the current circumstances.

He poured himself some vodka and switched on the television set. Somebody had video taped the explosion in his car earlier that day and the channel carried his picture on the top right corner. "The Senator has been taken into safe and secure custody by the SDPD. They have confirmed that he was not in the vehicle at the time of explosion," the newscaster reported. "As you all know, the Senator is on the top of the list of his party for a Presidential nomination in the upcoming elections," the newscaster paused, glanced sideways to a sheet of paper that was apparently handed over to her, looked up at the camera with a bewildered expression on her face and read the paper again just to confirm what she was about to report.

"We have just received some breaking news on this attack on Senator Timmons," she paused. Josh stopped midway to reach out for his glass from the side table—something was amiss.

"Our news channel has just received a fax message from someone named Billy, who is claiming complete responsibility for the attack on Senator Timmons this afternoon. Apparently, um…" she paused to read it again, hesitated, widened her eyes and continued to read. "Apparently, this man had called the Senator's office this morning asking him to pay up for all the supplies that he had ordered from Mexico for distribution in the United States. By supplies," she paused again to re-confirm. "By supplies, this message indicates narcotics and prohibited drugs. Excuse me," she paused, looked sideways from the camera with an inquisitive and puzzled expression on her face.

She returned to face the camera again and continued, "This is unconfirmed news, but in the interests of the general public, I will read this message to you word for word," she paused.

"The message says, and I quote, 'I claim complete responsibility for the two attacks on Senator Timmons this morning after he declined my request to pay up for all the supplies of unadulterated cocaine, brown sugar and marijuana that the Senator has been purchasing from our company in Mexico for the last couple of years. I had called him this morning in his office with a polite request to pay up but he would not want to even talk to me. He owes us over five million dollars. You must think this is a joke but trust me it is not. I encourage you to check the bottom of the trunk of his car in the compartment where an extra wheel is usually stored. You will see what I am talking about. He always keeps the stuff concealed in there. I hope this will make him pay us for the amount due. We send him all supplies in good faith but he has not returned the favor by making prompt payments. I have more evidence of his dealings with us that I will reveal to your channel if the Senator does not pay up,' unquote.

"We are going to take a short break and come back with an update on this developing story," the newscaster disappeared from the screen and some advertisement started to play.

Josh buried his head in his hands—he knew he was being framed. He had framed Bill twenty six years ago and now it was payback time for him. The telephone seemed to ring louder than he had ever heard before.

"What's all this in the news Josh?" the party secretary was not known for playing with words. "I am perplexed and so will be a whole bunch of others if I don't get an explanation. Two attacks on one day? I thought the explosion in your car was just the one and we thought it was just an accident. Senator Josh Timmons a drug peddler? Five million dollars in debt with some drug runners? Man what the hell is going on?"

"I am being framed, Curtis. I have no…" the phone beeped again. Josh checked the caller ID, Sergeant Mason was calling. "I promise to call you back right away, Curtis. Sergeant Mason of the SDPD is trying to reach me and I have to take that call," Josh switched over to the waiting call.

"Hello Sergeant," Josh said, "I guess you saw the news."

"Actually that is stale news you must be referring to. A few hours ago, we received a call from your opposition party office saying that they received an audio tape with the same message, asking them to have your car searched for narcotics," Carol said. "I cannot take names for reasons of confidentiality, but whoever sent that fax to the media, also contacted your opposition party folks before that."

"I'm listening," Josh had a million things going in his mind.

"Well, Senator, our narcotics guys checked out your car, exactly as the message indicated," she paused. "We did find five and a half pounds of cocaine in a sealed plastic bag in there. What do you have to say about that Sir?"

"Sergeant, I am being framed, surely you can see that" Josh sounded desperate.

"Based on what I have learned so far, I don't know what I am really sure of, quite candidly," Carol said. "You are in a tight spot Senator. Stay exactly where you are—no phone calls and no walks in the park. A warrant is being issued to place you under house arrest, till we know better. Am I clear Senator?"

"William McMillan is behind this, Sergeant. He planted those drugs in my car and it was he who blew up my trunk," Josh said in a quivering voice.

"Is that just another conjecture, Senator, or do you have any evidence to substantiate that?" Carol asked rhetorically. The silence from Josh answered her question. "Stay home, till you hear anything different from me. I will send someone over with the warrant. By the way, I think your opposition camp already knows about what we found. Sorry Senator, I thought you would want to know in advance.”

Josh sighed in disappointment. “Were you able to track down McMillan’s daughter?” Josh gambled.

“Yes,” Carol paused momentarily, “I checked, McMillan is not staying with her. I am still trying to track him down. I don’t want to sound like I am preaching to the choir here, Senator, but all we have against this man is your theory and your own accusations. None of that can be used to arrest this man. You know that. On the same lines, if he is indeed guilty of what you claim him to be and he comes after you with the intent to harm you, the SDPD will not hesitate to bring him down. I have already issued orders to shoot to kill if we have the opportunity. You have round the clock protection, Senator, so as long as you follow my directions, you are as secure as the gold in Fort Knox. I guess you have other things to worry about right now.” she disconnected.

Anita McMillan a.k.a Sergeant Carol Mason was no good for him anymore, Josh thought. If she found Anita McMillan, she definitely knew who she really was. A daughter would never hunt down her own father, let alone shoot him to death. Moreover, apart from circumstantial evidence, there was no proof that Bill was involved in any manner. Josh knew that he could not rely on Carol to help save his life.

He wanted to call the Chief of Police and request that another officer be assigned to the case. Then he realized that his phone lines were tapped and the SDPD was monitoring all inbound and outbound calls. Carol would know about everything and that might not have favorable consequences. Bill really had him pinned down on a corner and he had absolutely no wiggle room left. Bill had framed him up very well.

The telephone rang again and Josh picked it up wearily.

“What the hell have you been up to, Josh? You were supposed to call me back,” the party secretary was irritated. “Now they have found drugs in your car? Jeez man, what have you been hiding from us? We are having an urgent party meeting tomorrow morning to discuss your nomination. There is no way we can put up a candidate who has such a black spot on his profile—proven or not. Things are not looking good for you Josh. Be here at eight in the morning sharp, you don’t want to miss this one.”

“I-I can’t Curtis,” Josh stammered, “I am being placed under house arrest by the SDPD. I have been framed Curtis, believe me.”

“Well, who framed Roger Rabbit?” Curtis was sarcastic. “You’re not going to tell me that this is a political scandal sponsored by the opposition, are you?”

“No, the opposition is being used as a vehicle to get to me. They have nothing to do with this. It’s a long story, Curtis, and quite honestly, although I know in my heart the name of the person behind all of this, I don’t have any proof to substantiate any of it,” Josh sounded defeated. He wondered how Bill had managed to plant the drugs and explosives in the trunk of his car. The parking lot in the building had a few security cameras, but essentially unmanned otherwise. Bill could have easily sneaked in and managed to put everything in place.

"In the interests of the party, I think we have to pull your name off the nomination Josh," Curtis sounded sympathetic. "I recommend that you do this voluntarily instead of being asked the question—that may help salvage some of your image. Do you understand that?"

Josh grunted in approval.

He replaced the telephone in its cradle and collapsed in his sofa—he was finished. His career, his life, his dreams were all shattered. Bill had not even begun to release any of the actual evidence that he claimed to have in his possession. He wondered if Bill really had any substantial evidence that he had managed to conceal before his arrest or if he was simply trying to pull a fast one on him. That was one gamble Josh could no longer play. All his friends were dead, killed in the most brutal manner possible. He had run as much as he could and he was tired—there was no where left to hide. Bill had successfully imprisoned him in his own house, professionally and personally. Josh had never expected that to happen.

Josh knew exactly what he had to do to save himself from ultimate public humiliation, embarrassment within his party and even possible death. There was no other option left for him. He had played all his cards and was holding on to the wrong end of the stick. He had to act and he had to act fast if he had any hope of survival. But he desperately needed some rest—it had been the longest day for him.

He emptied his glass and then thoughtfully poured another. The alcohol had begun to take effect and clouded his mind even further, but that relaxed him. The nearly emptied glass slipped out of his lifeless grip and Josh slowly drifted into a slumber.

The television newscaster reported that his name was being dropped by his political party as a presidential candidate, for internal reasons. His party had made a statement that it did not believe in any of the allegations made and were organizing a thorough investigation to ascertain the truth. The newscaster went on to quote the party secretary saying that the Senator himself had voluntarily decided to withdraw his name in the interest of his party and the nation.

Josh was out cold, he never heard any of the television report. His telephone continued to ring several times before it gave up its effort to wake him up. It was the SDPD Narcotics department trying to reach Josh. They wanted to know who Josh was working for to manage the distribution of drugs. They were also curious about how he was able to own the most lavish chalet in far away Switzerland.

25

Josh was bleeding profusely. He was shot through both knees and through the hip. He joined his hands together and begged for mercy, but the man would not speak a word or show any emotion. He silently paced the room in front of him, surveying the damage he has done to Josh and trying to figure out where he would shoot next.

"Bill, I will admit everything to the press and in court. I have wronged you in the past and I have wronged this community in the past. Please forgive me for what I have done to you and to your family. Your daughter is still alive, man," Josh pleaded. "Anita McMillan is really Sergeant Carol Mason. She was adopted after your imprisonment and grew up to be a fine officer with the SDPD. You have not lost everything, Bill—you have to live for your daughter. Please stop this—I cannot bear such pain. I need medical attention, Bill. I am losing blood and feeling weaker every minute. Please get some help. I promise I will redeem your name, if you would just help me get some medical attention. Please, Bill, I beg of you. Oh God, Bill please…"

The Beretta boomed like a million explosives in his ear and his body jerked in reflex action. Josh fell off the couch and on the floor with a thud. He opened his eyes wide and looked around the room—everything was normal around him. There was nobody in the room and he was unhurt—no bullets, no damage to his body anywhere. Josh was sweating profusely and his heart was pounding inside his ribcage. He ran his fingers through his hair and realized he just had a nightmare. It was the worst he had ever imagined.

He picked himself up from the floor and collapsed on the couch again. The hangover made him feel nauseous and tired. He remembered how he had emptied a full bottle of Smirnoff literally on an empty stomach—something he would not have done under normal circumstances. He glanced at this watch. It was three in the morning. Some advertisement on health insurance was running silently on television.

Josh managed to undress himself and drag himself to the bathroom. He downed some hangover pills and stepped into the shower. The cold water seemed to refresh him as he leaned against the wall and let the water wash away his fatigue. He knew he had another long day ahead of him. All he had to do is somehow get on that nine o'clock flight to Zurich. With his dual citizenship status, it would be extremely difficult to extradite him to the US and moreover, he could disappear with a false identity and a new passport of some other country.

He put on a bathrobe and walked into his bedroom when the telephone rang. He let it ring for three times, hesitated and picked it up.

"Hello Senator, how's life treating you these days? You should have seen the terrified surprise when your pal Brant realized who the pizza delivery gal really was. I would say he suffered quite a bit before his body was blown to very small pieces. I heard they found torn body parts all over the lawn. Quite impressive, what explosives can do to a human body," the voice was cold and so unmistakably Bill.

"What happened Josh, the cat got your tongue, you piece of shit?" he paused. "I see, the SDPD is tapping this line, so you don't want to talk huh? How long will you feign innocence, Senator? Never mind—I'll do all the talking, you just listen carefully, ok?"

Another pause—Bill heard some heavy breathing on the other side.

"Good. Your house is about to blow up in exactly twenty minutes from now, oops correction, nineteen minutes and fifty one seconds," Bill said in a monotone. "There's nothing the SDPD or you can do to prevent this. The explosives were laid in the proper places, days before those stooges set up camp around your house and tapped into your phone line. I am sure you don't believe me and neither does the SDPD officers listening in on this conversation. Well, there is only one way to find out—just stay there and wait it out. At least they found Brant's body parts. I'm sorry I cannot guarantee they will be able to find any of yours."

Bill coughed to clear his throat.

"To the SDPD officers listening in—you may want to start evacuating the adjacent houses, because this is going to be a fairly loud bang," Bill advised. "So long Josh, my mission is complete. Nineteen minutes and three seconds," the line went dead.

Josh banged the phone down on its cradle and ran to his closet. He quickly slipped into a pair of jeans and pulled on a t-shirt, a pair of sneakers and a cap. He grabbed a small travel backpack, checked for his passport, wallet and his handgun that he had kept there for the past two weeks, just in case he needed to defend himself. He glanced at this watch. He had a little over sixteen minutes to go before the place blew up. Someone started to press his doorbell and frantically pound on his door. It was the SDPD trying to get in. They were definitely not in the mood to gamble.

The muted television caught his attention as he was about to leave the house. They were showing his picture with a caption saying that his presidential nomination was cancelled by his party. His political aspirations had bitten the dust. He opened the back door and realized that he had forgotten to disable the alarm. The blaring sound of the alarm cut through the quiet hours of the morning and the pounding on the door momentarily stopped.

Josh ran through his backyard, jumped the fence to his neighbor's yard and ran out to the street. There was substantial activity in the street with several police cruisers parked all over the street and had their lights flashing. They had apparently taken the threat seriously and already started the evacuation process. Josh ran like there was no tomorrow.

He flagged down a passing taxi, yanked the door open and yelled out to the driver, "LAX please, as fast as you can, my man. Here's five hundred dollars," he threw the bill on the passenger's seat next to the driver. "I have to catch a flight in three hours from now and I am late. I'll give you another thousand if I get there on time." The taxi took off like a bullet without a word. There was nobody behind him.

He sighed with relief—he had managed to slip past everybody. It would not take long for the SDPD to figure out that he had escaped, but it might take long for them to figure out where he was headed. He glanced at his watch, it was dark outside. He really had about five hours before his flight, which was ample time to reach the airport. The taxi was speeding without a doubt. The last thing that Josh wanted was to be pulled over by the CHP.

"All right, you can slow down now," he directed the driver. "Just stay a little over the speed limit and you should be fine."

The driver silently nodded.

"You're not too much of a talker are you?" Josh asked curiously.

The driver reached beside himself, handed a card over to Josh and switched on the rear seat light. "Disabled war veteran. I cannot speak, but I'm a good and safe driver," it read.

"I see, sorry about that," Josh said. "But you can hear, right?"

Another nod in the affirmative.

Josh fell silent and twisted around to see if anyone was following. He could not see anything unusual.

Carol had arrived at the scene after she was alerted about the threatening call by the officer in charge. She had seen the taxi take off like a rocket. She thought it might be a local resident trying to flee the neighborhood, so she had turned to speak to the officer in charge. Then something struck her and she shouted some orders and followed the taxi.

She thought about calling for backup, but there was little she knew about the taxi. It was still dark and the street lights were not bright enough to clearly see the plates. She had no description of the vehicle to go with.

She activated the police radio, "Jamie, listen very carefully," she got through to her assistant at the precinct. "Send out an alert for the CHP. They are looking for a taxi on Interstate Five heading northbound and should have just got on the ramp at Genesee Drive. It's got to be speeding, so it should not be too difficult to track. The taxi is probably carrying Senator Josh Timmons. I'm sure the CHP knows what Senator Timmons looks like. Keep me informed as soon as they turn anything up. I am already in pursuit. Give them my number so they can reach me directly if they turn up anything. Mason out."

From the tail lights, she could see the taxi enter the northbound freeway. She knew she had to catch up as quickly as she can, otherwise she could lose them in the not-too-light traffic in those wee hours of the morning.

"Hello, I want to make a reservation for the flight to Zurich at nine fifteen this morning, please," Josh spoke to the airline agent. With five hundred dollars beside him and the promise of another thousand when he reached LAX, the taxi driver had no hesitation to silently hand over his cellular phone over to Josh when he had requested.

Josh listened and gave his details to the booking agent who promised that he could pick up the first class tickets at the airport. "Thanks a ton, my man," Josh handed the phone over to the driver. "You're a life saver, you know?" They drove in silence. They were traveling a little over the speed limit but not too fast to attract attention.

They passed the last exit in Oceanside and into the open and uninhabited stretch of the freeway. Cars passed them like they were standing still. "I guess you can step it up a bit, huh?" Josh checked behind him and said. "Everybody seems to be doing ninety out here."

Another silent nod in the affirmative and the taxi accelerated. Josh glanced behind him again to check for the CHP, but in the dark it was pretty difficult to identify anything. He was so close to freedom from all the fear and disgrace, he could almost smell it. He just had to lay low till he boarded the plane and that was it—freedom beckoned. The Sergeant would have little to go on with. By the time she figured it out, he would probably be over the Atlantic patronizing his old friend, Jack Daniels.

"It looks like it will be a great day ahead of us," Josh commented as he rolled down his window to let the fresh morning air in. Something bothered him. The driver was speech impaired, but he still carried a cellular phone. He thought that was odd. Maybe the driver used the phone for listening in for dispatch instructions. The world had all kinds of people with all kinds of problems.

The brakes jammed on the rear wheels and brought the vehicle to a stop from ninety in five seconds. The taxi rolled down onto the ditch beside the road and came to an abrupt stop. The sudden change of momentum over the uneven unpaved ground literally threw Josh out his rear seat into the passenger's side beside the driver. His head hit the dashboard hard enough to show him a thousands flashbulbs exploding in his head. He realized too late before passing out that he had forgotten to wear his seatbelt in all the excitement.

When consciousness slowly returned, Josh felt that somebody was splashing water on his face and continuously slapping him on his cheeks—not too gently. He wondered if the slapping would ever stop but it didn't. He opened his eyes slowly. The first signs of daylight had begun to appear on the eastern sky over the mountains. He tried to sit up and a sharp streak of pain shot up though his spine and into his head. That made him nauseous. He collapsed on the ground again and winced in pain. The left side of his head felt wet and cold. He gingerly lifted his left hand to touch his head. It felt warm and sticky. The skull was definitely fractured from the concussion and he was bleeding.

Josh was becoming increasingly conscious by the moment and he realized that he was lying on his back on the ground among some wild brush. He squinted to focus on the person kneeling over him—it was taxi driver.

"Are you ok?" the driver asked as he propped Josh up first into a sitting position and then helped him stand up on his feet.

Josh gingerly massaged his head and neck, "I'm still alive, what happened?"

"I thought it was the end of the road and enough was enough," the driver said nonchalantly. "I guess you'll miss your flight now. The rear axle of my taxi is broken, so we're not going anywhere in a hurry."

"You've got to be kidding me," Josh was fully conscious and was rapidly regaining his strength. "What the heck do you mean by the end of the road? Speak up man." There was silence, the driver simply stood with his hands on his hips a few feet away from Josh. When the realization dawned on Josh, he froze with a newly discovered sense of fear.

He thought that the driver could not speak, and now he was talking just fine. The voice was not difficult for Josh to recognize. He had really been taken for a ride and most likely the last in his life.

"This is a disabled war veteran Senator. I cannot speak, but I drive rather well, don't I?" the voice was cold. There was no mistake anymore, Josh looked around—they were all alone. The freeway was about a hundred feet away and the high wild bushes obstructed the view. He could make out the outline of the taxi stranded on the ditch at an almost impossible angle.

"I've been at war for the last twenty six years Senator and I have not spoken much for a long time," Bill continued. "It is the end of the road for me. I'm tired and I am desperate to go home to my wife."

"Bill, we can work this out," Josh started, "please give me a chance to explain. I can't bring your wife back, but I know who and where your daughter is. Let me live and I will not only reconcile you with your daughter, I will also…"

"Sergeant Carol Mason, my daughter, should be here any minute," Bill cut him off. "She is sharper than both of us combined, Josh. I wonder how she grew up to be such a fine young woman when you literally made her an orphan. She will stop at nothing to prevent me from getting to you. Can you believe that?" Bill paused and Josh listened open-mouthed. Bill knew everything about Anita.

"A daughter is protecting the killer of her own mother and the architect of the complete destruction of her own father. That will make headlines for a month," Bill gave a short laugh. "She knows who I am, Josh just like I know who she is. But she does not have any evidence to prove that you are guilty, although she knows everything—I told her everything," he stressed.

"But still she pursues me and does not hesitate to protect those that the law considers as innocent. Do you know why? It's called integrity, something you never had or ever intended to have. She will shoot her own father against her better judgment to protect her code of service. In her professional mind, you are innocent as long as she does not have any evidence. I gave her no evidence, Josh, which to her, translates to just one thing—you are innocent. Of all the things life has given me, my daughter is the best gift of them all. She is unfortunate to have a father like me, but I can tell you God never gave a better daughter to any father."

"You never had any evidence, did you Bill?" Josh was trying to keep the conversation going. Daylight was not too far away and if he had any hope of survival he had to buy time. "We burnt it all up when we burnt your house down. Dave did a rather thorough job. Too bad your family was in it. The evidence was all I was after, Bill. I had tried several times to have you hand over all that evidence to us and none of this would have ever happened. You brought this on yourself, Bill. You should have looked the other way and let us on with our merry lives."

Bill laughed, "I did not expect anything more than that from you, Josh. Once a scumbag always remains the same scumbag. By the way, I do have a lot of evidence—tapes, photographs, copies of deeds and real estate transactions. I have them all, Josh. I promised the Sergeant to hand everything over to her as soon as I'm done. So long, this is the end of the road for you, Josh" Bill aimed his Beretta at Josh's chest.

"Drop your weapon Mr. McMillan, I will not hesitate to shoot," Carol's voice cut through the silence behind Bill. She had followed as fast as she could without her warning lights, carefully scanning every taxi that she had passed. Her radio had remained silent—the CHP had not been able to turn up anything. She had contemplated calling in helicopter support, but decided against it. Her headlights had picked up the dark tracks of tires that ran off the freeway and she had seen the taxi on the ditch. She had turned off her lights to take cover of the darkness and stopped about a hundred yards ahead. She reported her position on the radio and called for backup.

With her weapon drawn, she had run back to the where the taxi lay abandoned and knew in her mind what had happened. She looked around and had seen the outline of two men standing in the distance and engaged in some conversation. She had no doubts about who they were. She had crept up silently and seen Bill pull his gun and take aim on Josh.

"You see Josh, your protection has arrived, just like I said," Bill smiled. "To her, I'm just McMillan—a suspect and a killer, not her father. You know why? It's because she has no evidence against you."

"You know I can't Sergeant," Bill shouted and kept his aim steady on Josh. "I am on my home stretch and my wife is waiting for me. This is one last job I have to finish," he winced as the pain from his left arm where Anita had shot him, sent a warning not to make sharp movements.

"Dad," Anita pleaded. "Please don't make me do this. Let me handle this by the law. Give me the evidence and I will see to it that justice is delivered. I promise you Dad, I will bring this man down—just give me the evidence. I implore you."

Josh furtively looked around. He desperately needed a gun. His bag was in the taxi, which was some distance away from where he stood. Moreover Bill would shoot at the slightest movement.

"You will get the evidence after I complete my mission, Anita. We've had this discussion before," Bill said without turning. "Please don't approach me any closer, I will not hesitate to shoot if you come in my way. Goodbye Josh."

The wail of sirens and flashing lights filled the early morning air as several CHP vehicles approached from the south.

"Dear God, please forgive me," Carol prayed silently.

The sound of gunfire cut through the din of the approaching reinforcements and the gun went flying from Bill's hand. The bullet struck his right arm. He collapsed to the ground clutching his right arm with his left and cried out in pain as the left arm revolted from the previous wound.

Josh threw himself on the ground, picked up the Beretta and fired at Bill's prostrate body. The body jerked a few times and then went limp. Josh turned and lined up his gun on Carol, who was surprised by the sudden turn of events. She could see from the corner of her eye that officers were rushing out of their vehicles and sprinting towards them.

Josh fired again and the bullet struck Anita just above her right breast and threw her backwards. "I can't let you live Sergeant. You know too much and I have a career and a life to live. Sorry, you asked for this."

He started to squeeze the trigger. Then he felt something small and hard strike the back of his head, go straight through his brains and fly out from between his eyes, drenching him in a warm pool of blood. Then he felt nothing.

Carol pushed herself up to see Bill slowly collapse back on the ground. He had carried a gun in his ankle holster and used all the strength he could summon to get a clean shot on his last target—his mission was complete

Officers rushed towards Carol to attend to her wounds, but she brushed them aside. She dragged herself along the ground to where Bill lay and slowly removed the handgun from his hands and tossed it aside.

She knelt beside Bill and waved the officers away. The hole in his left chest was soaked and a small red stream dripped on the ground. If it was not the heart, clearly the aorta was pierced when Josh had fired. "I need a paramedic here, right now," she screamed at one of the CHP patrolmen, "I have an officer down. For goodness sake, hurry." The patrolman hurried away.

She turned to Bill and cradled his head in her hands. "I'm sorry Dad, you obstinate man. Why did you make me do this? I know you are innocent. How much you have suffered all these years. I am such an ungrateful daughter, I could do nothing to help you and I shot you twice instead. Oh God Dad, this is a scar that will remain with me all my life."

"You're a very bad markswoman, lady," blood welled from his mouth as Bill gave a wry smile and tried to speak. "I know you had shot to incapacitate and not to kill, so I wouldn't worry that pretty head too much."

"You completed your mission, Dad notwithstanding all our efforts to stop you," Anita cried. She knew medical attention could do nothing to save her father. He must have been shot through his lungs and probably the aorta was severed as well. "Somebody please get a medic in here fast for God's sake," she yelled again. She was bleeding herself, but that was the last thing on her mind.

"I owe you something, Anita," the voice sounded more like a gurgle as blood oozed from his mouth. "My arms are useless, so I need your help. Reach into my right trouser pocket."

Anita did as she was told and found a voice recorder and a bank locker key.

"Interesting conversation in that recorder," Bill gasped for breath. "What you are looking for is in locker one zero five two at the bank down the street from where we once had our home," he rolled his eyes and coughed more blood out from his lungs.

He looked at his daughter with all the love he had in his dying heart. "I love you with all my heart Anita. I know you could have been born to a better father, but I could not have ever hoped for a better daughter. God bless you my child. Remember you will always have us by your side," the breaths were becoming shorter and shorter.

"Stay with me Dad, please don't leave me. Dear God," she turned around to see paramedics rushing towards them. "You'll be fine Dad, the medics…", the body had already gone completely limp in her hands and Anita herself collapsed beside her father.

She didn't know if the bullet was still lodged inside her to have gone right through her rib cage. All she knew was that she was bleeding profusely herself. She kissed Bill on his cheek and closed his lifeless eyes, "Go home in peace, Dad. Mom could not have asked for a more doting husband who was always ready to sacrifice his own life for her," she murmured.

The last thing she saw was a medic hovering around her asking something that she could not understand and then she remembered nothing.

26

"While this court does not condone the brutal crimes committed by William McMillan, the reasons for his actions are clear to us. Flaws in our legal system had forced an honest man and a dedicated and accomplished police officer to adopt such measures. That is where the law had fallen short of his expectations," the judge paused and scanned the courtroom that was filled to capacity.

"He lost faith in the power of the law, which led him to believe that justice could not be served unto him. This is why he had decided to take the law in his hands. He has done what anyone would have done if our legal system had failed to deliver the promise of fair and equal justice to every citizen of these United States. After all we are only human," he paused again.

"It is possible that to the common man, William McMillan is guilty of the four murders that he is committed and this court is in complete agreement. However, it will be a terrible injustice on our part if we overlook the service that he has served this community, this city and the United States."

"Based on the evidence presented to this court by the San Diego Police Department it leaves no doubt that the four deceased were criminals in the most appropriate sense of the word. They had taken advantage of our legal system to mislead the public and caused serious damage to the community. Without these pieces of evidence, the truth would never have come to daylight and maybe one day a felon could have been elected to the highest office of this nation. Imagine what that would have done to the integrity of our constitution and to the faith and trust of the millions of Americans. William McMillan has saved us and the constitution of this great nation from the most embarrassing disgrace. Although this court does not condone the methods used to fulfill his duties, William McMillan has served his country and his code that he had been sworn into as an officer of the SDPD." The court reporter was typing away as fast as she could.

"This court is sending a message to everybody engaged in law enforcement in this country. Take every precaution and to ensure that true justice is served to each and every citizen in the manner described in our constitution. Otherwise there will be other William McMillans who will arise to take law in their hands. To every citizen who has been trying to take advantage of our legal system to commit crimes, let this be a warning that if the law cannot get to you, someone somewhere will arise to bring you down just like William McMillan did."

"This courtroom had wronged William McMillan twenty six years ago. Despite that, he has served our community and this country in the most unprecedented and unique manner. So this court is going to make an effort redeem itself. While the past cannot be undone, this court requests the SDPD to restore full service honors posthumously to Lieutenant William McMillan."

"The life of a police officer is definitely not a walk in the park. Service before self is easier said than done. Sergeant Carol Mason, or should we address you as Anita McMillan, ma'am?" the judge smiled at Anita seated in the courtroom. "You have set an example of how a true police officer should conduct herself or himself in the most selfless manner. This court salutes you for your courage and commitment to serve. Your parents, both living and dead must be very proud of you and they should be. We thank you for your service to this community. I am glad to personally make your acquaintance."

Anita's dropped her head down and her eyes welled up with emotion. Carla and Nathan McIntyre seated on either side, tried to console her. Every eye in the courtroom was on Anita. They stood up and gave a standing ovation. The media had been carrying the story in the front pages for several days now and the part that Anita played in the case was a popular topic of discussion in almost all walks of life

The judge paused to allow the courtroom to settle down. "This has been the most intriguing case of my career in more ways than one. I am sure many of the men and women present in this courtroom will agree. At the end justice has been duly served, so all's well that ends well. Court is adjourned," the judge beat his gavel.

They walked down the walkway in the cemetery together, the McIntyres and Anita. They were the only living family she was left with and she loved them most dearly. She had buried Bill next to her mother's grave.

The keys to Bill's locker revealed everything that she needed to clear his name. For the first time in her life, she made the media her ally and they grabbed the opportunity as if it was the last piece of news on the planet. The publicity that the story received had been monumental. She interviewed on radio and on the papers, but stayed away from the television networks. She had to gain the support of the public if she had a fighting chance to clear her father's name.

To her utmost surprise she had also found the will that her father had left for her. His last gift to her was a handsome enough inheritance. "I could not give you anything all your life, my dear Anita. Hopefully you can make use of this," Bill had left a handwritten note for her on the will.

She knelt on the ground between the two graves, lit candles and placed them on both. She placed floral wreaths and smiled, "There you go Mom and Dad. You're finally together. They re-instated your position in the SDPD, Lieutenant William McMillan," she raised her hand in a salute. "They think you saved the community and this nation from the most embarrassing dis- grace in history. The court apologized for their failure to deliver justice to you. Dad, they still think that you should not have taken the law into your hands."

"I am proud to have been born to parents such as the two of you and consider myself unfortunate that I could not share much of my life with you. But Dad, I know you have always loved Mom more than you ever loved yourself," she paused. "I know you have always loved me. You will always remain in my heart. I have the comfort to know that you are finally together and in peace. Don't worry about me, I am blessed to have two wonderful parents," she reached out to hold the hands of Nathan and Carla McIntyre and pulled them down beside her. "They will take care of me."

"I guess we should start calling you Anita McMillan from now on, my dear," Nathan smiled and looked at Anita.

"No, Sir," she smiled, "Caroline Anita McIntyre would suit me just fine."

The cool refreshing breeze drifted in from the ocean beyond where the orange sun had just disappeared over the horizon. The gathering darkness paved the road for a new day ahead.

Part Four

Present Day

The chill of the evening breeze punctuated the silence that had fallen around. Anita had bottled up her emotions and her secret for such a long time. She had slipped into a trance as she related her story to Kyle. The events had unfolded just like it happened just yesterday right in front of her eyes.

She hung her head and wiped tears off her eyes. Kyle saw a mother like he had never seen before. She had always been strong and steadfast like a rock in the face of life's trials. She had been the strength and the driving force in his life. It grieved him to see a totally different and miserable side of his mother.

He came around and hugged Anita and she embraced him.

"Don't cry Mom," Kyle said softly. "My respect and love for you just escalated to a new high. You carried all this in your heart, but you never let us know the suffering you had gone through all these years? You are simply amazing!" he looked at her in wonder.

"Was I," Anita hesitated. "Was I right in my decision, Kyle?"

"I just realized that my Mom is really the superwoman that we always thought you were when Bobby and I were kids. Any lesser man or woman would have acted differently and taken Grandpa's statements at face value without any evidence. But you didn't Mom. What you did takes more than courage to fight your own demons and uphold the law," Kyle smiled. "Of course you were right—no questions."

"I have always debated with myself ever since Dad passed away if I could have done this any differently that could have somehow saved him," Anita sobbed. "He would have been alive today and sitting right here with us, but I had failed him."

"No, you didn't fail him Mom," Kyle was certain. "If you did anything otherwise, you would have failed him. He had the good fortune to see that you grew up to be an honest citizen and a police officer dedicated to your code. I am sure he was proud of his daughter, even more than I am proud of you today. He wanted you to do your duty, be true and honest. That is what any good father would advise his child to do. That is exactly what he did, Mom. He showed you the right path. I am beginning to love this man. I wish I could meet him."

Anita smiled, "Thanks for listening and understanding, Kyle. I never thought I could ever express myself properly to anyone. As you see, the life of a police officer is not a walk in the park. If you want to be dedicated to your code, chances are that you may have to live the rest of your life with the deepest scar that will come to haunt you over and over again. Trust me it is a challenge to fight your own demons and keep things straight. There are more temptations than one can possibly handle."

They sat there silently for a while.

"I have never discouraged you on what you want to do in life and I won't change that now. But I wanted you to know my story. Hopefully it will help you make your decision. So do you still want to be a police officer, Kyle?"

"More than ever Mom," Kyle was confident. "Grandpa was a police officer, you are one, someone's got to keep the family tradition, you know?" he chuckled.

"As you wish, my dear," Anita sighed. "Let me know how I can help."

"I will Mom, I will need to learn a lot—I just had my first lesson, you know?" they both laughed. "How's Bobby doing Ma? Are things any better?"

Anita leaned back on her chair and exhaled heavily, "I don't know Kyle. Bobby worries me very much. Ever since that incident when he was seven years old, he thinks I am his enemy. I don't like the company he keeps. I have tried to talk to him about it. He just wouldn't listen. I did what I had to, Kyle. I was doing my job. I lost your father in my line of duty, for Christ's sake, but Bobby will probably never understand me."

Kyle held her hand, "I'll talk to him, Mom. I am sure he will understand."

Anita sighed, "Good luck, son. I just hope he will come around. This is one battle I am not sure I am winning and I fear where this might lead us. My life is quite a story, isn't it?"

The birds had stopped chirping and the darkness had set in. Anita wondered if the silence was the calm before the beginning of another storm.

To Be
Continued...

Printed in the United States
96145LV00001B/1-48/A